FOILED

Written by **Jane Yolen**   Artwork by **Mike Cavallaro**

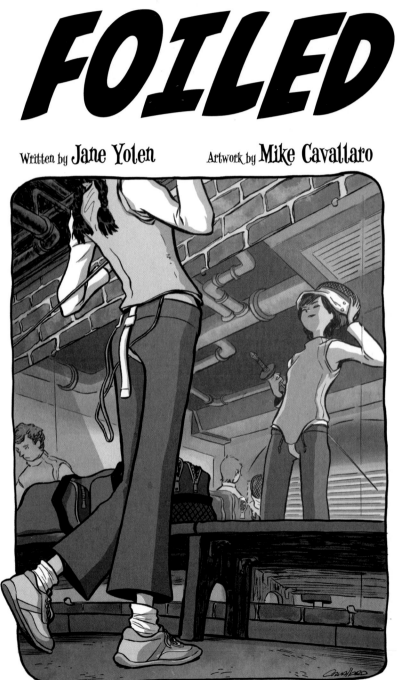

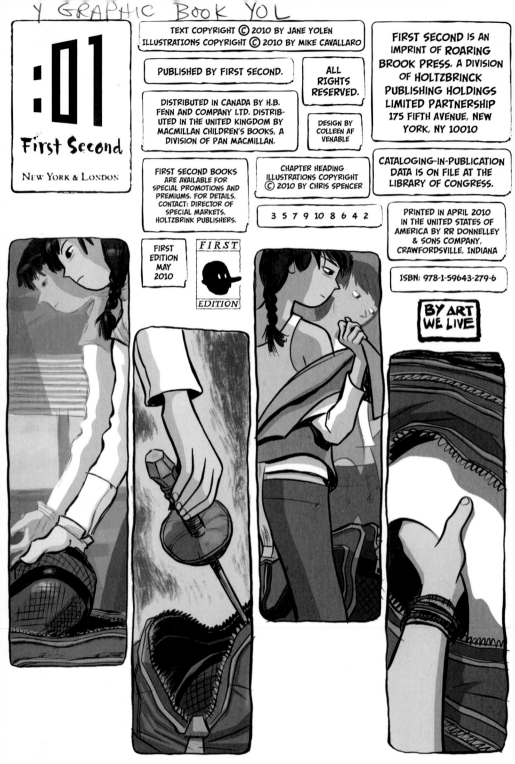

:01
First Second
NEW YORK & LONDON

TEXT COPYRIGHT © 2010 BY JANE YOLEN
ILLUSTRATIONS COPYRIGHT © 2010 BY MIKE CAVALLARO

PUBLISHED BY FIRST SECOND.

DISTRIBUTED IN CANADA BY H.B. FENN AND COMPANY LTD. DISTRIBUTED IN THE UNITED KINGDOM BY MACMILLAN CHILDREN'S BOOKS, A DIVISION OF PAN MACMILLAN.

FIRST SECOND BOOKS ARE AVAILABLE FOR SPECIAL PROMOTIONS AND PREMIUMS. FOR DETAILS, CONTACT: DIRECTOR OF SPECIAL MARKETS, HOLTZBRINK PUBLISHERS.

ALL RIGHTS RESERVED.

DESIGN BY COLLEEN AF VENABLE

CHAPTER HEADING ILLUSTRATIONS COPYRIGHT © 2010 BY CHRIS SPENCER

3 5 7 9 10 8 6 4 2

FIRST EDITION MAY 2010

FIRST EDITION

FIRST SECOND IS AN IMPRINT OF ROARING BROOK PRESS, A DIVISION OF HOLTZBRINCK PUBLISHING HOLDINGS LIMITED PARTNERSHIP 175 FIFTH AVENUE, NEW YORK, NY 10010

CATALOGING-IN-PUBLICATION DATA IS ON FILE AT THE LIBRARY OF CONGRESS.

PRINTED IN APRIL 2010 IN THE UNITED STATES OF AMERICA BY RR DONNELLEY & SONS COMPANY, CRAWFORDSVILLE, INDIANA

ISBN: 978-1-59643-279-6

BY ART WE LIVE

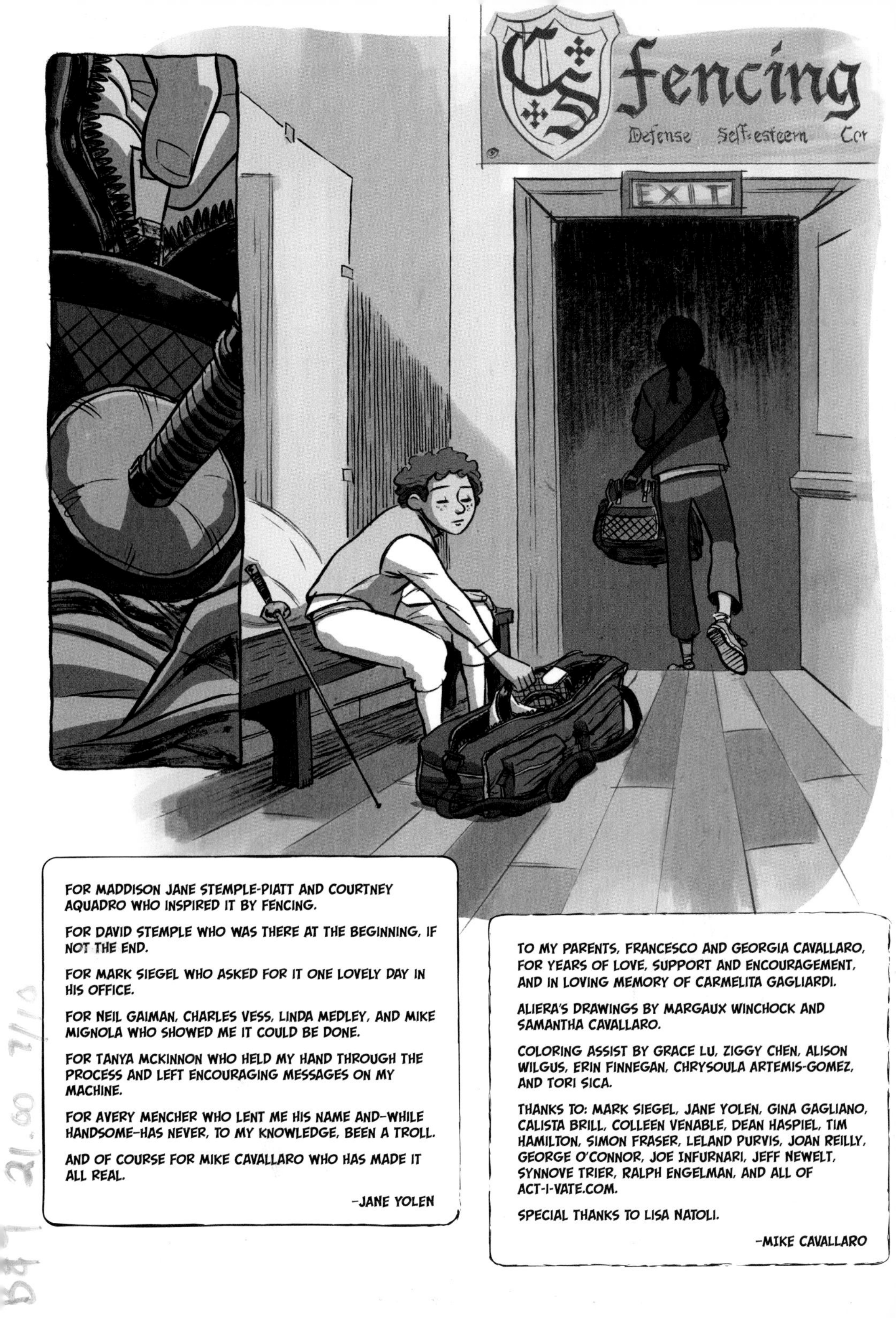
fencing
Defense Self-esteem Cor
EXIT

FOR MADDISON JANE STEMPLE-PIATT AND COURTNEY AQUADRO WHO INSPIRED IT BY FENCING.

FOR DAVID STEMPLE WHO WAS THERE AT THE BEGINNING, IF NOT THE END.

FOR MARK SIEGEL WHO ASKED FOR IT ONE LOVELY DAY IN HIS OFFICE.

FOR NEIL GAIMAN, CHARLES VESS, LINDA MEDLEY, AND MIKE MIGNOLA WHO SHOWED ME IT COULD BE DONE.

FOR TANYA MCKINNON WHO HELD MY HAND THROUGH THE PROCESS AND LEFT ENCOURAGING MESSAGES ON MY MACHINE.

FOR AVERY MENCHER WHO LENT ME HIS NAME AND–WHILE HANDSOME–HAS NEVER, TO MY KNOWLEDGE, BEEN A TROLL.

AND OF COURSE FOR MIKE CAVALLARO WHO HAS MADE IT ALL REAL.

–JANE YOLEN

TO MY PARENTS, FRANCESCO AND GEORGIA CAVALLARO, FOR YEARS OF LOVE, SUPPORT AND ENCOURAGEMENT, AND IN LOVING MEMORY OF CARMELITA GAGLIARDI.

ALIERA'S DRAWINGS BY MARGAUX WINCHOCK AND SAMANTHA CAVALLARO.

COLORING ASSIST BY GRACE LU, ZIGGY CHEN, ALISON WILGUS, ERIN FINNEGAN, CHRYSOULA ARTEMIS-GOMEZ, AND TORI SICA.

THANKS TO: MARK SIEGEL, JANE YOLEN, GINA GAGLIANO, CALISTA BRILL, COLLEEN VENABLE, DEAN HASPIEL, TIM HAMILTON, SIMON FRASER, LELAND PURVIS, JOAN REILLY, GEORGE O'CONNOR, JOE INFURNARI, JEFF NEWELT, SYNNOVE TRIER, RALPH ENGELMAN, AND ALL OF ACT-I-VATE.COM.

SPECIAL THANKS TO LISA NATOLI.

–MIKE CAVALLARO

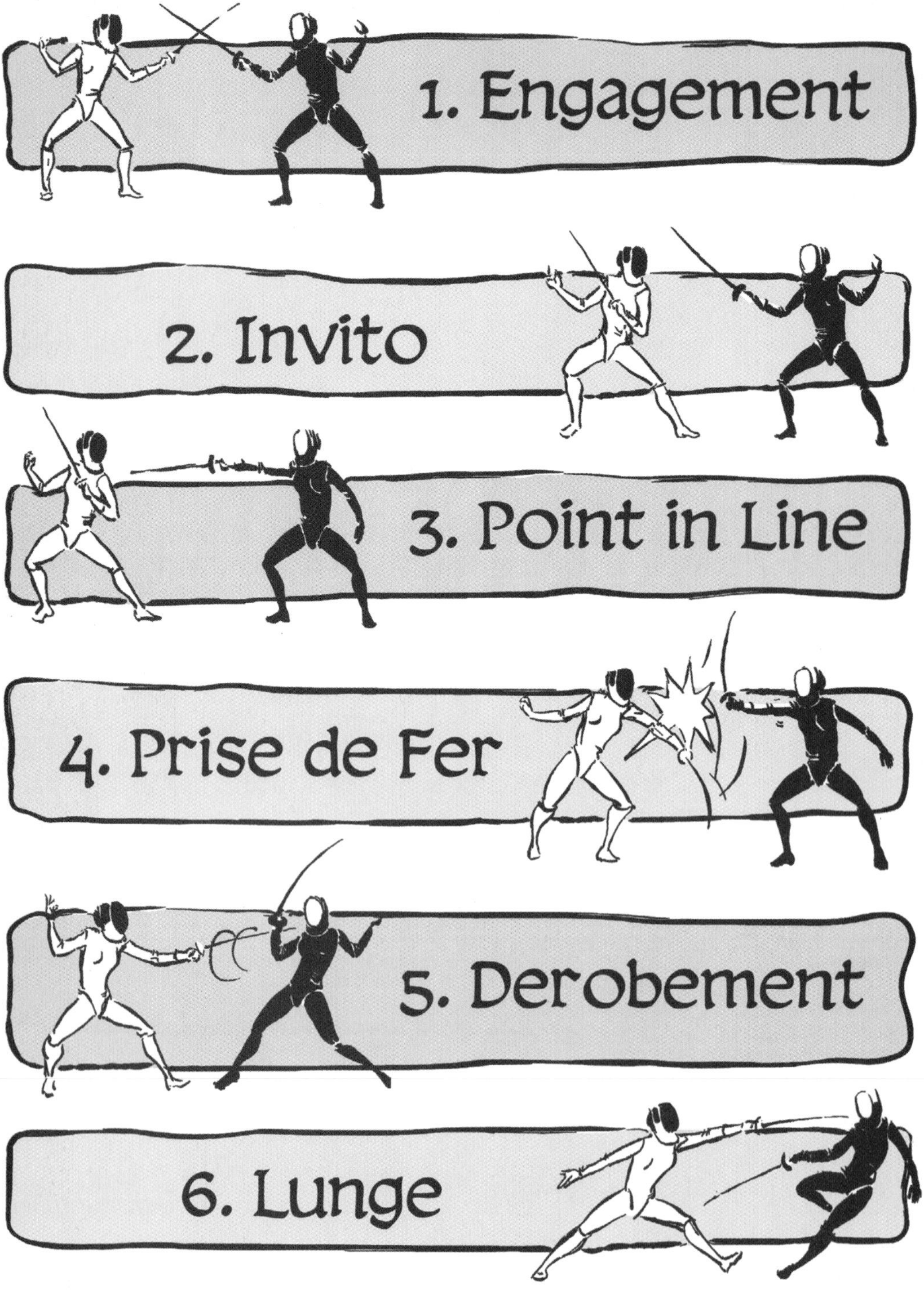
1. Engagement
2. Invito
3. Point in Line
4. Prise de Fer
5. Derobement
6. Lunge

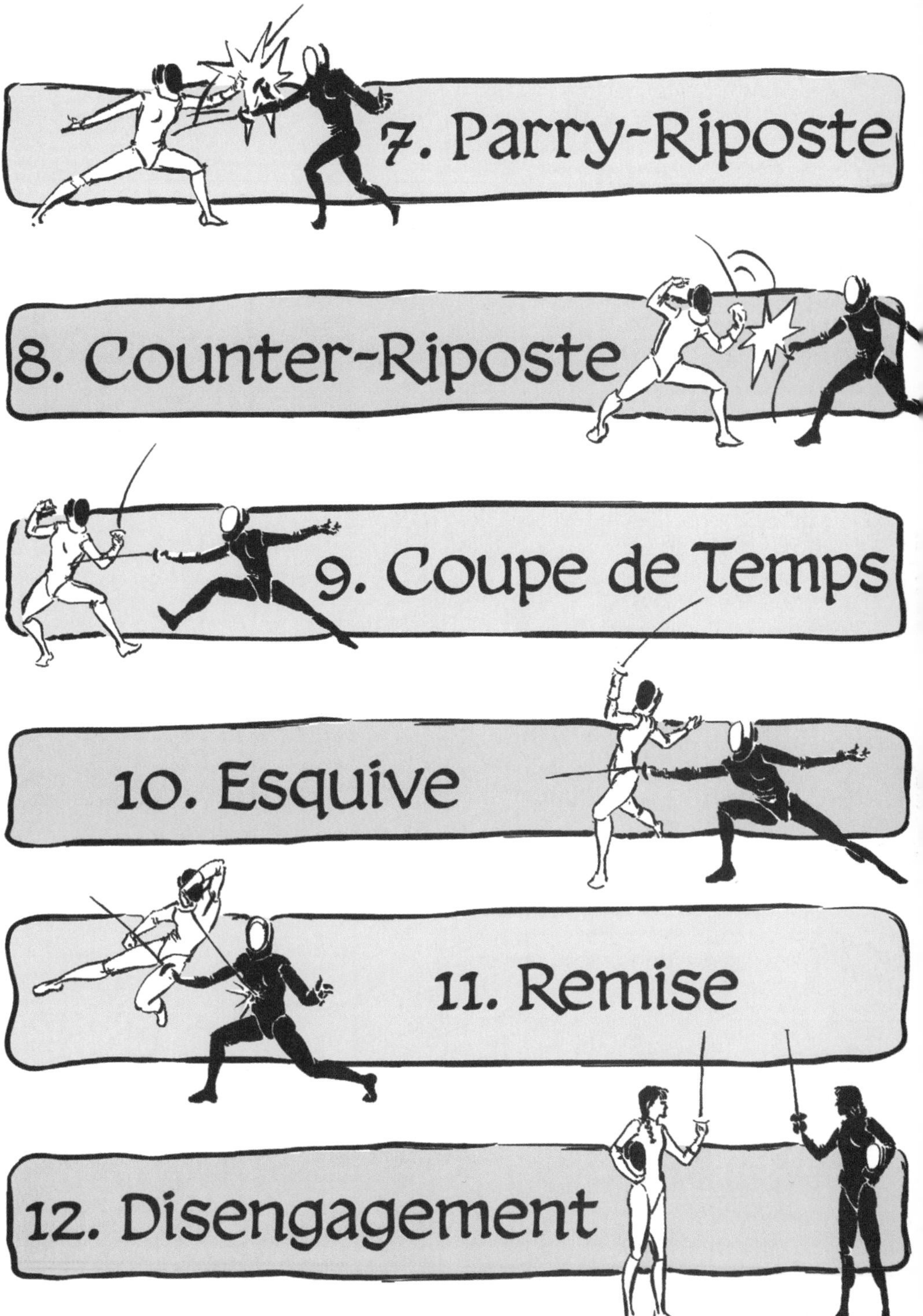
7. Parry-Riposte
8. Counter-Riposte
9. Coupe de Temps
10. Esquive
11. Remise
12. Disengagement

1. Engagement

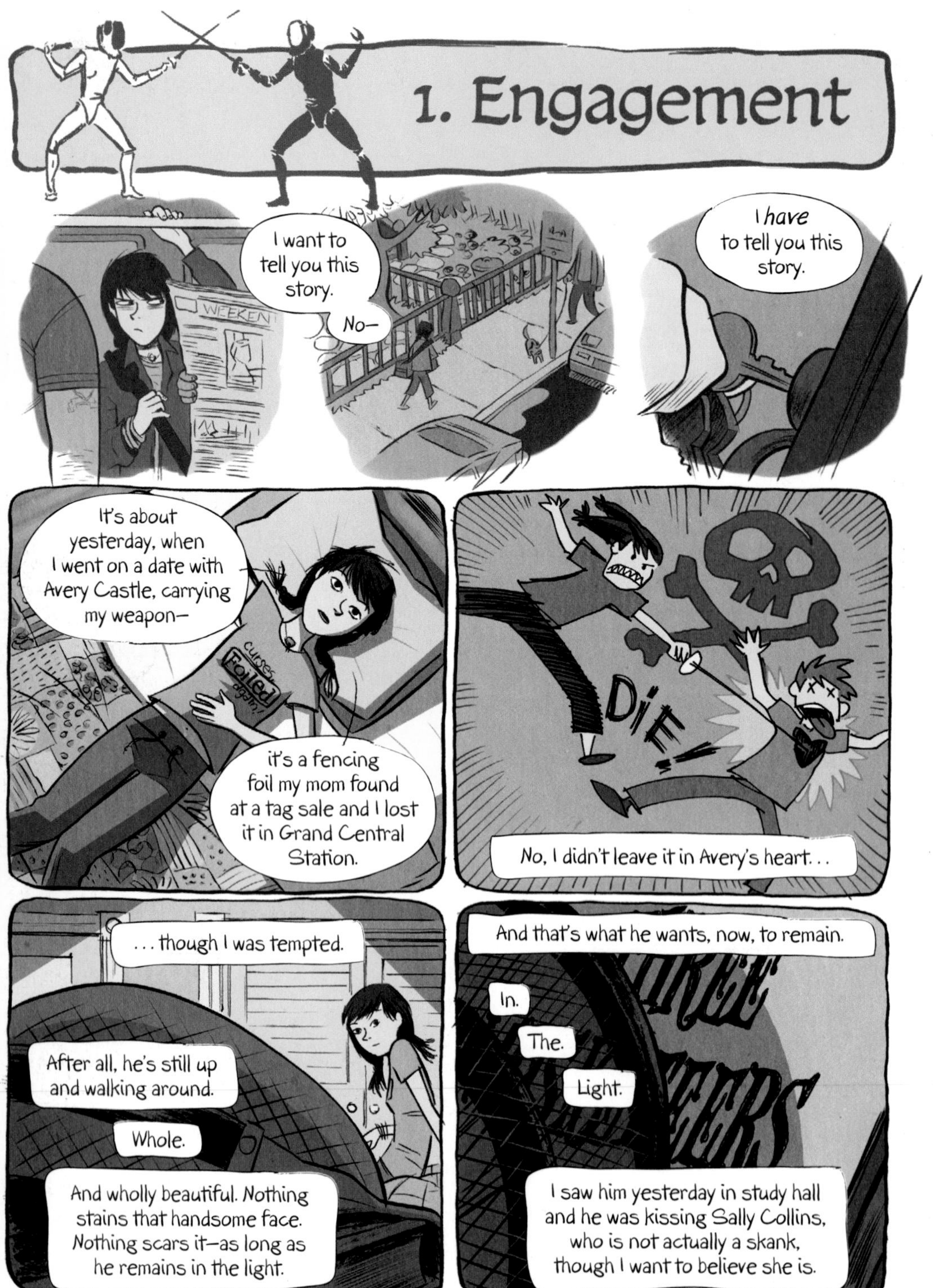
I want to tell you this story.
No—
I *have* to tell you this story.
It's about yesterday, when I went on a date with Avery Castle, carrying my weapon—
curses, Foiled again!
it's a fencing foil my mom found at a tag sale and I lost it in Grand Central Station.
DiE!
No, I didn't leave it in Avery's heart...
...though I was tempted.
After all, he's still up and walking around.
Whole.
And wholly beautiful. Nothing stains that handsome face. Nothing scars it—as long as he remains in the light.
And that's what he wants, now, to remain.
In.
The.
Light.
I saw him yesterday in study hall and he was kissing Sally Collins, who is not actually a skank, though I want to believe she is.

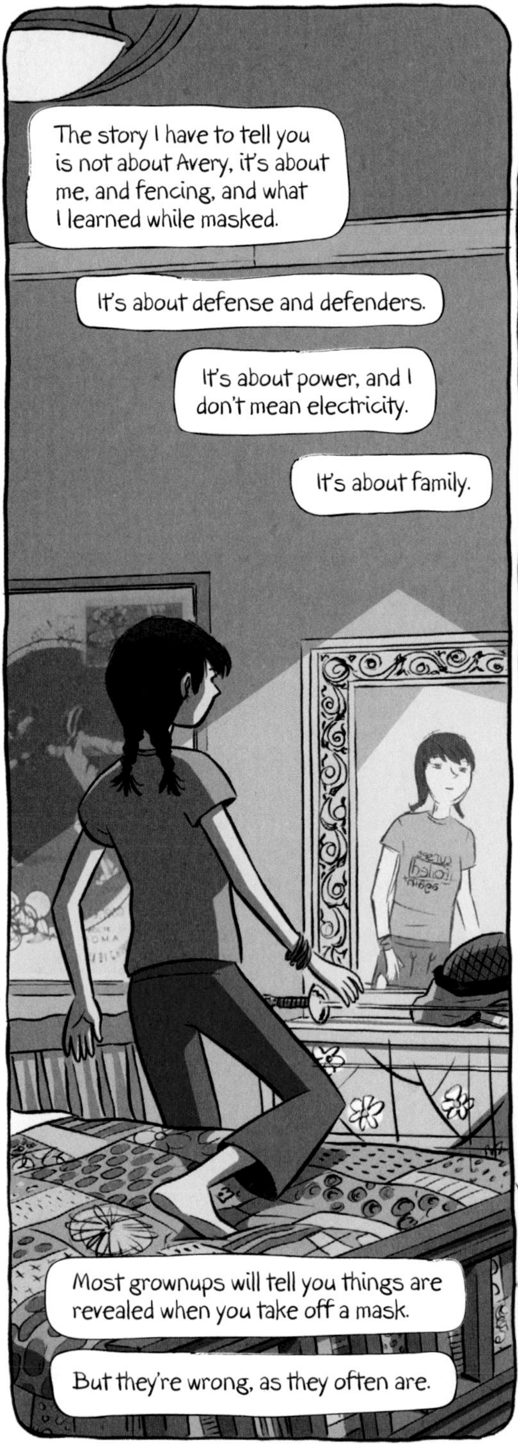

The story I have to tell you is not about Avery, it's about me, and fencing, and what I learned while masked.
It's about defense and defenders.
It's about power, and I don't mean electricity.
It's about family.
Most grownups will tell you things are revealed when you take off a mask.
But they're wrong, as they often are.

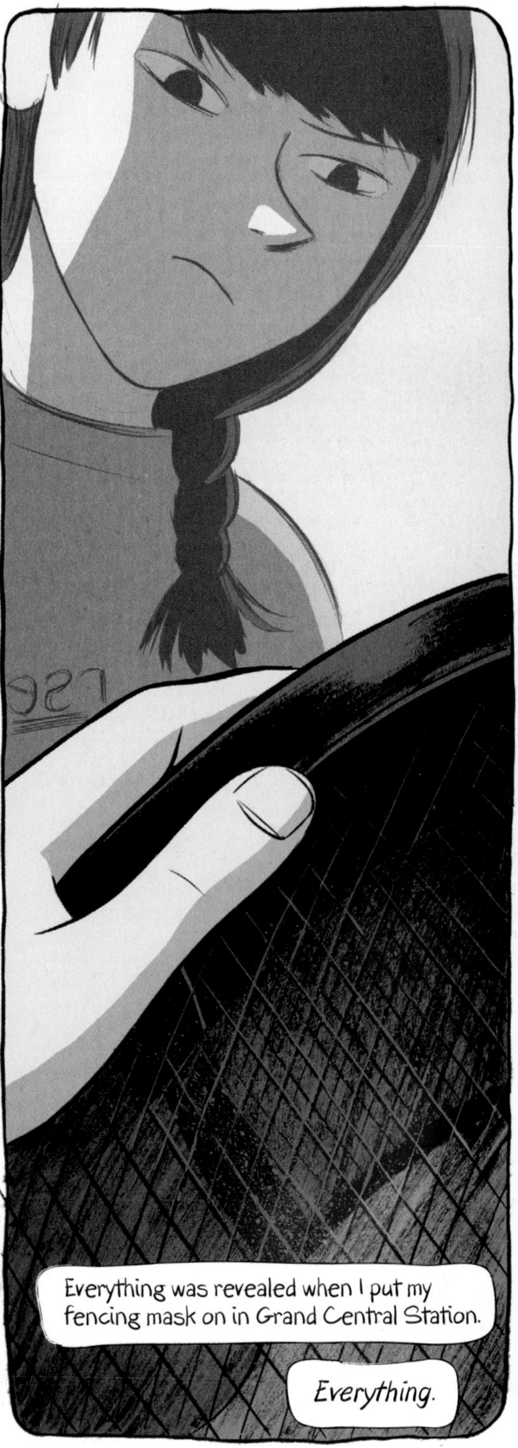

Everything was revealed when I put my fencing mask on in Grand Central Station.
Everything.

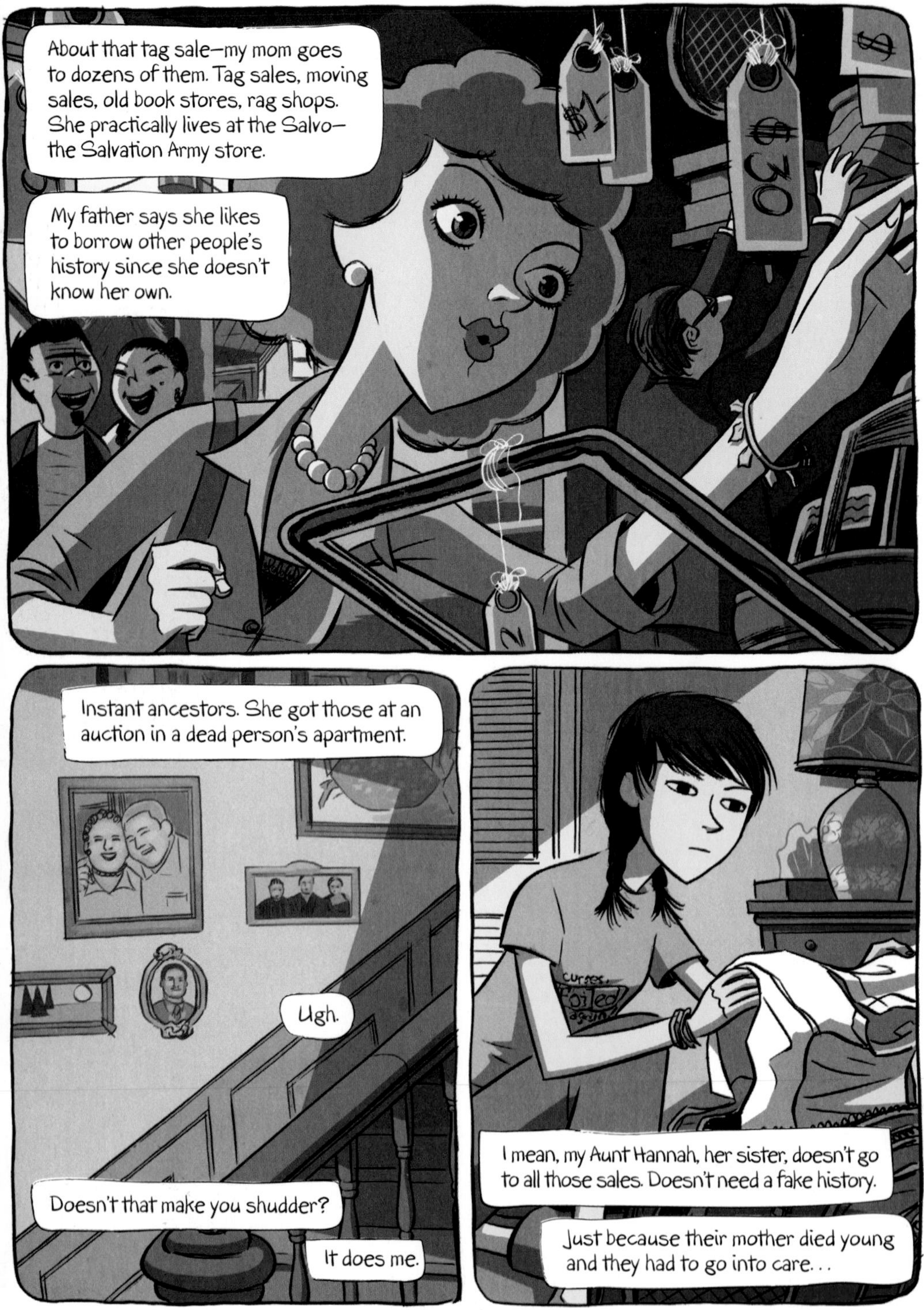

About that tag sale—my mom goes to dozens of them. Tag sales, moving sales, old book stores, rag shops. She practically lives at the Salvo—the Salvation Army store.
My father says she likes to borrow other people's history since she doesn't know her own.
$1
$30
Instant ancestors. She got those at an auction in a dead person's apartment.
Ugh.
Doesn't that make you shudder?
It does me.
I mean, my Aunt Hannah, her sister, doesn't go to all those sales. Doesn't need a fake history.
Just because their mother died young and they had to go into care. . .

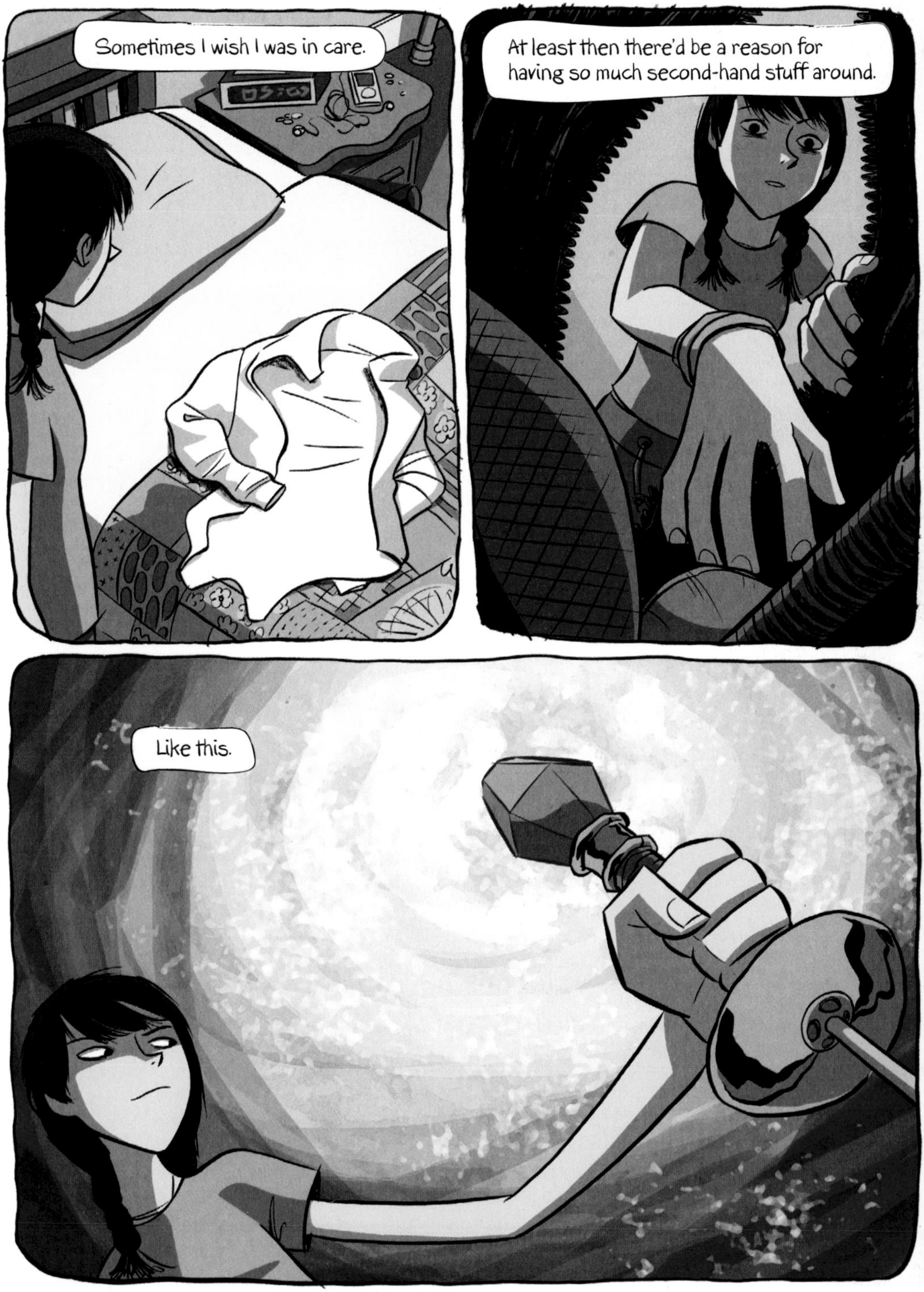
Sometimes I wish I was in care.
At least then there'd be a reason for having so much second-hand stuff around.
Like this.

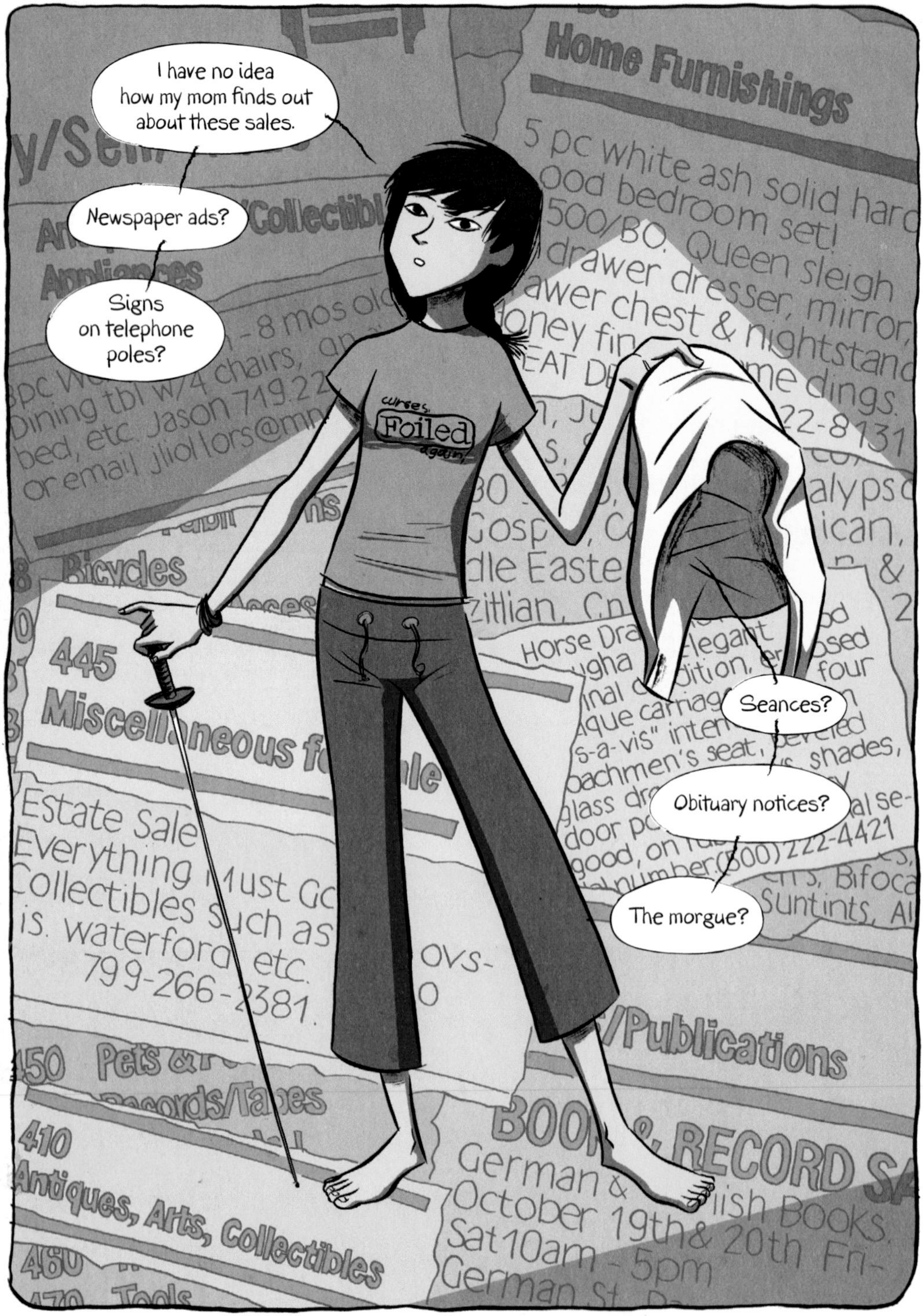

I have no idea how my mom finds out about these sales.
Newspaper ads?
Signs on telephone poles?
curses, Foiled again,
Seances?
Obituary notices?
The morgue?

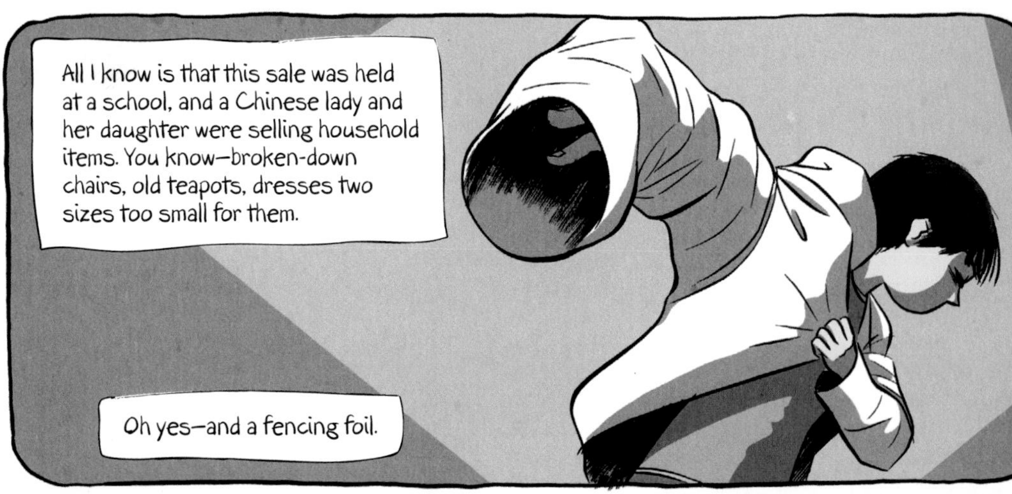
All I know is that this sale was held at a school, and a Chinese lady and her daughter were selling household items. You know—broken-down chairs, old teapots, dresses two sizes too small for them.
Oh yes—and a fencing foil.

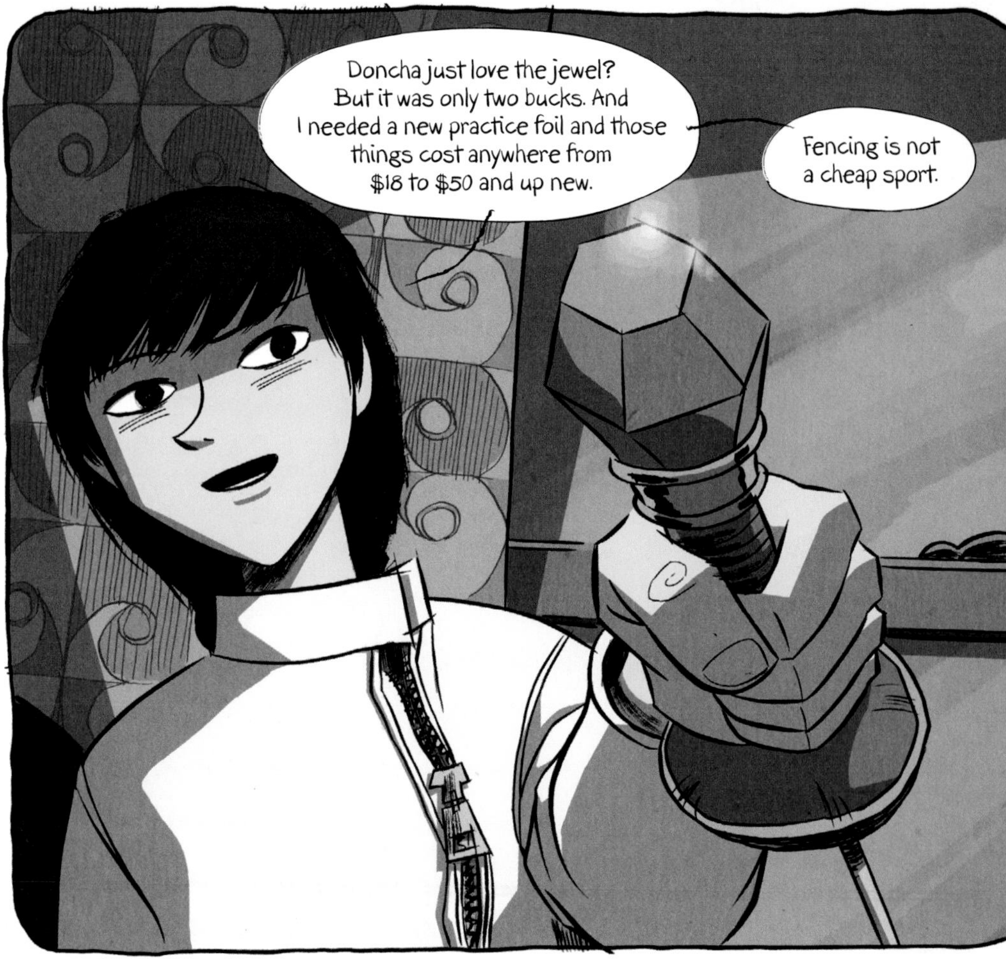
Doncha just love the jewel? But it was only two bucks. And I needed a new practice foil and those things cost anywhere from $18 to $50 and up new.
Fencing is not a cheap sport.

2. Invito

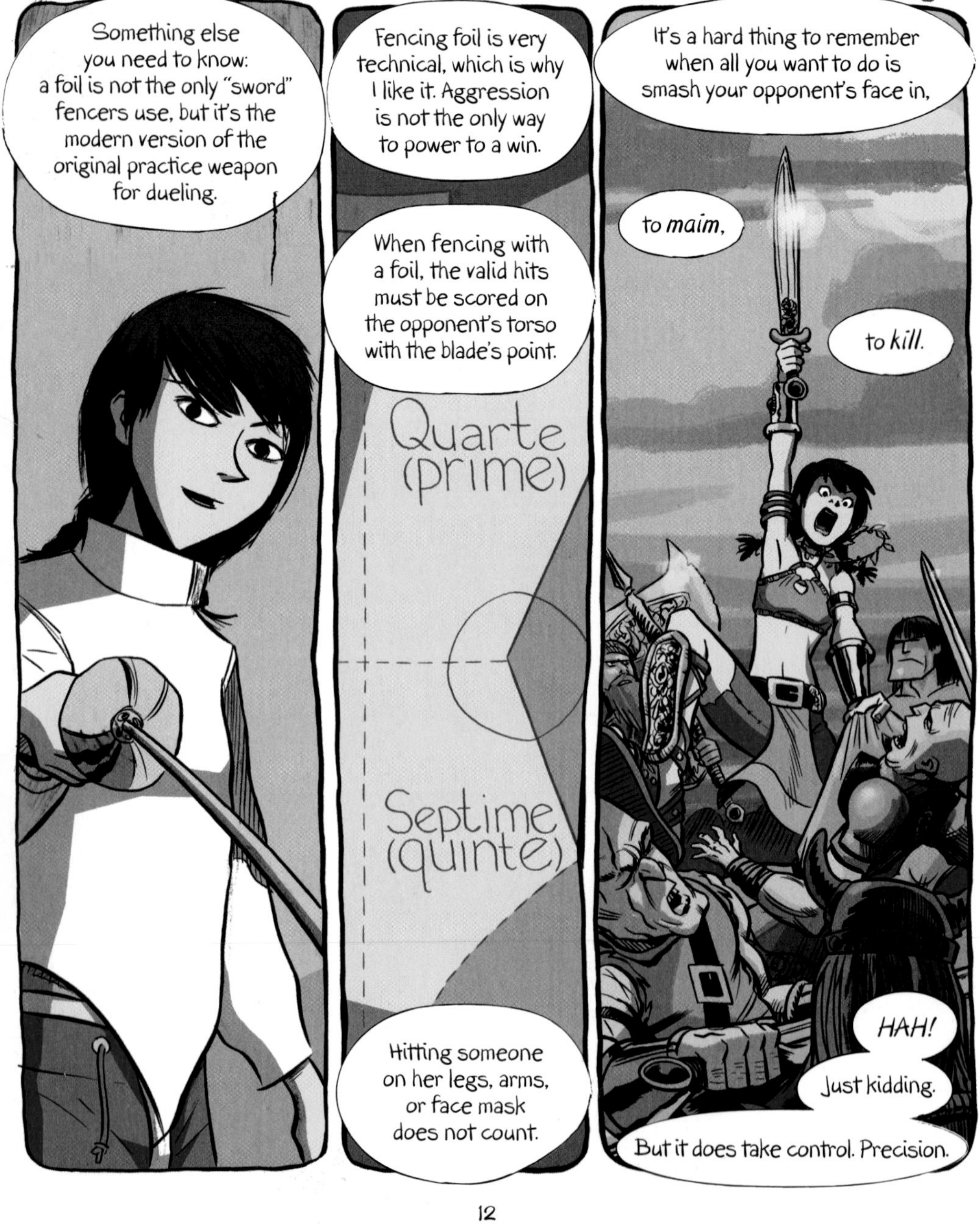
Something else you need to know: a foil is not the only "sword" fencers use, but it's the modern version of the original practice weapon for dueling.
Fencing foil is very technical, which is why I like it. Aggression is not the only way to power to a win.
When fencing with a foil, the valid hits must be scored on the opponent's torso with the blade's point.
Quarte (prime)
Septime (quinte)
Hitting someone on her legs, arms, or face mask does not count.
It's a hard thing to remember when all you want to do is smash your opponent's face in,
to *maim*,
to *kill*.
HAH!
Just kidding.
But it does take control. Precision.

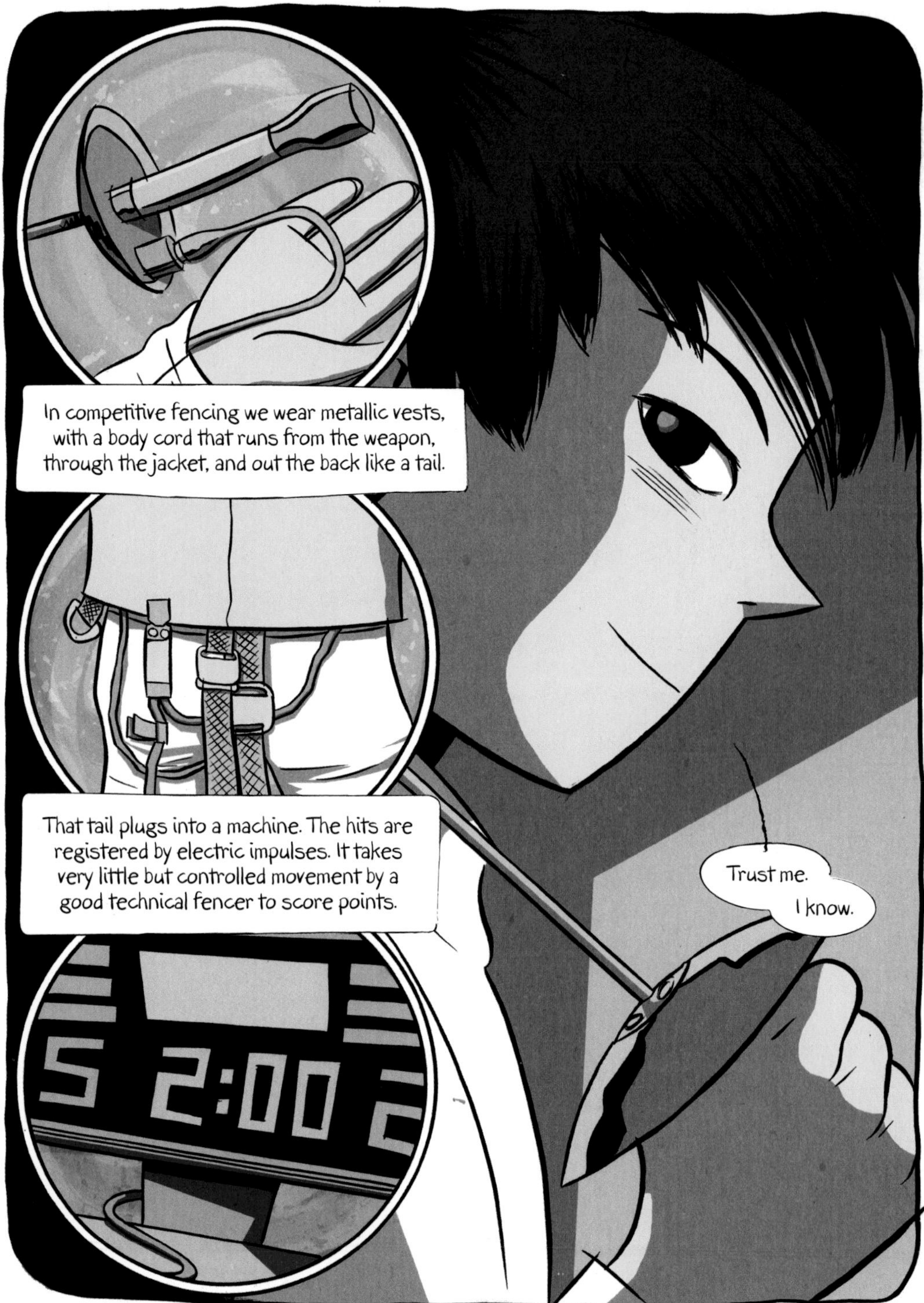
In competitive fencing we wear metallic vests, with a body cord that runs from the weapon, through the jacket, and out the back like a tail.
That tail plugs into a machine. The hits are registered by electric impulses. It takes very little but controlled movement by a good technical fencer to score points.
Trust me.
I know.
5 2:00 2

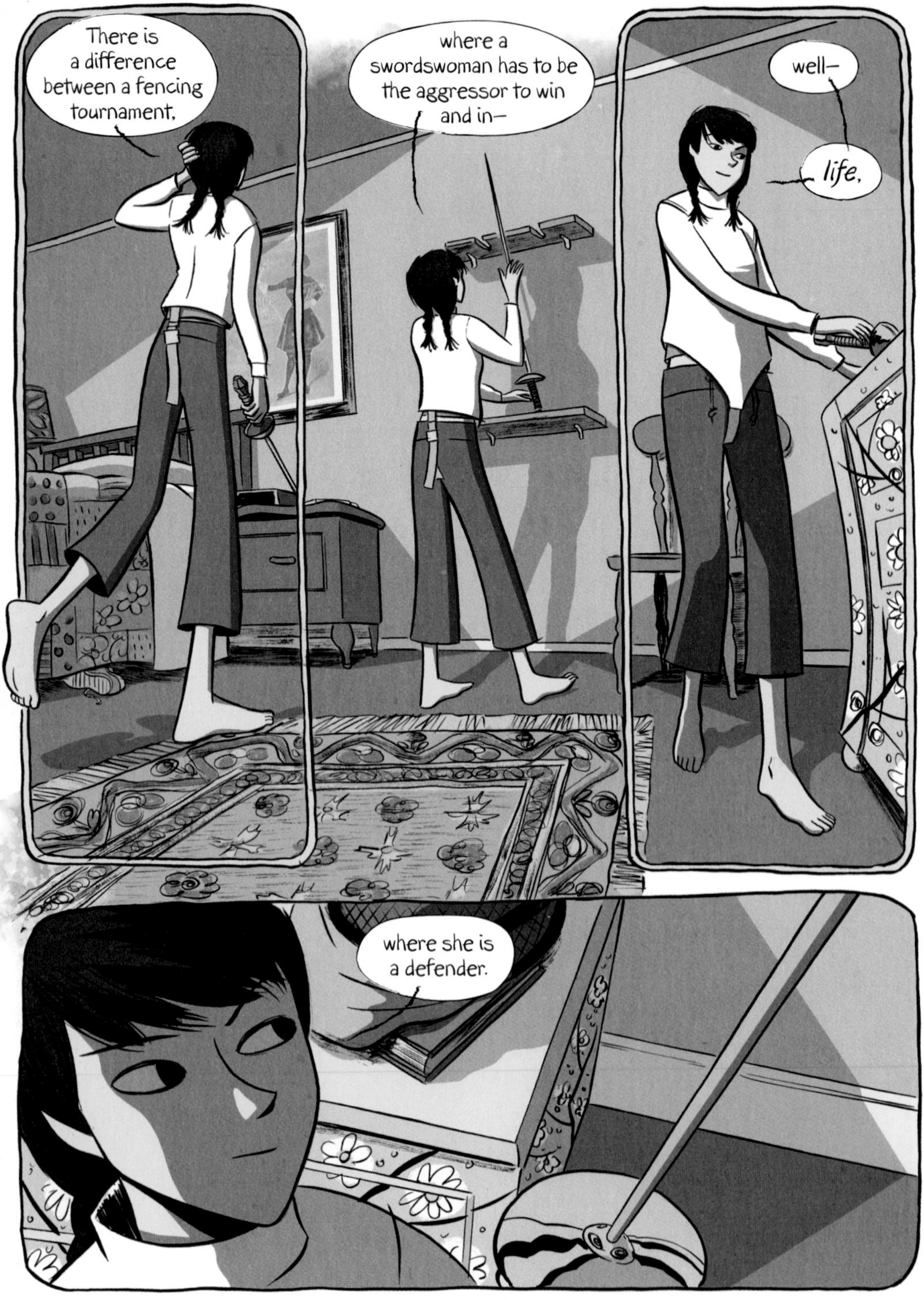
There is a difference between a fencing tournament,
where a swordswoman has to be the aggressor to win and in—
well—
life,
where she is a defender.

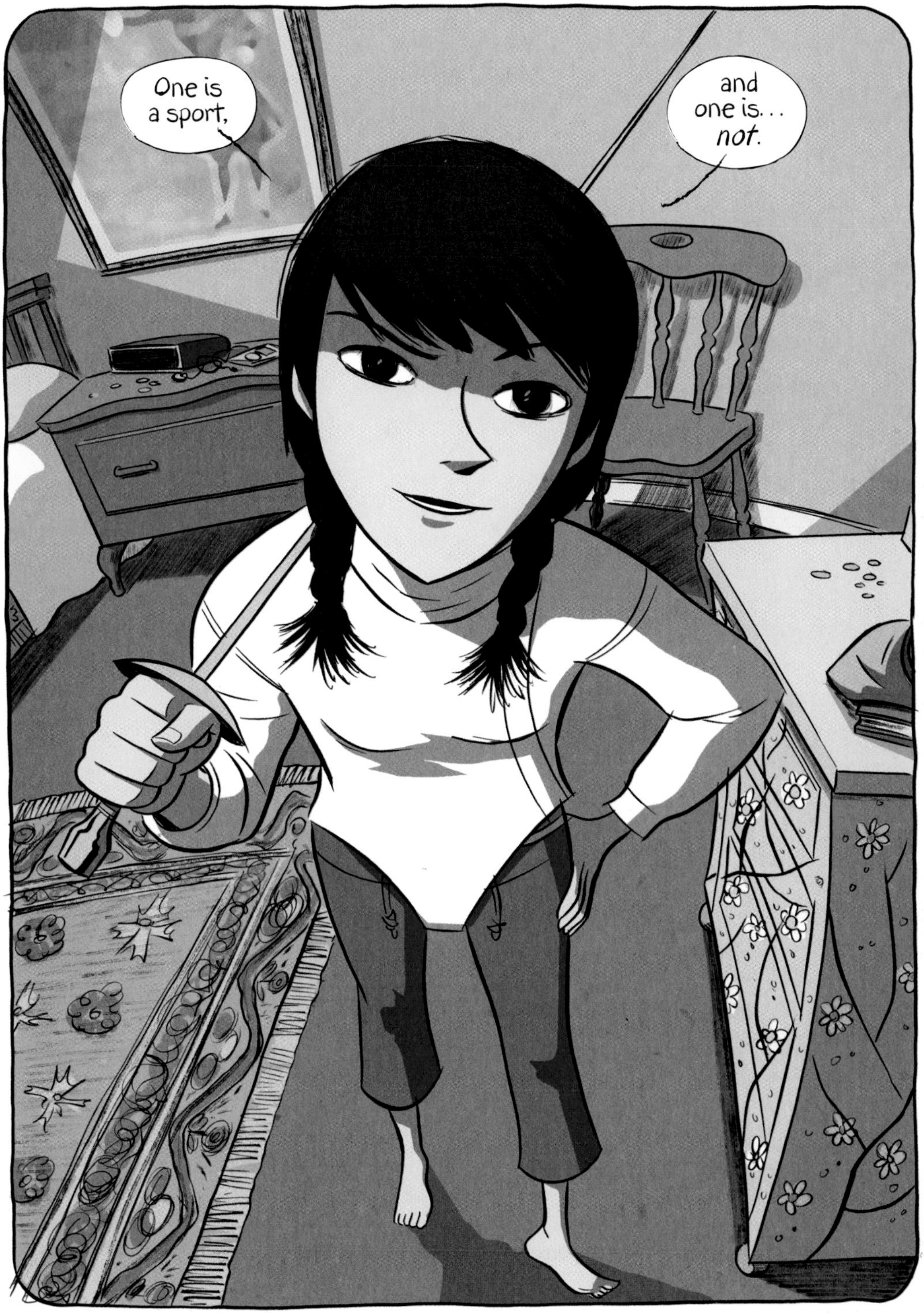
One is a sport,
and one is... *not*.

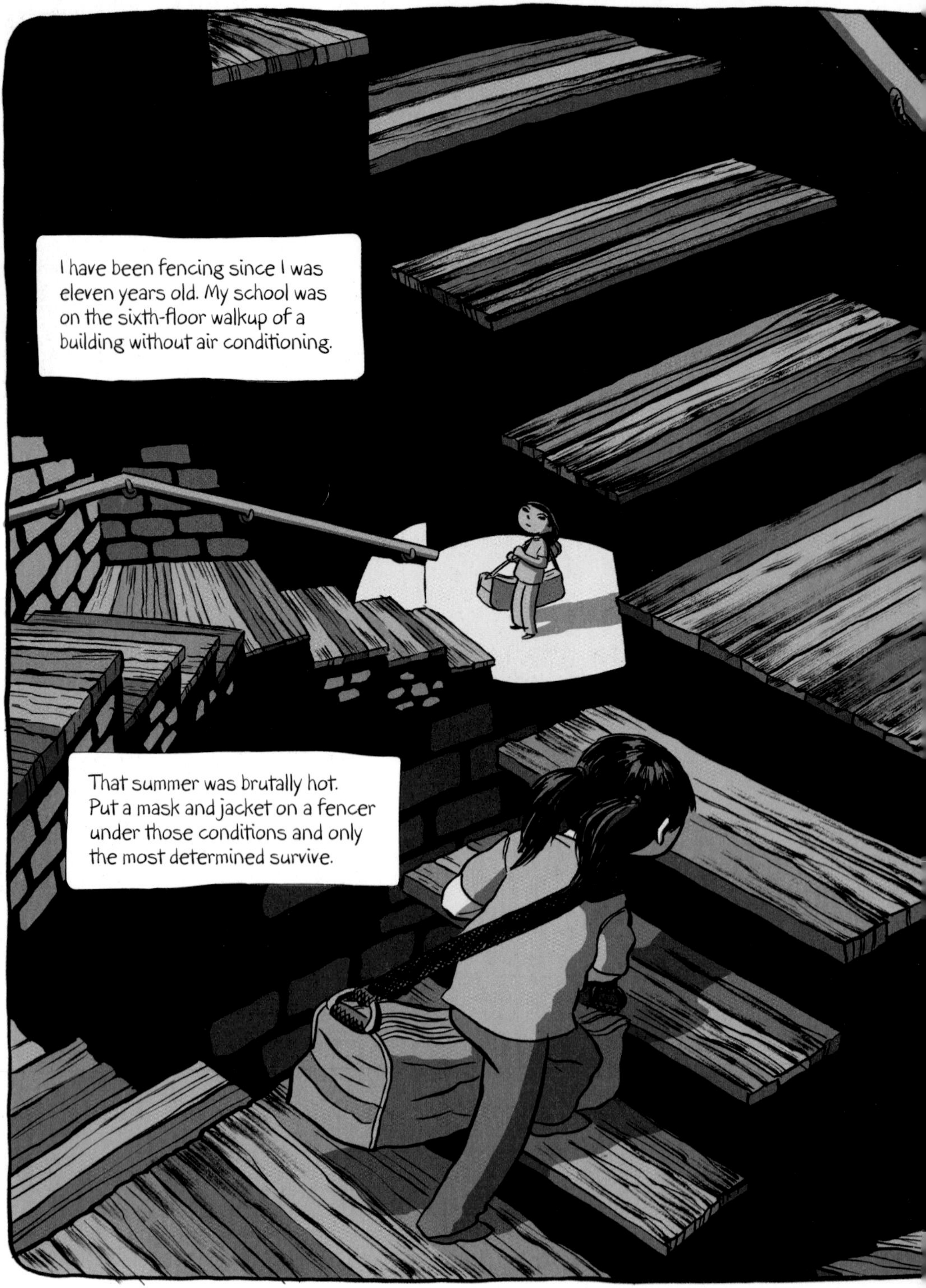
I have been fencing since I was eleven years old. My school was on the sixth-floor walkup of a building without air conditioning.
That summer was brutally hot. Put a mask and jacket on a fencer under those conditions and only the most determined survive.

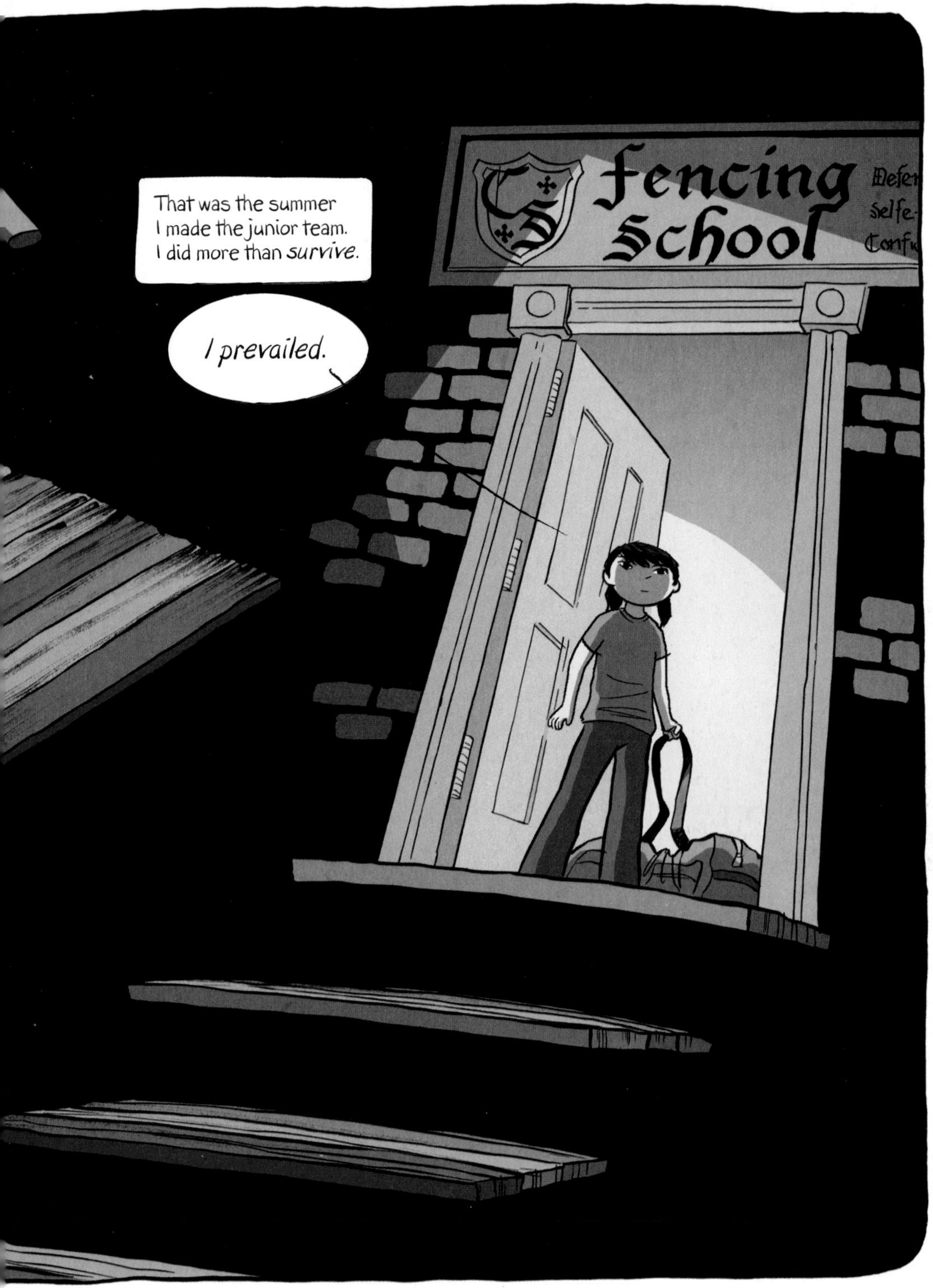

That was the summer I made the junior team. I did more than *survive*.
I prevailed.
Fencing School

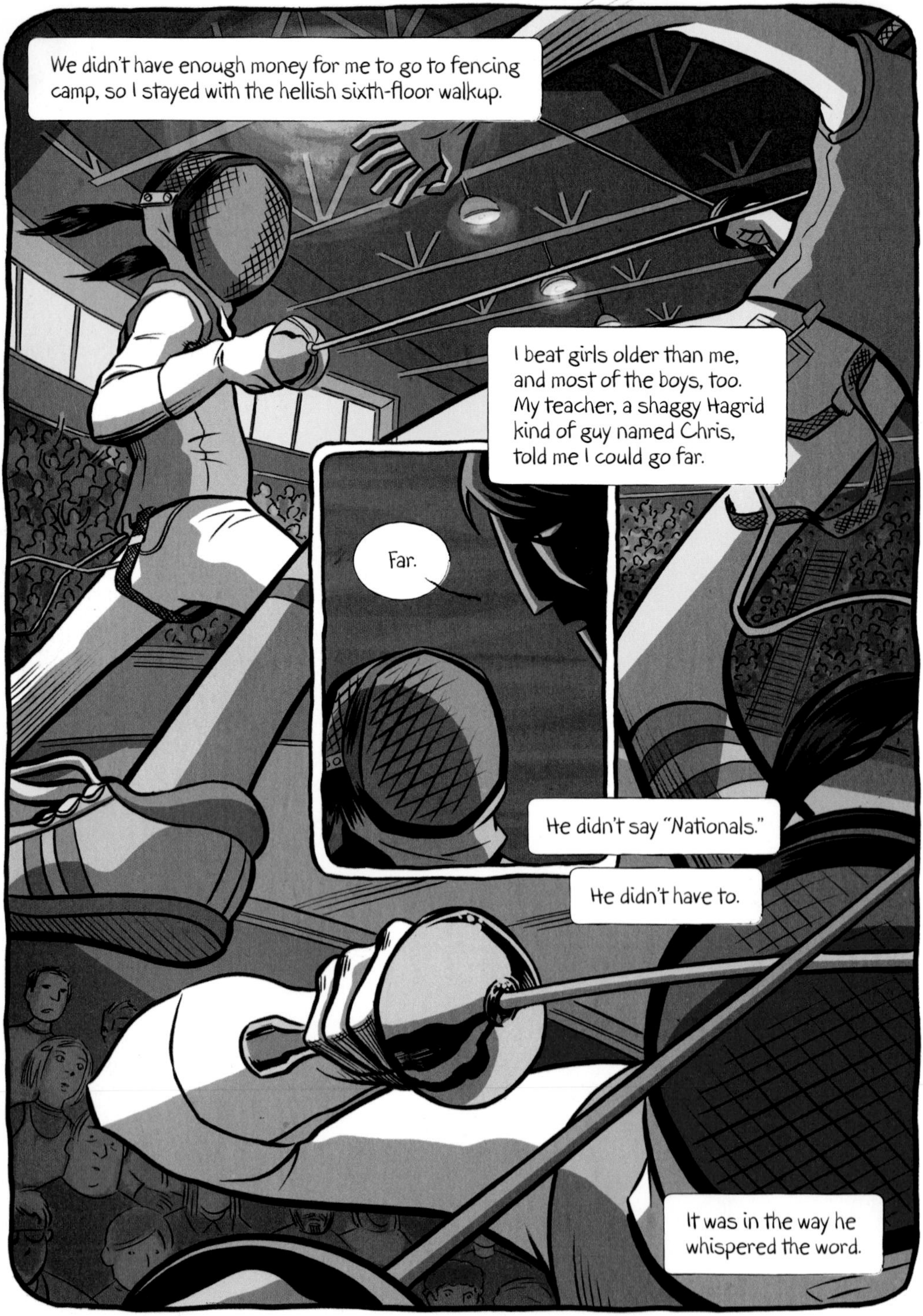
We didn't have enough money for me to go to fencing camp, so I stayed with the hellish sixth-floor walkup.
I beat girls older than me, and most of the boys, too. My teacher, a shaggy Hagrid kind of guy named Chris, told me I could go far.
Far.
He didn't say "Nationals."
He didn't have to.
It was in the way he whispered the word.

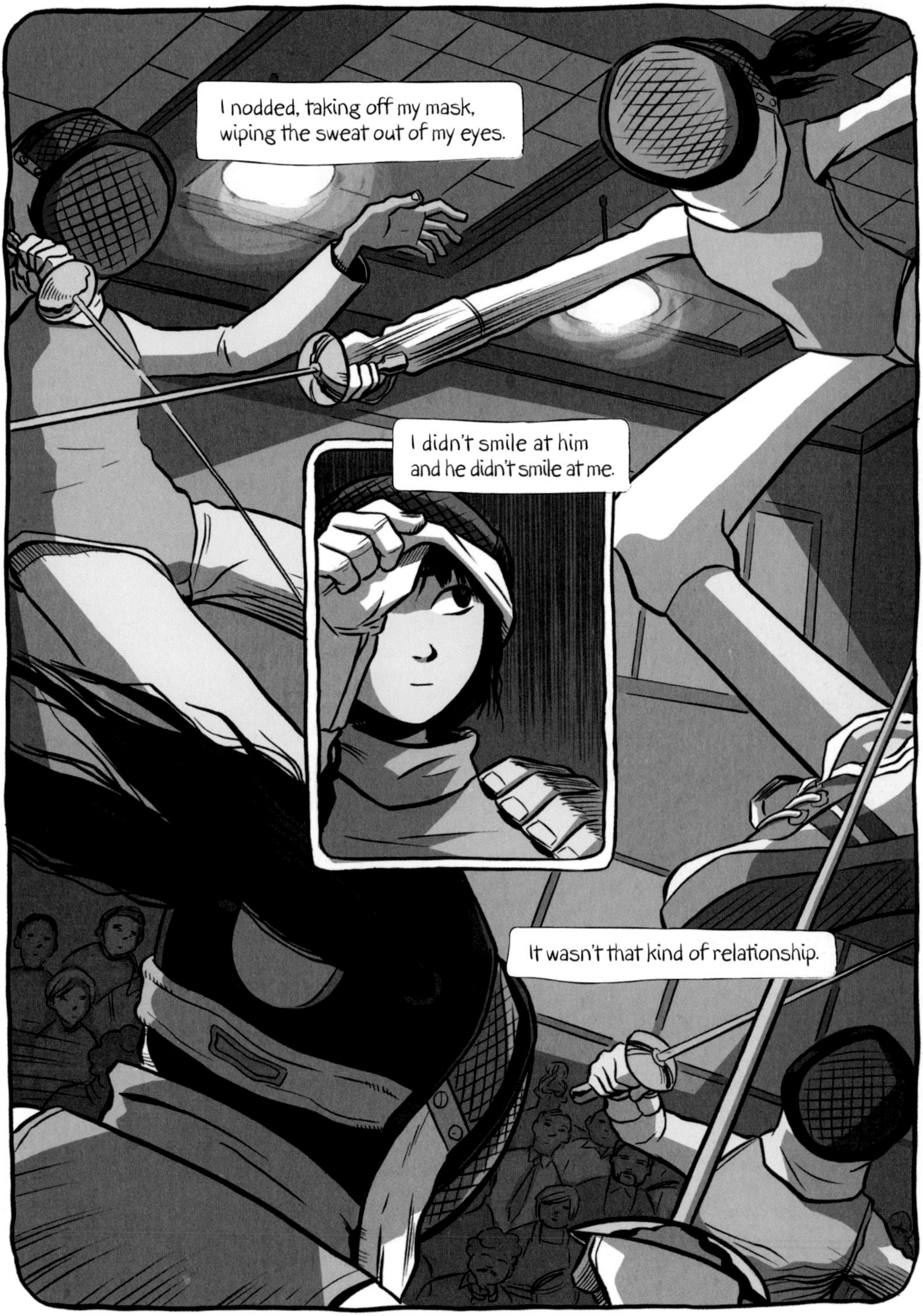
I nodded, taking off my mask, wiping the sweat out of my eyes.
I didn't smile at him and he didn't smile at me.
It wasn't that kind of relationship.

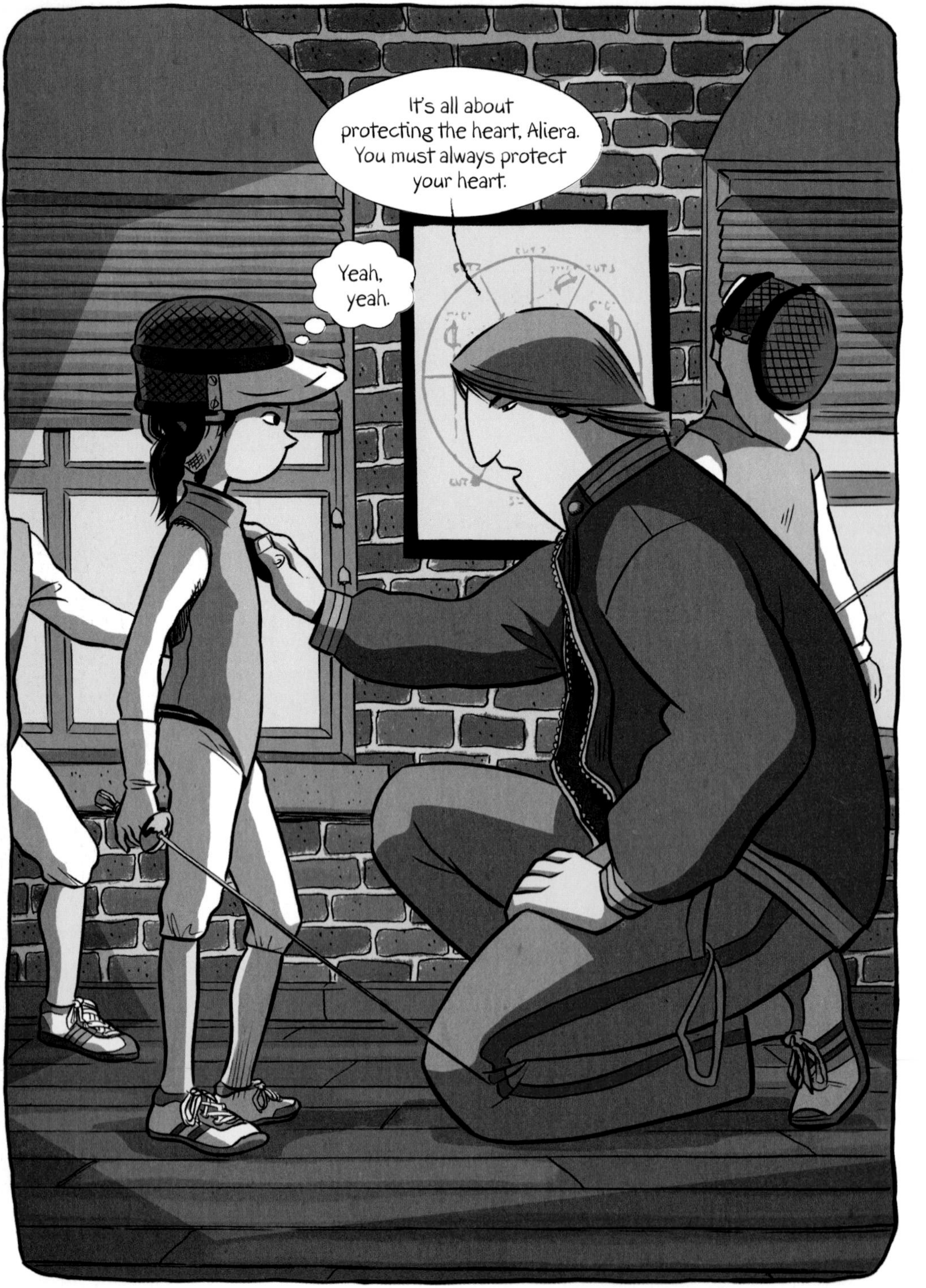
It's all about protecting the heart, Aliera. You must always protect your heart.
Yeah, yeah.

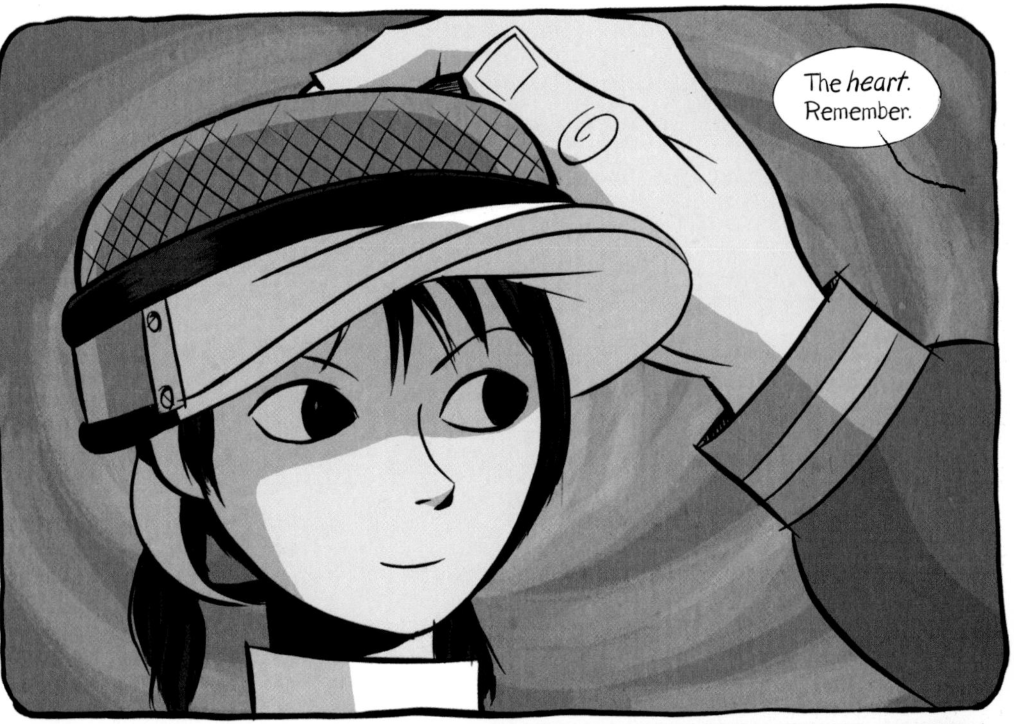
The *heart*. Remember.

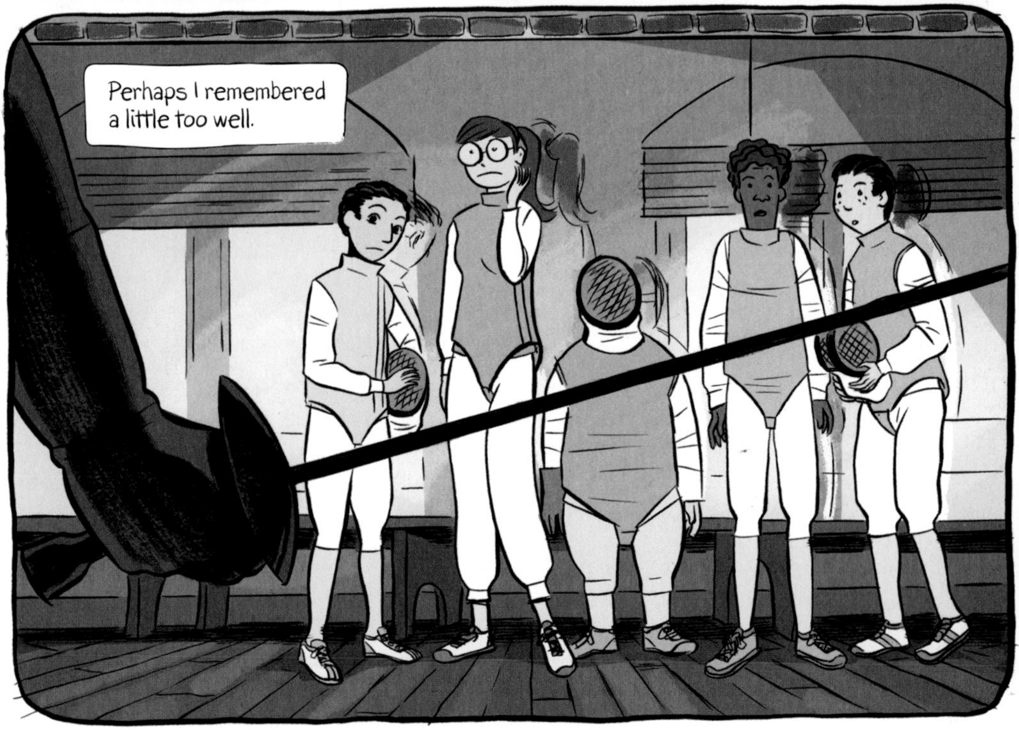
Perhaps I remembered a little too well.

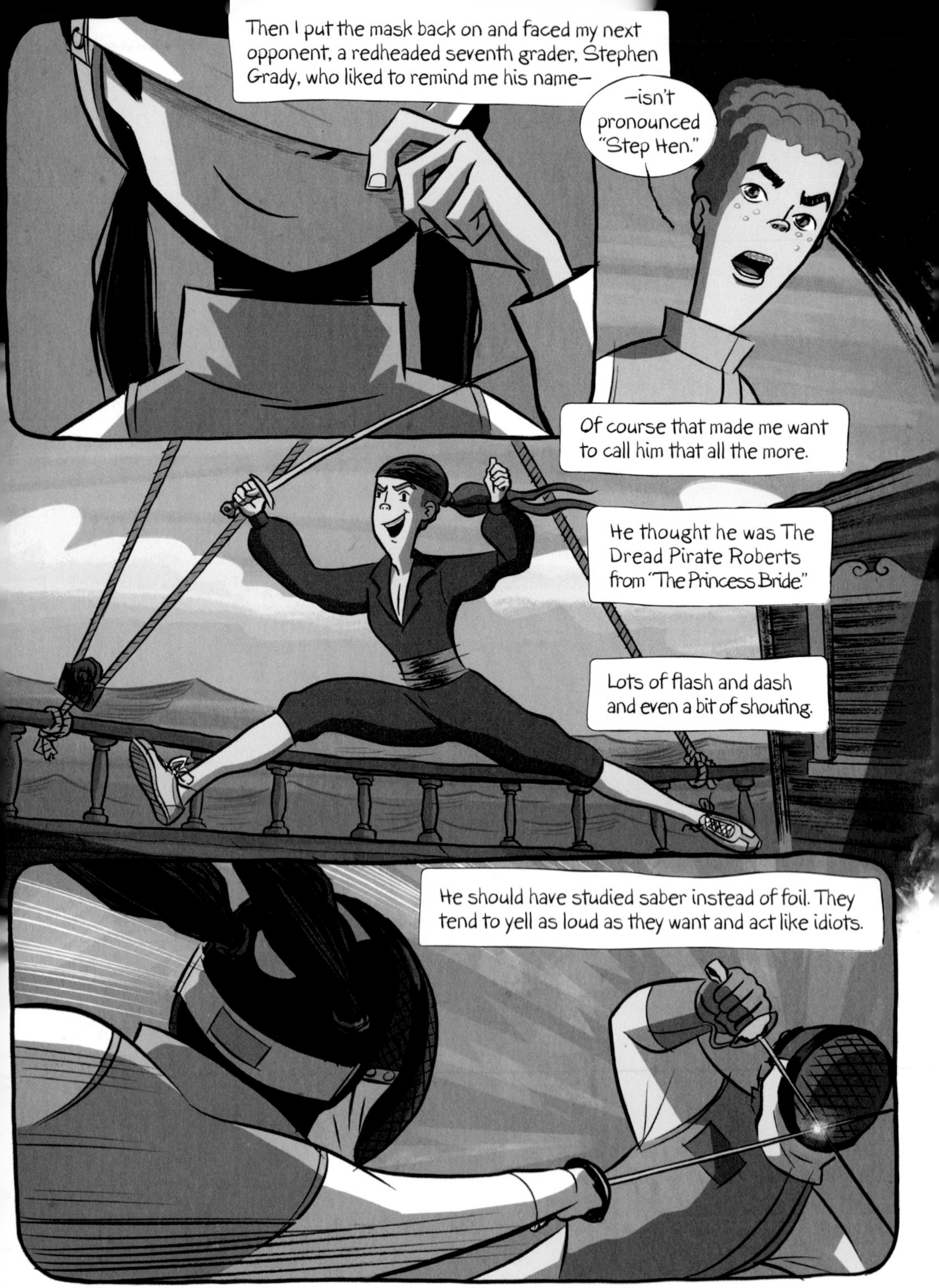

Then I put the mask back on and faced my next opponent, a redheaded seventh grader, Stephen Grady, who liked to remind me his name—
—isn't pronounced "Step Hen."
Of course that made me want to call him that all the more.
He thought he was The Dread Pirate Roberts from "The Princess Bride."
Lots of flash and dash and even a bit of shouting.
He should have studied saber instead of foil. They tend to yell as loud as they want and act like idiots.

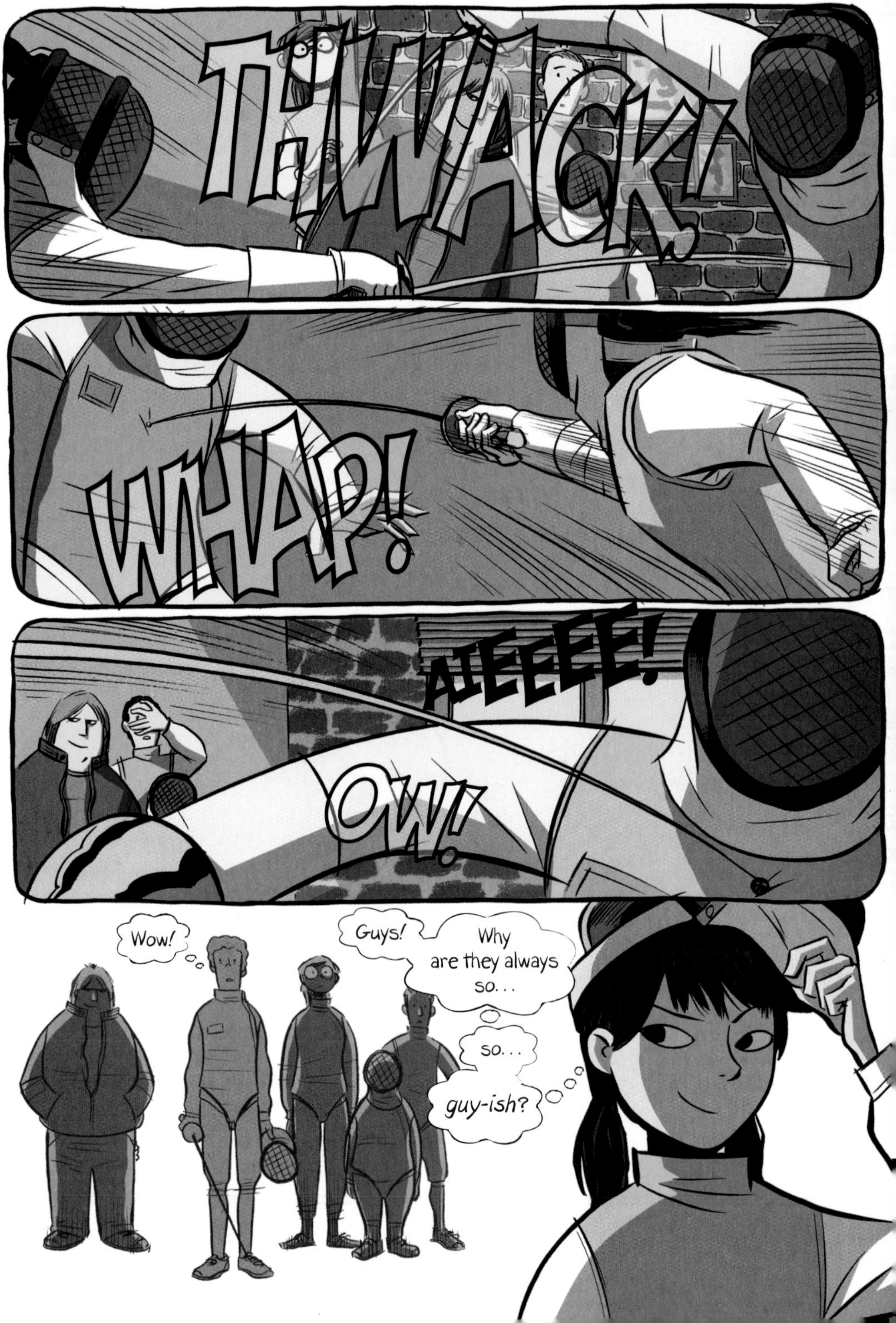
THWACK!
WHAP!
AIEEEEE!
OW!
Wow!
Guys!
Why are they always so...
so...
guy-ish?

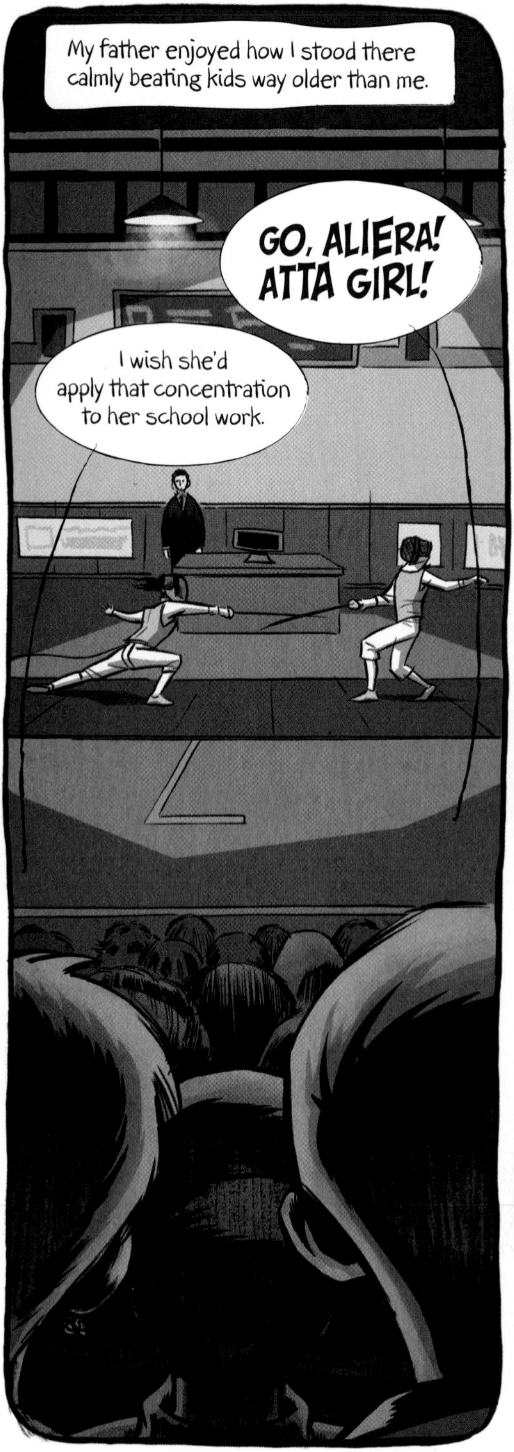
My father enjoyed how I stood there calmly beating kids way older than me.
GO, ALIERA! ATTA GIRL!
I wish she'd apply that concentration to her school work.

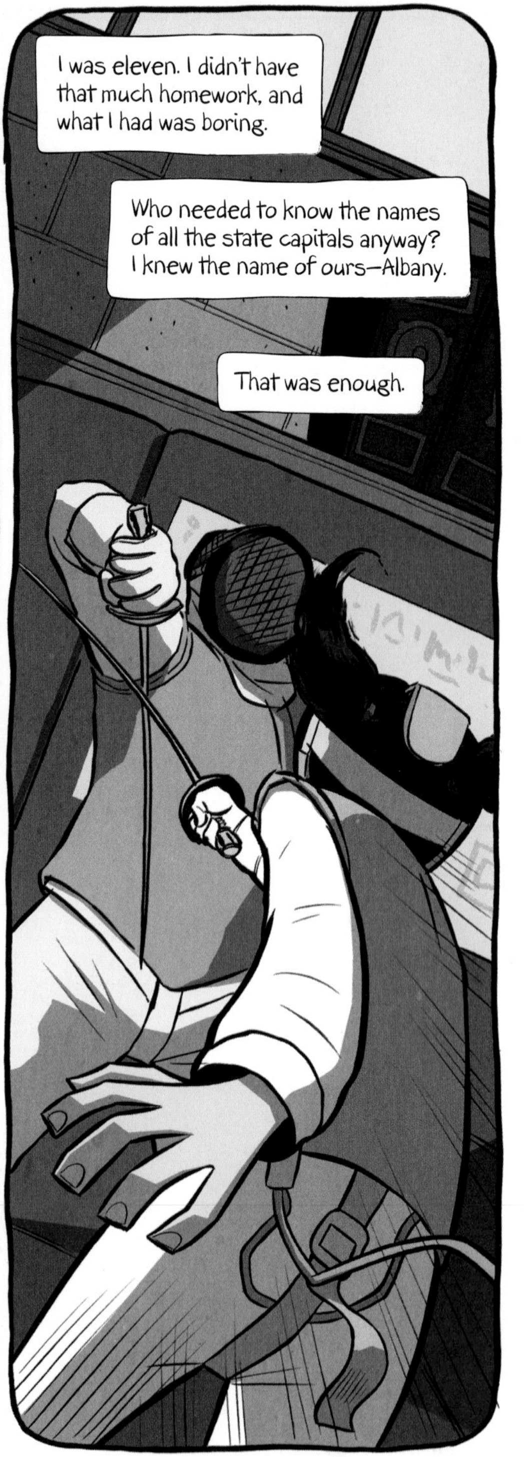
I was eleven. I didn't have that much homework, and what I had was boring.
Who needed to know the names of all the state capitals anyway? I knew the name of ours—Albany.
That was enough.

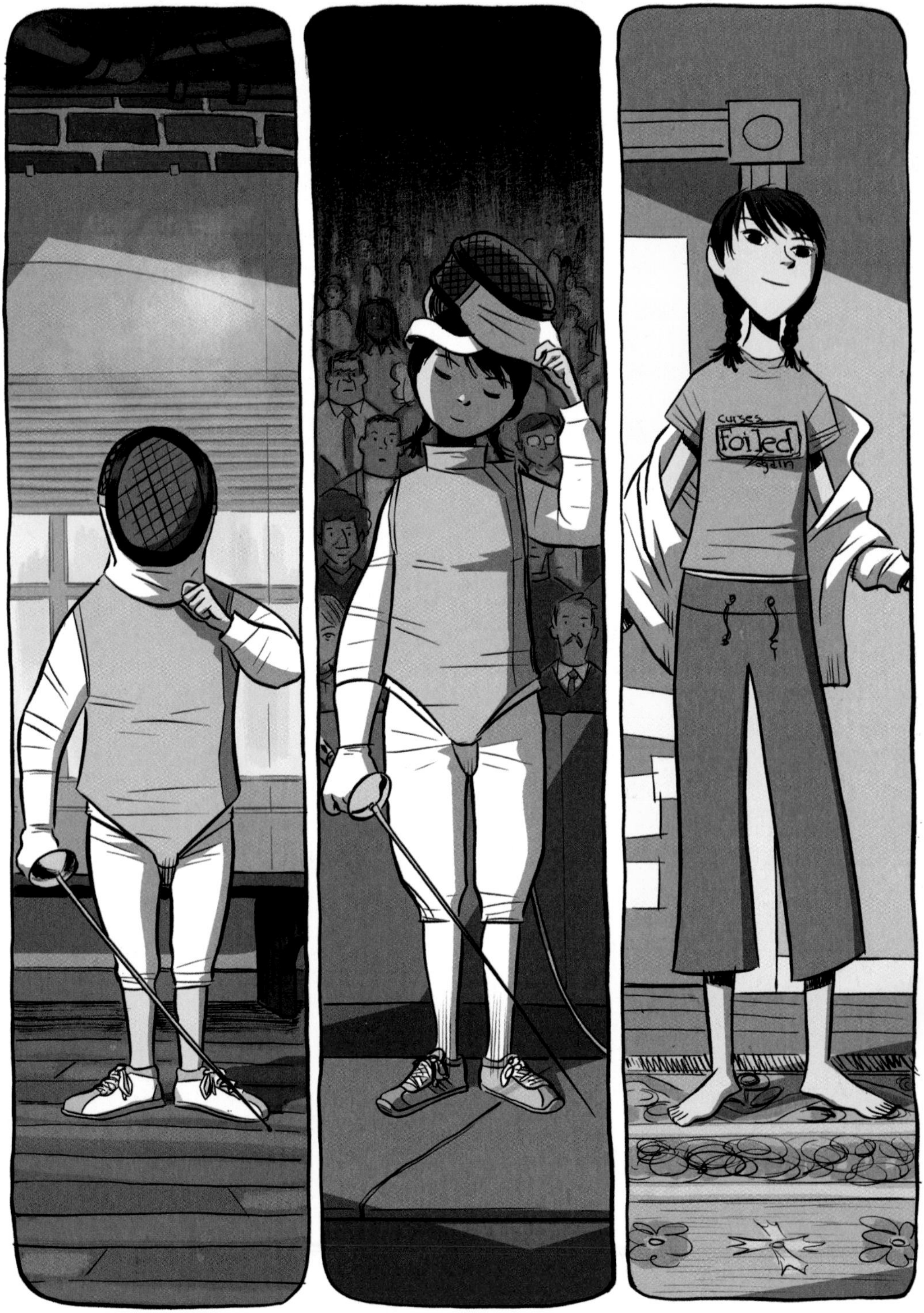

curses
Foiled
again

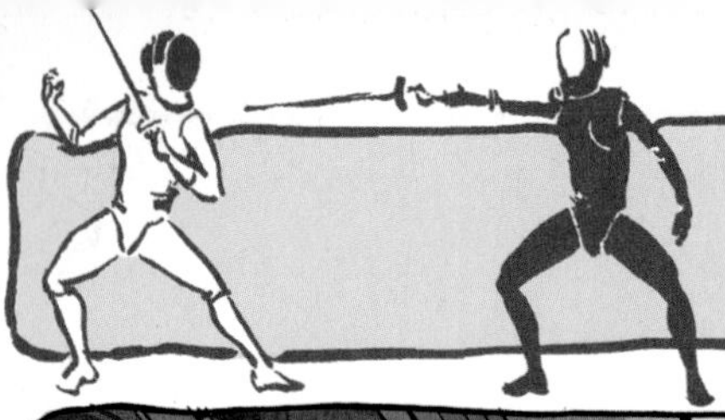

3. Point in Line

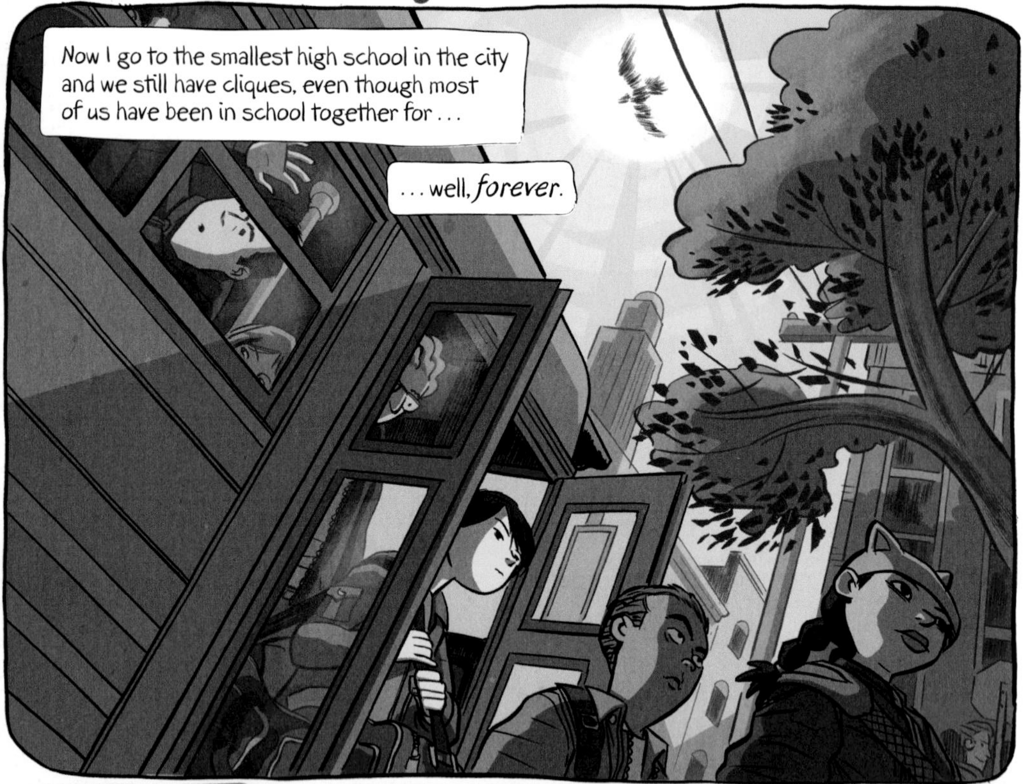
Now I go to the smallest high school in the city and we still have cliques, even though most of us have been in school together for . . .
. . . well, *forever*.

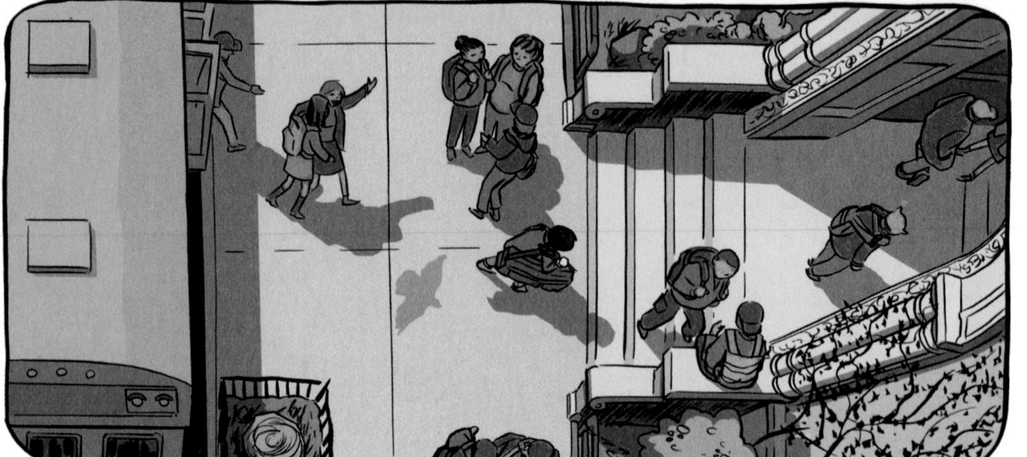

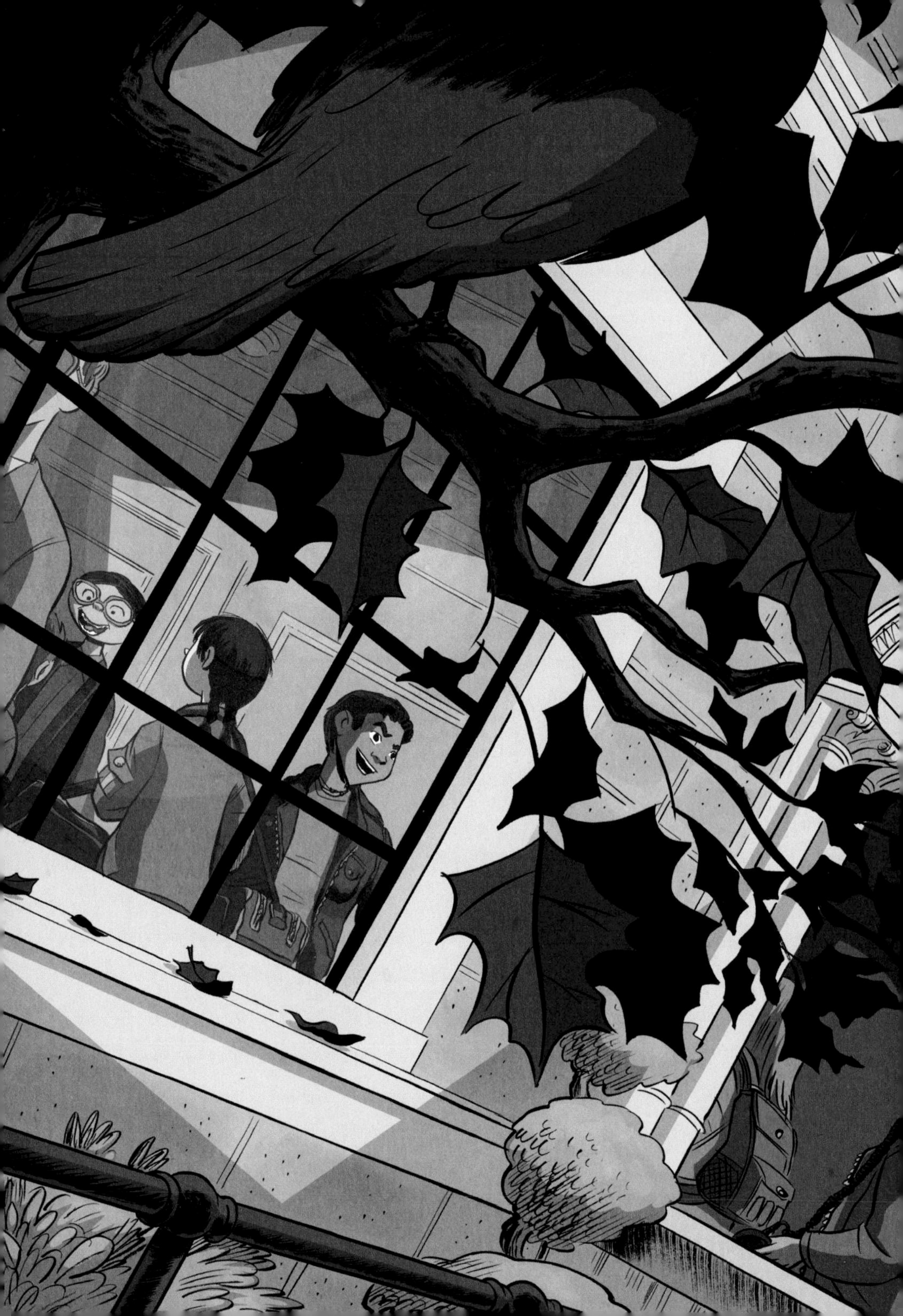

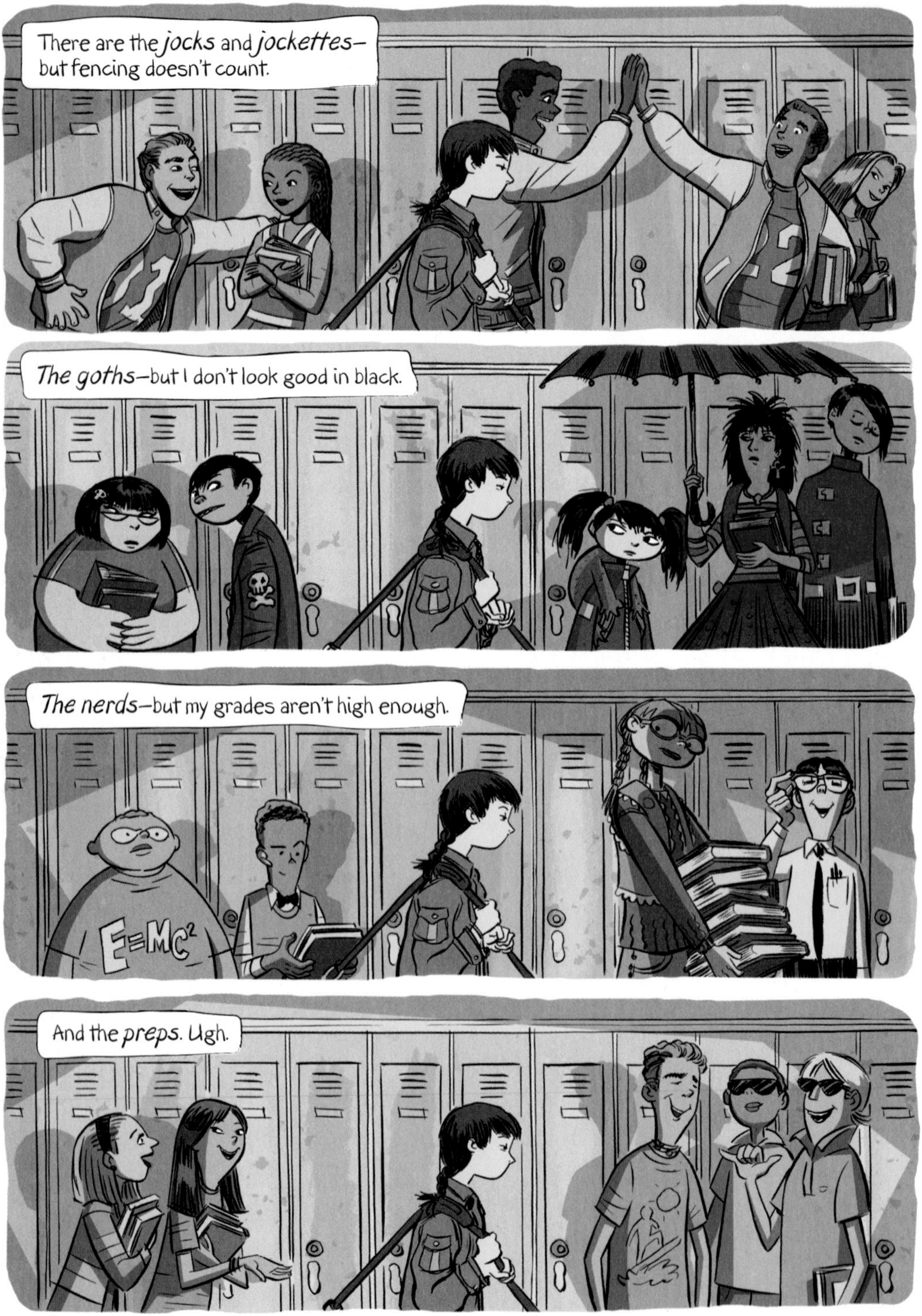
There are the *jocks* and *jockettes*—but fencing doesn't count.
22
The goths—but I don't look good in black.
The nerds—but my grades aren't high enough.
E=MC²
And the *preps*. Ugh.

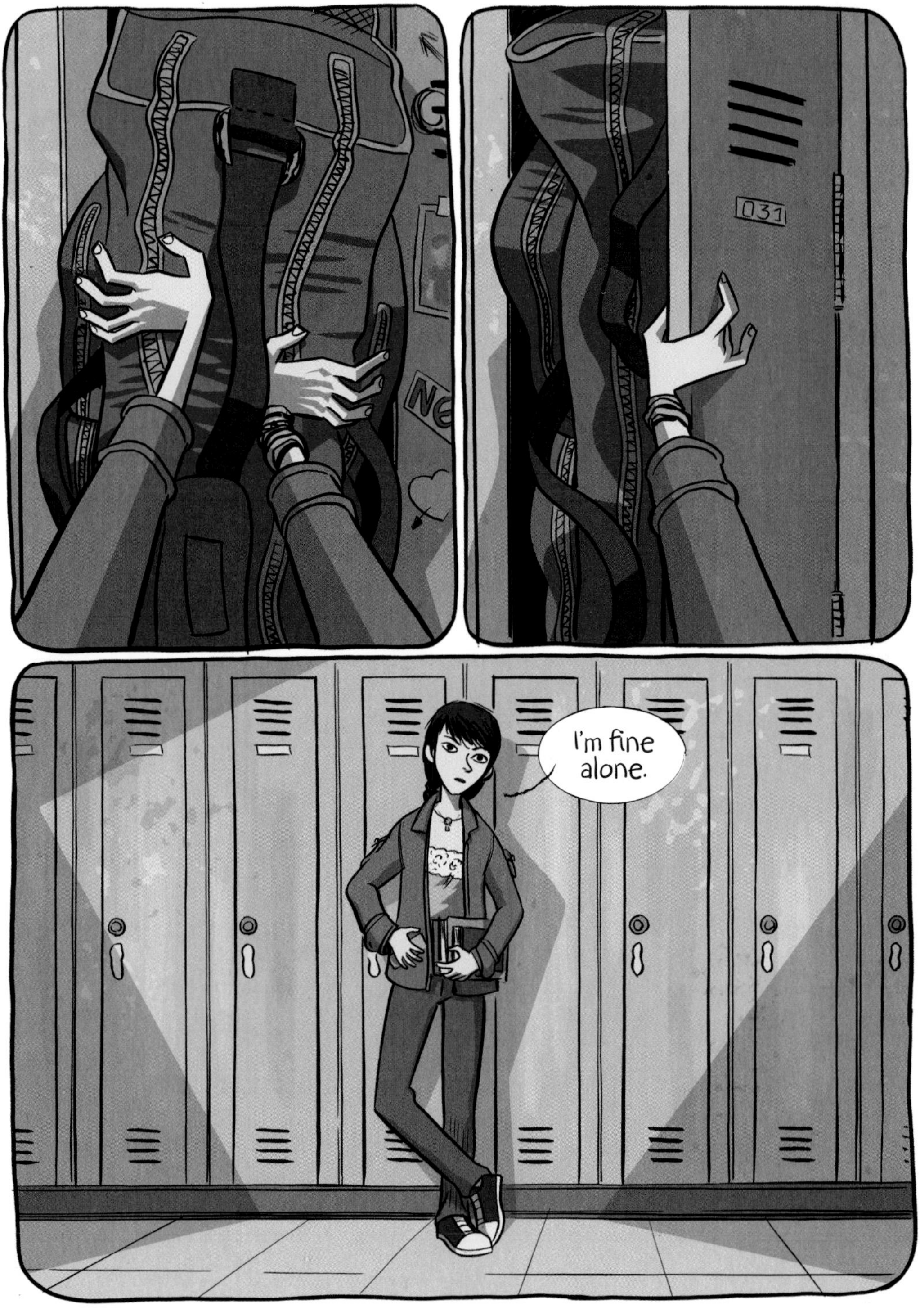
031
I'm fine alone.

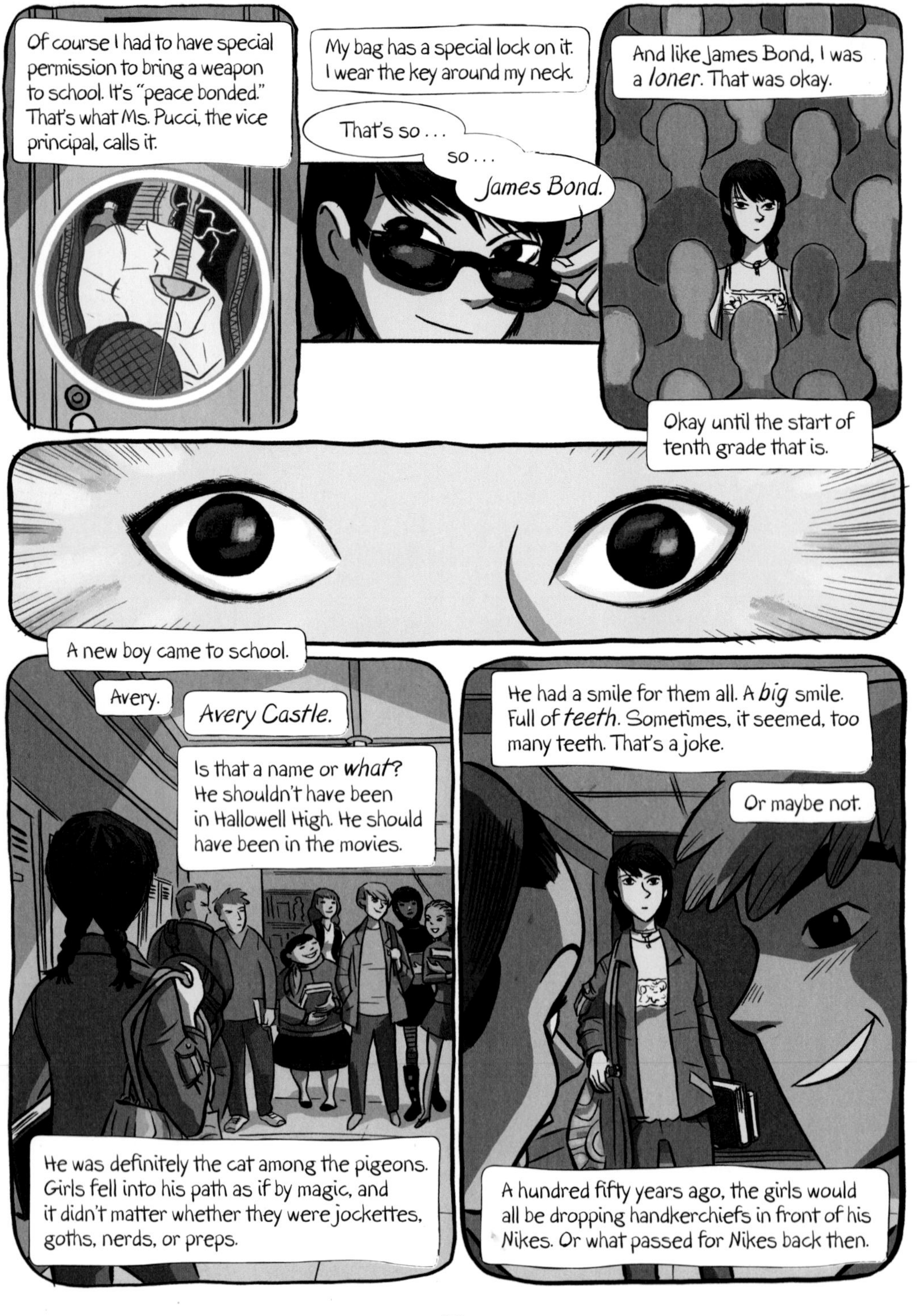
Of course I had to have special permission to bring a weapon to school. It's "peace bonded." That's what Ms. Pucci, the vice principal, calls it.
My bag has a special lock on it. I wear the key around my neck.
That's so . . .
so . . .
James Bond.
And like James Bond, I was a *loner*. That was okay.
Okay until the start of tenth grade that is.
A new boy came to school.
Avery.
Avery Castle.
Is that a name or *what*? He shouldn't have been in Hallowell High. He should have been in the movies.
He was definitely the cat among the pigeons. Girls fell into his path as if by magic, and it didn't matter whether they were jockettes, goths, nerds, or preps.
He had a smile for them all. A *big* smile. Full of *teeth*. Sometimes, it seemed, too many teeth. That's a joke.
Or maybe not.
A hundred fifty years ago, the girls would all be dropping handkerchiefs in front of his Nikes. Or what passed for Nikes back then.

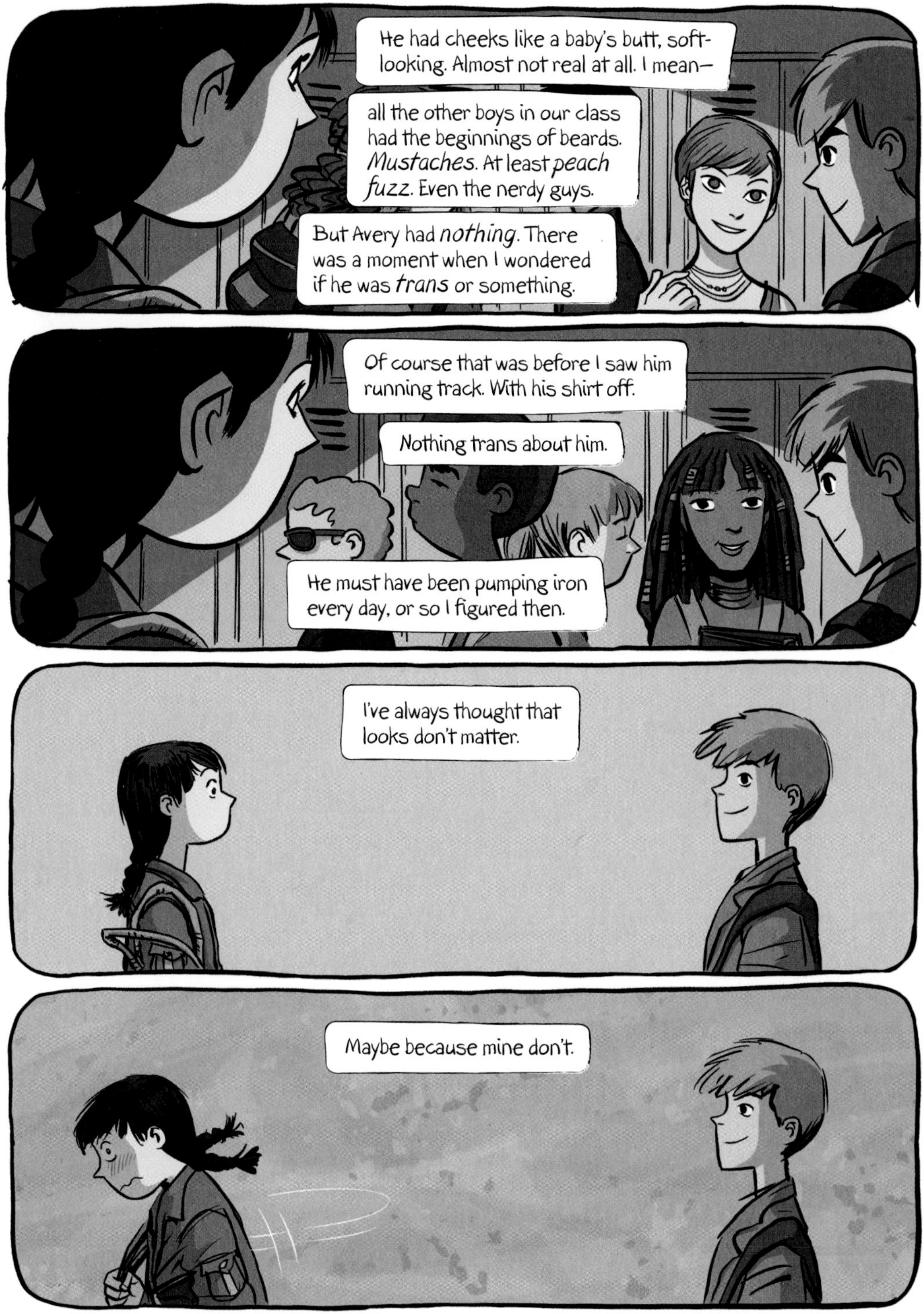
He had cheeks like a baby's butt, soft-looking. Almost not real at all. I mean—
all the other boys in our class had the beginnings of beards. *Mustaches*. At least *peach fuzz*. Even the nerdy guys.
But Avery had *nothing*. There was a moment when I wondered if he was *trans* or something.
Of course that was before I saw him running track. With his shirt off.
Nothing trans about him.
He must have been pumping iron every day, or so I figured then.
I've always thought that looks don't matter.
Maybe because mine don't.

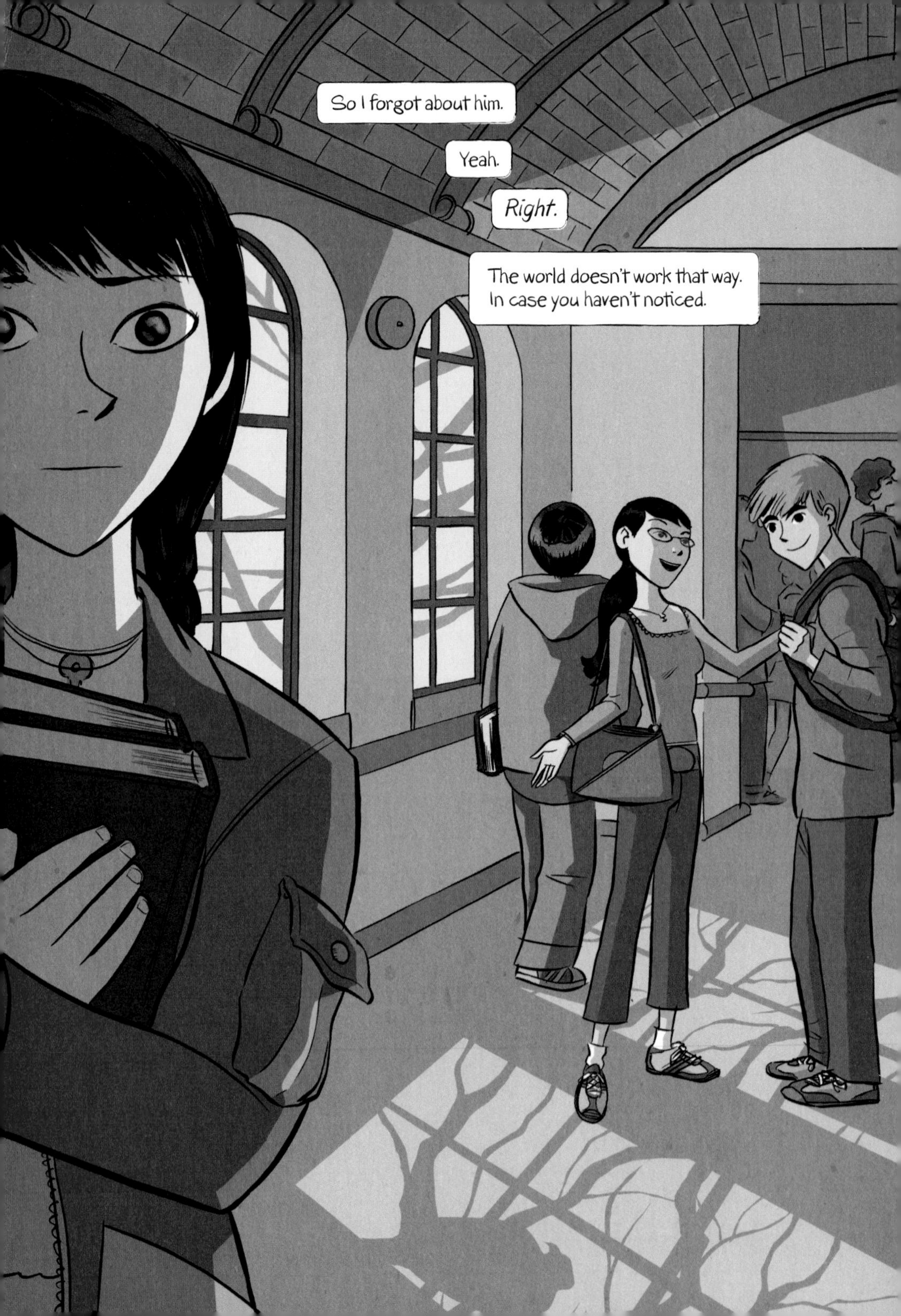
So I forgot about him.
Yeah.
Right.
The world doesn't work that way. In case you haven't noticed.

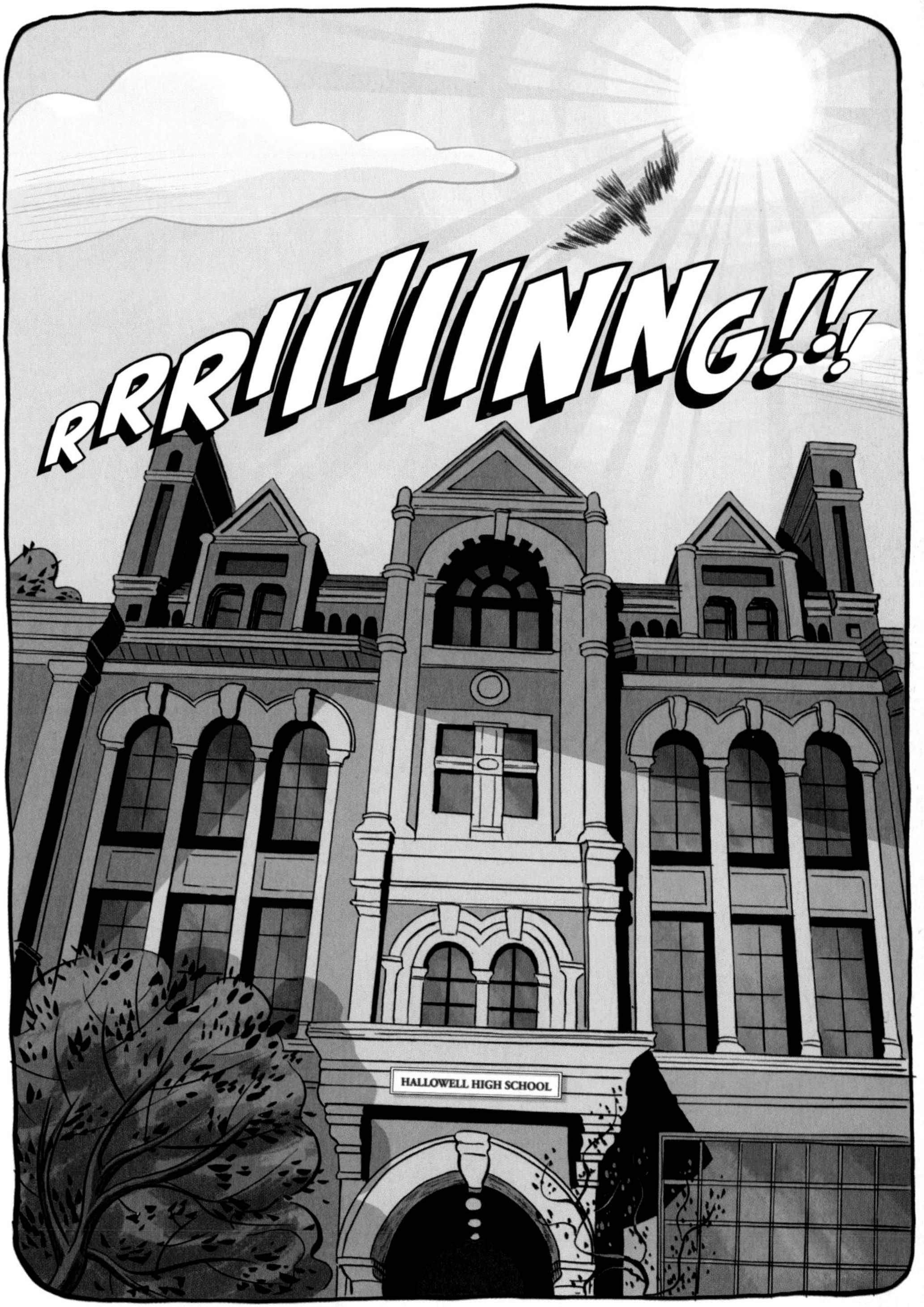
RRRIIIIIINNG!!!
HALLOWELL HIGH SCHOOL

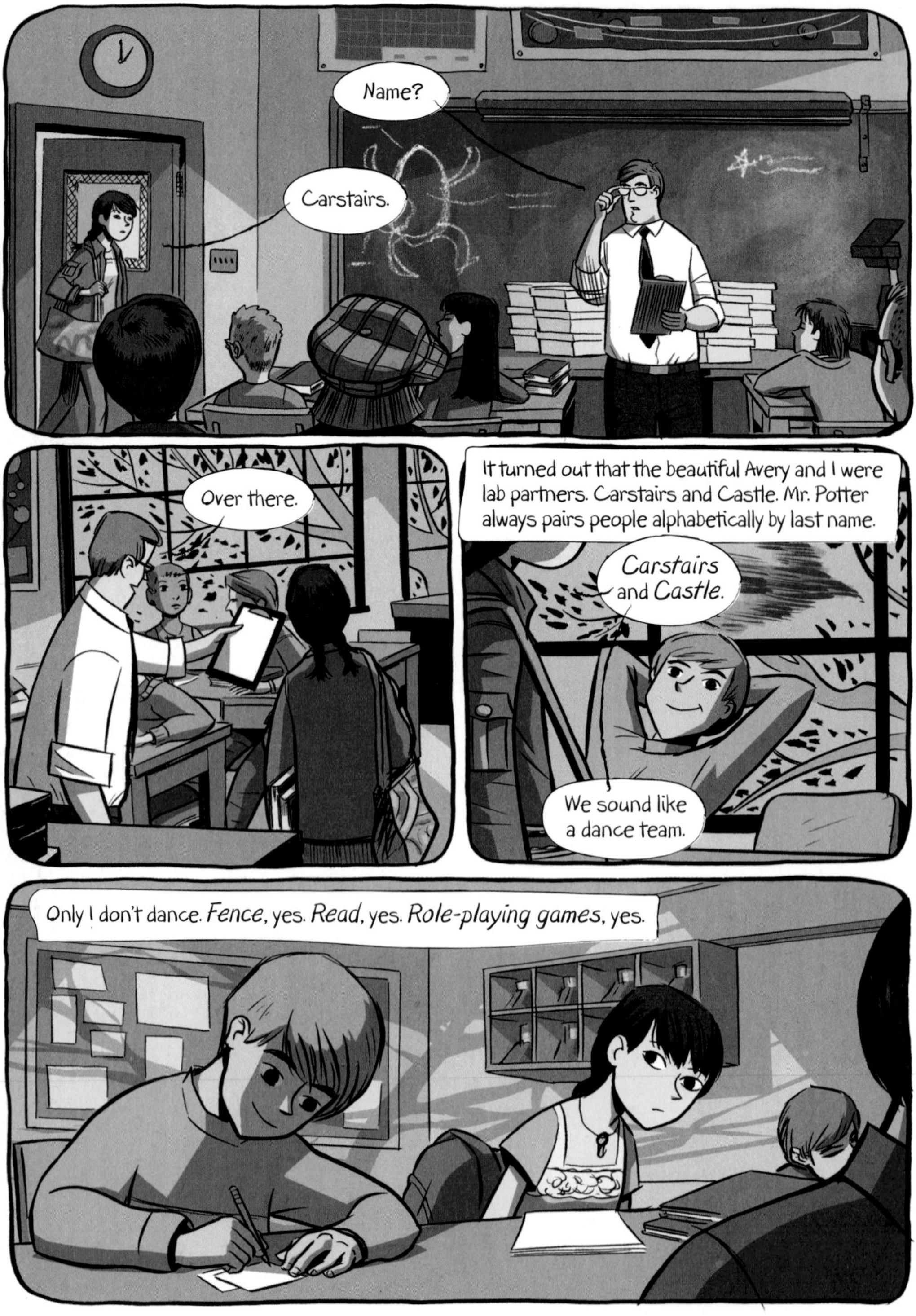
Name?
Carstairs.
Over there.
It turned out that the beautiful Avery and I were lab partners. Carstairs and Castle. Mr. Potter always pairs people alphabetically by last name.
Carstairs and *Castle.*
We sound like a dance team.
Only I don't dance. *Fence*, yes. *Read*, yes. *Role-playing games*, yes.

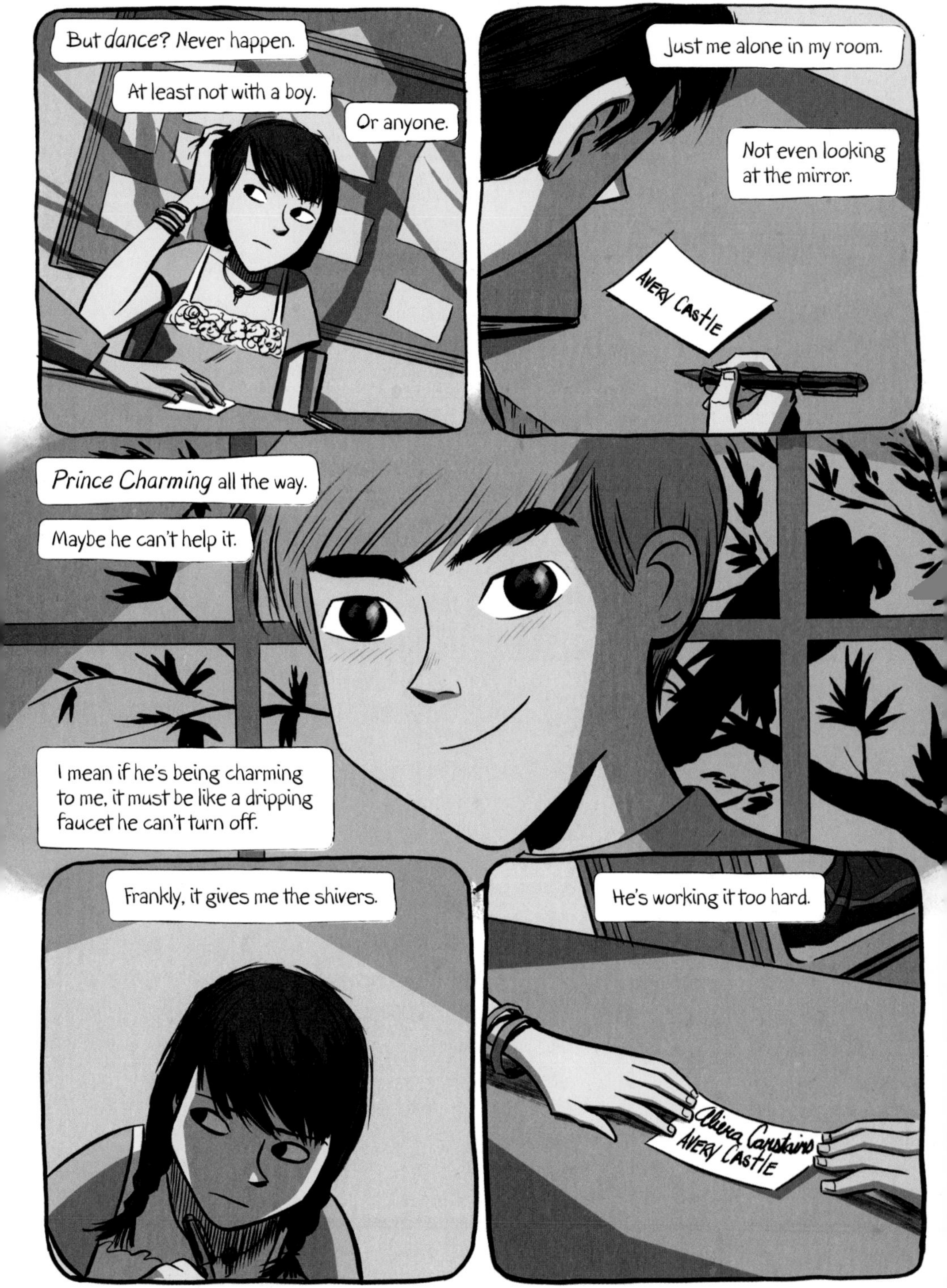
But *dance*? Never happen.
At least not with a boy.
Or anyone.
Just me alone in my room.
Not even looking at the mirror.
AVERY CASTLE
Prince Charming all the way.
Maybe he can't help it.
I mean if he's being charming to me, it must be like a dripping faucet he can't turn off.
Frankly, it gives me the shivers.
He's working it too hard.
Aliera Carstairs
AVERY CASTLE

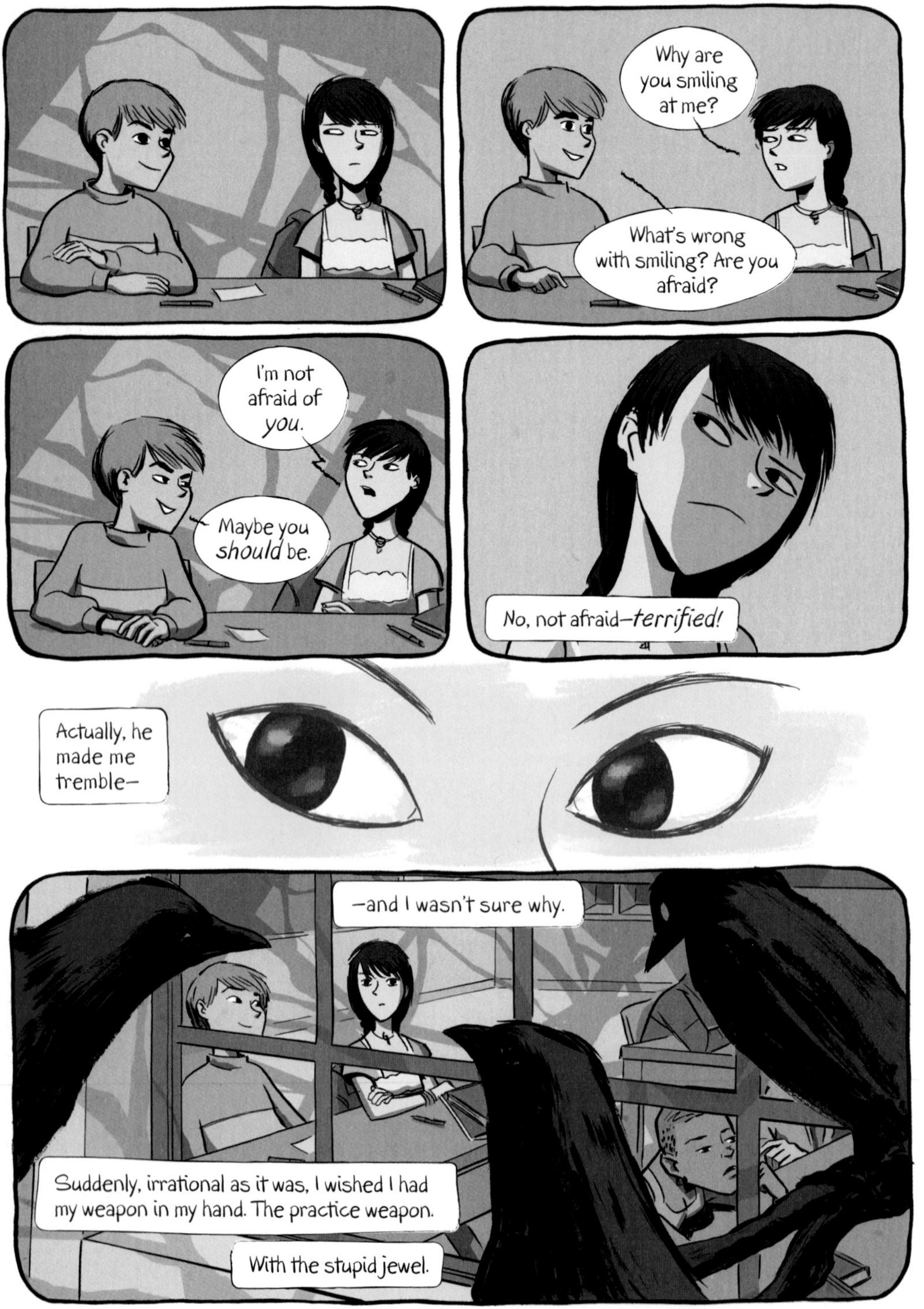
Why are you smiling at me?
What's wrong with smiling? Are you afraid?
I'm not afraid of *you*.
Maybe you *should* be.
No, not afraid—*terrified!*
Actually, he made me tremble—
—and I wasn't sure why.
Suddenly, irrational as it was, I wished I had my weapon in my hand. The practice weapon.
With the stupid jewel.

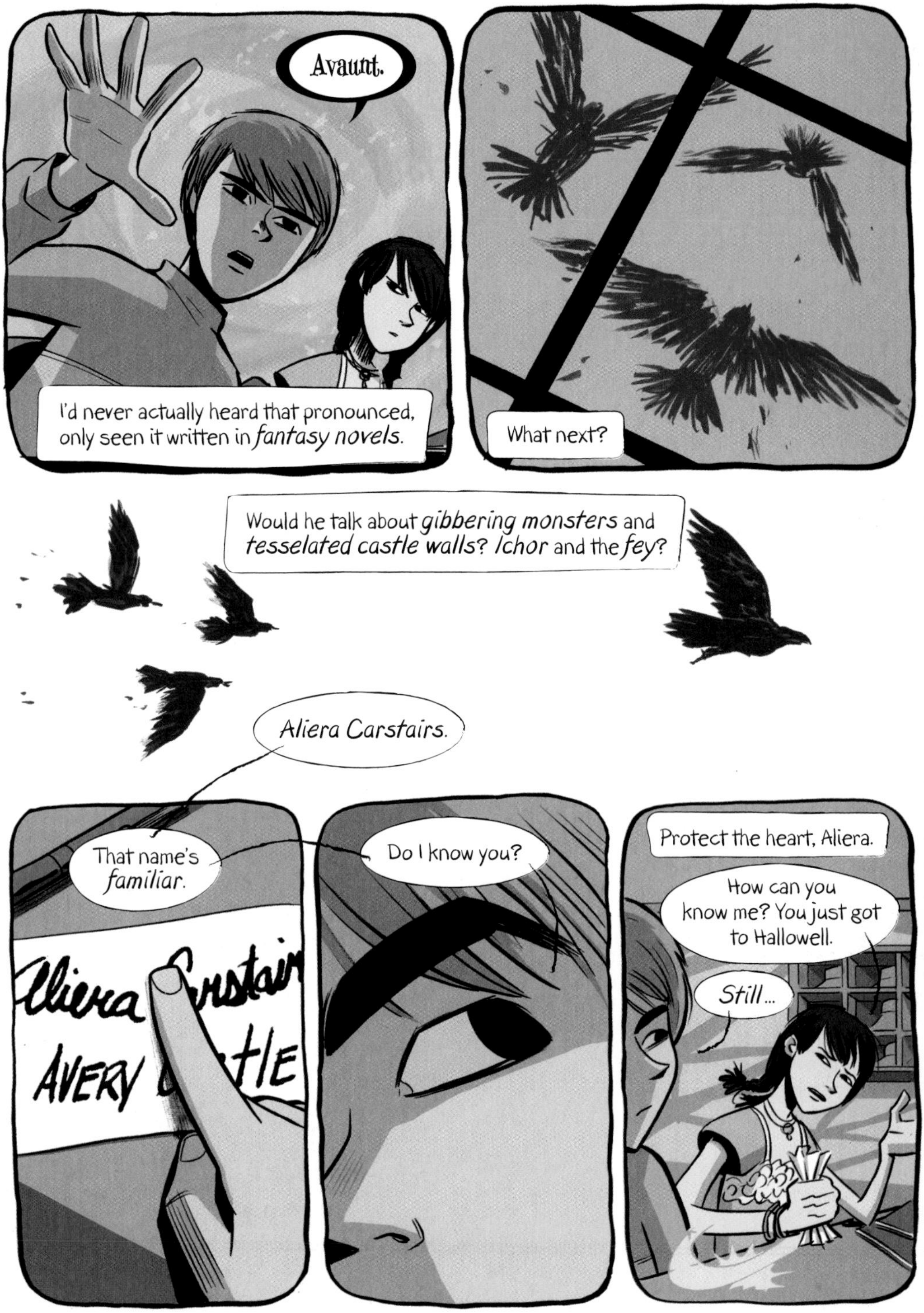
Avaunt.
I'd never actually heard that pronounced, only seen it written in *fantasy novels*.
What next?
Would he talk about *gibbering monsters* and *tesselated castle walls? Ichor* and the *fey*?
Aliera Carstairs.
Aliera Carstairs
AVERY
tle
That name's *familiar*.
Do I know you?
Protect the heart, Aliera.
How can you know me? You just got to Hallowell.
Still...

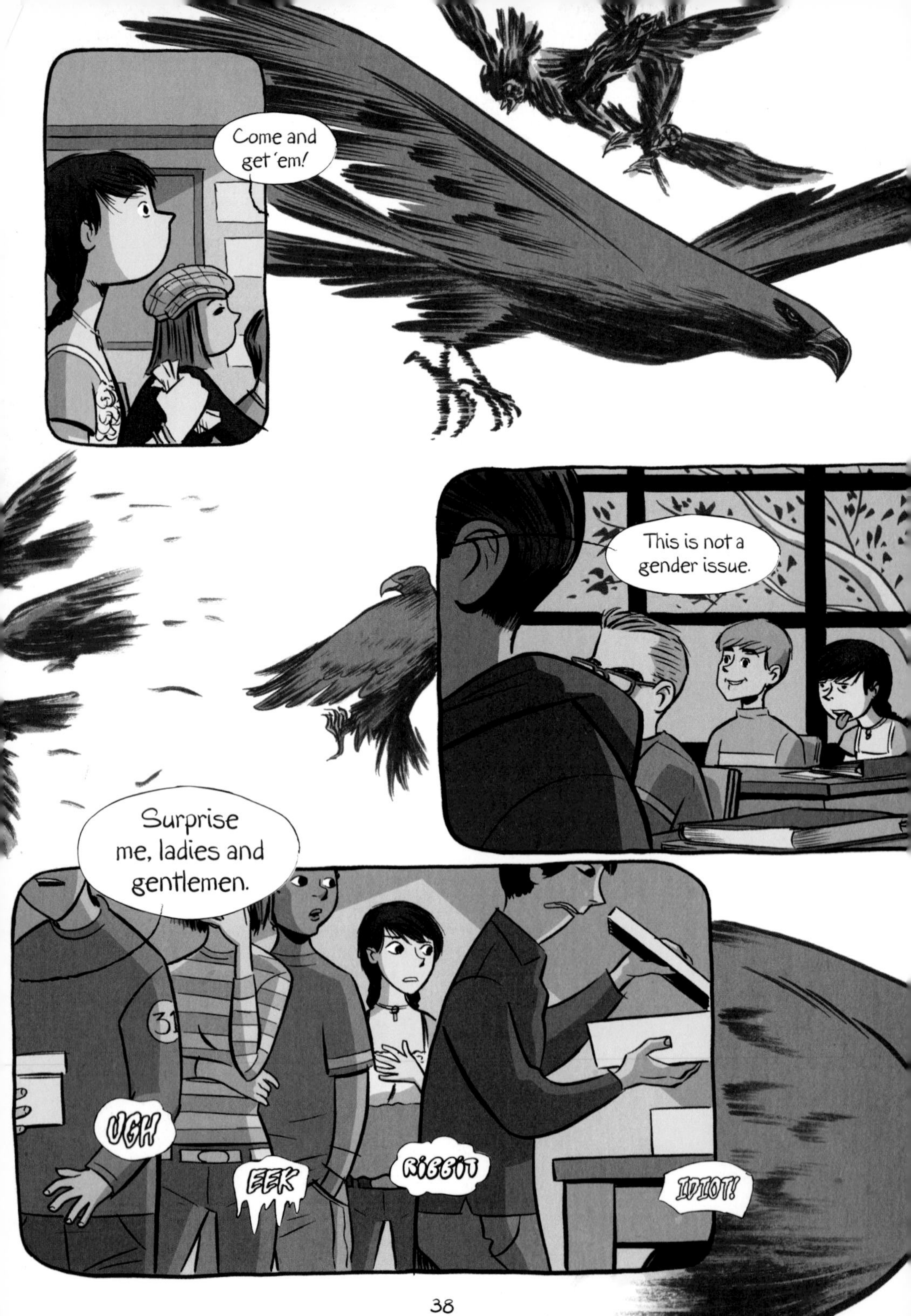

Come and get 'em!
This is not a gender issue.
Surprise me, ladies and gentlemen.
UGH
EEK
RIBBIT
IDIOT!

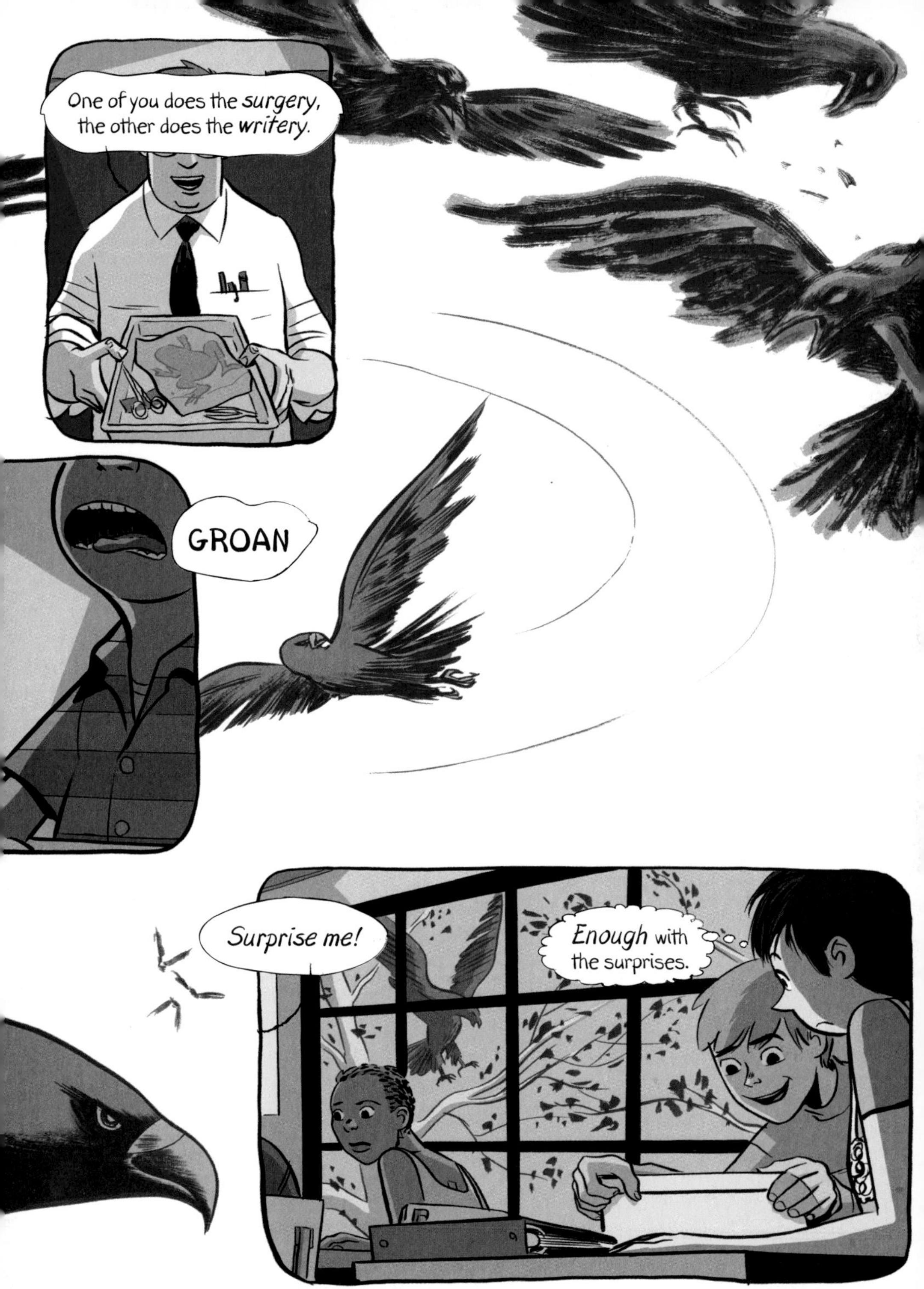

One of you does the *surgery*, the other does the *writery*.
GROAN
Surprise me!
Enough with the surprises.

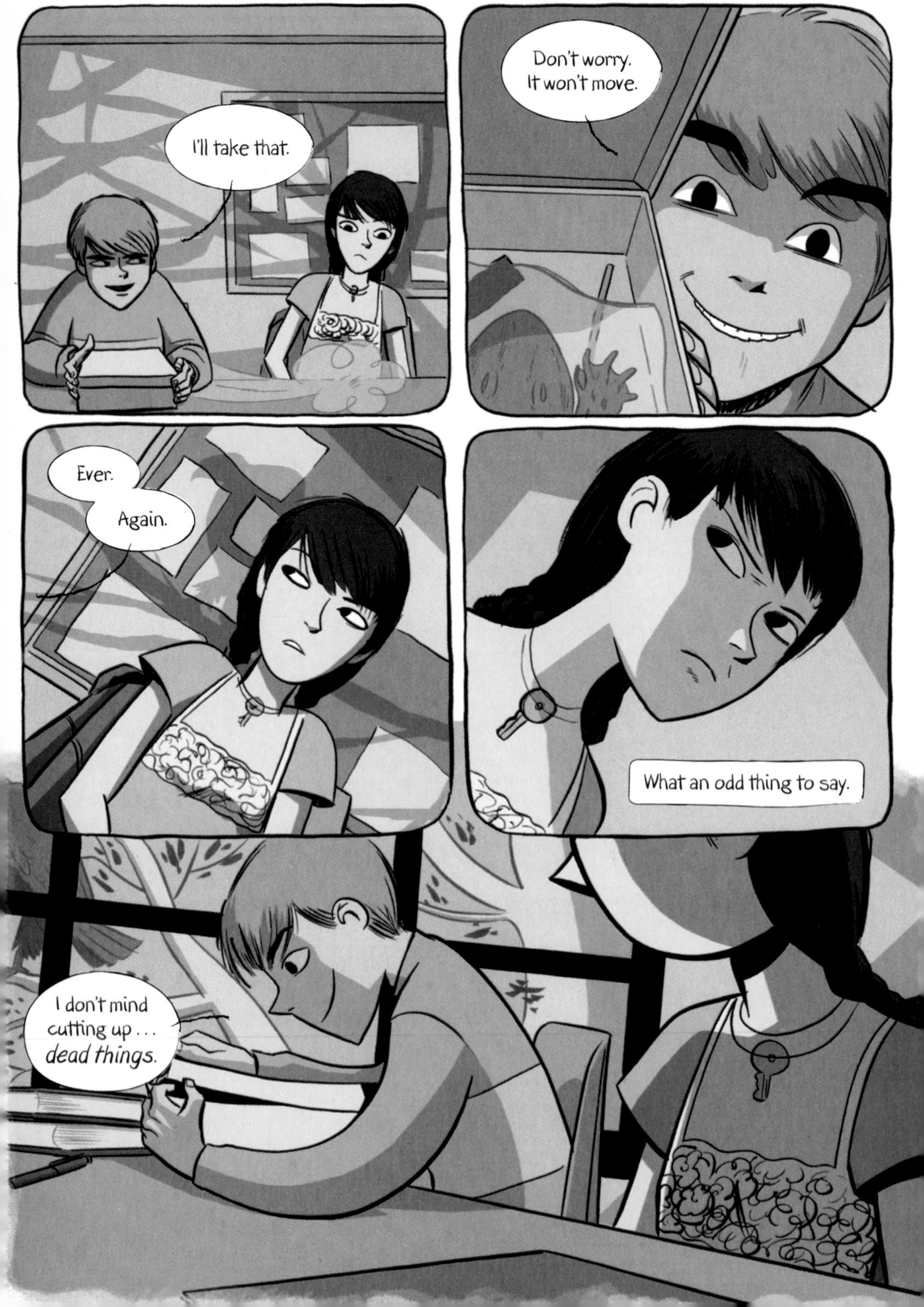
I'll take that.
Don't worry. It won't move.
Ever.
Again.
What an odd thing to say.
I don't mind cutting up . . . *dead things.*

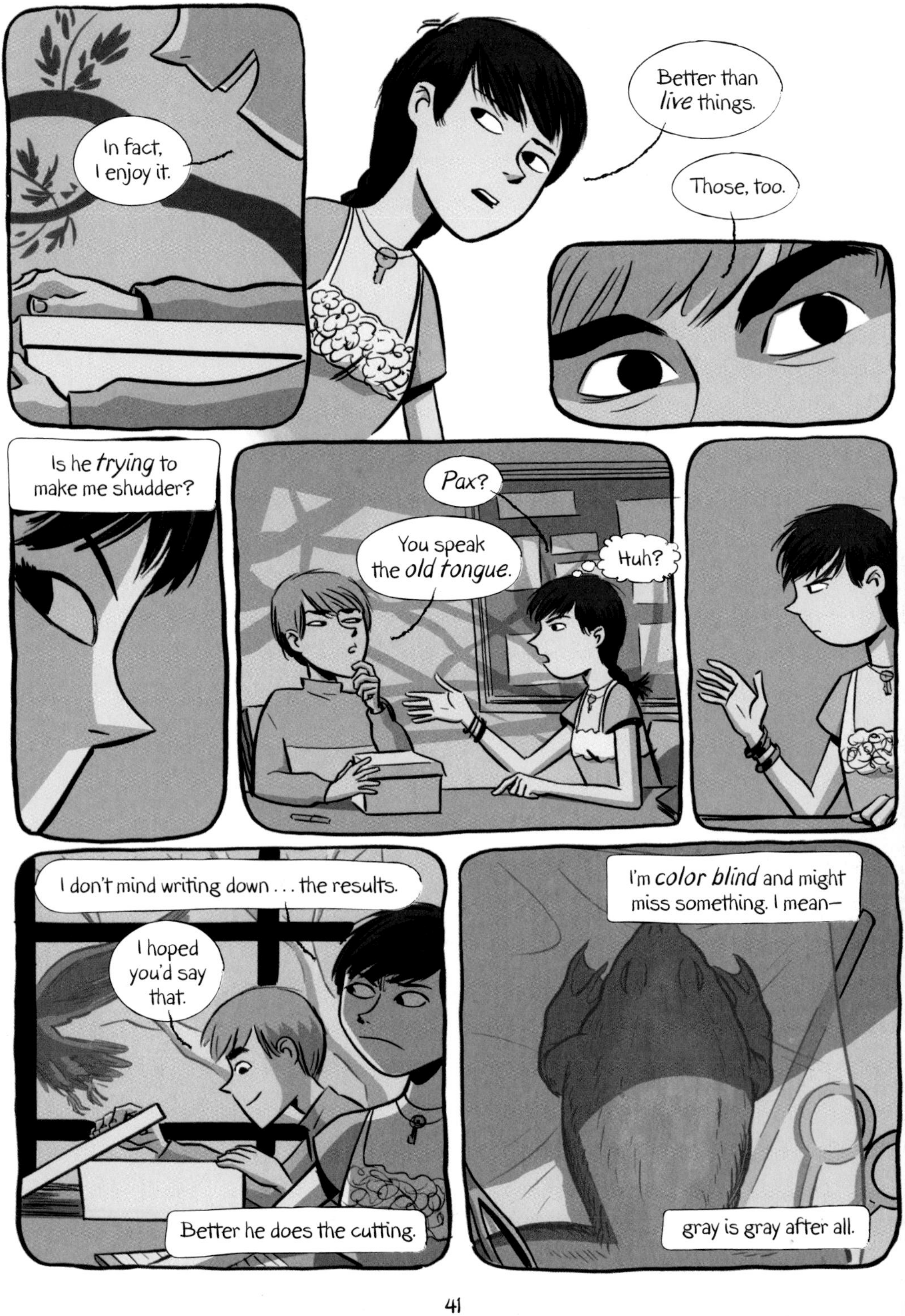
In fact, I enjoy it.
Better than *live* things.
Those, too.
Is he *trying* to make me shudder?
Pax?
You speak the *old tongue.*
Huh?
I don't mind writing down . . . the results.
I hoped you'd say that.
Better he does the cutting.
I'm *color blind* and might miss something. I mean—
gray is gray after all.

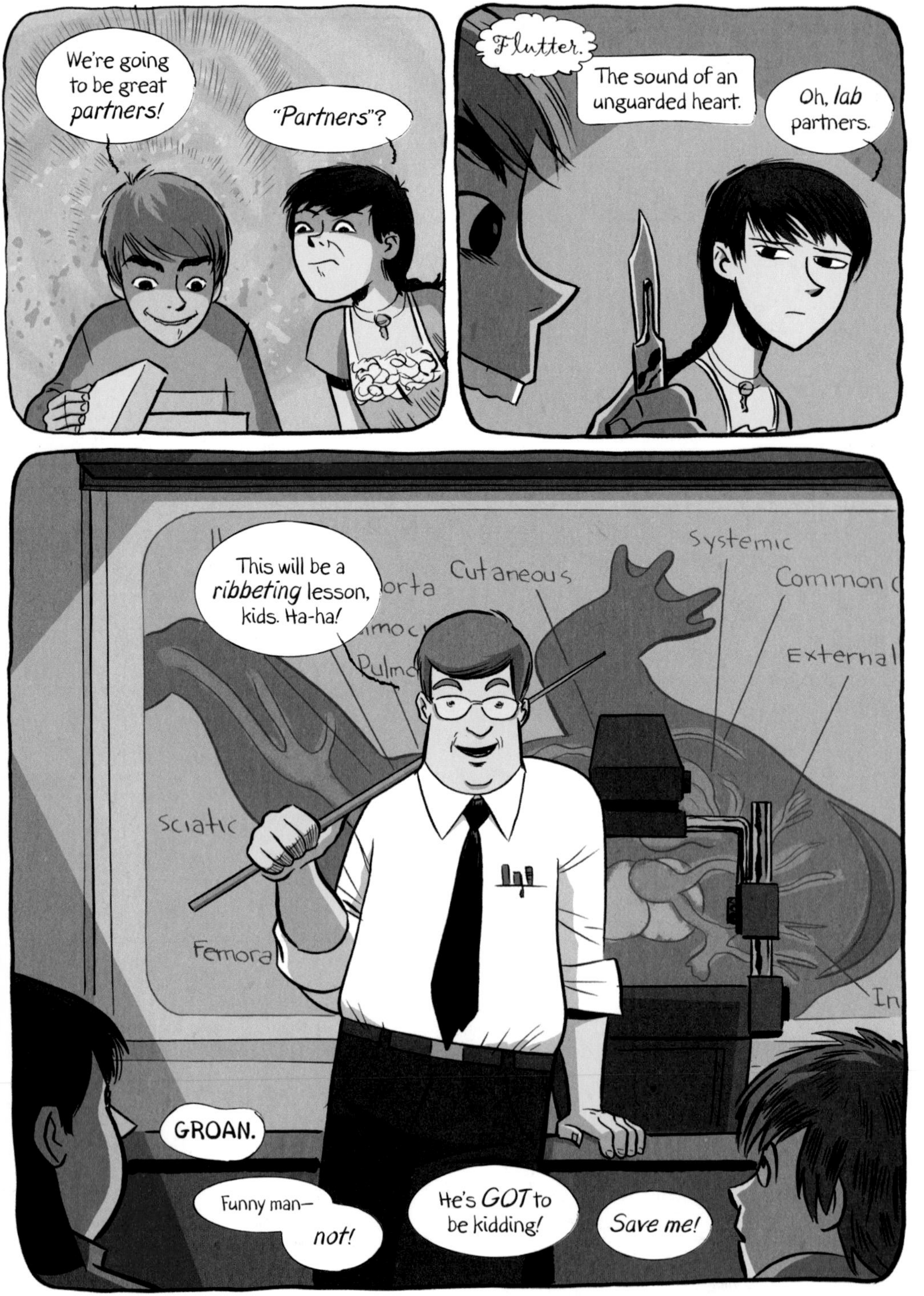
We're going to be great *partners!*
"*Partners*"?
Flutter.
The sound of an unguarded heart.
Oh, *lab* partners.
Systemic
Cutaneous
Common c
orta
This will be a *ribbeting* lesson, kids. Ha-ha!
External
Pulmo
Sciatic
Femora
In
GROAN.
Funny man— *not!*
He's *GOT* to be kidding!
Save me!

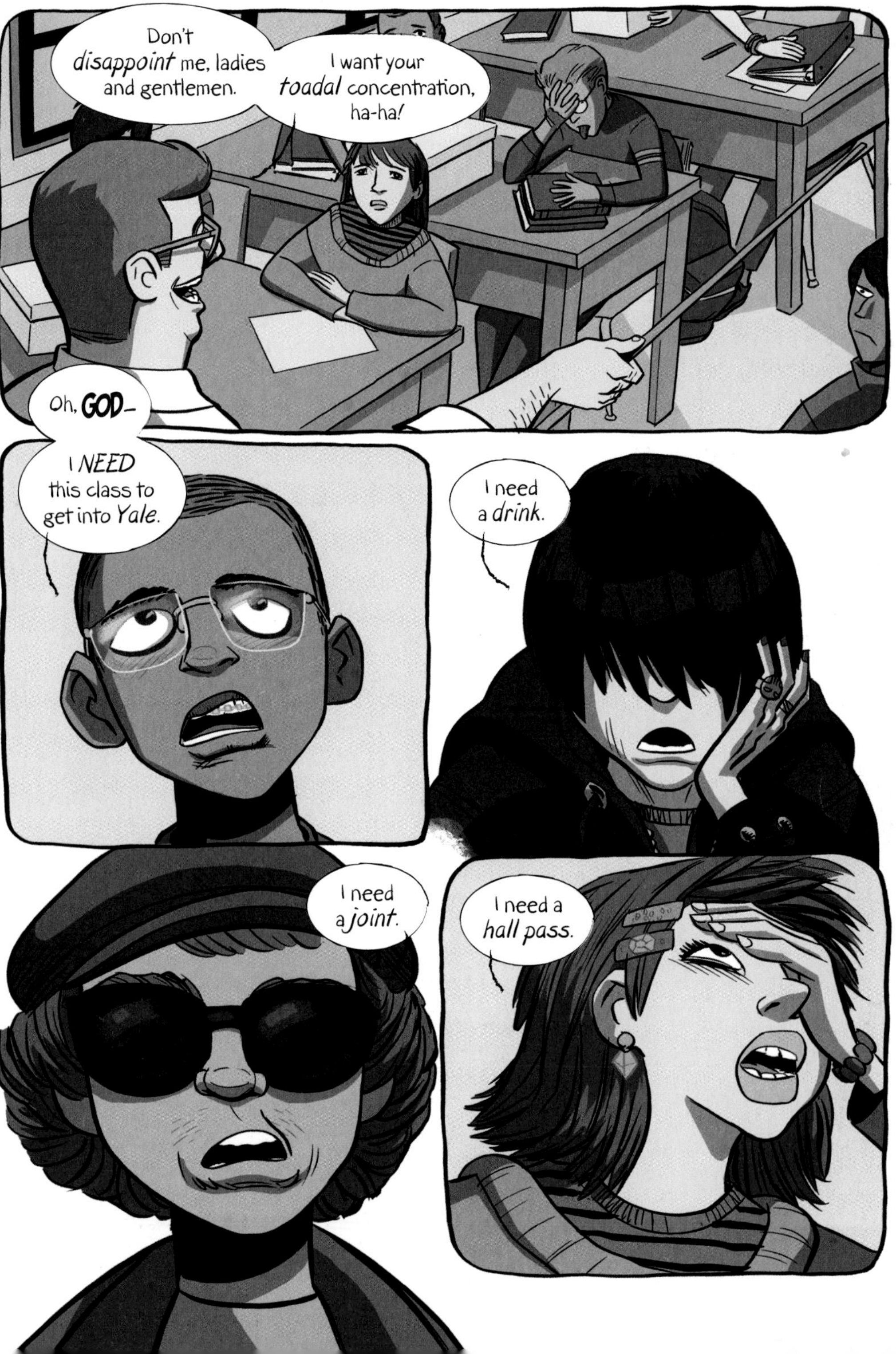
Don't *disappoint* me, ladies and gentlemen.
I want your *toadal* concentration, ha-ha!
Oh, **GOD**–
I *NEED* this class to get into *Yale*.
I need a *drink*.
I need a *joint*.
I need a *hall pass*.

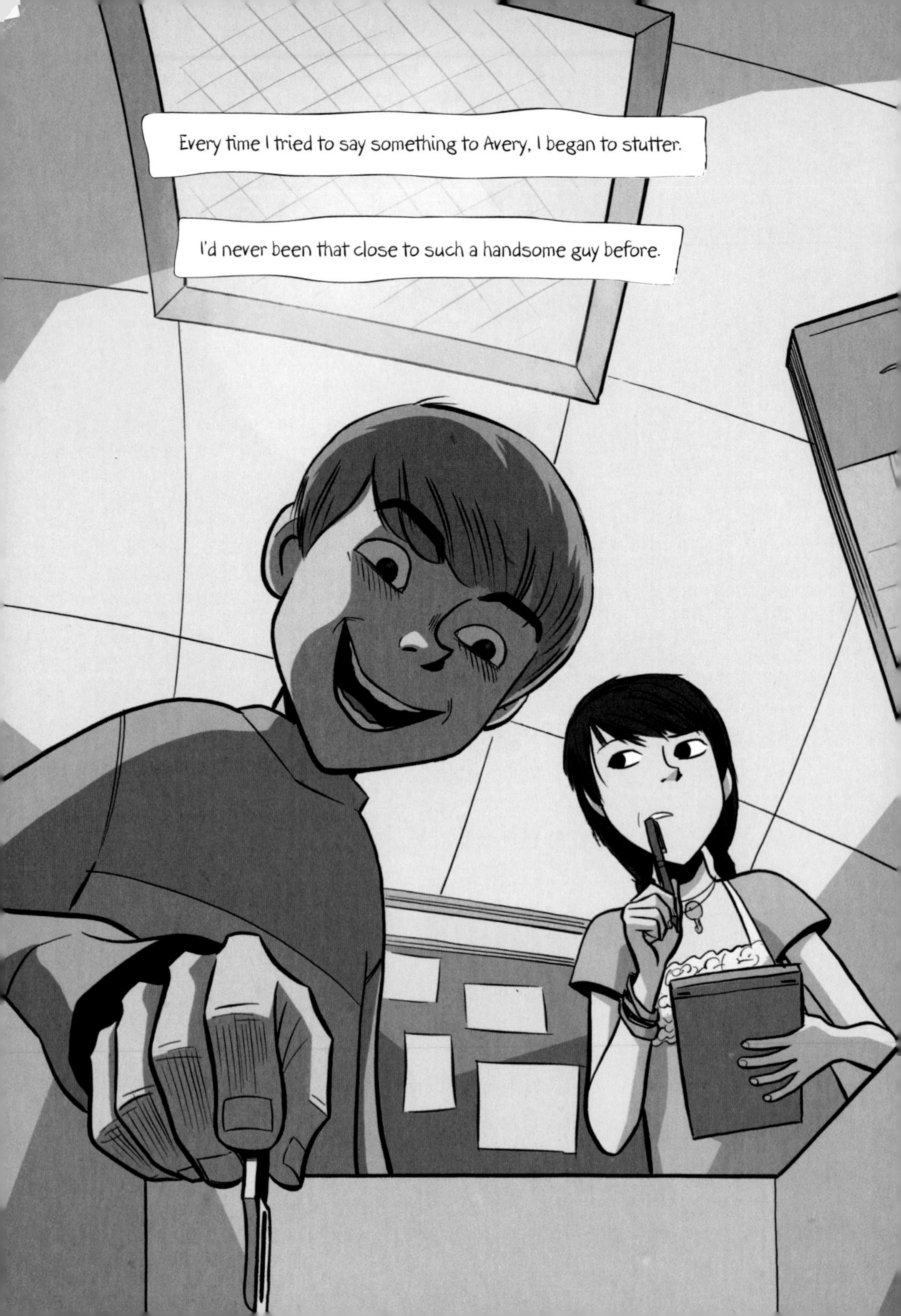
Every time I tried to say something to Avery, I began to stutter.
I'd never been that close to such a handsome guy before.

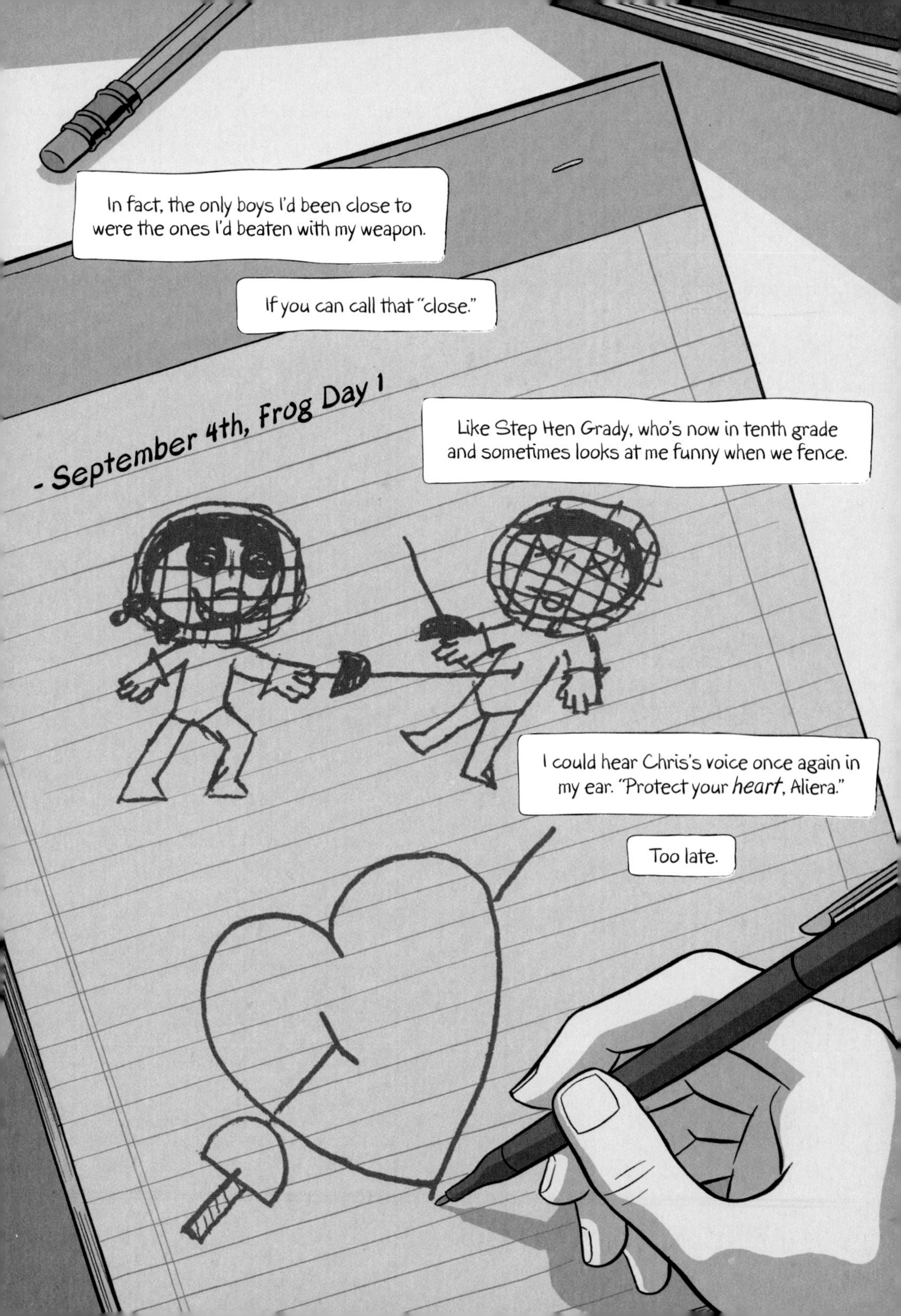
In fact, the only boys I'd been close to were the ones I'd beaten with my weapon.
If you can call that "close."
- September 4th, Frog Day 1
Like Step Hen Grady, who's now in tenth grade and sometimes looks at me funny when we fence.
I could hear Chris's voice once again in my ear. "Protect your *heart*, Aliera."
Too late.

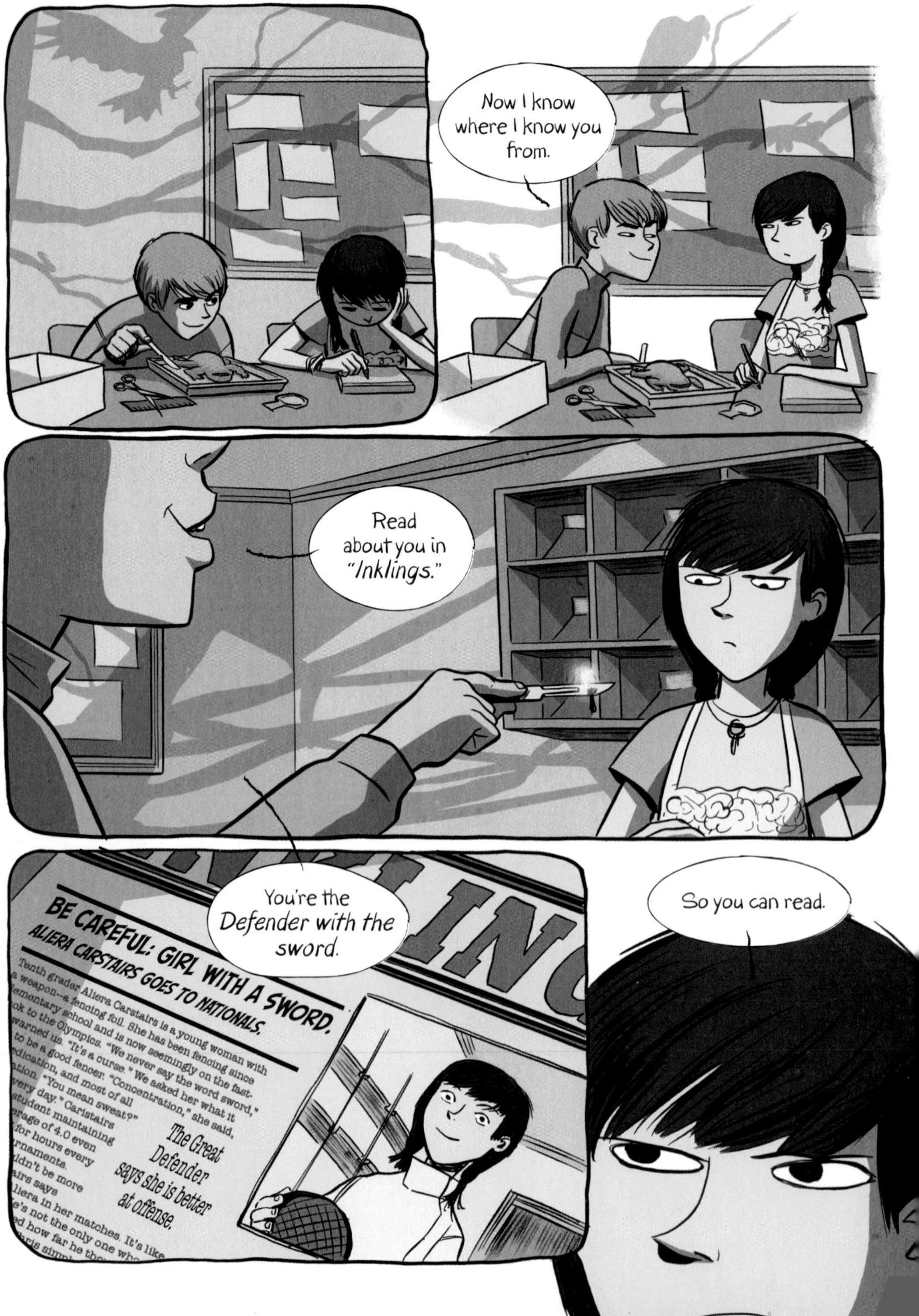

Now I know where I know you from.
Read about you in "Inklings."
You're the Defender with the sword.
BE CAREFUL: GIRL WITH A SWORD.
ALIERA CARSTAIRS GOES TO NATIONALS.
The Great Defender says she is better at offense.
So you can read.

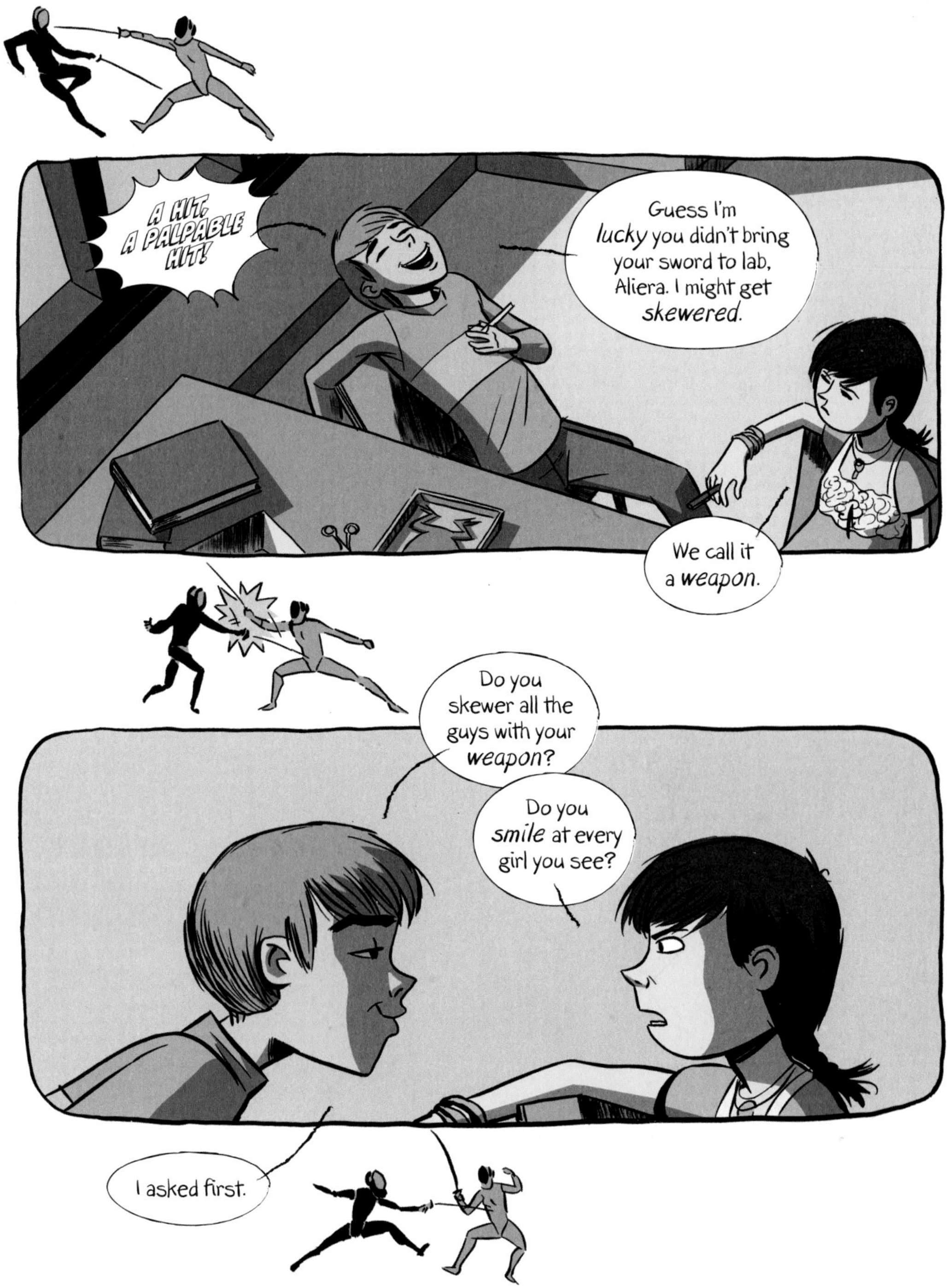
A HIT, A PALPABLE HIT!
Guess I'm lucky you didn't bring your sword to lab, Aliera. I might get skewered.
We call it a weapon.
Do you skewer all the guys with your weapon?
Do you smile at every girl you see?
I asked first.

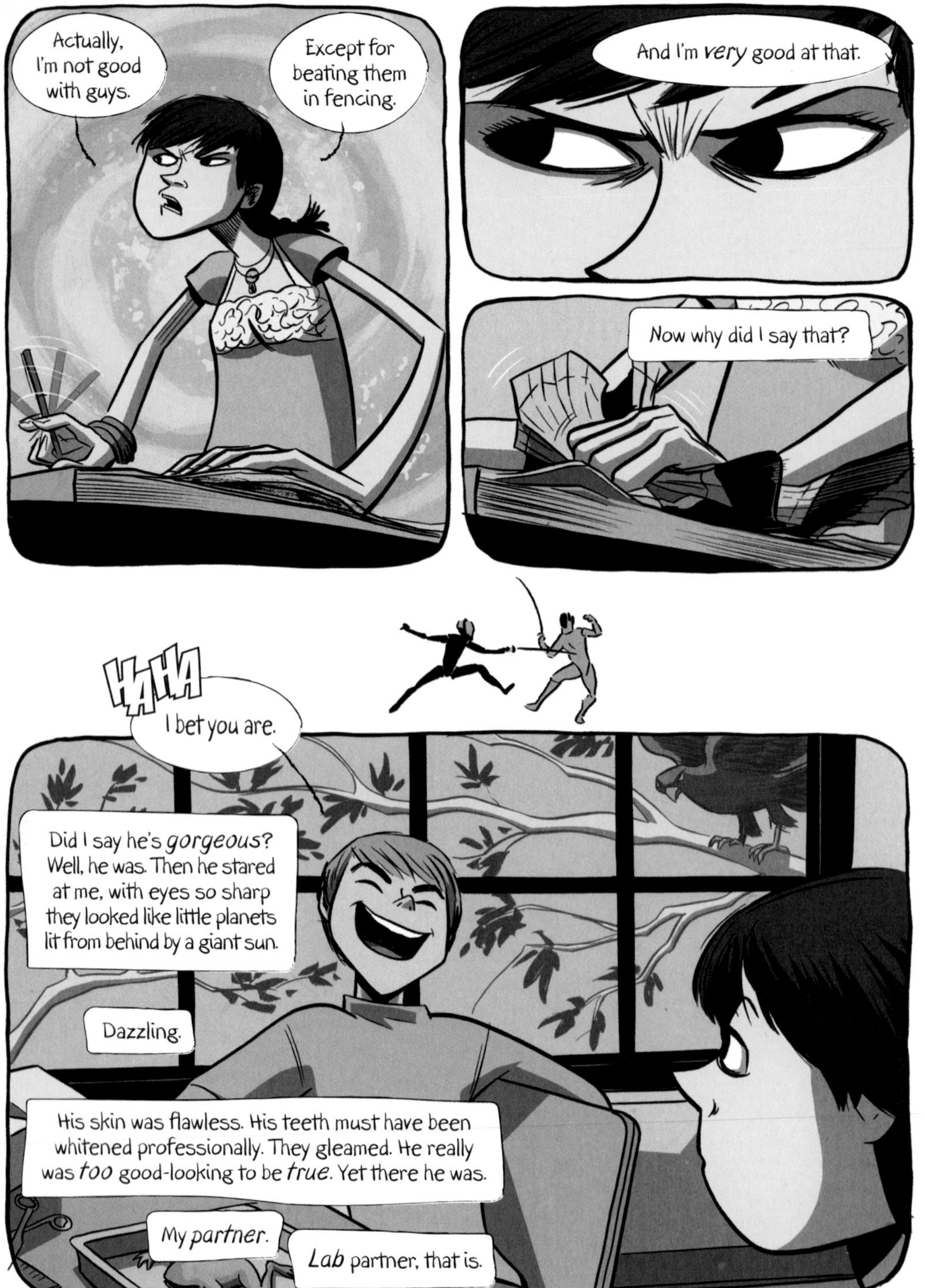
Actually, I'm not good with guys.
Except for beating them in fencing.
And I'm *very* good at that.
Now why did I say that?
HAHA
I bet you are.
Did I say he's *gorgeous*? Well, he was. Then he stared at me, with eyes so sharp they looked like little planets lit from behind by a giant sun.
Dazzling.
His skin was flawless. His teeth must have been whitened professionally. They gleamed. He really was *too* good-looking to be *true*. Yet there he was.
My *partner*.
Lab partner, that is.

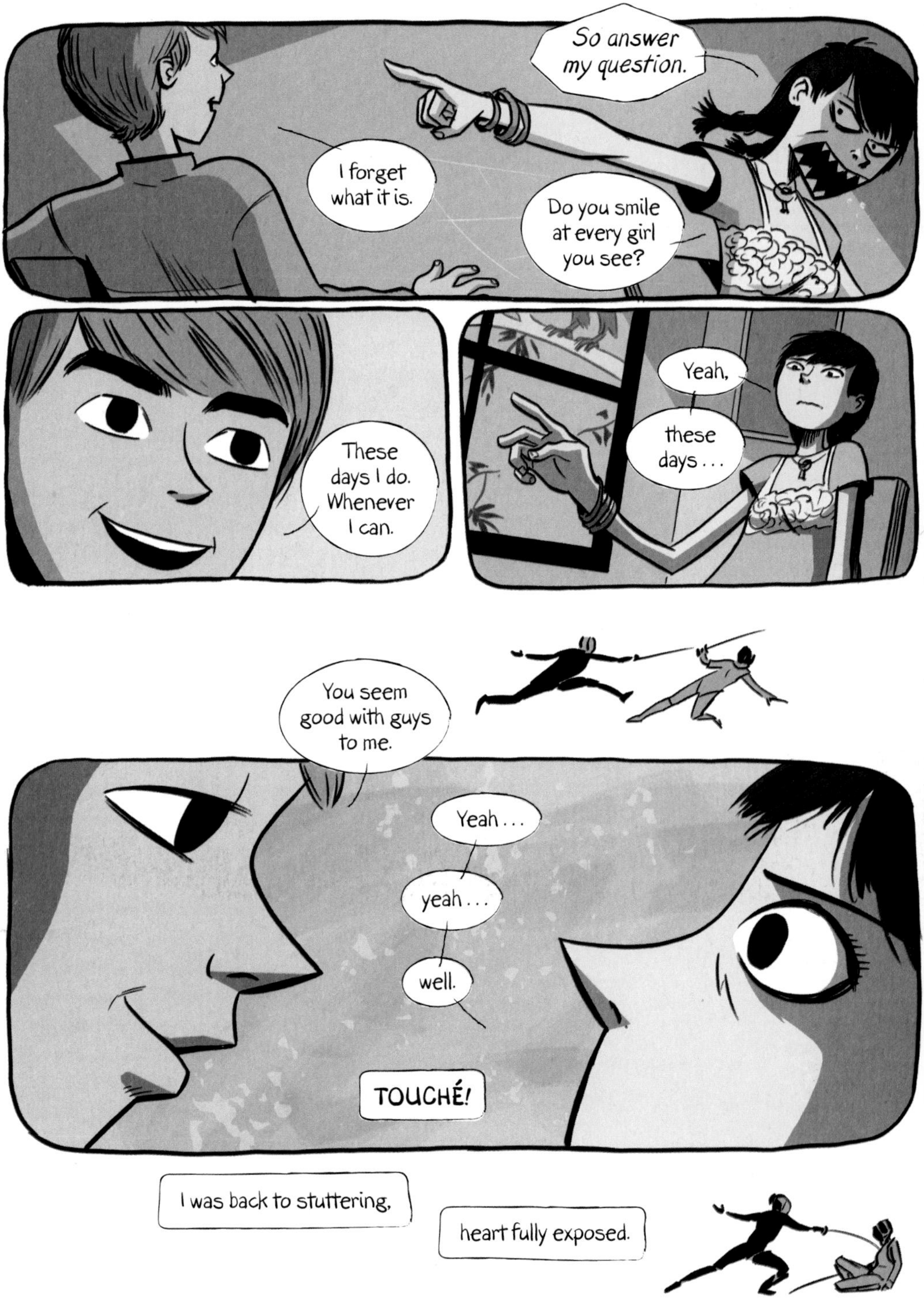

So answer my question.
I forget what it is.
Do you smile at every girl you see?
These days I do. Whenever I can.
Yeah,
these days . . .
You seem good with guys to me.
Yeah . . .
yeah . . .
well.
TOUCHÉ!
I was back to stuttering,
heart fully exposed.

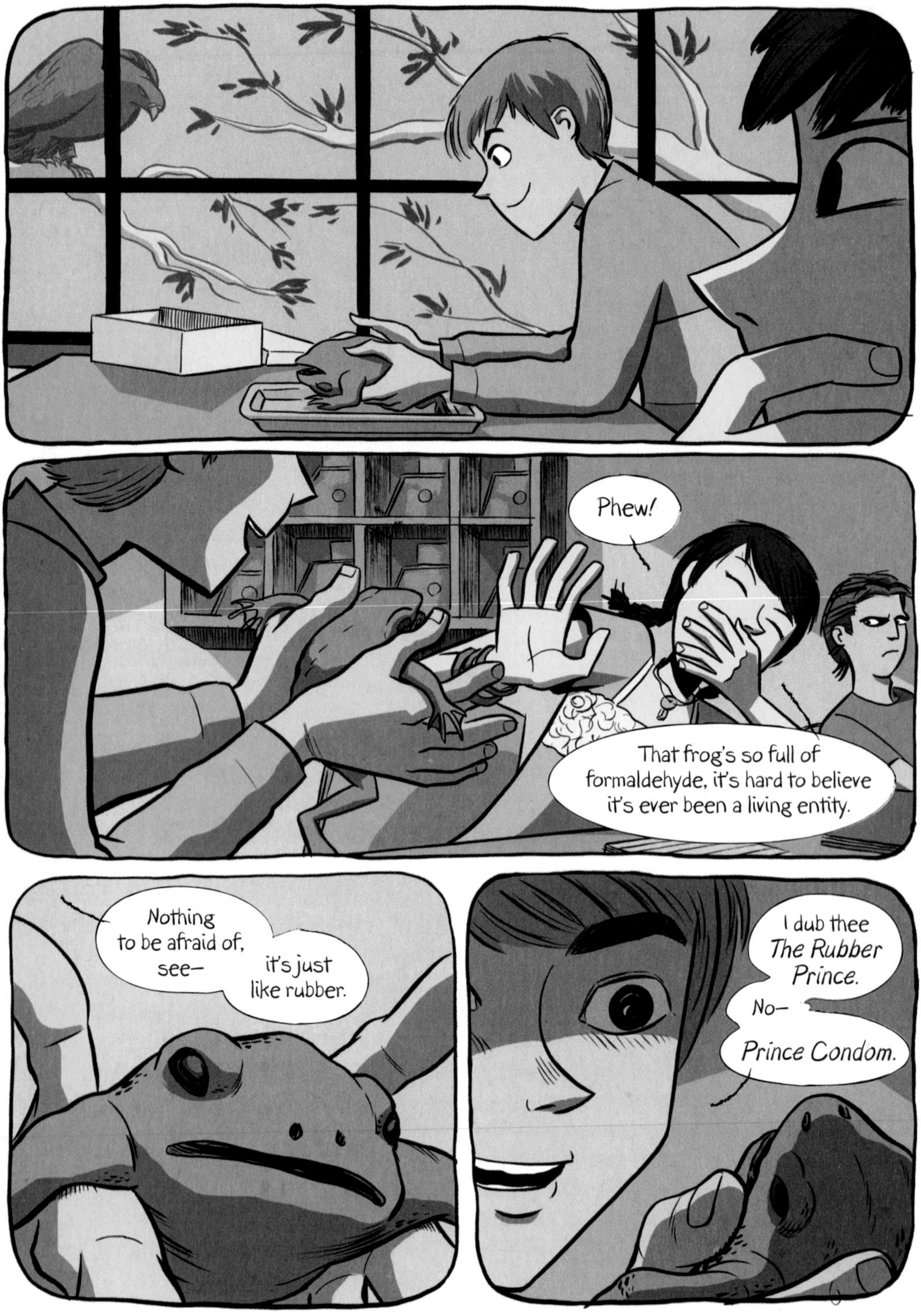
Phew!
That frog's so full of formaldehyde, it's hard to believe it's ever been a living entity.
Nothing to be afraid of, see—
it's just like rubber.
I dub thee *The Rubber Prince.*
No—
Prince Condom.

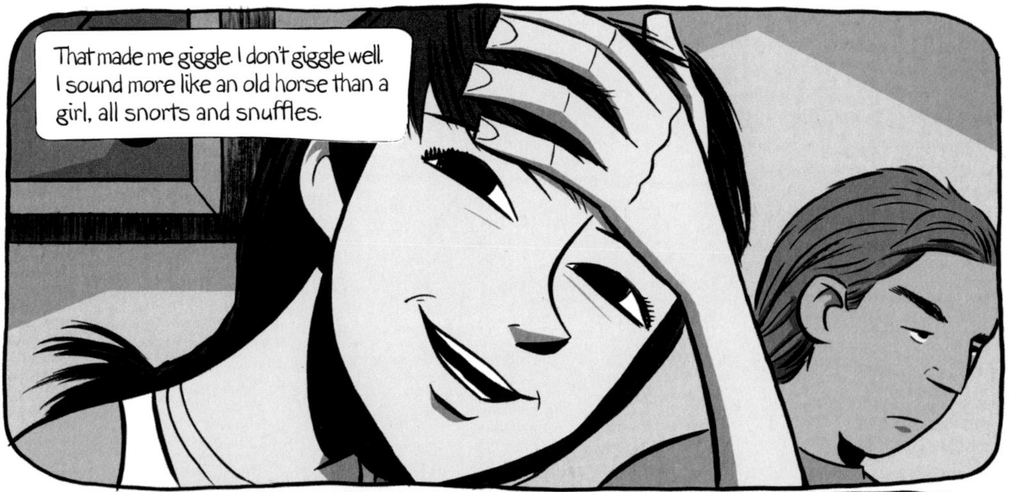
That made me giggle. I don't giggle well. I sound more like an old horse than a girl, all snorts and snuffles.

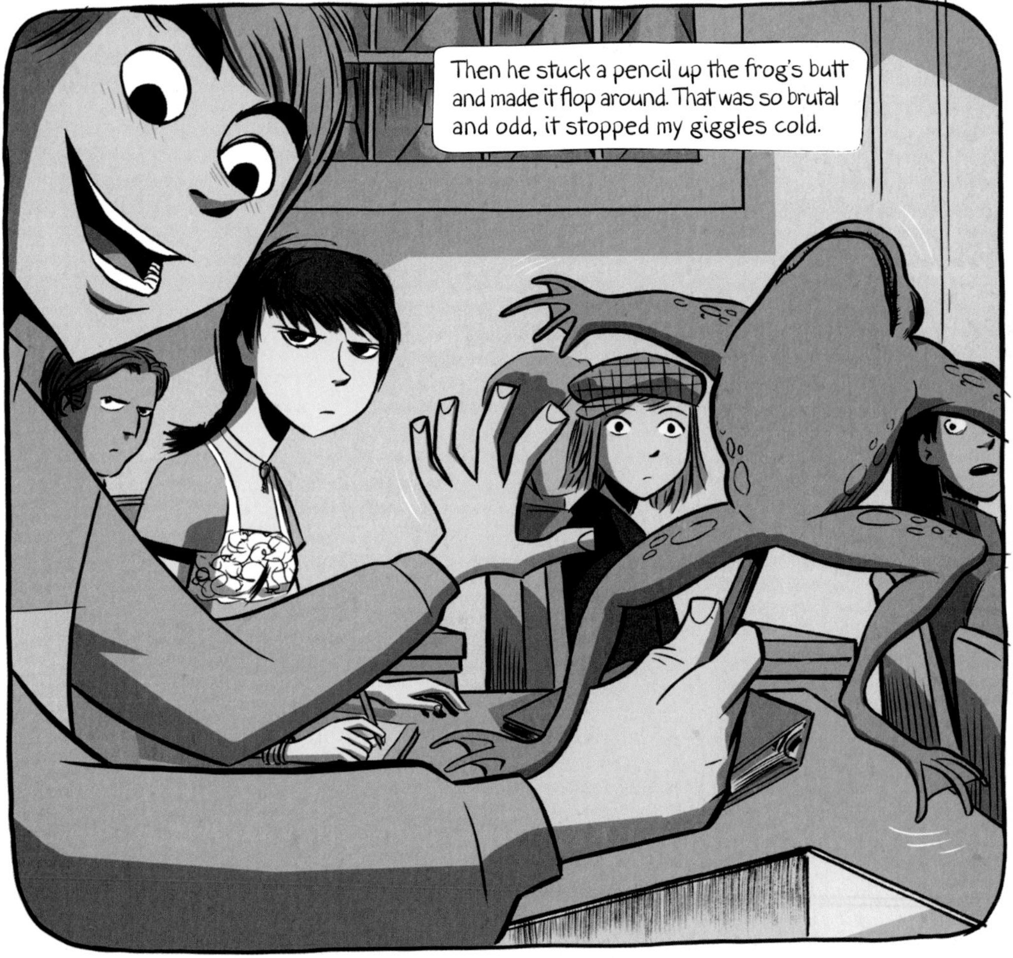
Then he stuck a pencil up the frog's butt and made it flop around. That was so brutal and odd, it stopped my giggles cold.

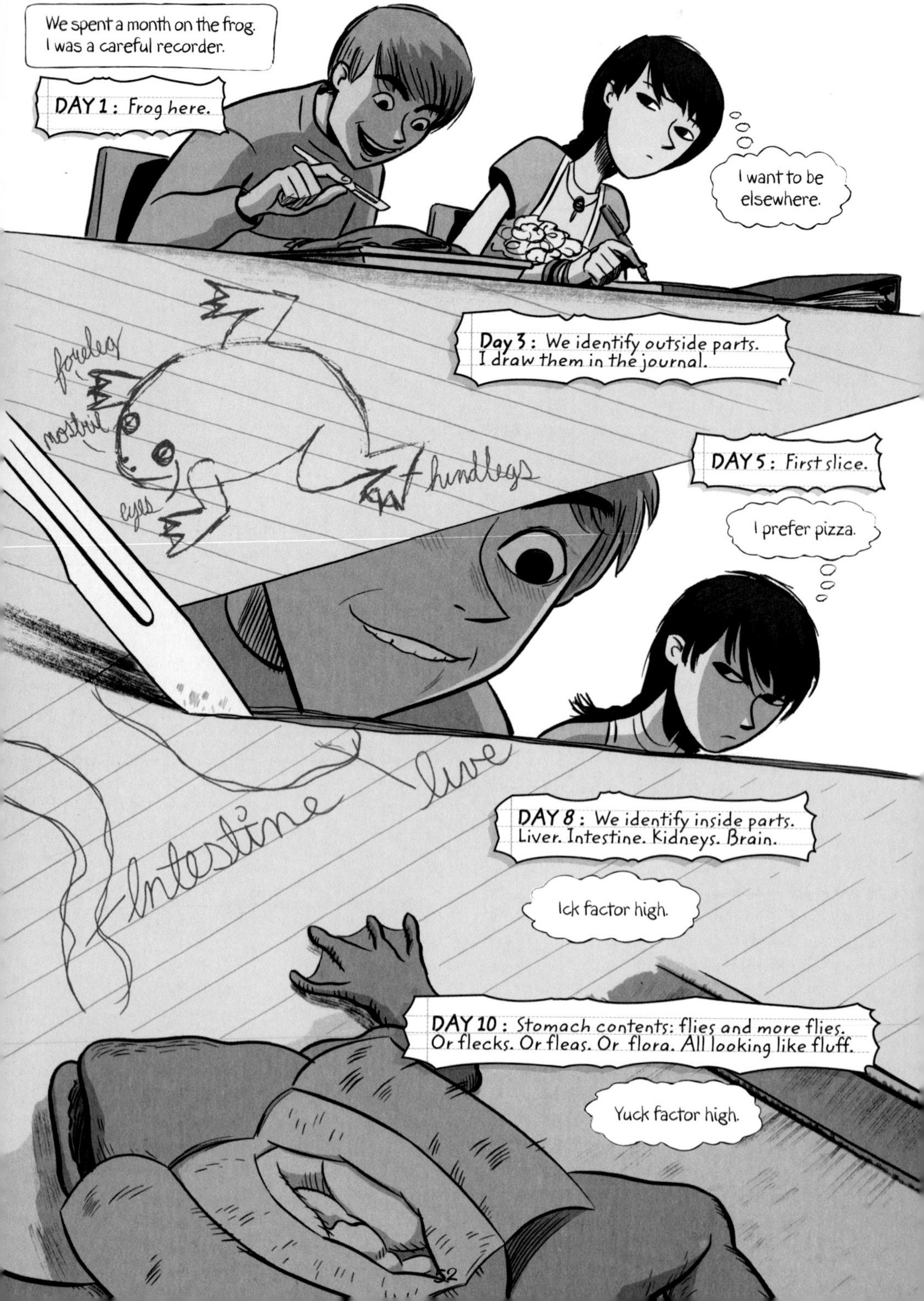
We spent a month on the frog. I was a careful recorder.
DAY 1: Frog here.
I want to be elsewhere.
Day 3: We identify outside parts. I draw them in the journal.
foreleg
nostril
eyes
hindlegs
DAY 5: First slice.
I prefer pizza.
Intestine
live
DAY 8: We identify inside parts. Liver. Intestine. Kidneys. Brain.
Ick factor high.
DAY 10: Stomach contents: flies and more flies. Or flecks. Or fleas. Or flora. All looking like fluff.
Yuck factor high.

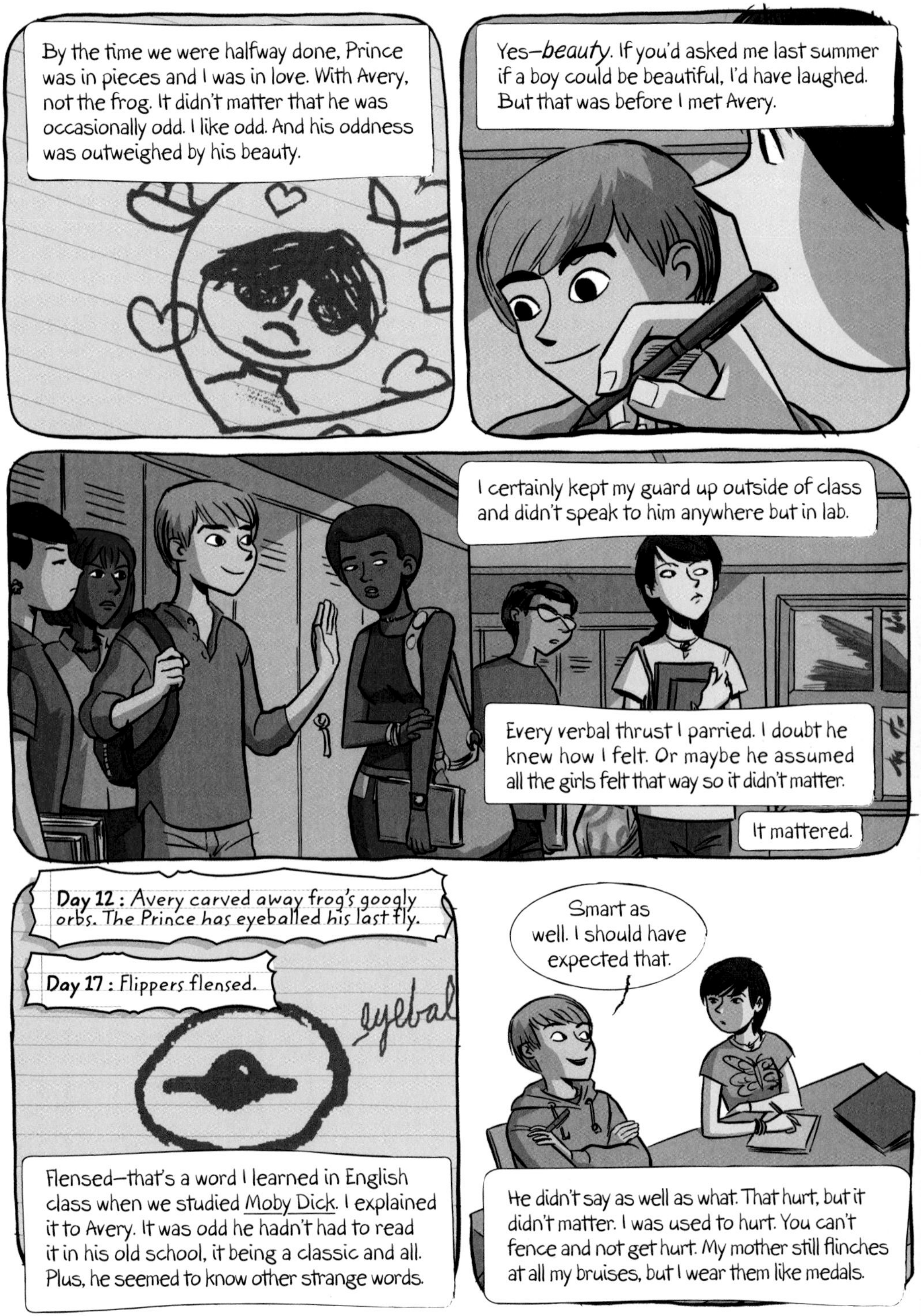
By the time we were halfway done, Prince was in pieces and I was in love. With Avery, not the frog. It didn't matter that he was occasionally odd. I like odd. And his oddness was outweighed by his beauty.
Yes—*beauty*. If you'd asked me last summer if a boy could be beautiful, I'd have laughed. But that was before I met Avery.
I certainly kept my guard up outside of class and didn't speak to him anywhere but in lab.
Every verbal thrust I parried. I doubt he knew how I felt. Or maybe he assumed all the girls felt that way so it didn't matter.
It mattered.
Day 12 : Avery carved away frog's googly orbs. The Prince has eyeballed his last fly.
Day 17 : Flippers flensed.
Flensed—that's a word I learned in English class when we studied Moby Dick. I explained it to Avery. It was odd he hadn't had to read it in his old school, it being a classic and all. Plus, he seemed to know other strange words.
Smart as well. I should have expected that.
He didn't say as well as what. That hurt, but it didn't matter. I was used to hurt. You can't fence and not get hurt. My mother still flinches at all my bruises, but I wear them like medals.

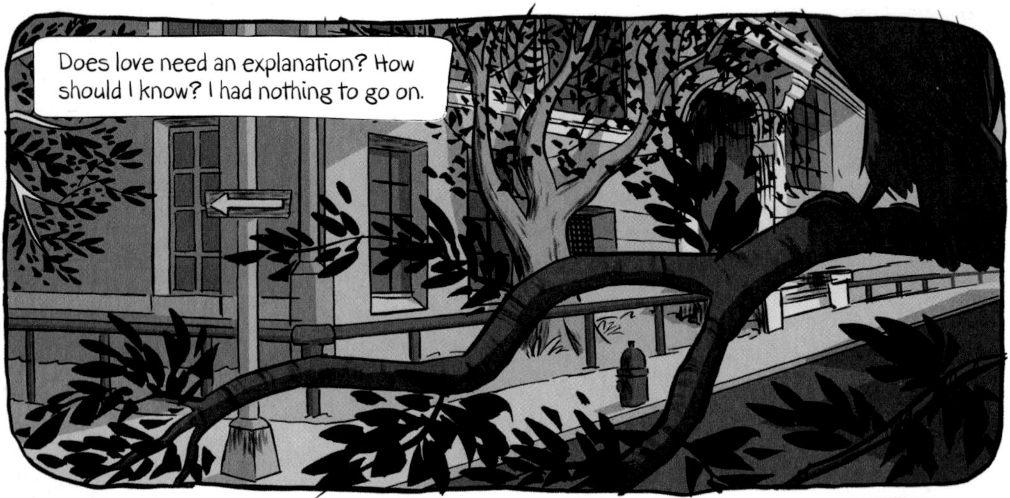
Does love need an explanation? How should I know? I had nothing to go on.

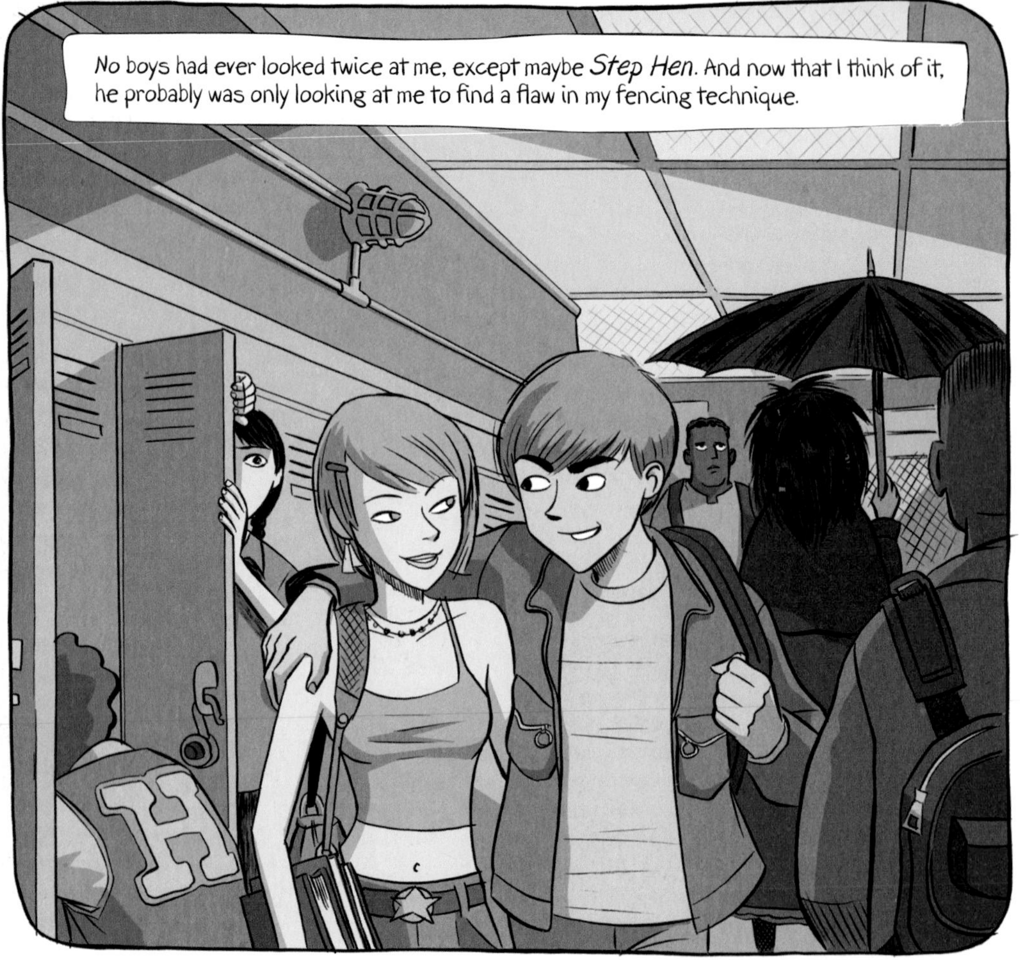
No boys had ever looked twice at me, except maybe *Step Hen*. And now that I think of it, he probably was only looking at me to find a flaw in my fencing technique.

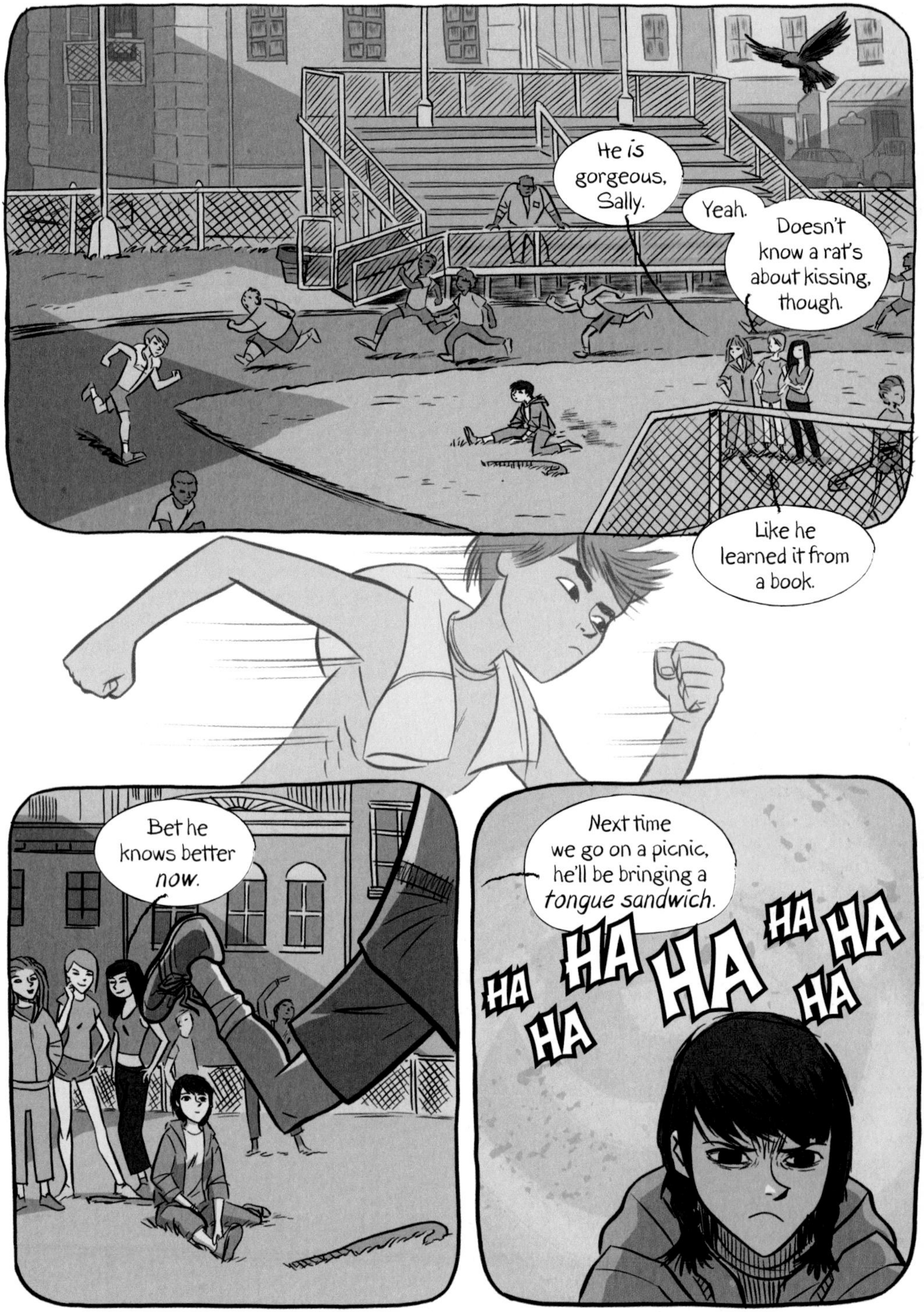
He *is* gorgeous, Sally.
Yeah.
Doesn't know a rat's about kissing, though.
Like he learned it from a book.
Bet he knows better *now*.
Next time we go on a picnic, he'll be bringing a *tongue sandwich*.
HA HA HA HA HA HA HA HA

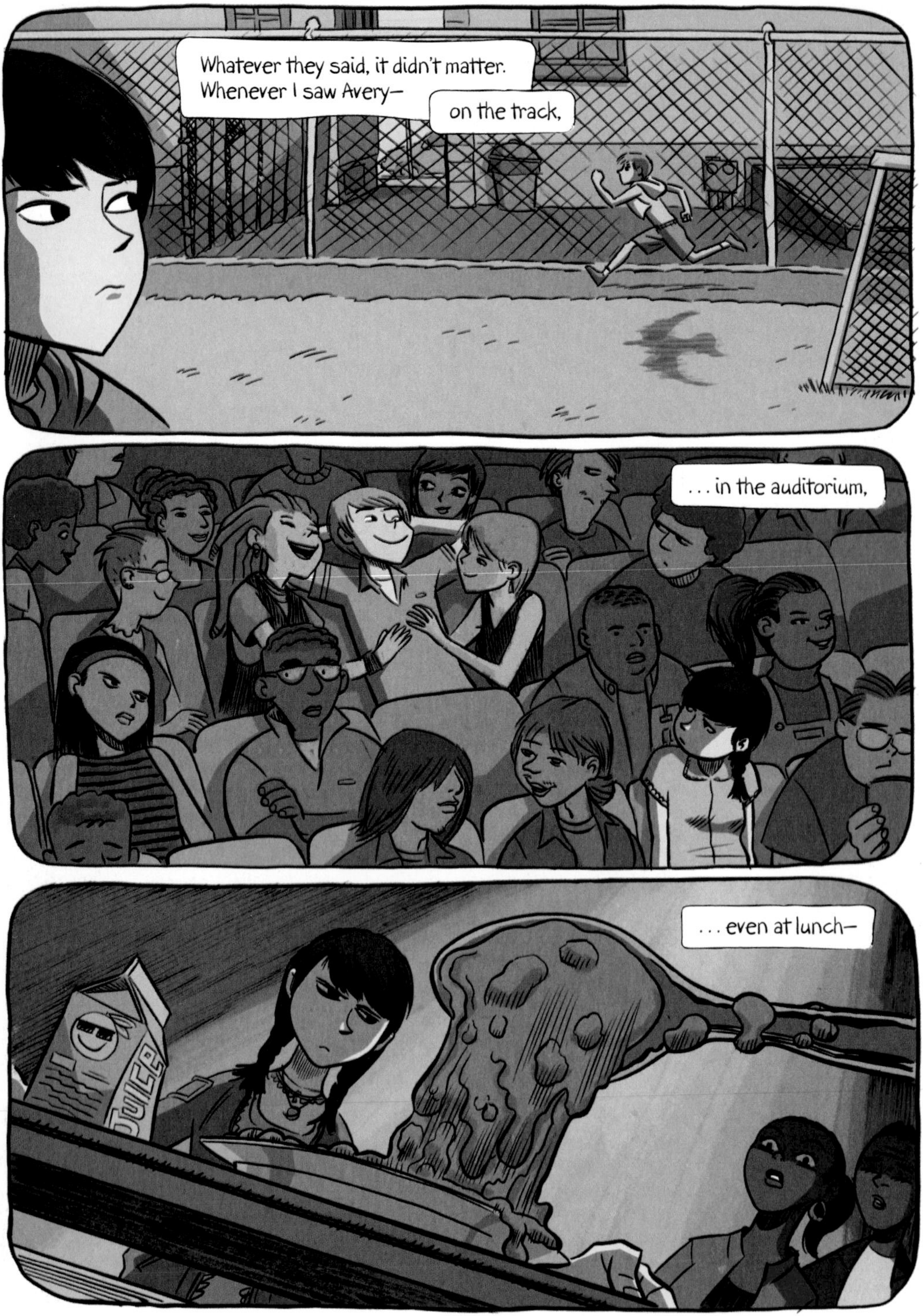
Whatever they said, it didn't matter.
Whenever I saw Avery—
on the track,
. . . in the auditorium,
. . . even at lunch—
Juice

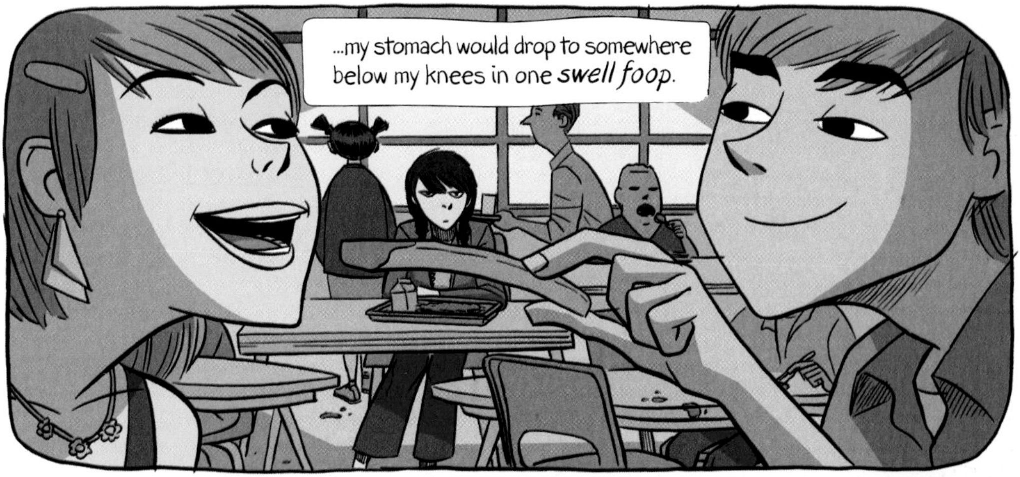
...my stomach would drop to somewhere below my knees in one *swell foop*.

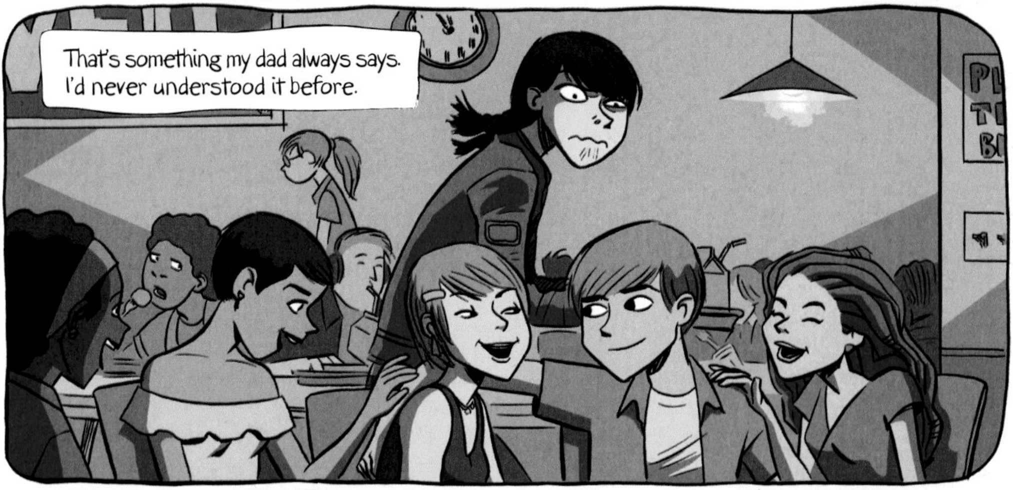
That's something my dad always says. I'd never understood it before.

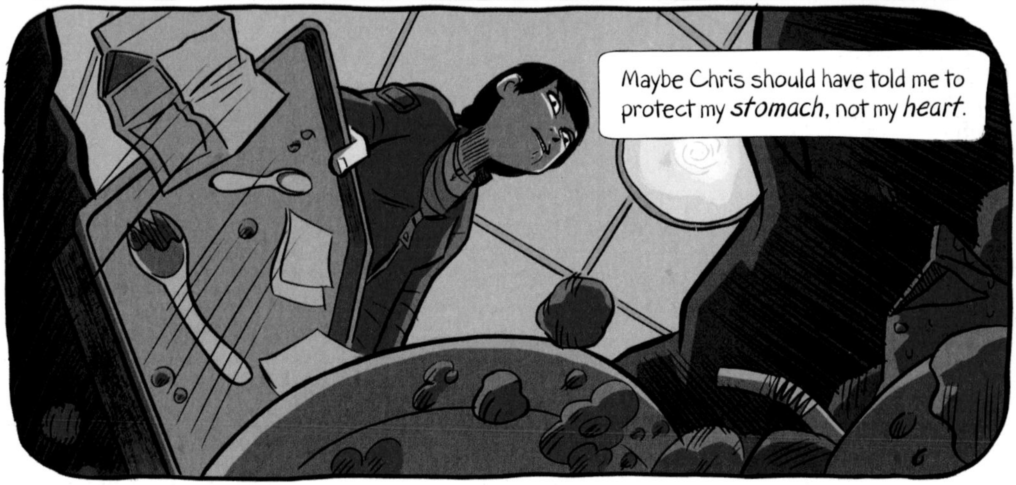
Maybe Chris should have told me to protect my *stomach*, not my *heart*.

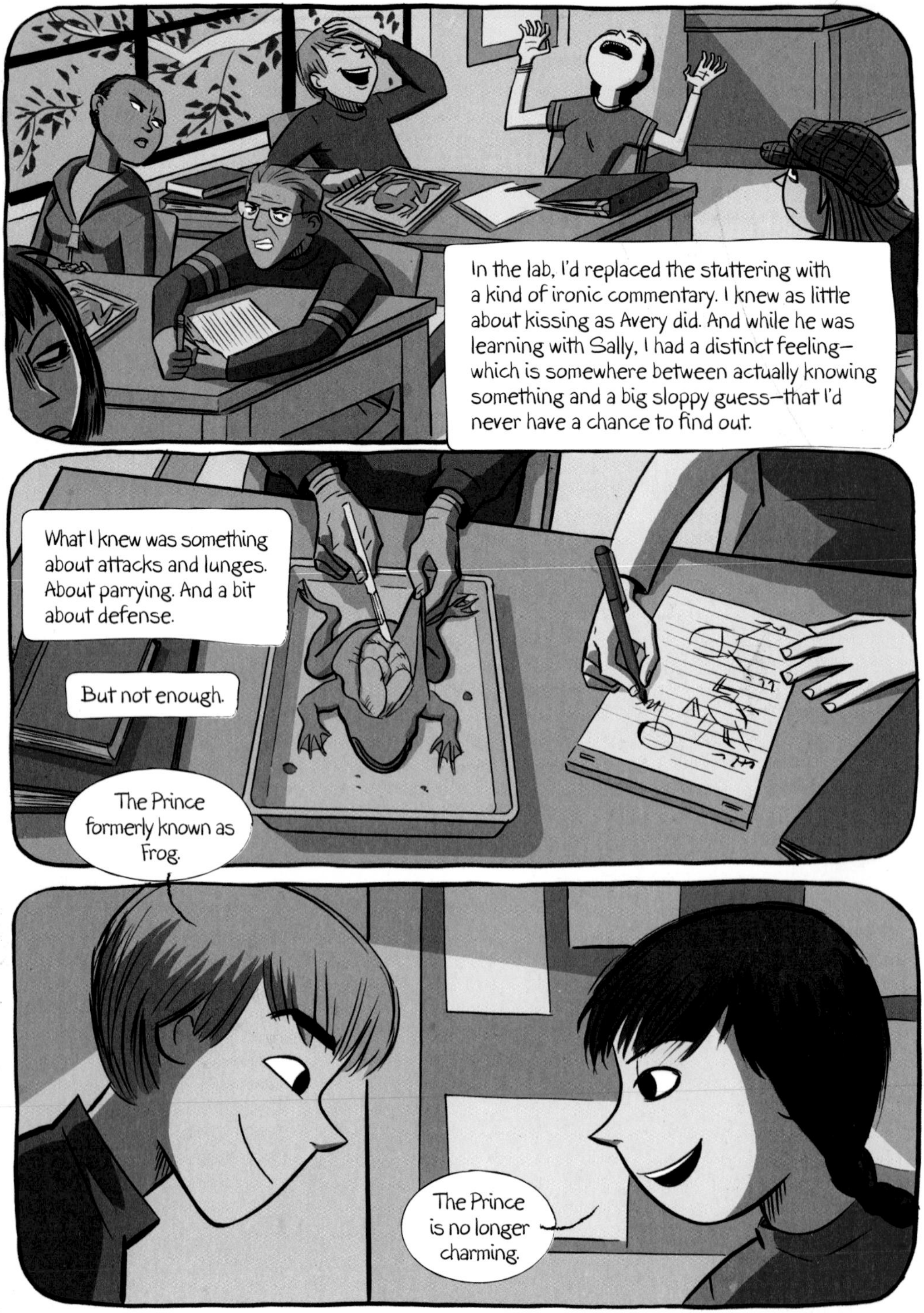
In the lab, I'd replaced the stuttering with a kind of ironic commentary. I knew as little about kissing as Avery did. And while he was learning with Sally, I had a distinct feeling—which is somewhere between actually knowing something and a big sloppy guess—that I'd never have a chance to find out.
What I knew was something about attacks and lunges. About parrying. And a bit about defense.
But not enough.
The Prince formerly known as Frog.
The Prince is no longer charming.

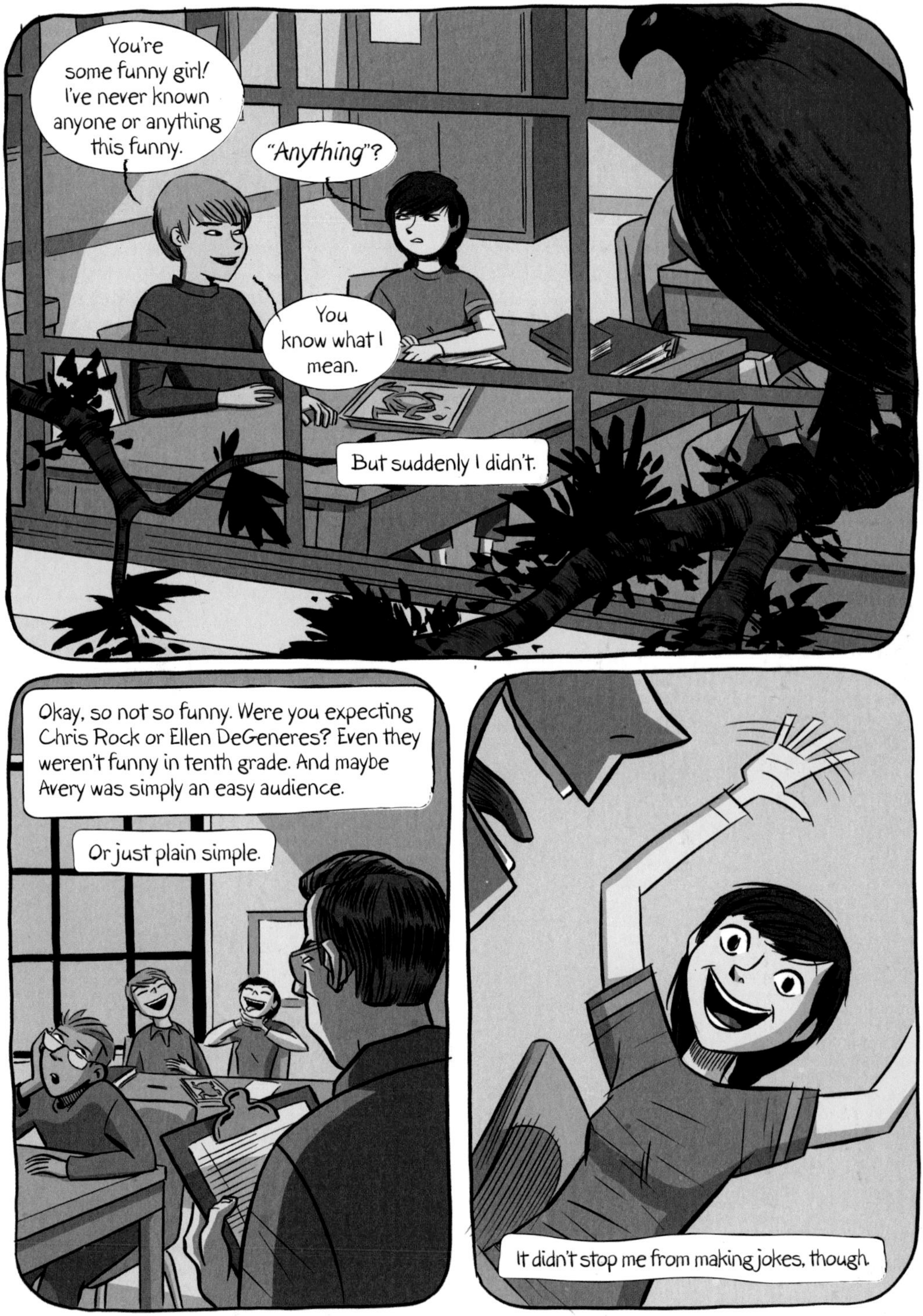
You're some funny girl! I've never known anyone or anything this funny.
"Anything"?
You know what I mean.
But suddenly I didn't.
Okay, so not so funny. Were you expecting Chris Rock or Ellen DeGeneres? Even they weren't funny in tenth grade. And maybe Avery was simply an easy audience.
Or just plain simple.
It didn't stop me from making jokes, though.

4. Prise de Fer

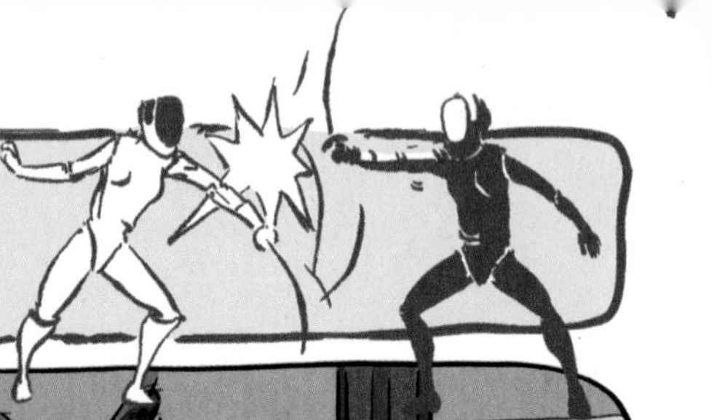

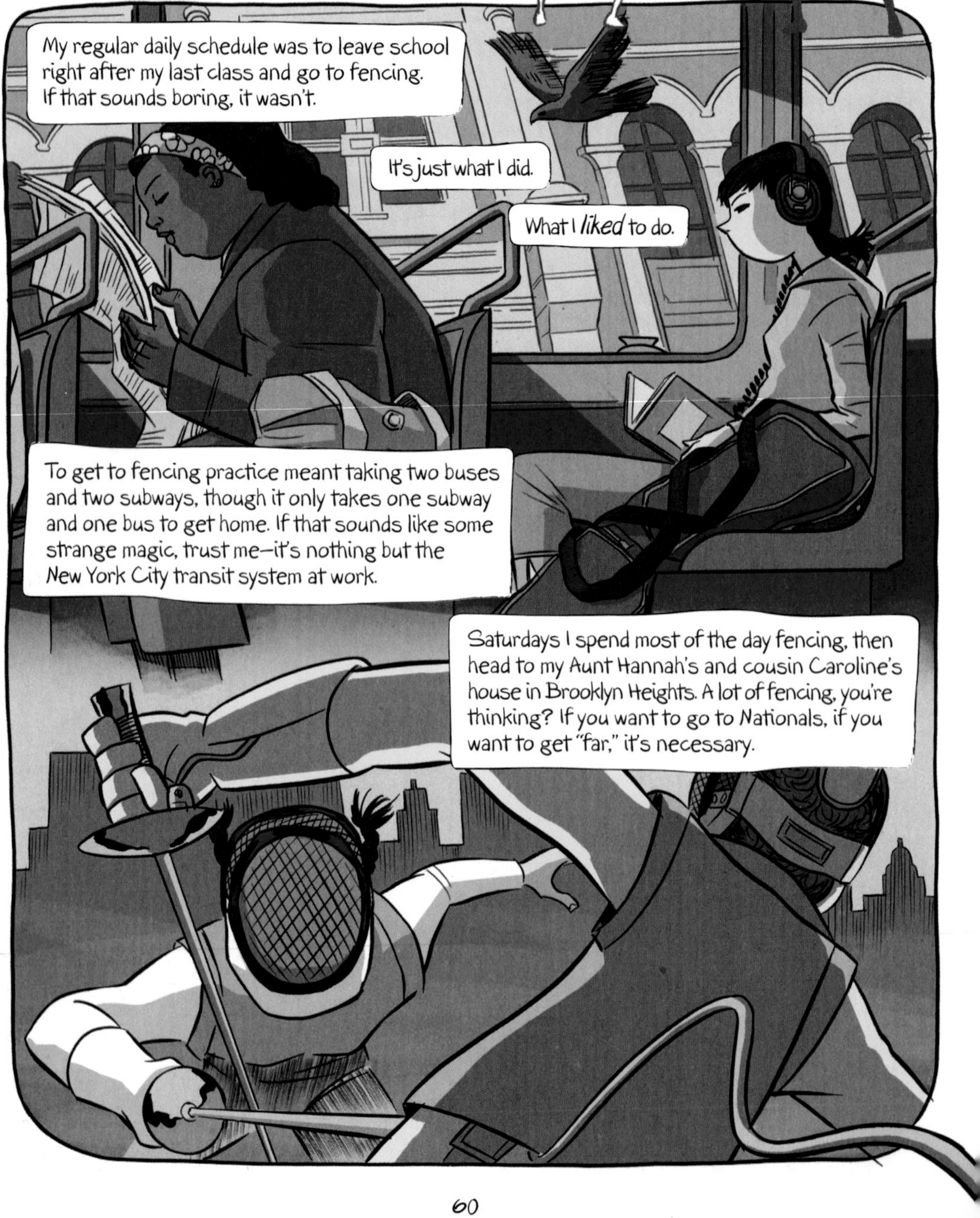

My regular daily schedule was to leave school right after my last class and go to fencing. If that sounds boring, it wasn't.
It's just what I did.
What I *liked* to do.
To get to fencing practice meant taking two buses and two subways, though it only takes one subway and one bus to get home. If that sounds like some strange magic, trust me—it's nothing but the New York City transit system at work.
Saturdays I spend most of the day fencing, then head to my Aunt Hannah's and cousin Caroline's house in Brooklyn Heights. A lot of fencing, you're thinking? If you want to go to Nationals, if you want to get "far," it's necessary.

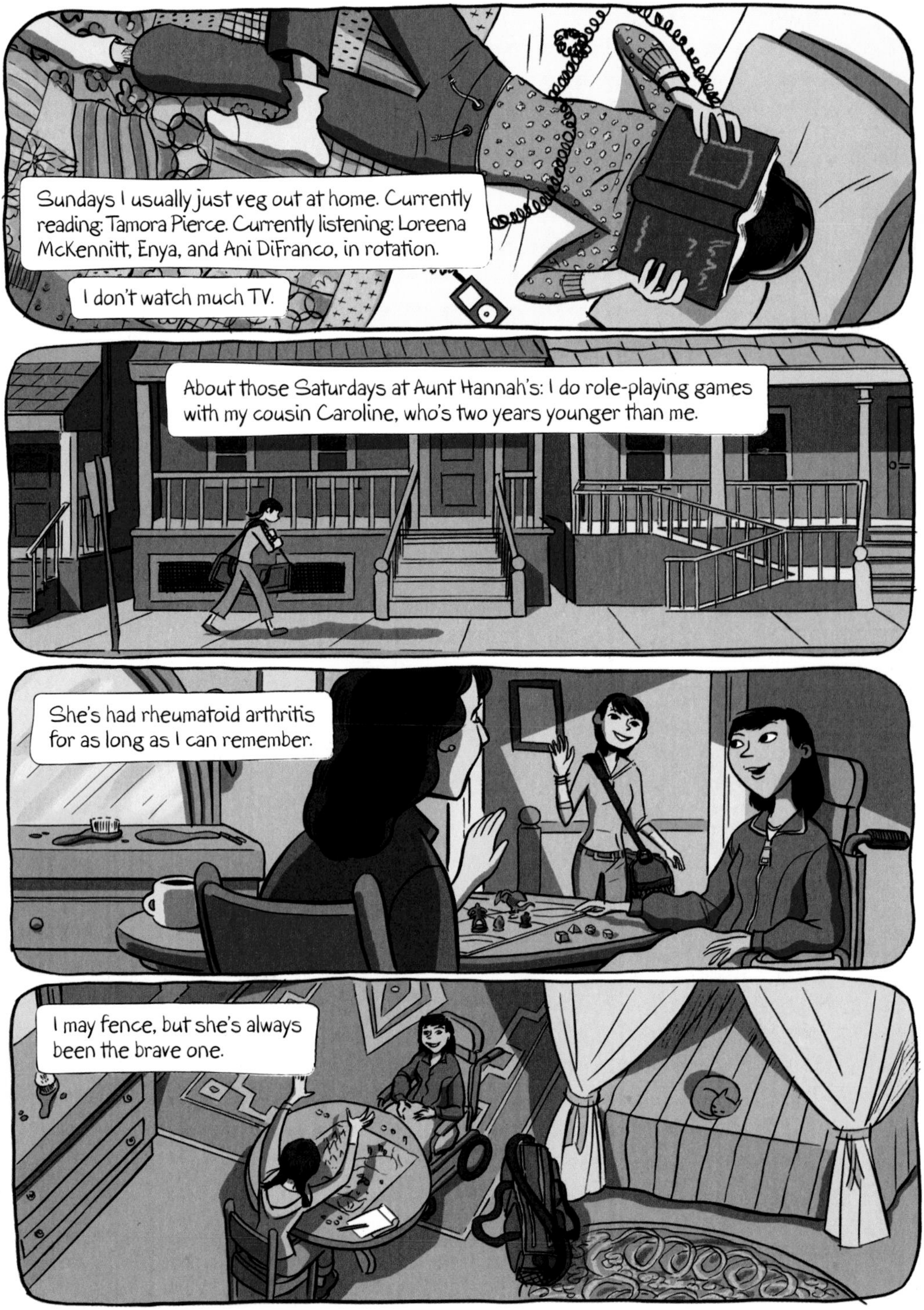
Sundays I usually just veg out at home. Currently reading: Tamora Pierce. Currently listening: Loreena McKennitt, Enya, and Ani DiFranco, in rotation.
I don't watch much TV.
About those Saturdays at Aunt Hannah's: I do role-playing games with my cousin Caroline, who's two years younger than me.
She's had rheumatoid arthritis for as long as I can remember.
I may fence, but she's always been the brave one.

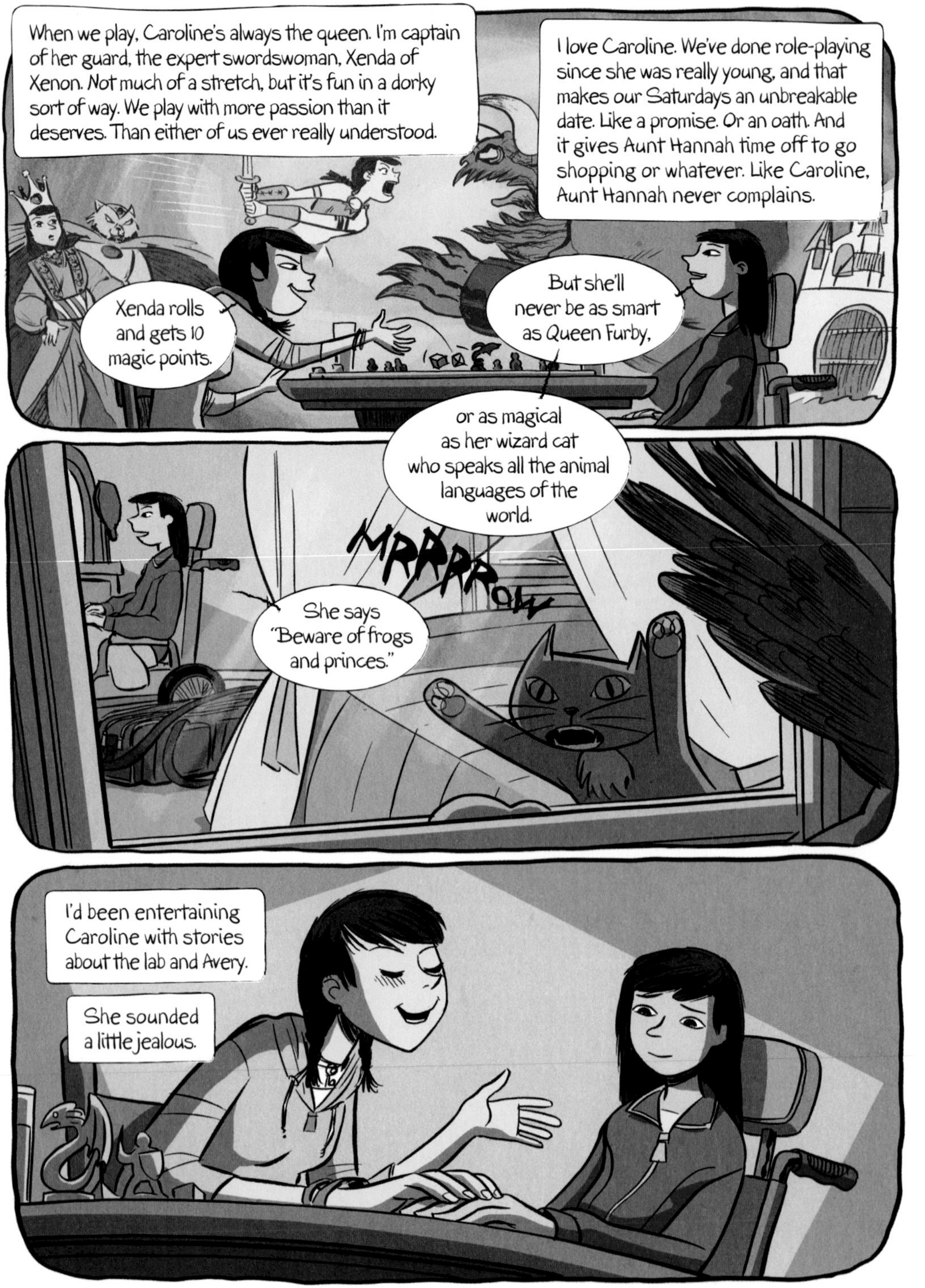

When we play, Caroline's always the queen. I'm captain of her guard, the expert swordswoman, Xenda of Xenon. Not much of a stretch, but it's fun in a dorky sort of way. We play with more passion than it deserves. Than either of us ever really understood.
I love Caroline. We've done role-playing since she was really young, and that makes our Saturdays an unbreakable date. Like a promise. Or an oath. And it gives Aunt Hannah time off to go shopping or whatever. Like Caroline, Aunt Hannah never complains.
Xenda rolls and gets 10 magic points.
But she'll never be as smart as Queen Furby,
or as magical as her wizard cat who speaks all the animal languages of the world.
MRRRROW
She says "Beware of frogs and princes."
I'd been entertaining Caroline with stories about the lab and Avery.
She sounded a little jealous.

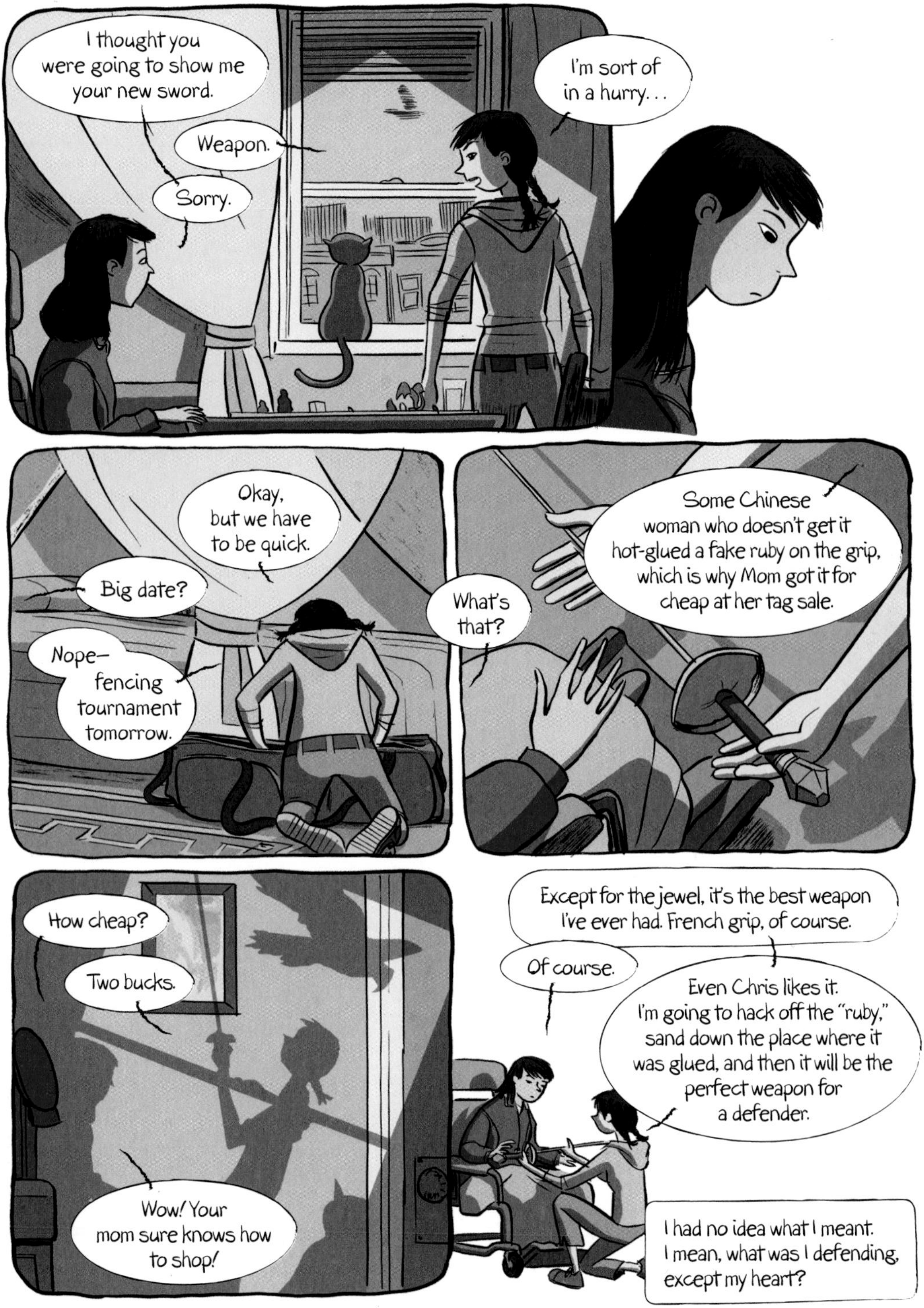
I thought you were going to show me your new sword.
Weapon.
Sorry.
I'm sort of in a hurry. . .
Okay, but we have to be quick.
Big date?
Nope— fencing tournament tomorrow.
What's that?
Some Chinese woman who doesn't get it hot-glued a fake ruby on the grip, which is why Mom got it for cheap at her tag sale.
How cheap?
Two bucks.
Wow! Your mom sure knows how to shop!
Except for the jewel, it's the best weapon I've ever had. French grip, of course.
Of course.
Even Chris likes it. I'm going to hack off the "ruby," sand down the place where it was glued, and then it will be the perfect weapon for a defender.
I had no idea what I meant. I mean, what was I defending, except my heart?

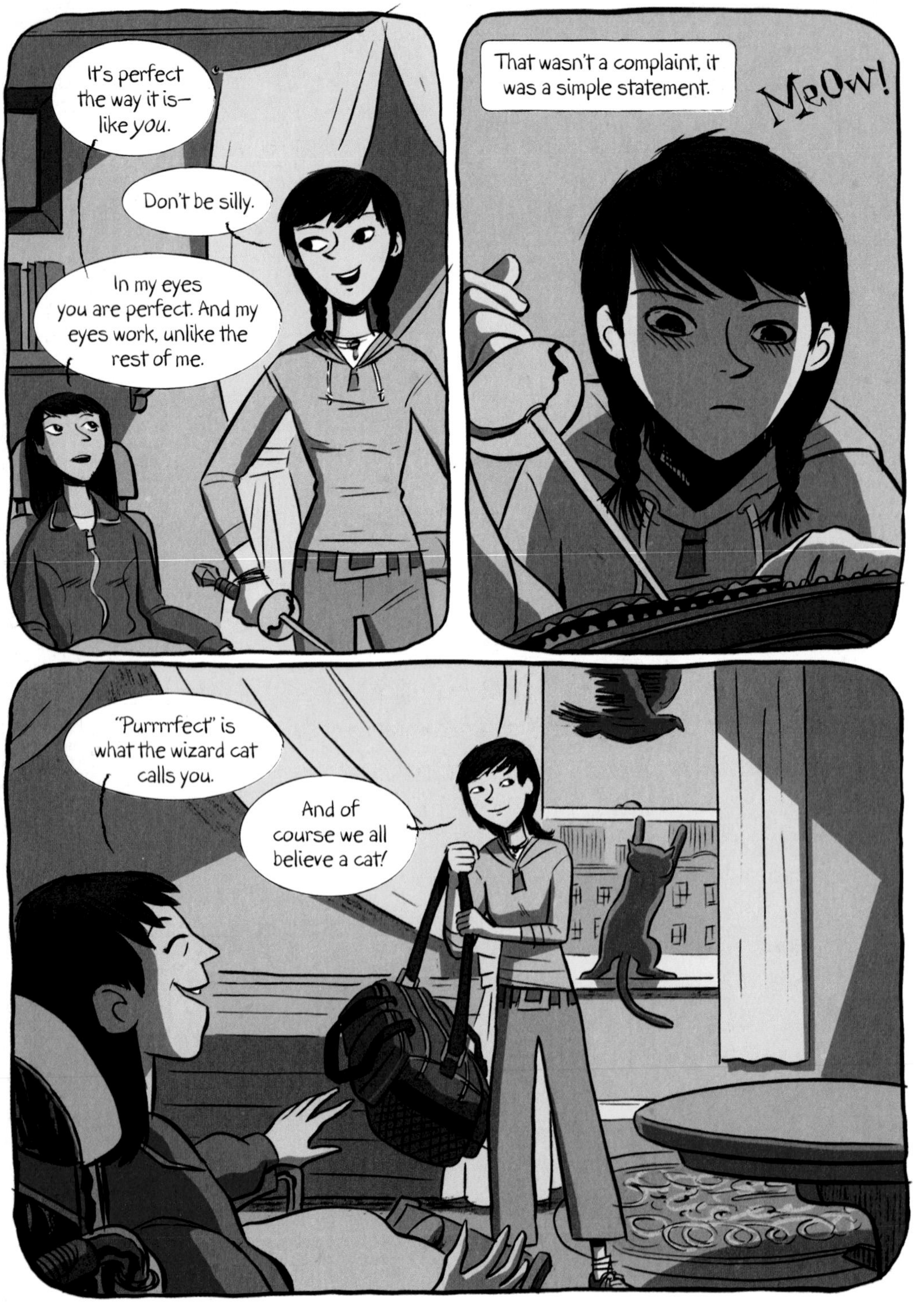
It's perfect the way it is— like *you*.
Don't be silly.
In my eyes you are perfect. And my eyes work, unlike the rest of me.
That wasn't a complaint, it was a simple statement.
MeOw!
"Purrrrfect" is what the wizard cat calls you.
And of course we all believe a cat!

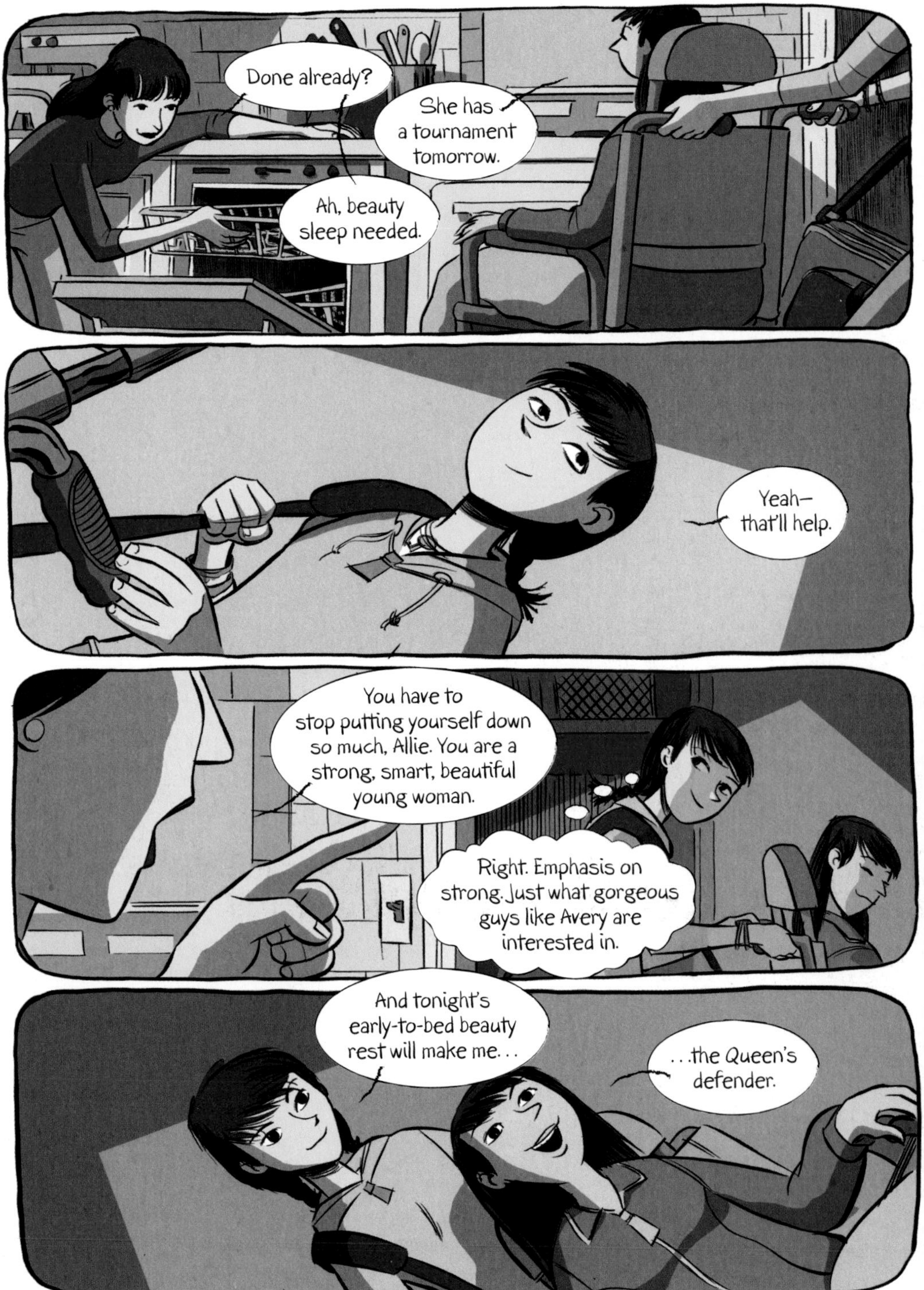
Done already?
She has a tournament tomorrow.
Ah, beauty sleep needed.
Yeah— that'll help.
You have to stop putting yourself down so much, Allie. You are a strong, smart, beautiful young woman.
Right. Emphasis on strong. Just what gorgeous guys like Avery are interested in.
And tonight's early-to-bed beauty rest will make me. . .
. . .the Queen's defender.

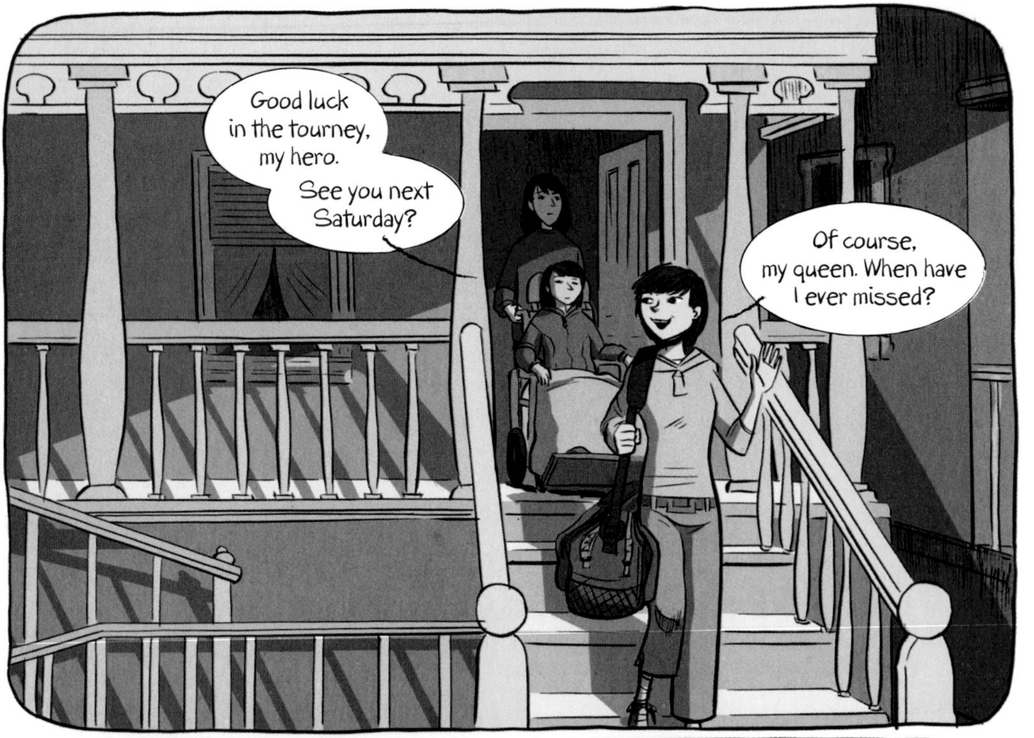
Good luck in the tourney, my hero.
See you next Saturday?
Of course, my queen. When have I ever missed?

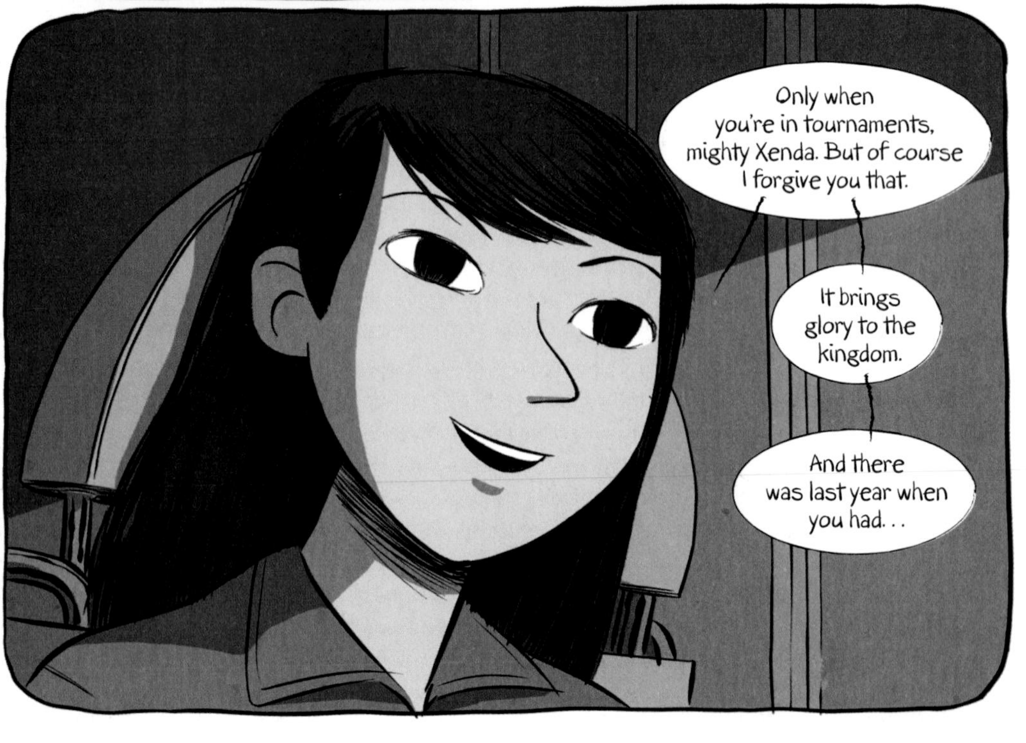
Only when you're in tournaments, mighty Xenda. But of course I forgive you that.
It brings glory to the kingdom.
And there was last year when you had. . .

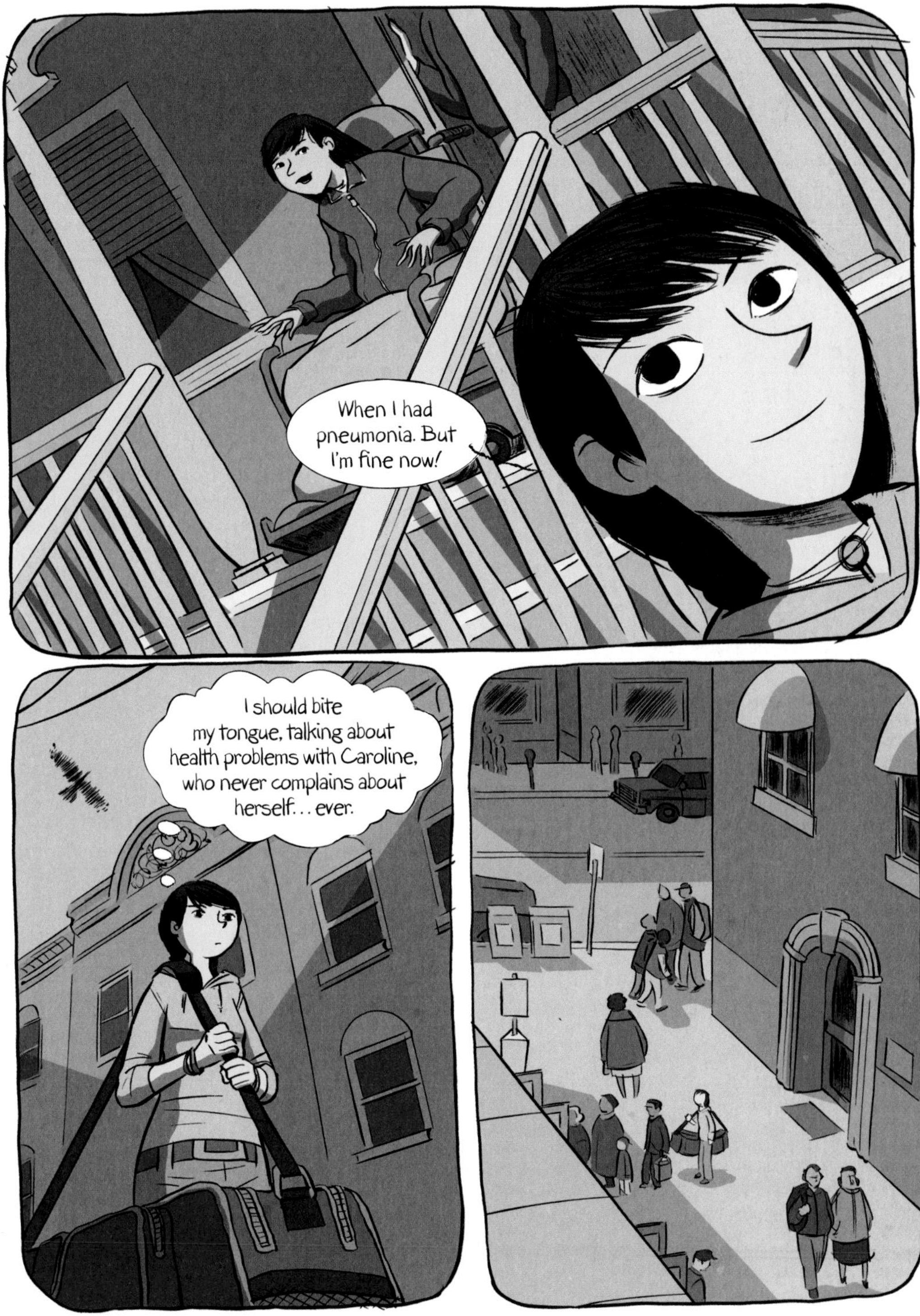
When I had pneumonia. But I'm fine now!
I should bite my tongue, talking about health problems with Caroline, who never complains about herself... ever.

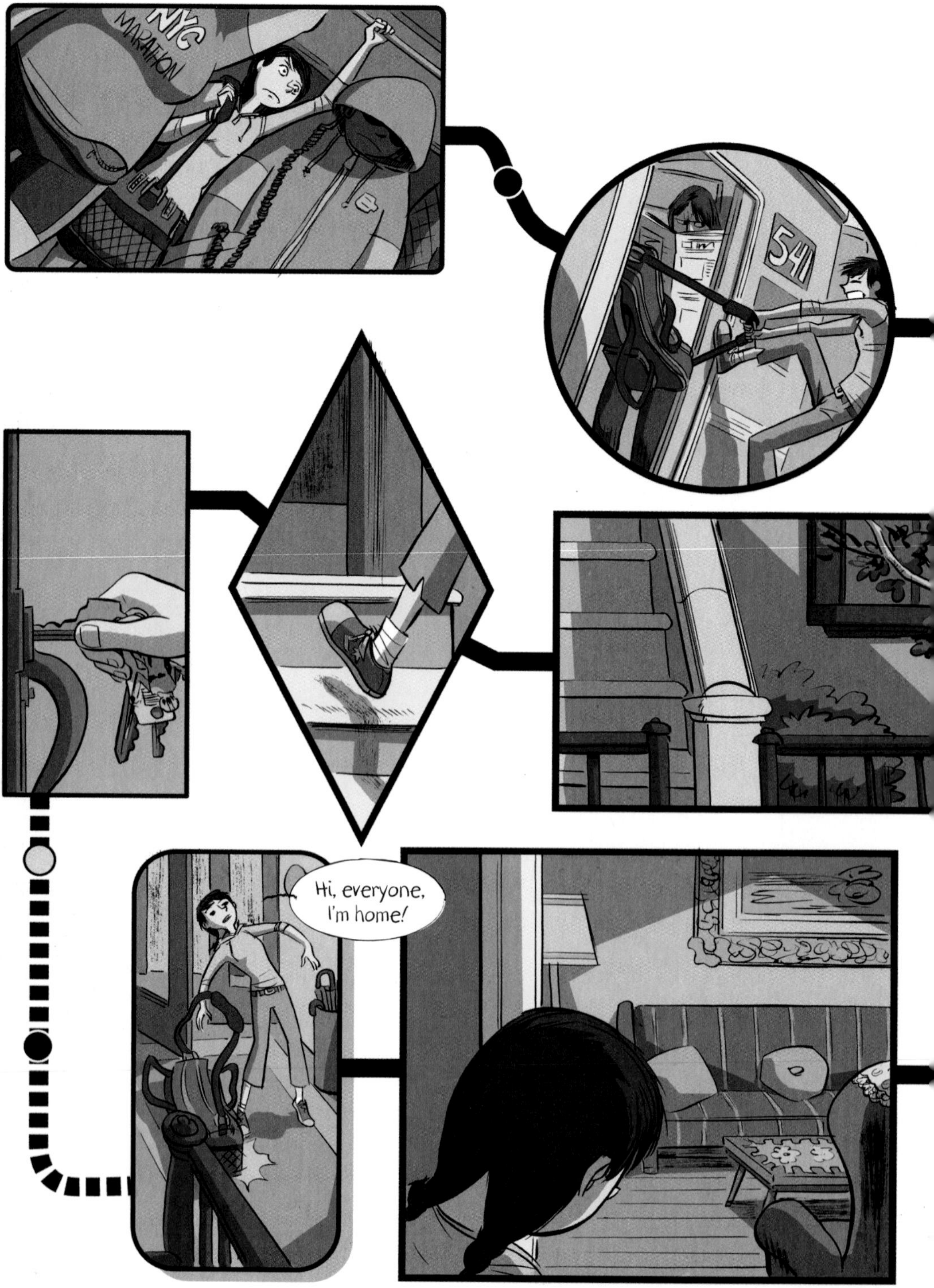
NYC
MARATHON
541
Hi, everyone, I'm home!

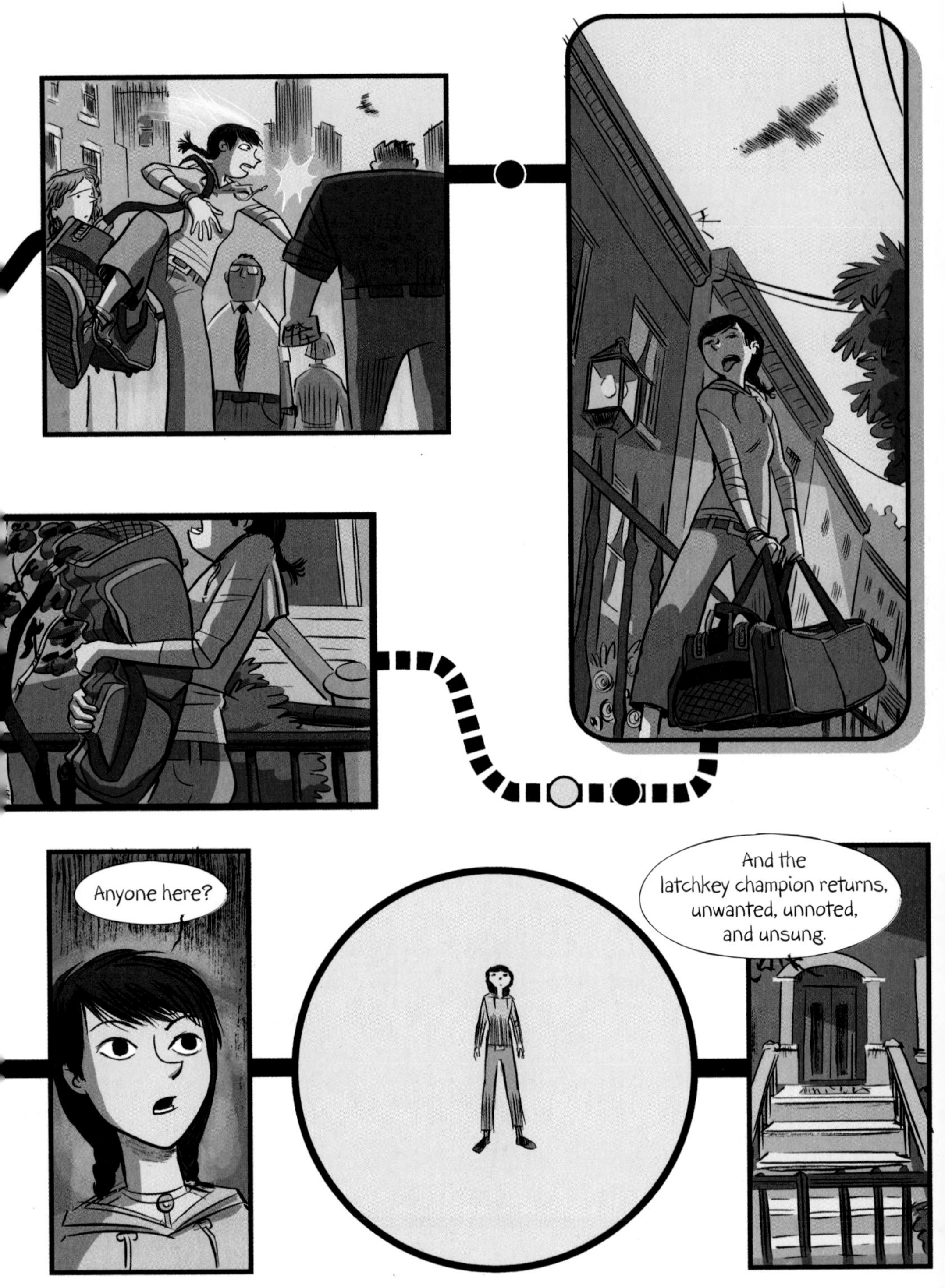
Anyone here?
And the latchkey champion returns, unwanted, unnoted, and unsung.

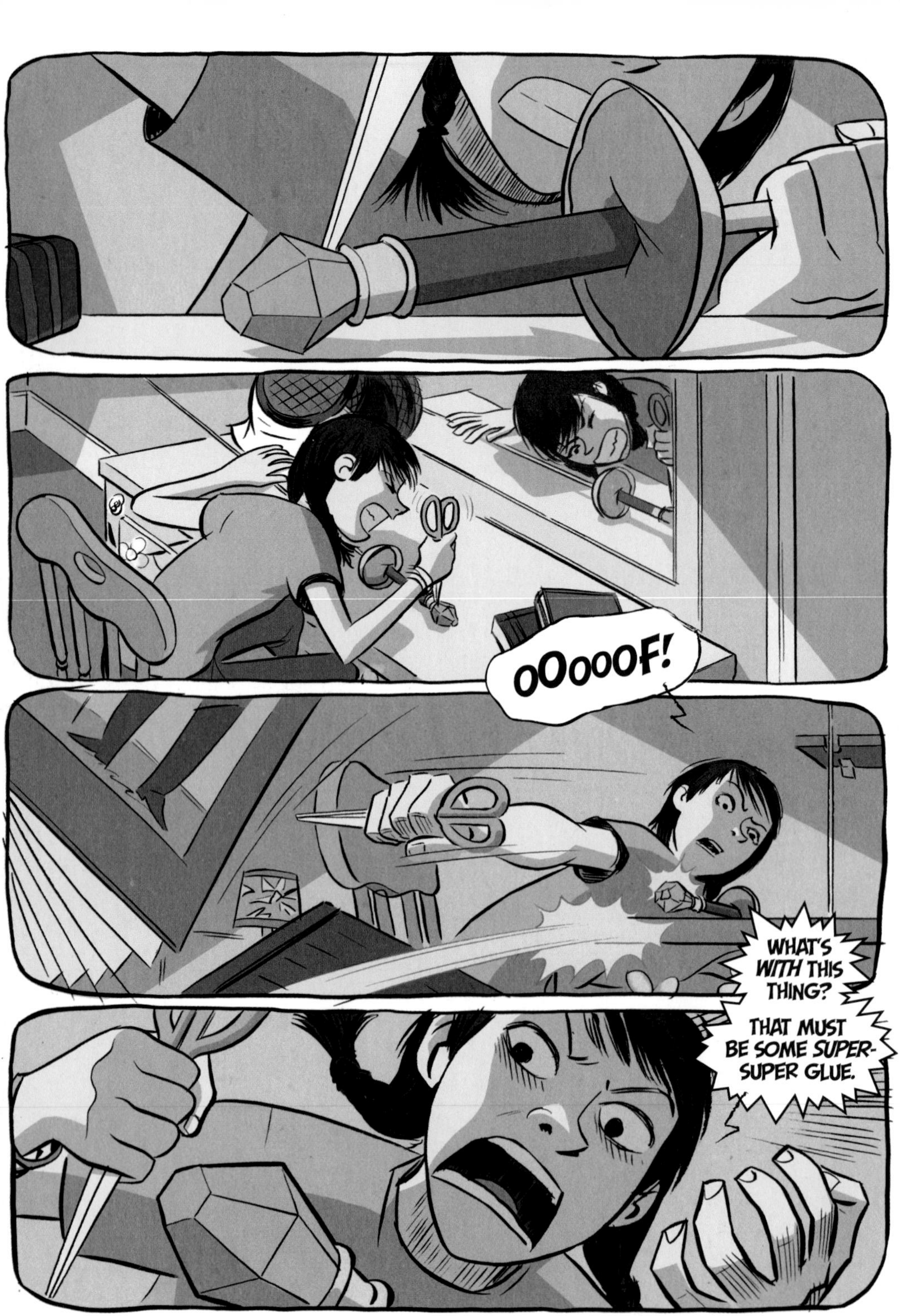
OOOOOF!
WHAT'S *WITH* THIS THING?
THAT MUST BE SOME *SUPER*-SUPER GLUE.

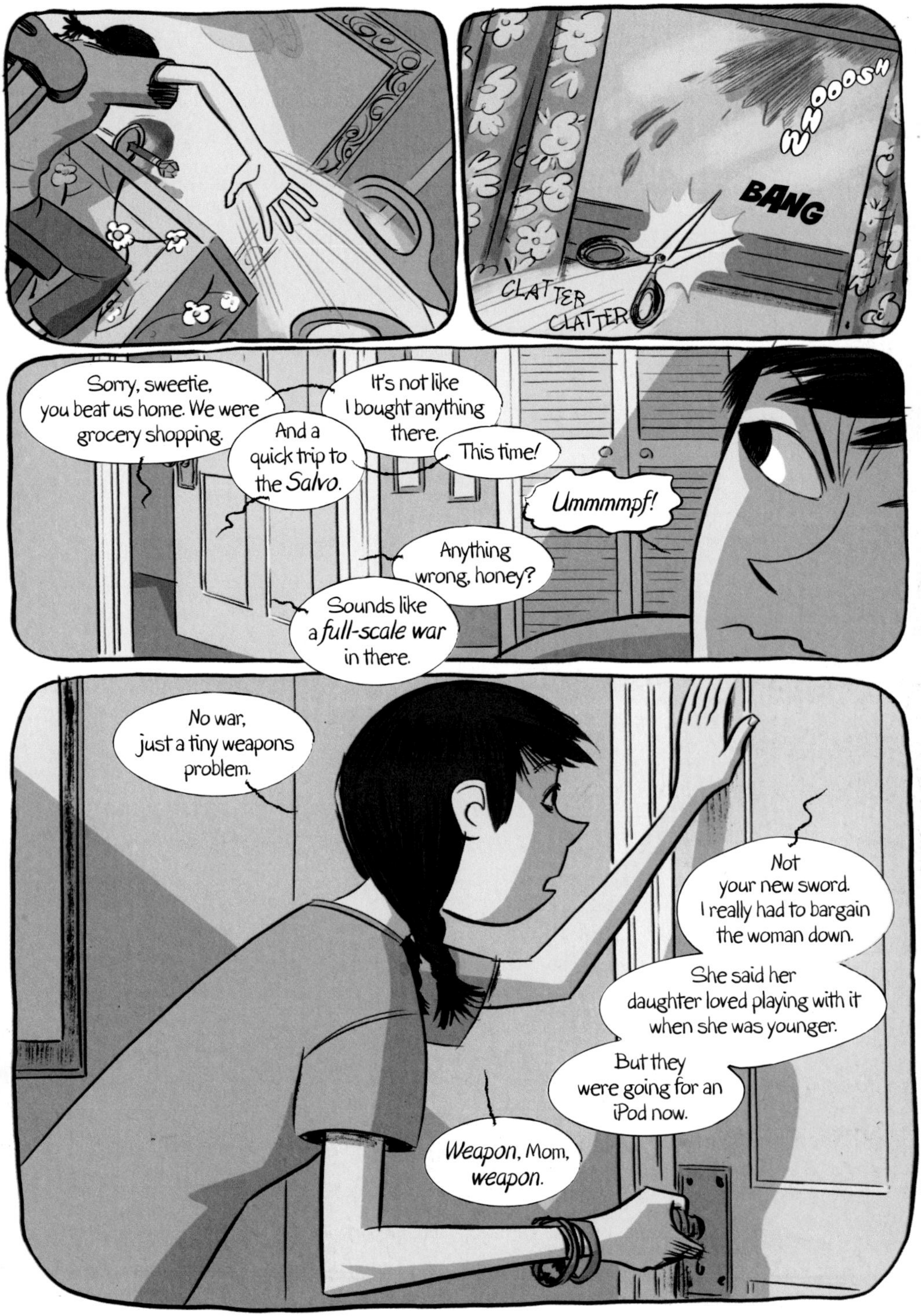
WHOOOSH
BANG
CLATTER
CLATTER
Sorry, sweetie, you beat us home. We were grocery shopping.
It's not like I bought anything there.
And a quick trip to the *Salvo*.
This time!
Ummmmpf!
Anything wrong, honey?
Sounds like a *full-scale war* in there.
No war, just a tiny weapons problem.
Not your new sword. I really had to bargain the woman down.
She said her daughter loved playing with it when she was younger.
But they were going for an iPod now.
Weapon, Mom, *weapon*.

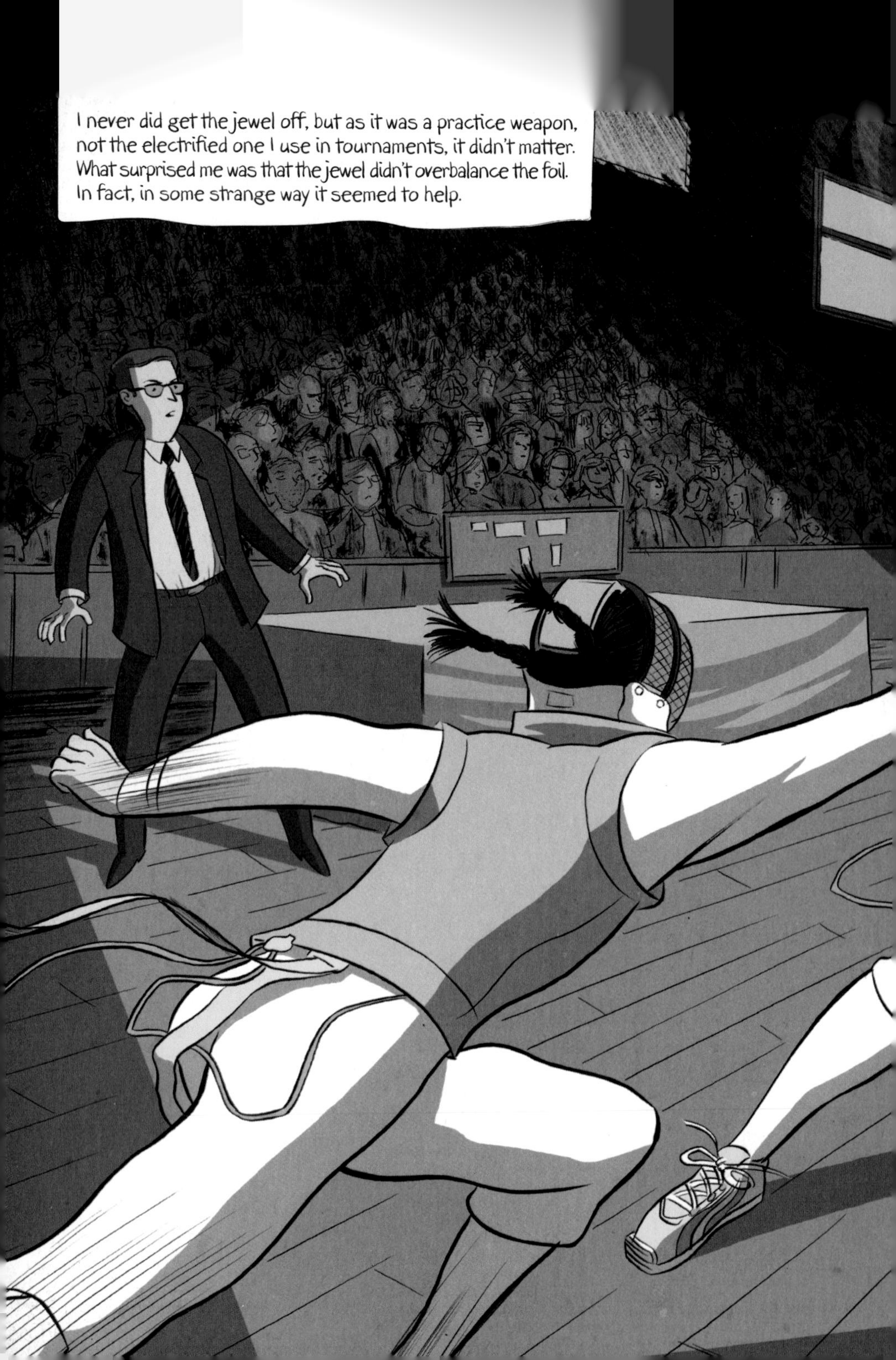
I never did get the jewel off, but as it was a practice weapon, not the electrified one I use in tournaments, it didn't matter. What surprised me was that the jewel didn't overbalance the foil. In fact, in some strange way it seemed to help.

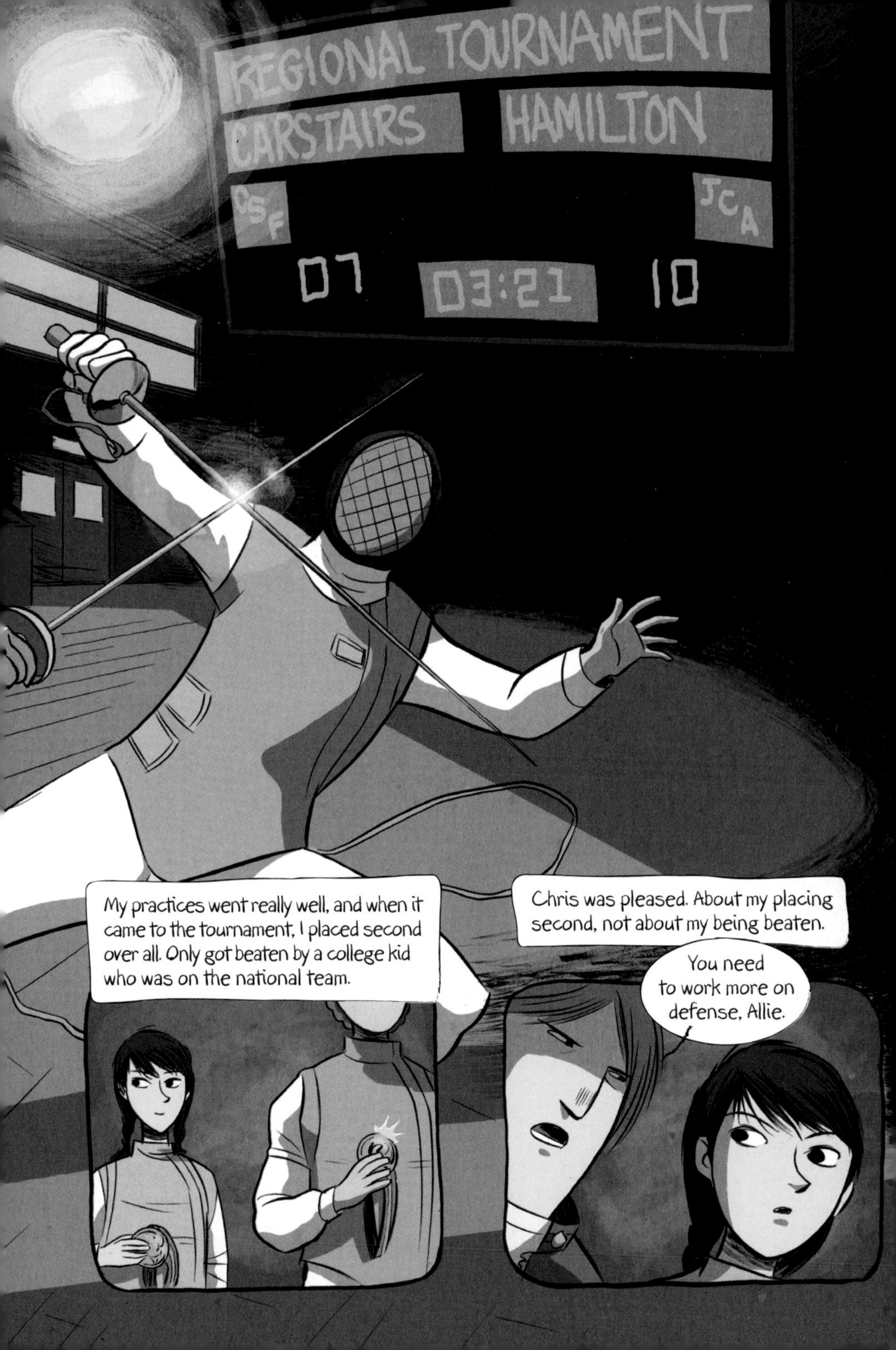
REGIONAL TOURNAMENT
CARSTAIRS
HAMILTON
CSF
JCA
07
03:21
10
My practices went really well, and when it came to the tournament, I placed second over all. Only got beaten by a college kid who was on the national team.
Chris was pleased. About my placing second, not about my being beaten.
You need to work more on defense, Allie.

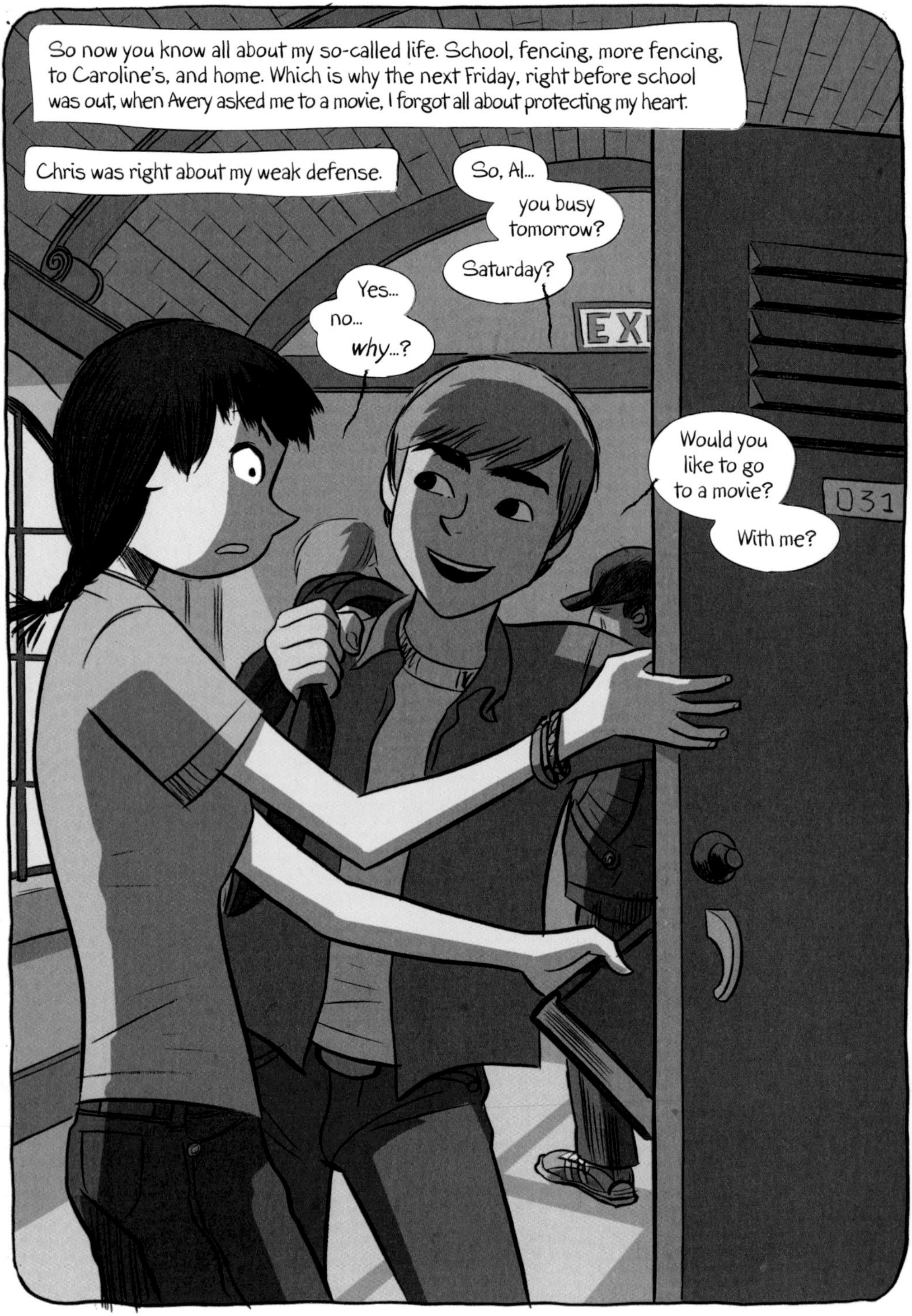

So now you know all about my so-called life. School, fencing, more fencing, to Caroline's, and home. Which is why the next Friday, right before school was out, when Avery asked me to a movie, I forgot all about protecting my heart.
Chris was right about my weak defense.
So, Al...
you busy tomorrow?
Saturday?
Yes... no... why...?
Would you like to go to a movie?
With me?
EXI
031

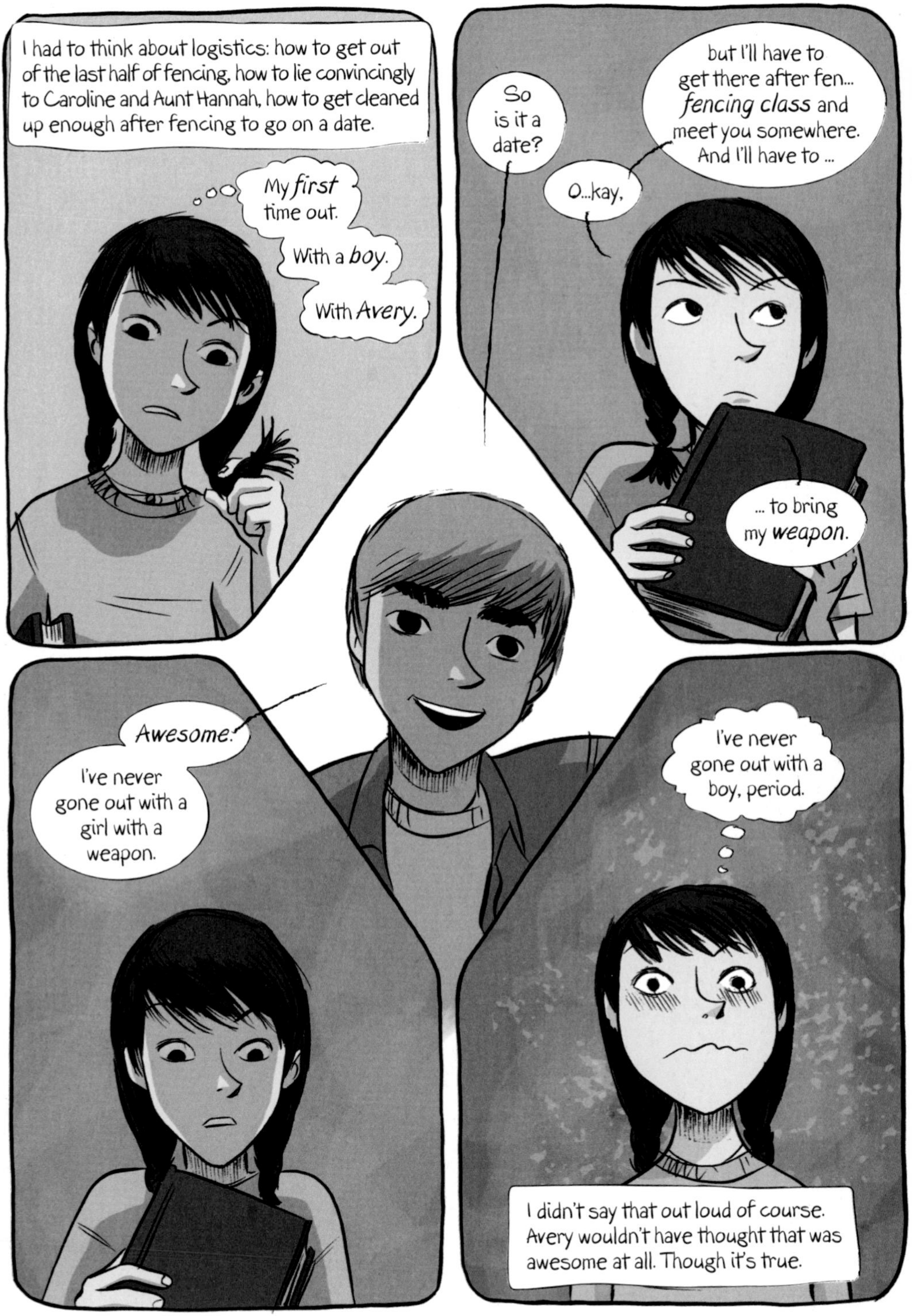
I had to think about logistics: how to get out of the last half of fencing, how to lie convincingly to Caroline and Aunt Hannah, how to get cleaned up enough after fencing to go on a date.
My *first* time out.
With a *boy*.
With *Avery*.
So is it a date?
O...kay,
but I'll have to get there after fen... *fencing class* and meet you somewhere. And I'll have to ...
... to bring my **weapon**.
Awesome.
I've never gone out with a girl with a weapon.
I've never gone out with a boy, period.
I didn't say that out loud of course. Avery wouldn't have thought that was awesome at all. Though it's true.

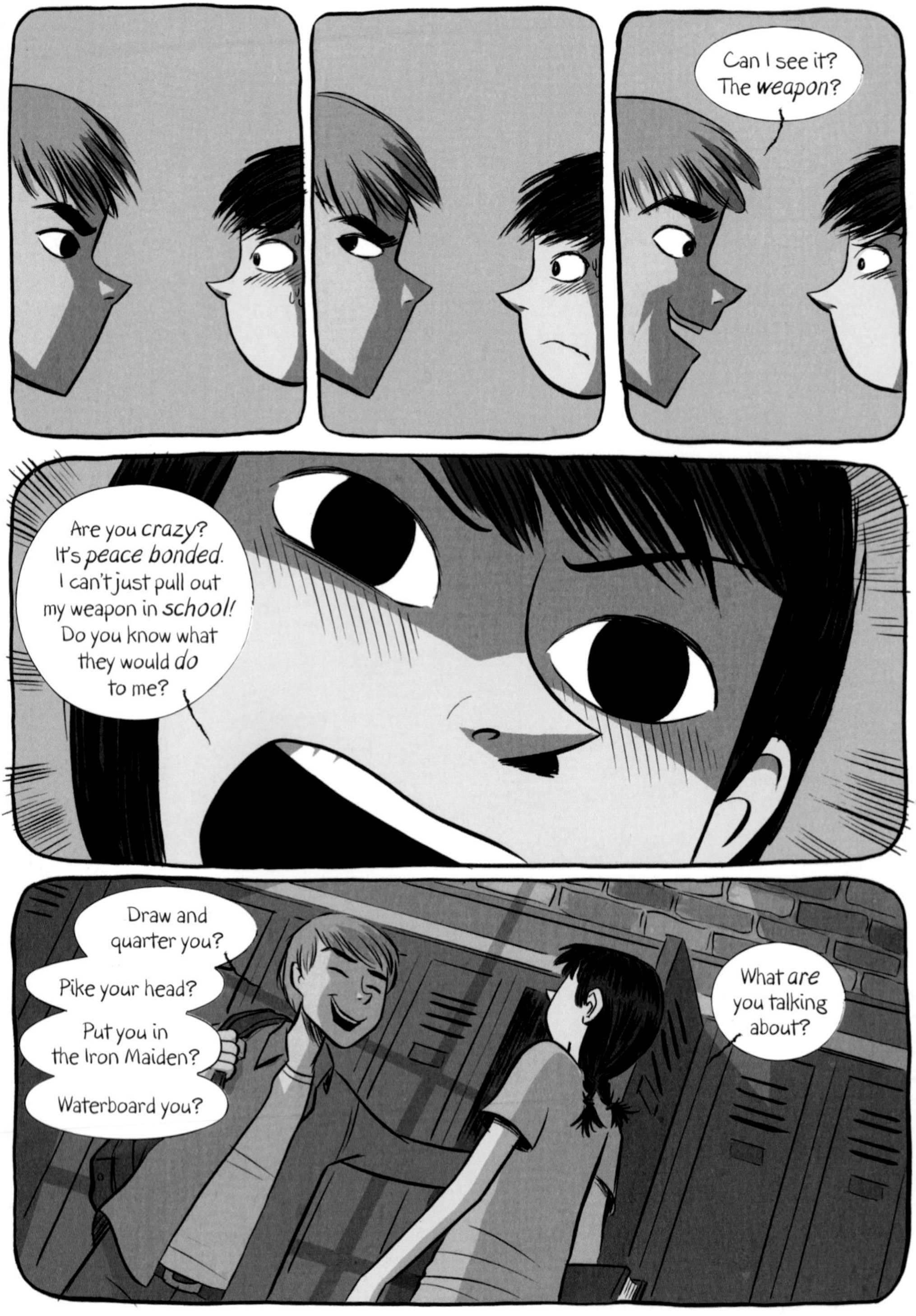
Can I see it? The *weapon*?
Are you *crazy*? It's *peace bonded*. I can't just pull out my weapon in *school*! Do you know what they would *do* to me?
Draw and quarter you?
Pike your head?
Put you in the Iron Maiden?
Waterboard you?
What *are* you talking about?

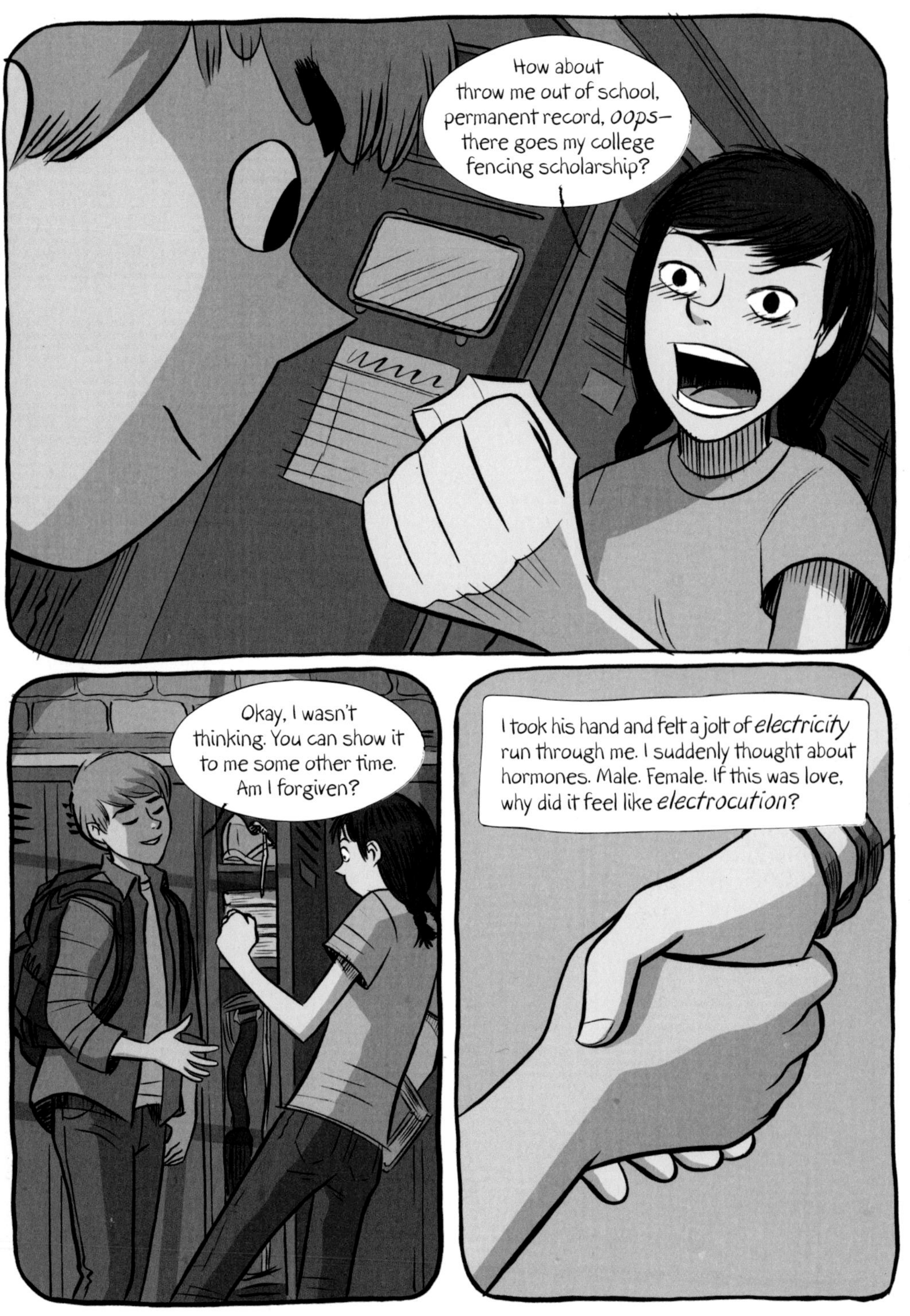
How about throw me out of school, permanent record, *oops*— there goes my college fencing scholarship?
Okay, I wasn't thinking. You can show it to me some other time. Am I forgiven?
I took his hand and felt a jolt of *electricity* run through me. I suddenly thought about hormones. Male. Female. If this was love, why did it feel like *electrocution*?

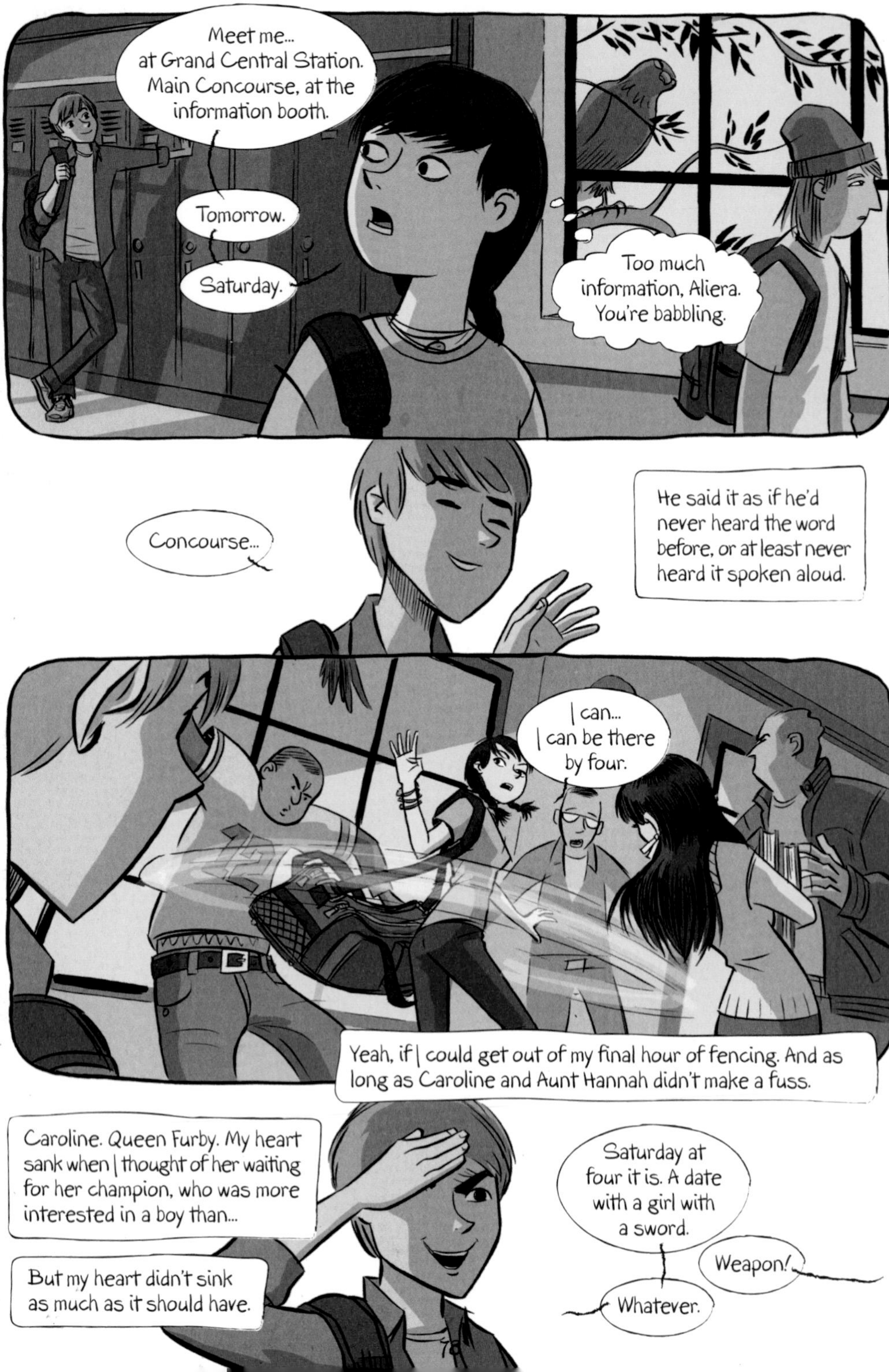
Meet me... at Grand Central Station. Main Concourse, at the information booth.
Tomorrow.
Saturday.
Too much information, Aliera. You're babbling.
Concourse...
He said it as if he'd never heard the word before, or at least never heard it spoken aloud.
I can... I can be there by four.
Yeah, if I could get out of my final hour of fencing. And as long as Caroline and Aunt Hannah didn't make a fuss.
Caroline. *Queen Furby*. My heart sank when I thought of her waiting for her champion, who was more interested in a boy than...
But my heart didn't sink as much as it should have.
Saturday at four it is. A date with a girl with a sword.
Weapon!
Whatever.

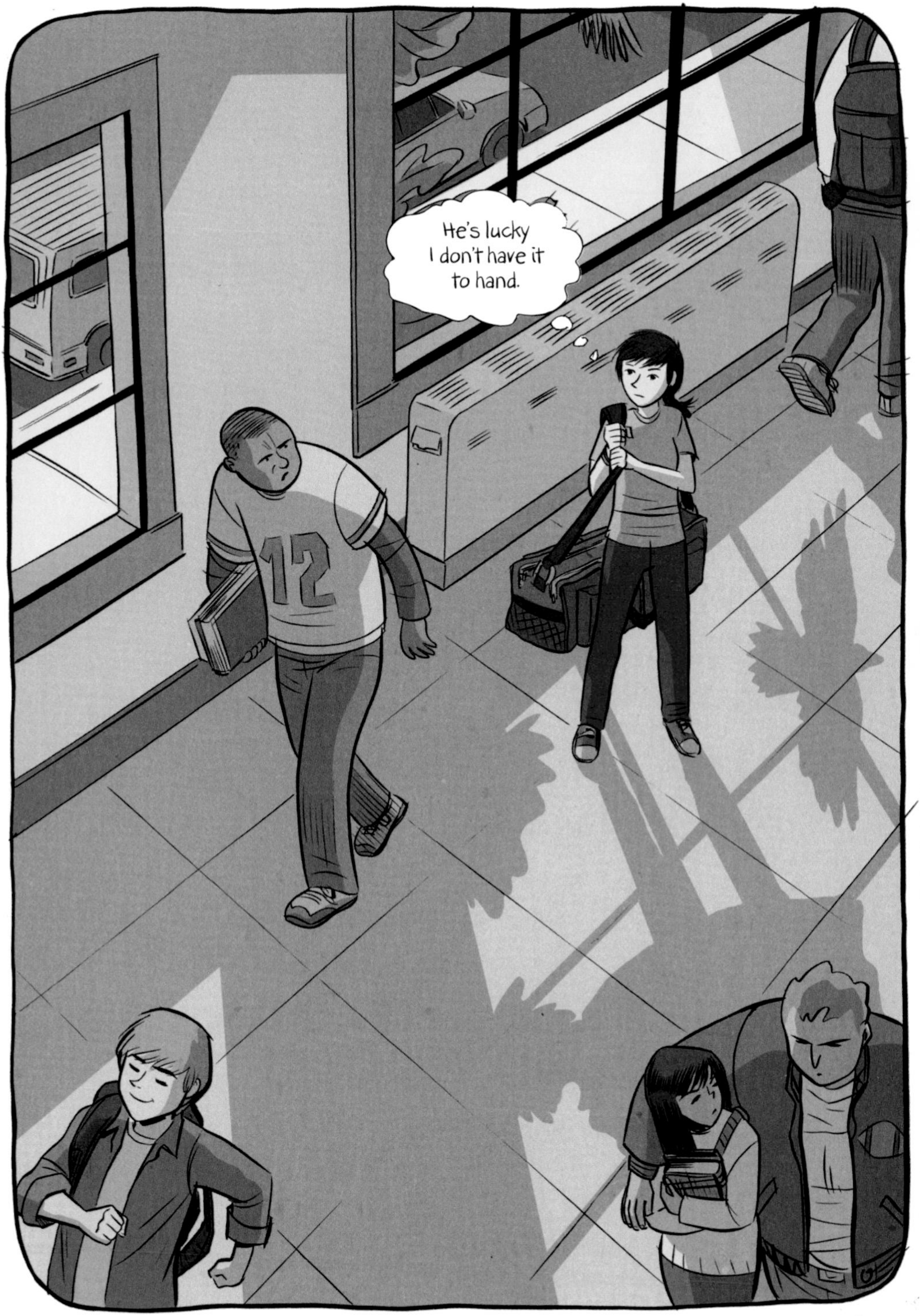
He's lucky
I don't have it
to hand.
12

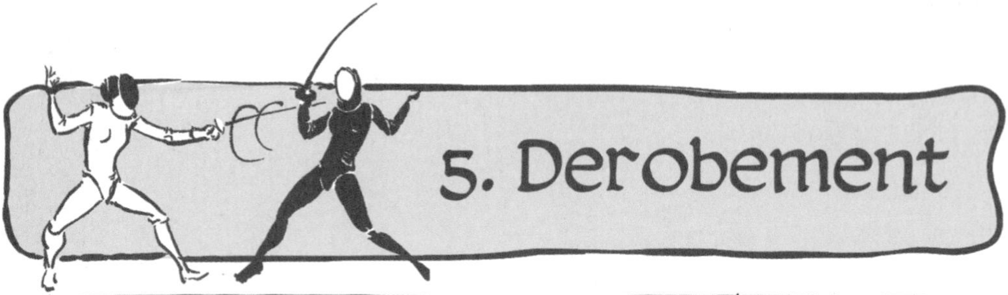
5. Derobement

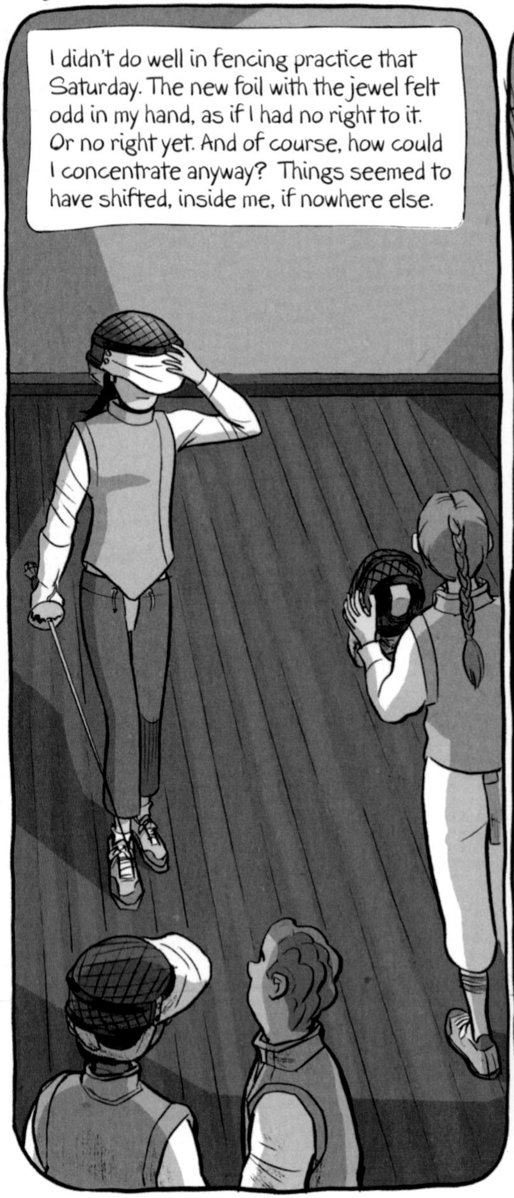
I didn't do well in fencing practice that Saturday. The new foil with the jewel felt odd in my hand, as if I had no right to it. Or no right yet. And of course, how could I concentrate anyway? Things seemed to have shifted, inside me, if nowhere else.

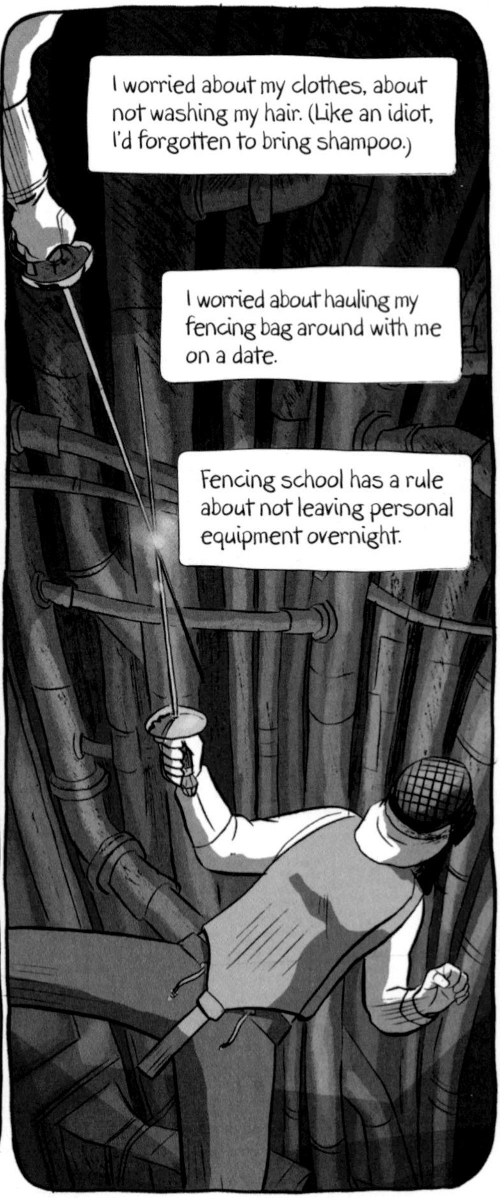
I worried about my clothes, about not washing my hair. (Like an idiot, I'd forgotten to bring shampoo.)
I worried about hauling my fencing bag around with me on a date.
Fencing school has a rule about not leaving personal equipment overnight.

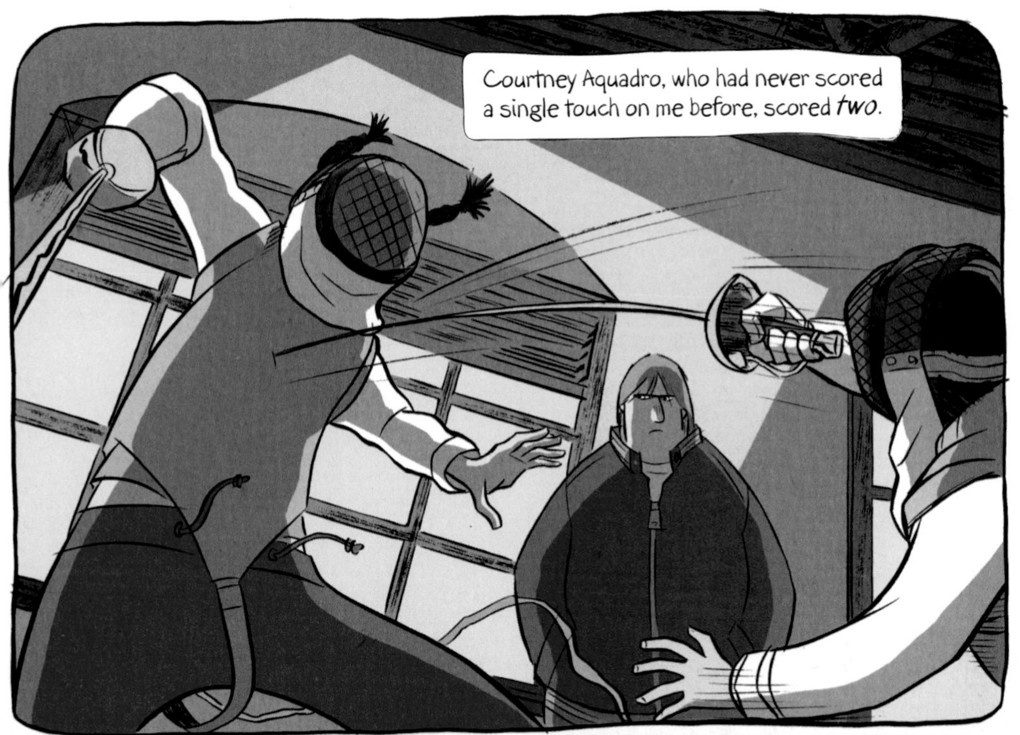
Courtney Aquadro, who had never scored a single touch on me before, scored *two*.

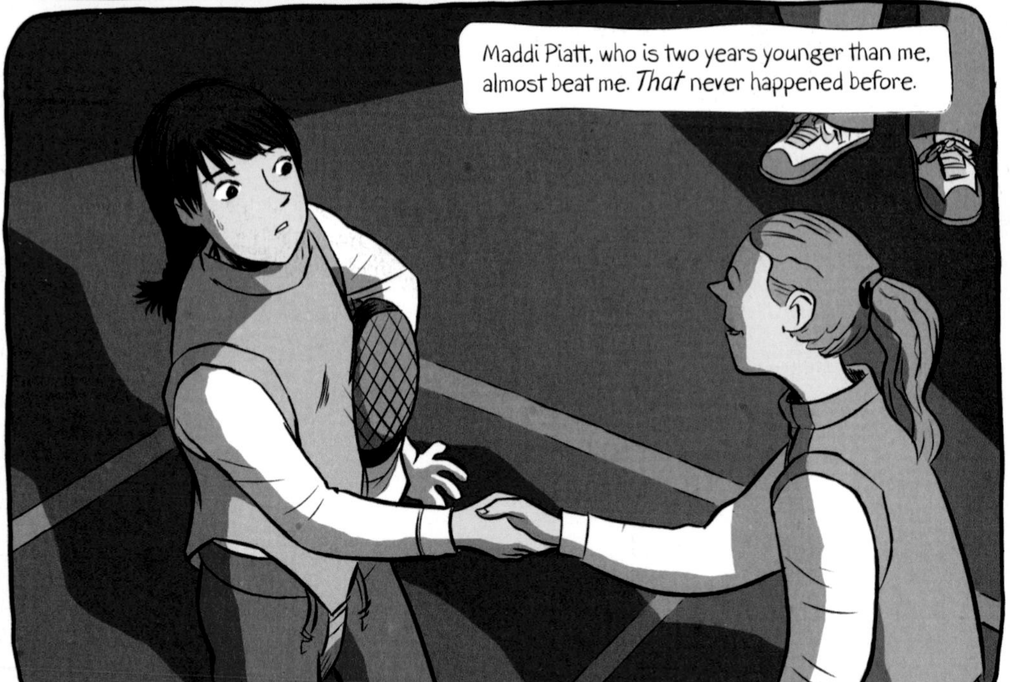
Maddi Piatt, who is two years younger than me, almost beat me. *That* never happened before.

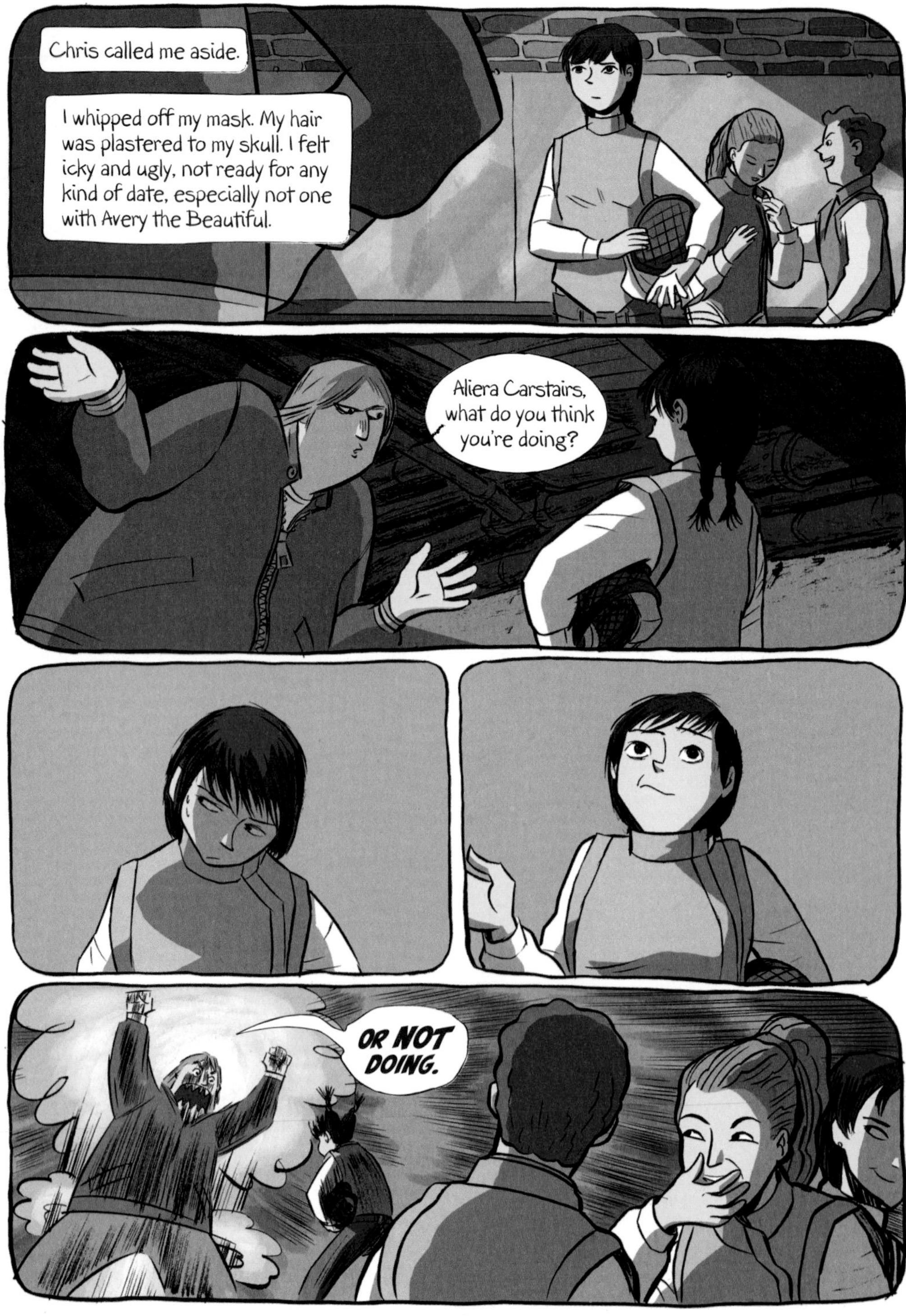
Chris called me aside.
I whipped off my mask. My hair was plastered to my skull. I felt icky and ugly, not ready for any kind of date, especially not one with Avery the Beautiful.
Aliera Carstairs, what do you think you're doing?
OR NOT DOING.

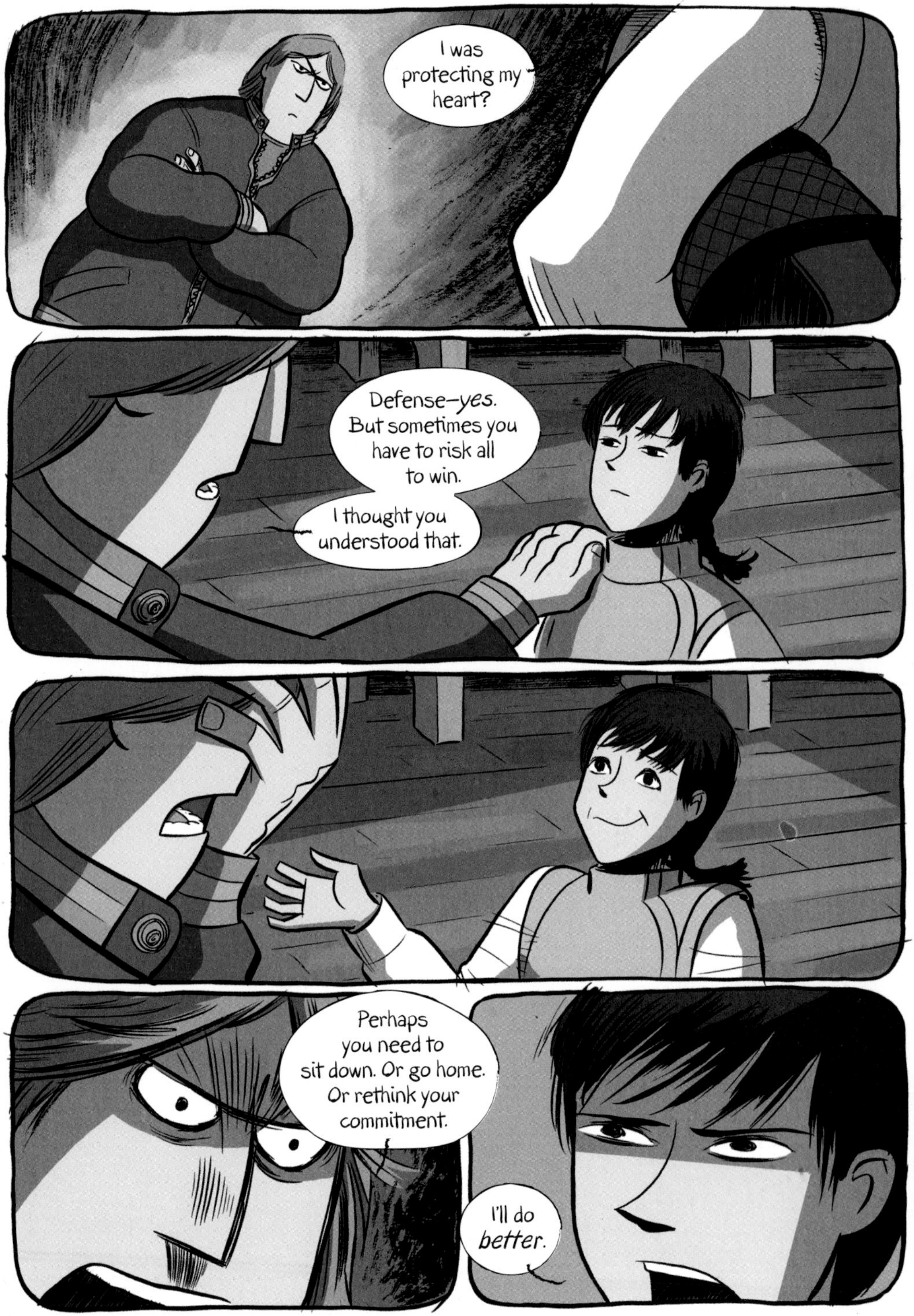
I was protecting my heart?
Defense—*yes.* But sometimes you have to risk all to win.
I thought you understood that.
Perhaps you need to sit down. Or go home. Or rethink your commitment.
I'll do *better.*

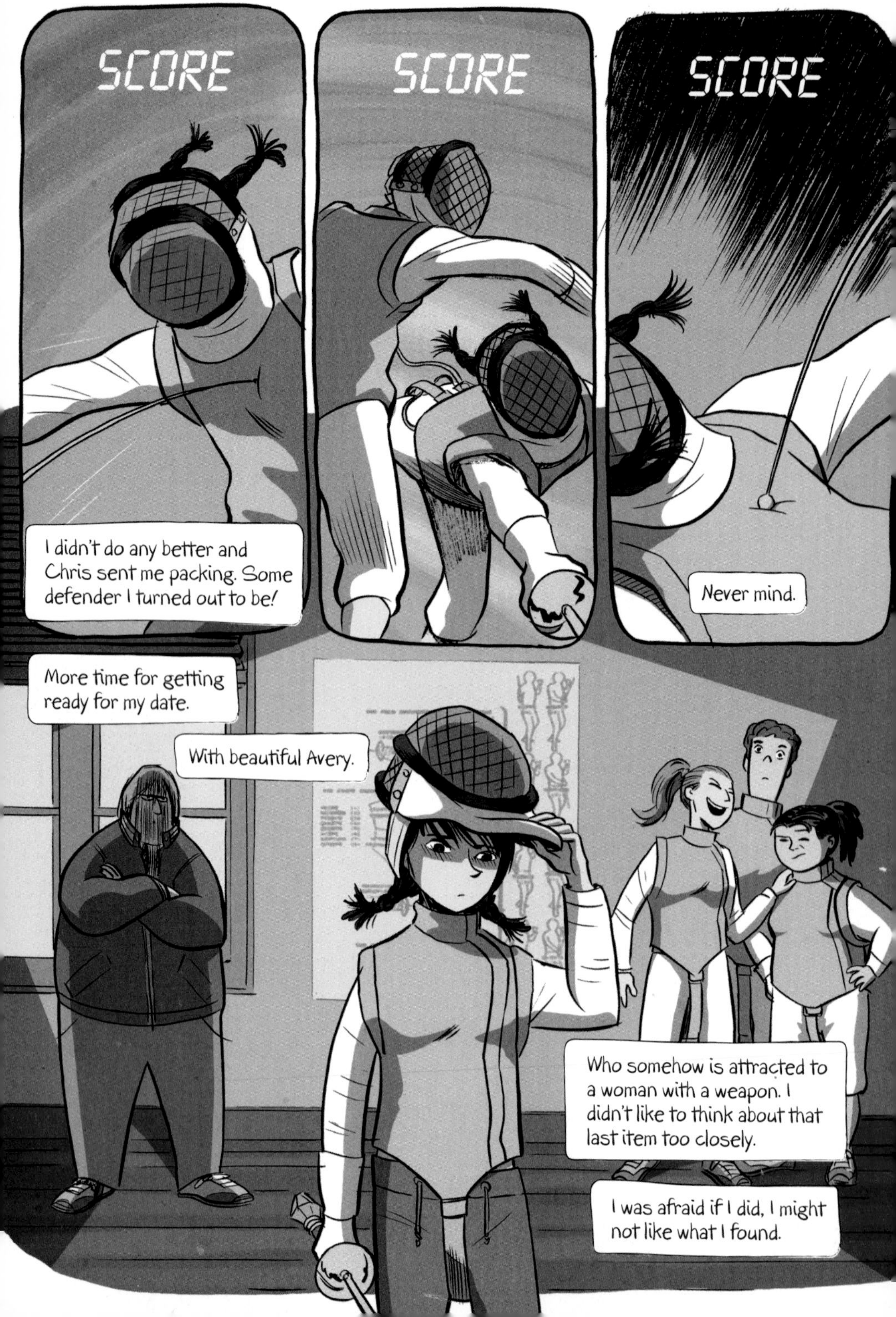
SCORE
SCORE
SCORE
I didn't do any better and Chris sent me packing. Some defender I turned out to be!
Never mind.
More time for getting ready for my date.
With beautiful Avery.
Who somehow is attracted to a woman with a weapon. I didn't like to think about that last item too closely.
I was afraid if I did, I might not like what I found.

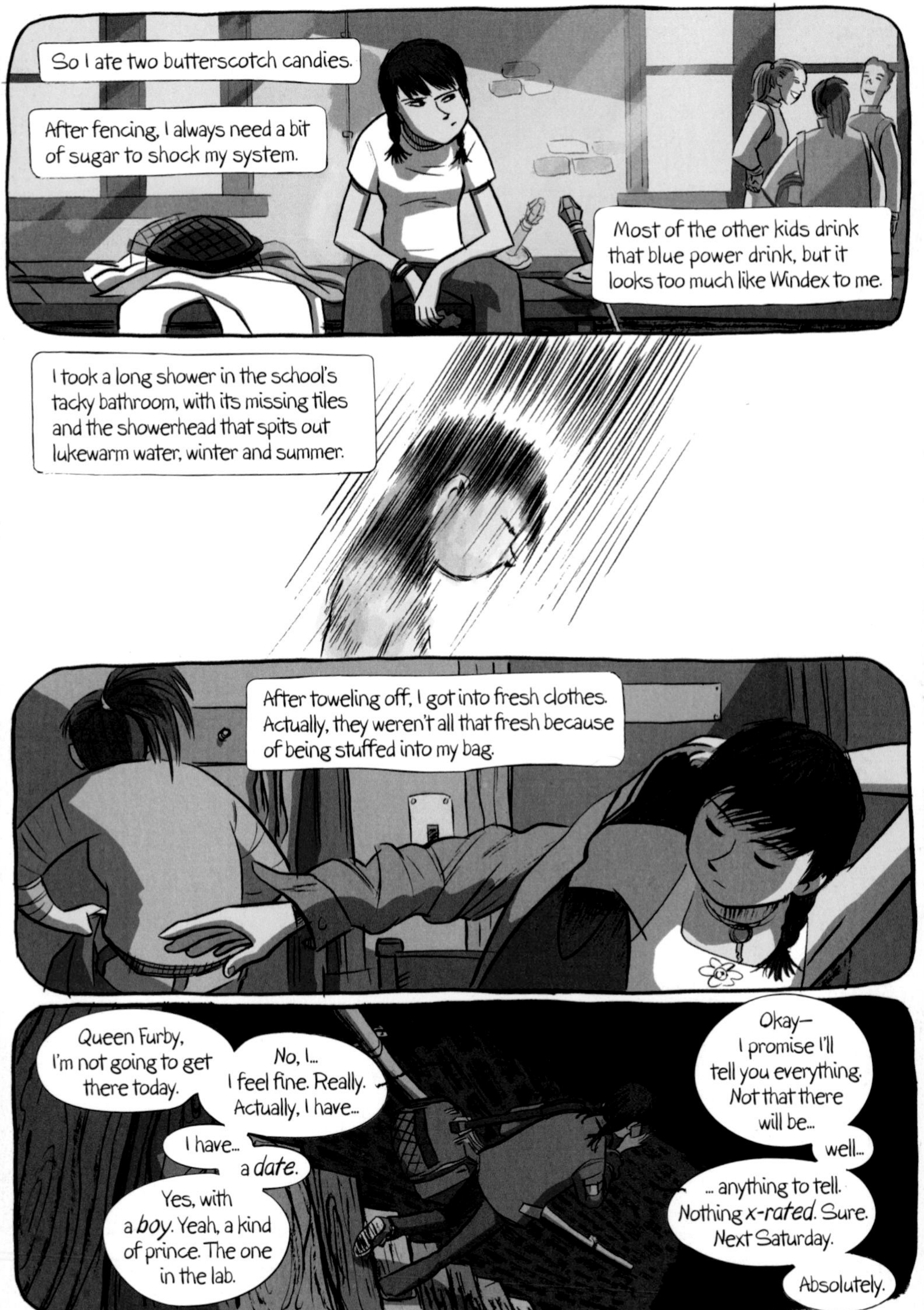

So I ate two butterscotch candies.
After fencing, I always need a bit of sugar to shock my system.
Most of the other kids drink that blue power drink, but it looks too much like Windex to me.
I took a long shower in the school's tacky bathroom, with its missing tiles and the showerhead that spits out lukewarm water, winter and summer.
After toweling off, I got into fresh clothes. Actually, they weren't all that fresh because of being stuffed into my bag.
Queen Furby, I'm not going to get there today.
No, I... I feel fine. Really. Actually, I have...
I have... a *date*.
Yes, with a *boy*. Yeah, a kind of prince. The one in the lab.
Okay— I promise I'll tell you everything. Not that there will be...
well...
... anything to tell. Nothing *x-rated*. Sure. Next Saturday.
Absolutely.

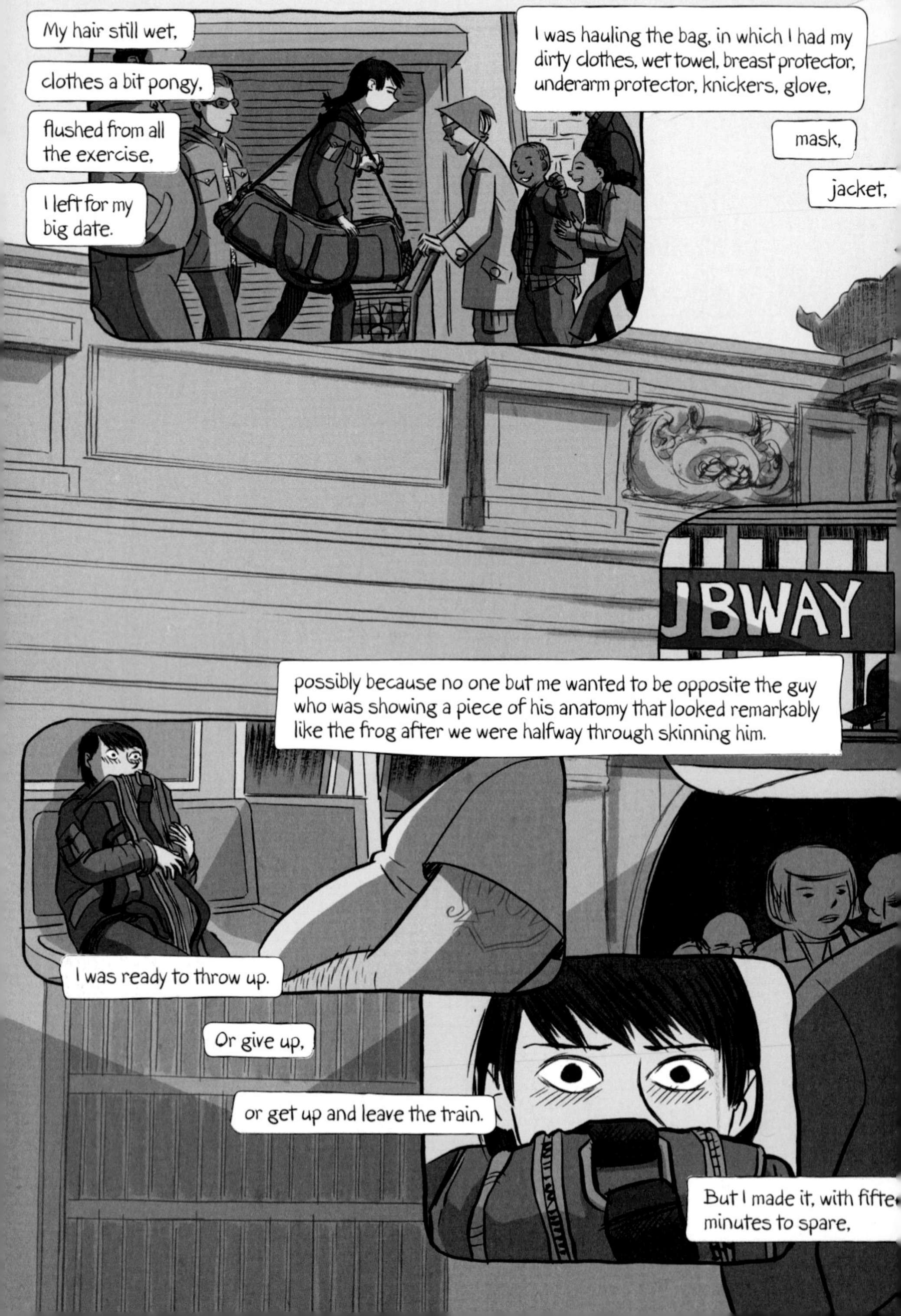
My hair still wet,
clothes a bit pongy,
flushed from all the exercise,
I left for my big date.
I was hauling the bag, in which I had my dirty clothes, wet towel, breast protector, underarm protector, knickers, glove,
mask,
jacket,
JBWAY
possibly because no one but me wanted to be opposite the guy who was showing a piece of his anatomy that looked remarkably like the frog after we were halfway through skinning him.
I was ready to throw up.
Or give up,
or get up and leave the train.
But I made it, with fifte
minutes to spare,

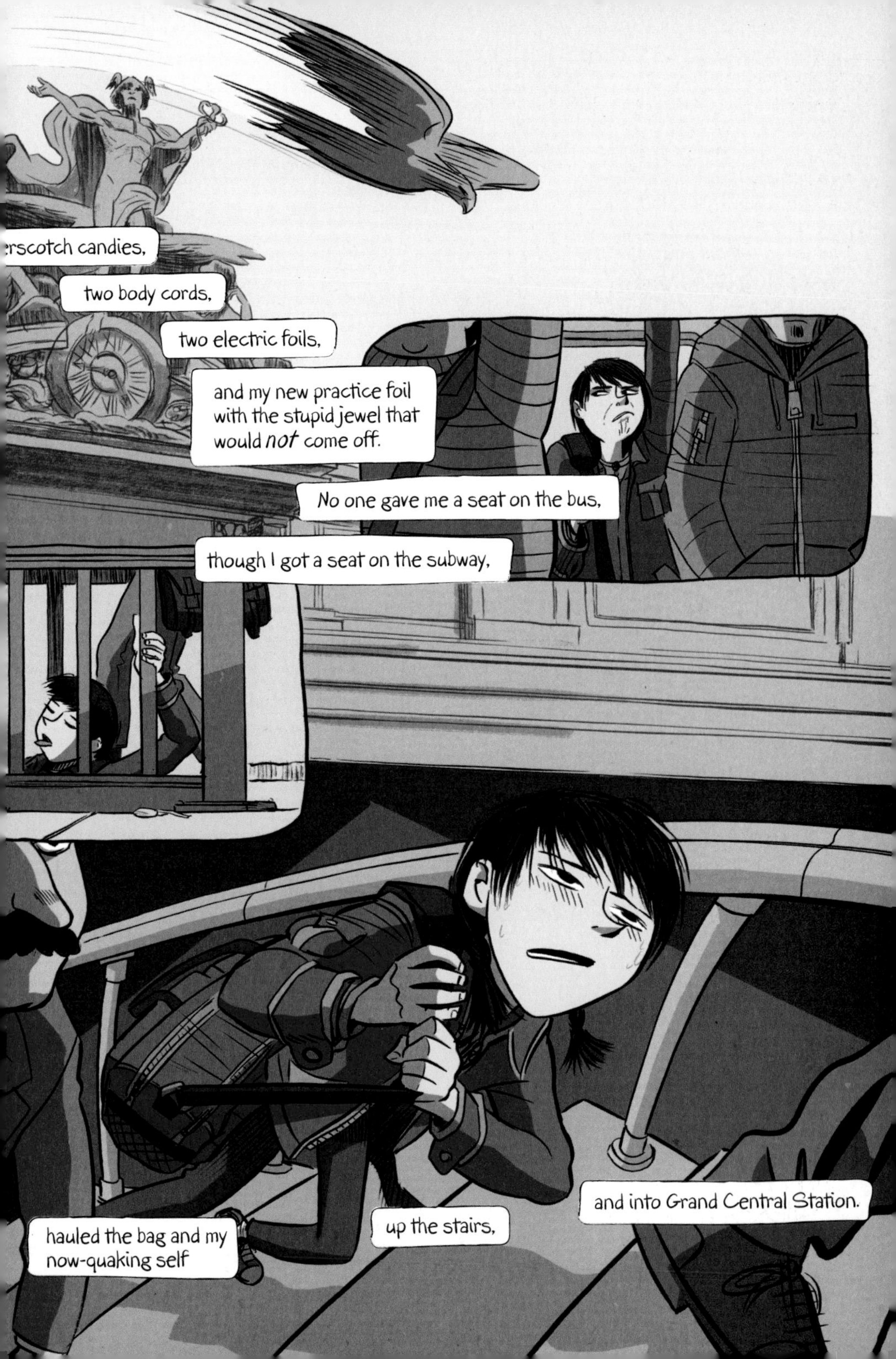

rscotch candies,
two body cords,
two electric foils,
and my new practice foil with the stupid jewel that would *not* come off.
No one gave me a seat on the bus,
though I got a seat on the subway,
hauled the bag and my now-quaking self
up the stairs,
and into Grand Central Station.

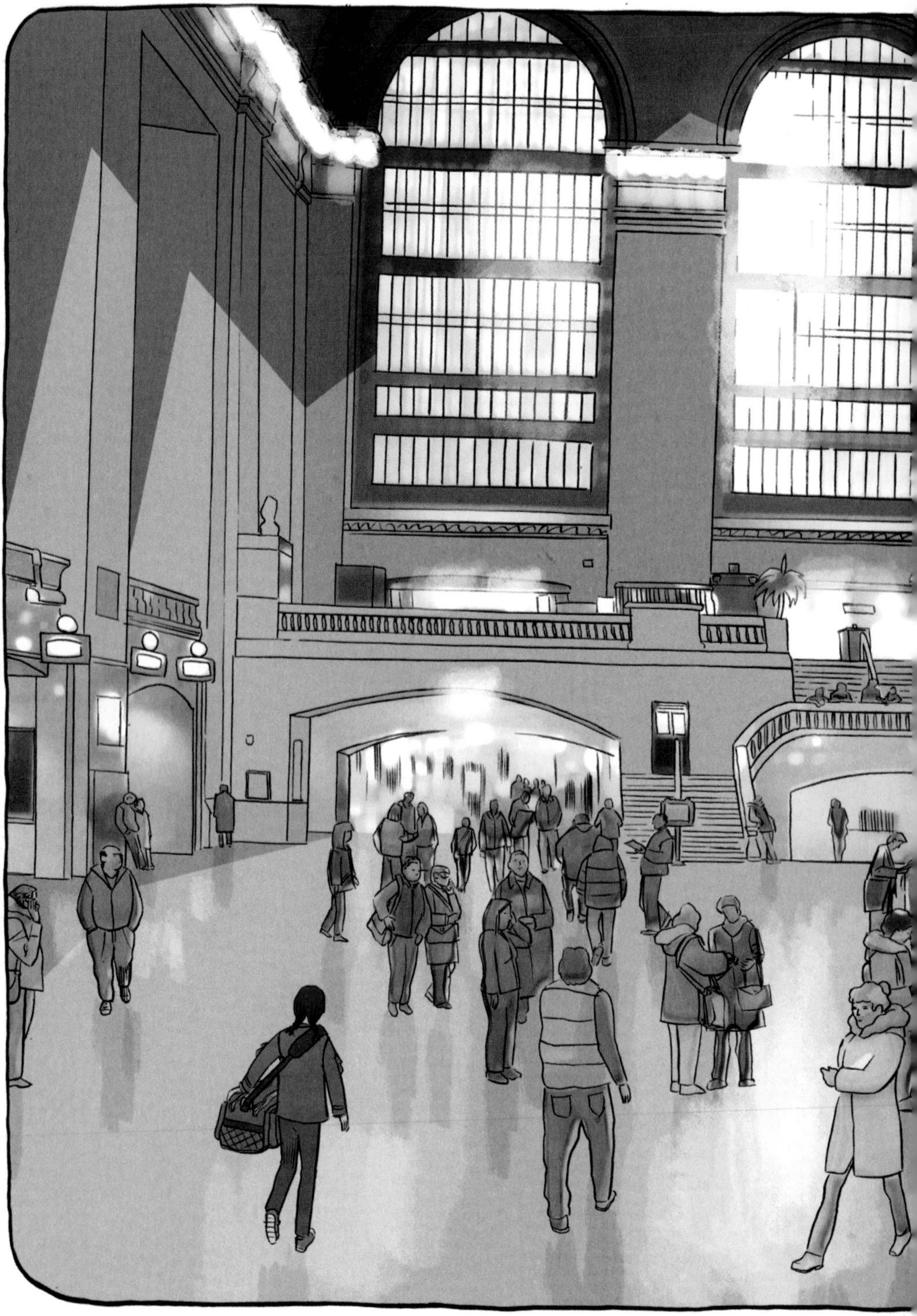

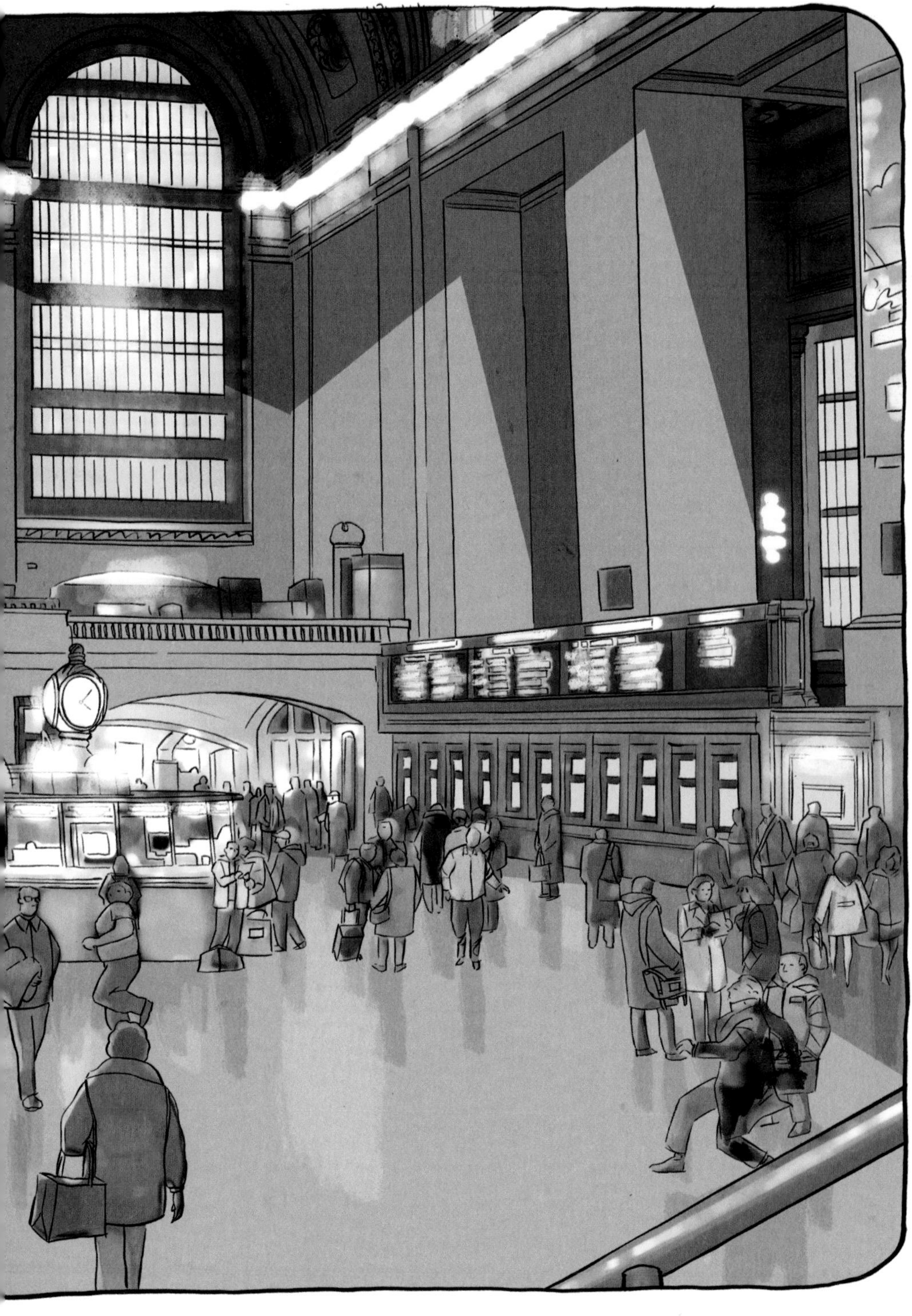

6. Lunge

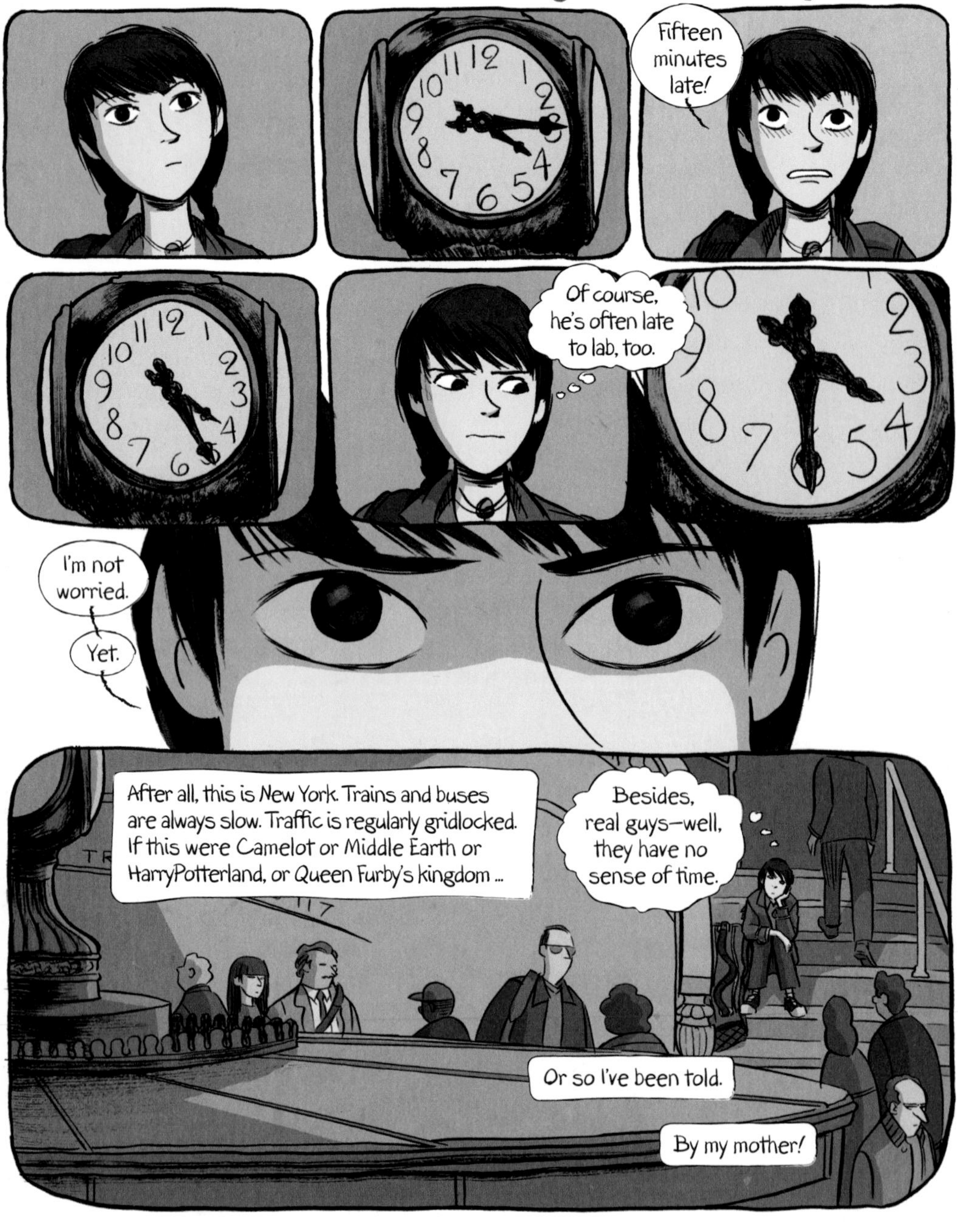
Fifteen minutes late!
Of course, he's often late to lab, too.
I'm not worried.
Yet.
After all, this is New York. Trains and buses are always slow. Traffic is regularly gridlocked. If this were Camelot or Middle Earth or HarryPotterland, or Queen Furby's kingdom ...
Besides, real guys—well, they have no sense of time.
Or so I've been told.
By my mother!

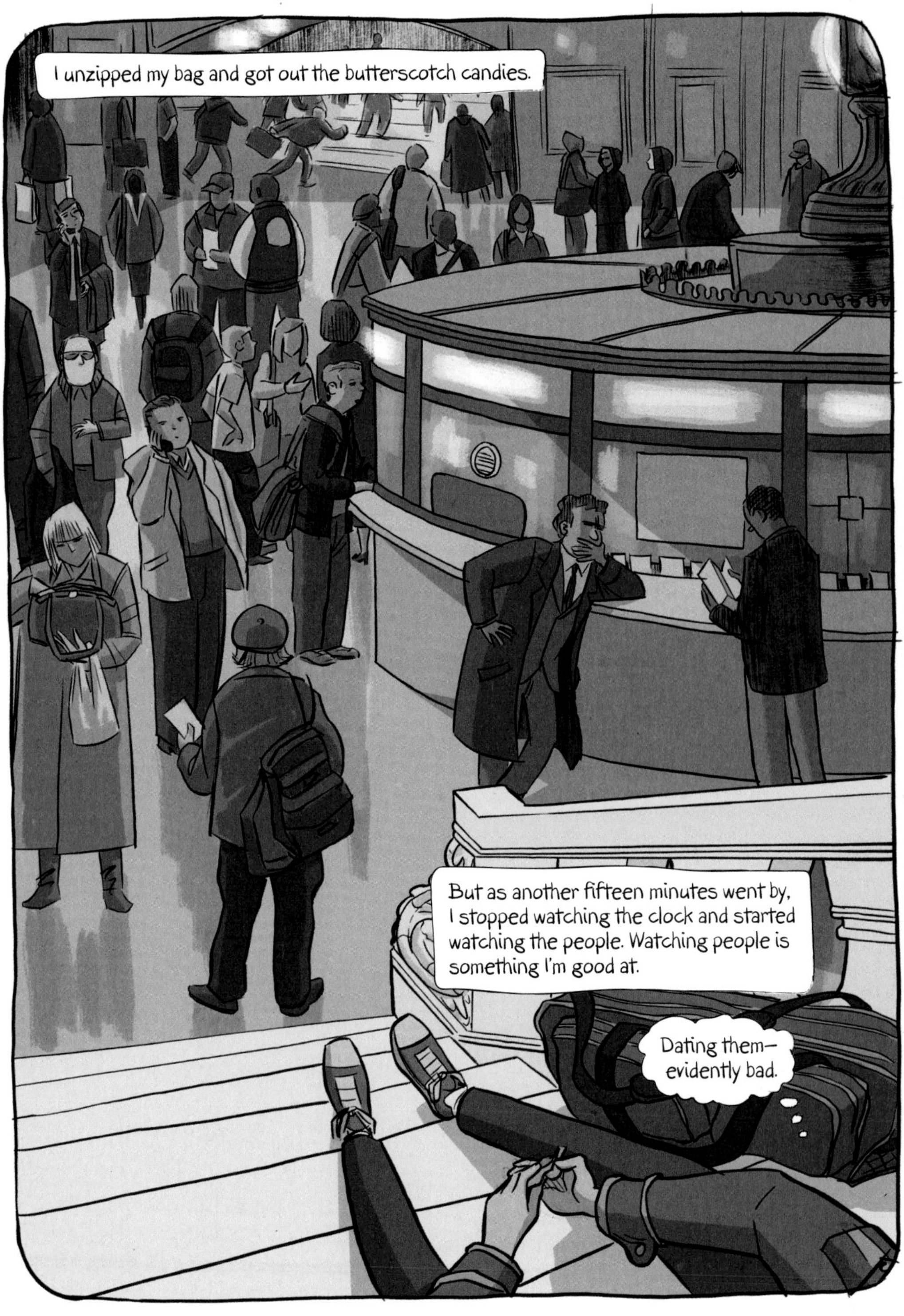
I unzipped my bag and got out the butterscotch candies.
But as another fifteen minutes went by, I stopped watching the clock and started watching the people. Watching people is something I'm good at.
Dating them—evidently bad.

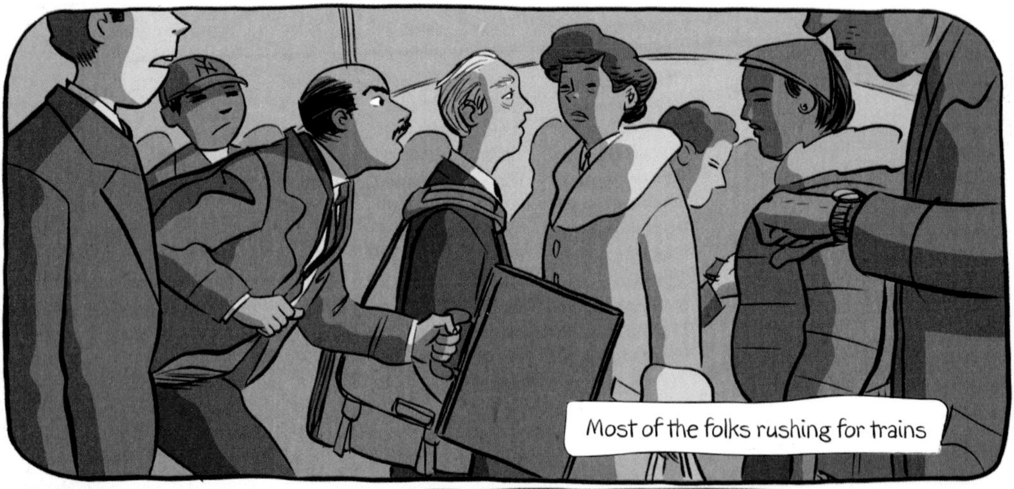
Most of the folks rushing for trains

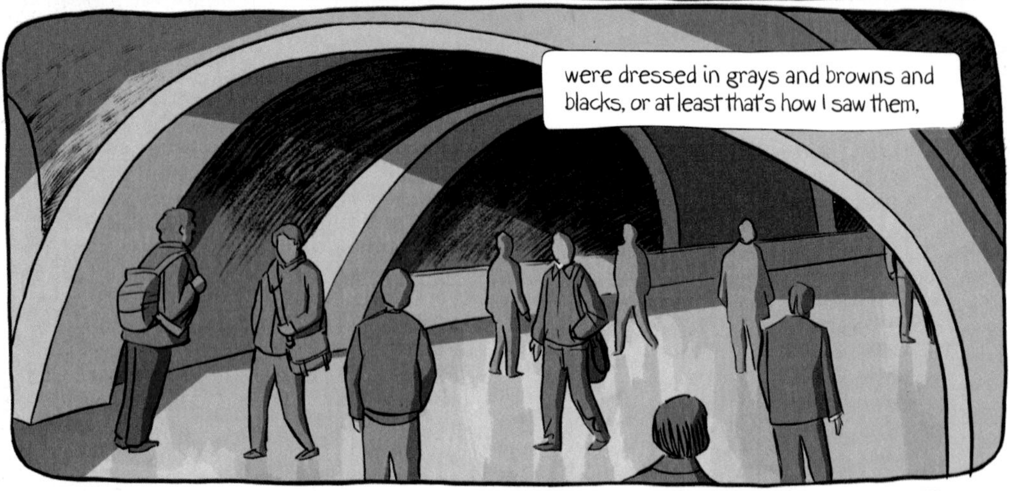
were dressed in grays and browns and blacks, or at least that's how I saw them,

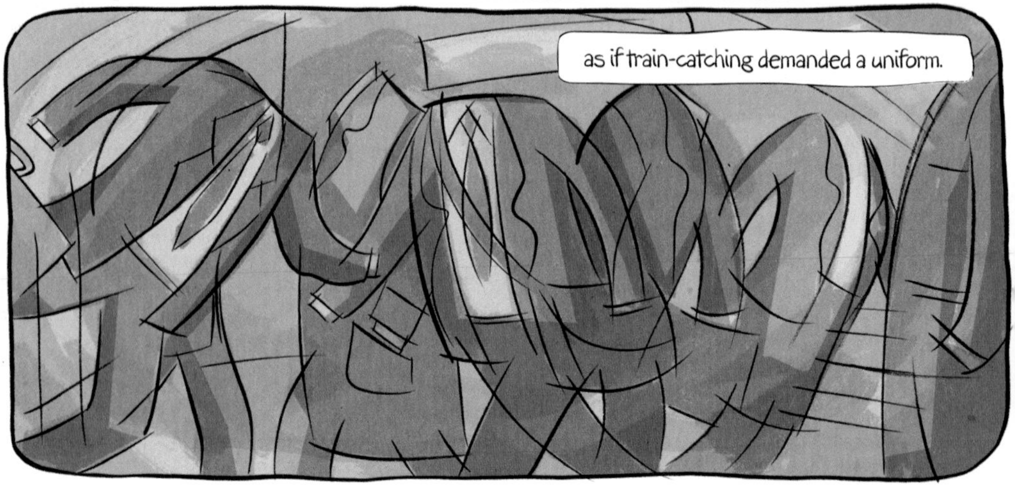
as if train-catching demanded a uniform.

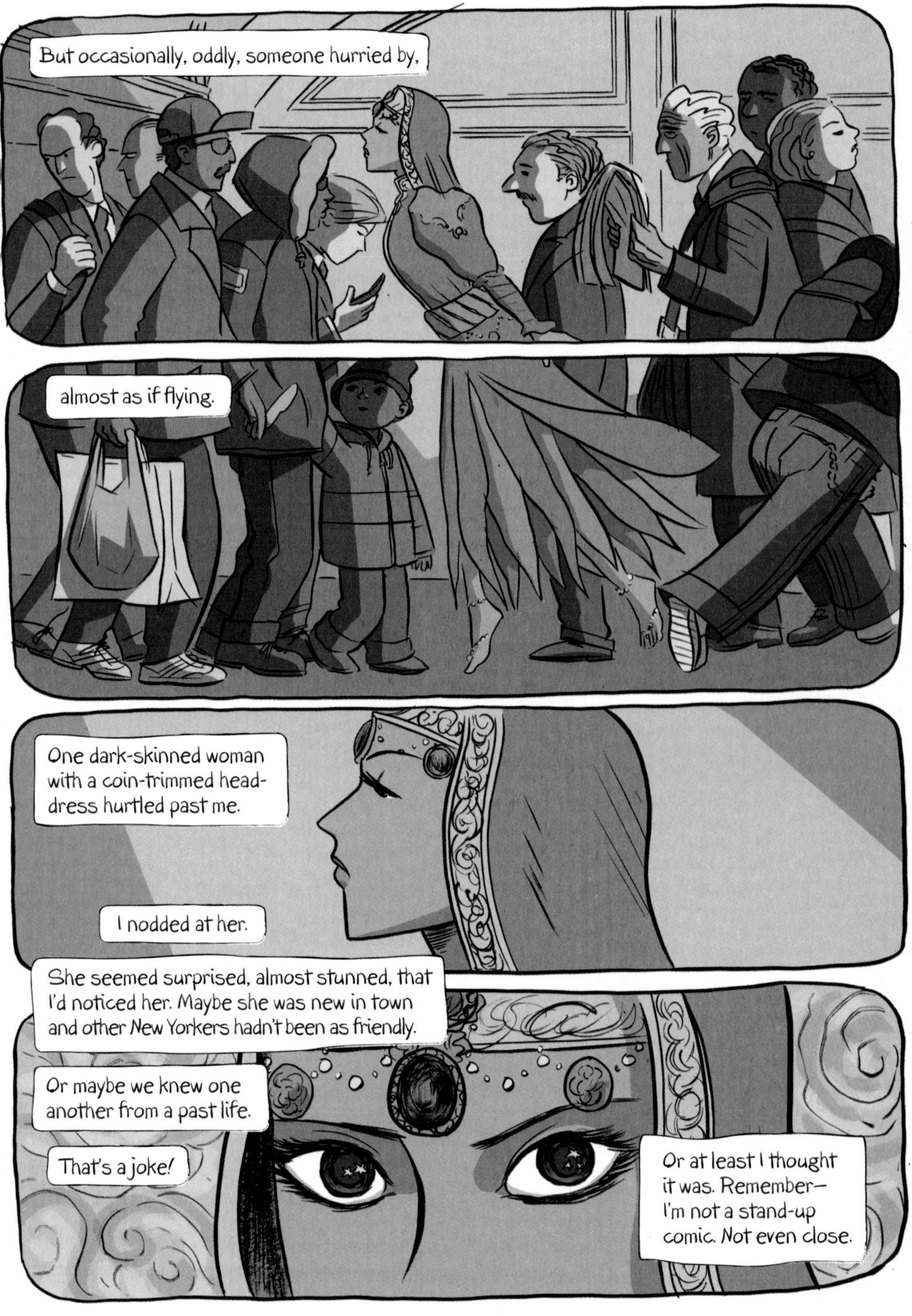
But occasionally, oddly, someone hurried by,
almost as if flying.
One dark-skinned woman with a coin-trimmed head-dress hurtled past me.
I nodded at her.
She seemed surprised, almost stunned, that I'd noticed her. Maybe she was new in town and other New Yorkers hadn't been as friendly.
Or maybe we knew one another from a past life.
That's a joke!
Or at least I thought it was. Remember— I'm not a stand-up comic. Not even close.

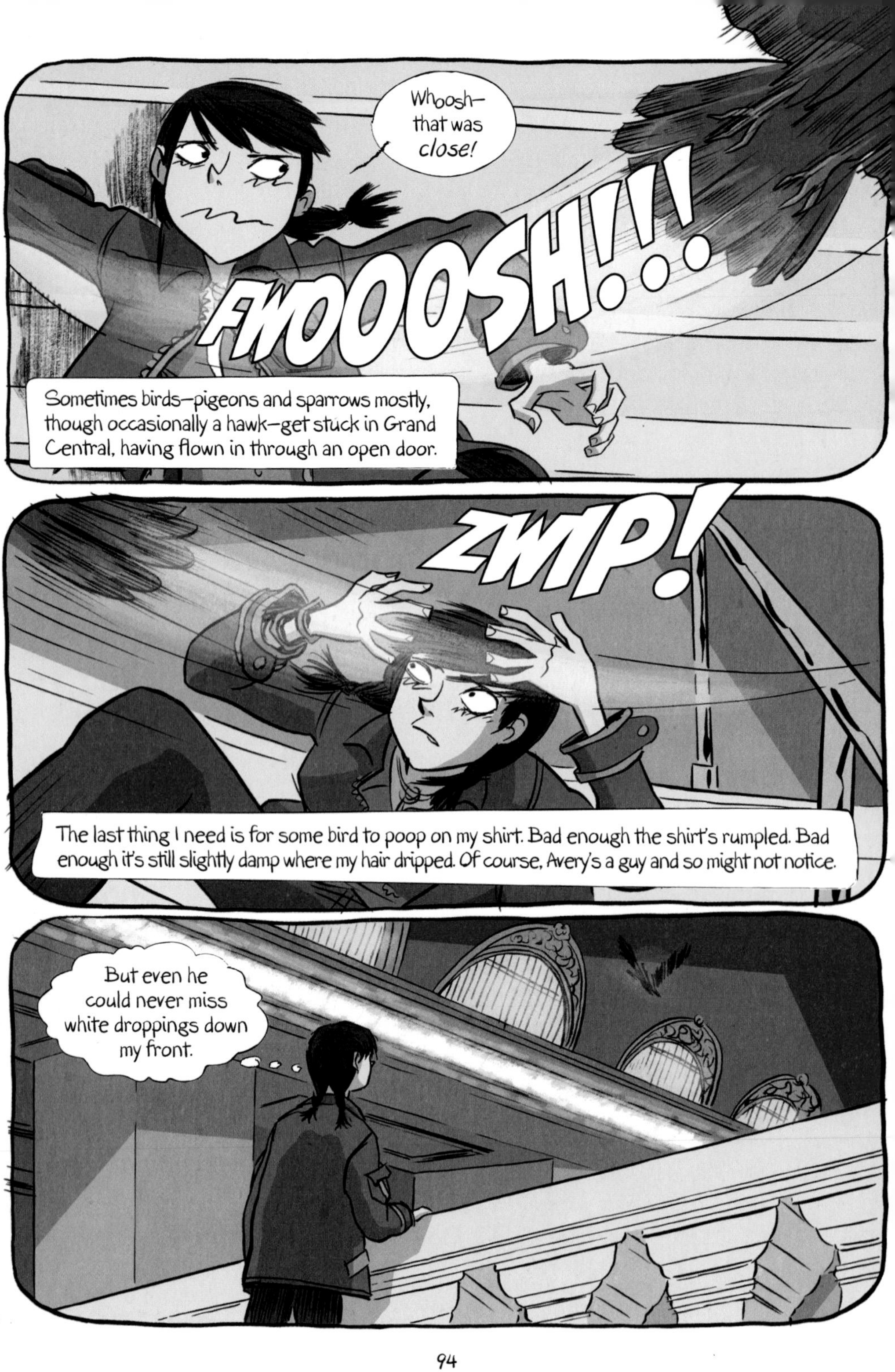
Whoosh—
that was
close!
FWOOOSH!!!
Sometimes birds—pigeons and sparrows mostly, though occasionally a hawk—get stuck in Grand Central, having flown in through an open door.
ZWIP!
The last thing I need is for some bird to poop on my shirt. Bad enough the shirt's rumpled. Bad enough it's still slightly damp where my hair dripped. Of course, Avery's a guy and so might not notice.
But even he could never miss white droppings down my front.

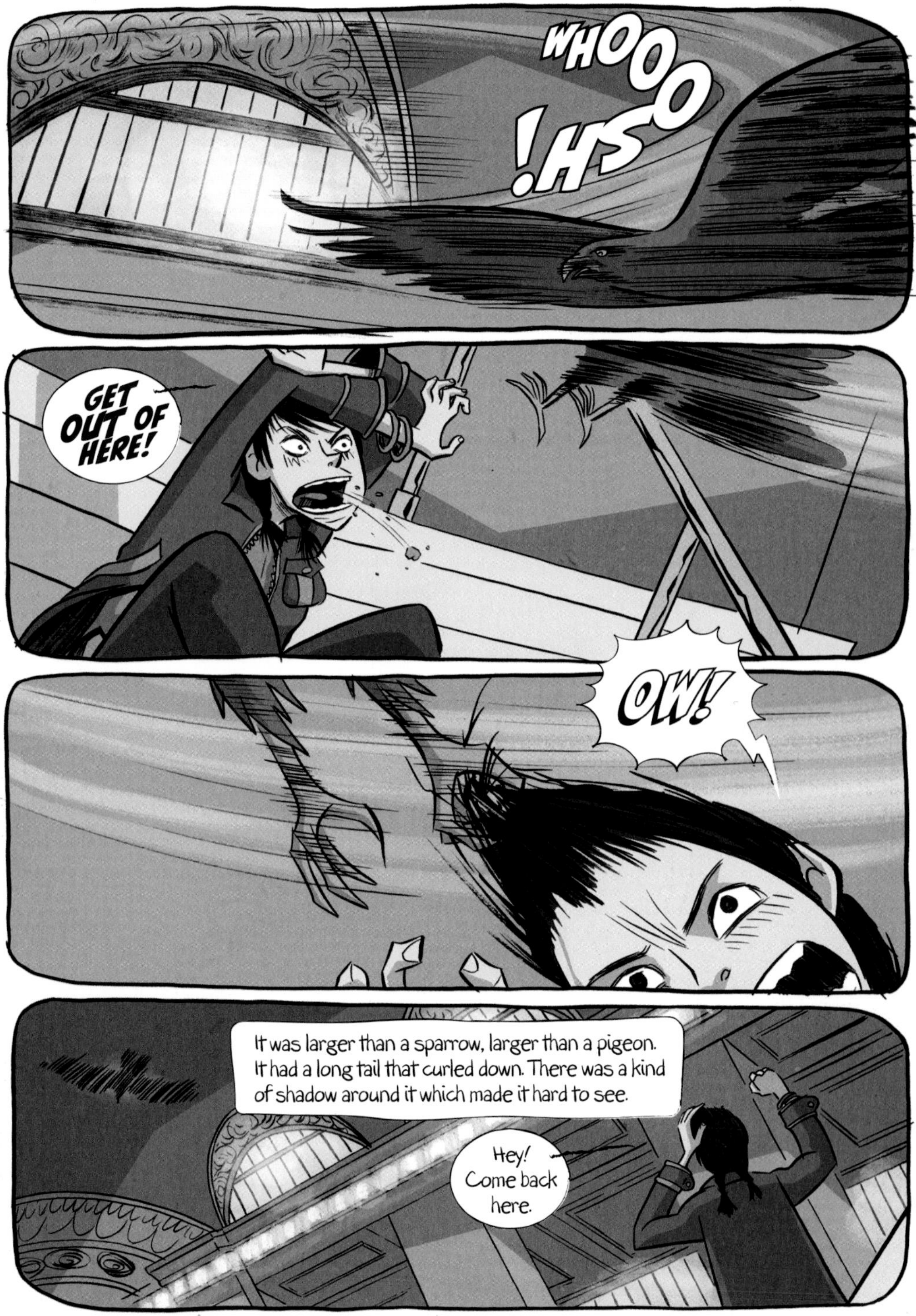
WHOOOOSH!
GET OUT OF HERE!
OW!
It was larger than a sparrow, larger than a pigeon. It had a long tail that curled down. There was a kind of shadow around it which made it hard to see.
Hey! Come back here.

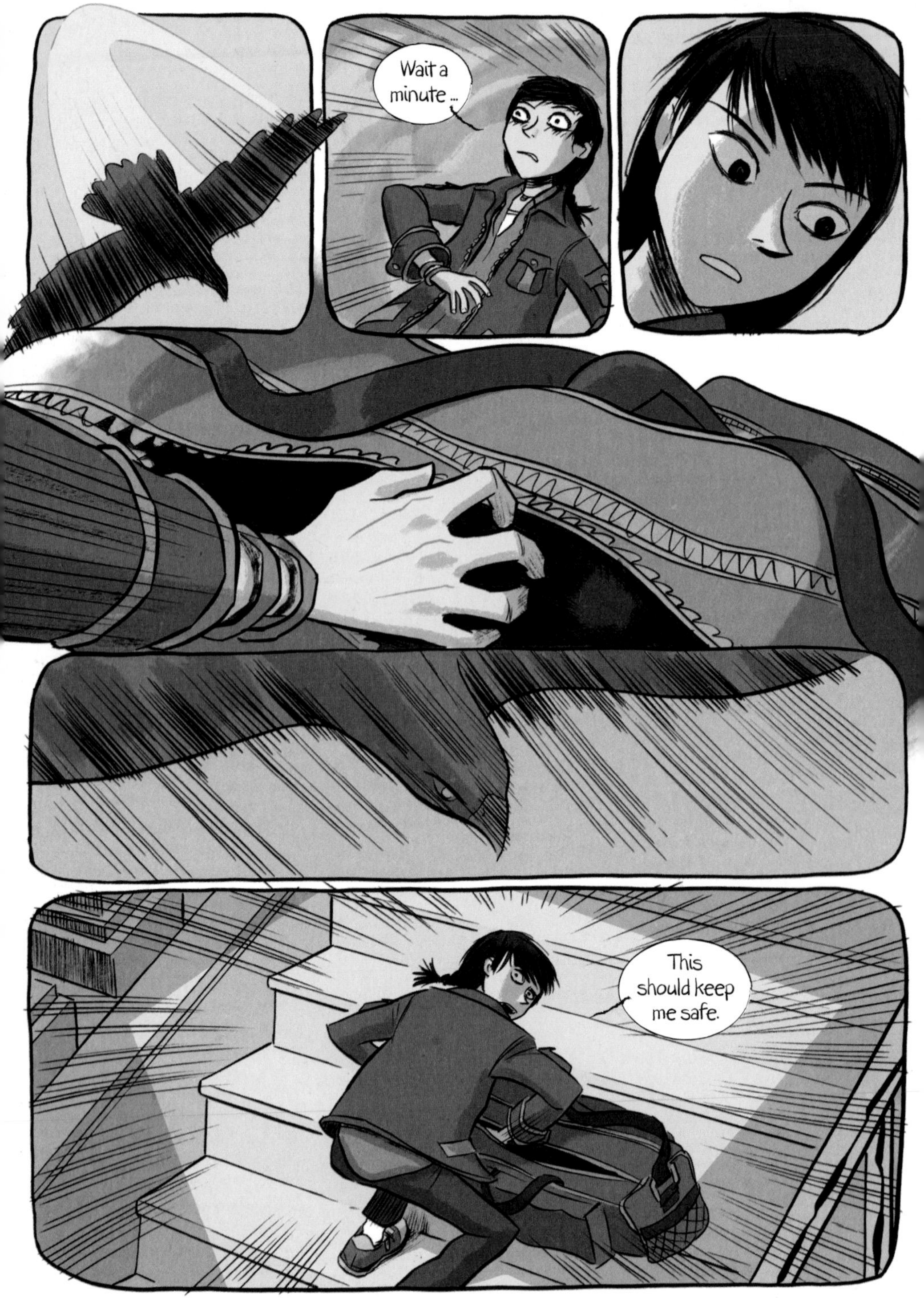
Wait a minute ...
This should keep me safe.

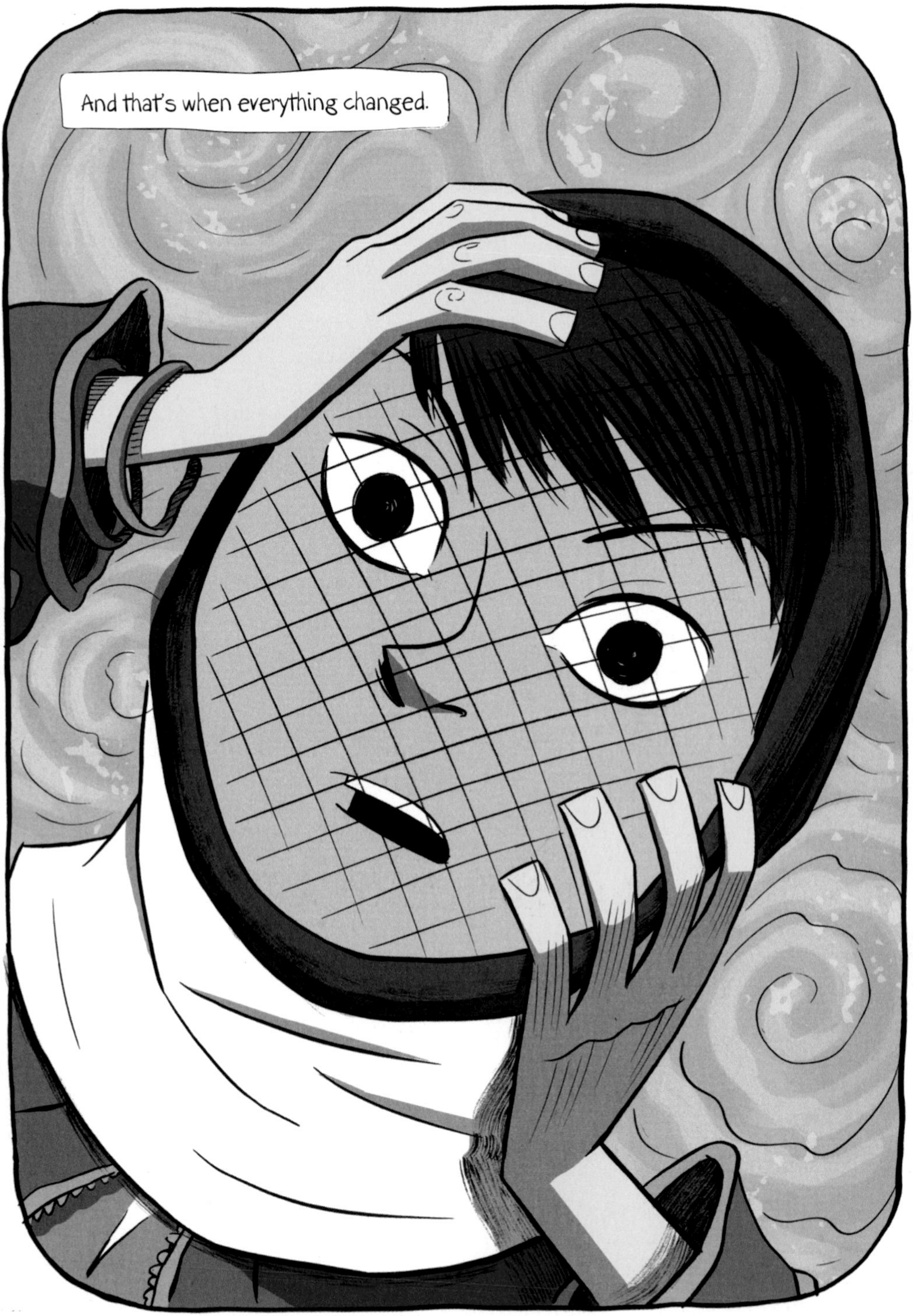
And that's when everything changed.

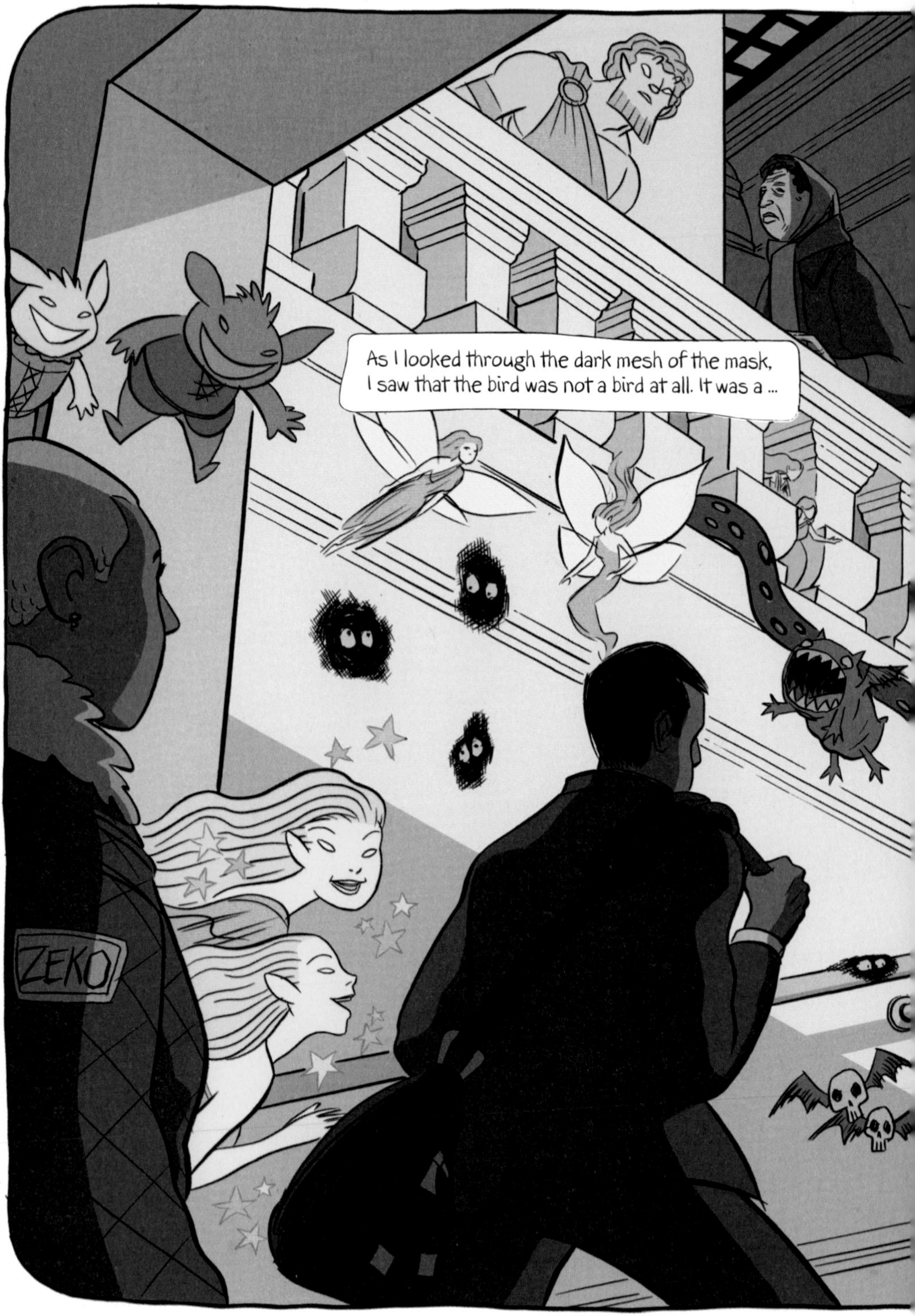
As I looked through the dark mesh of the mask, I saw that the bird was not a bird at all. It was a ...
ZEKO

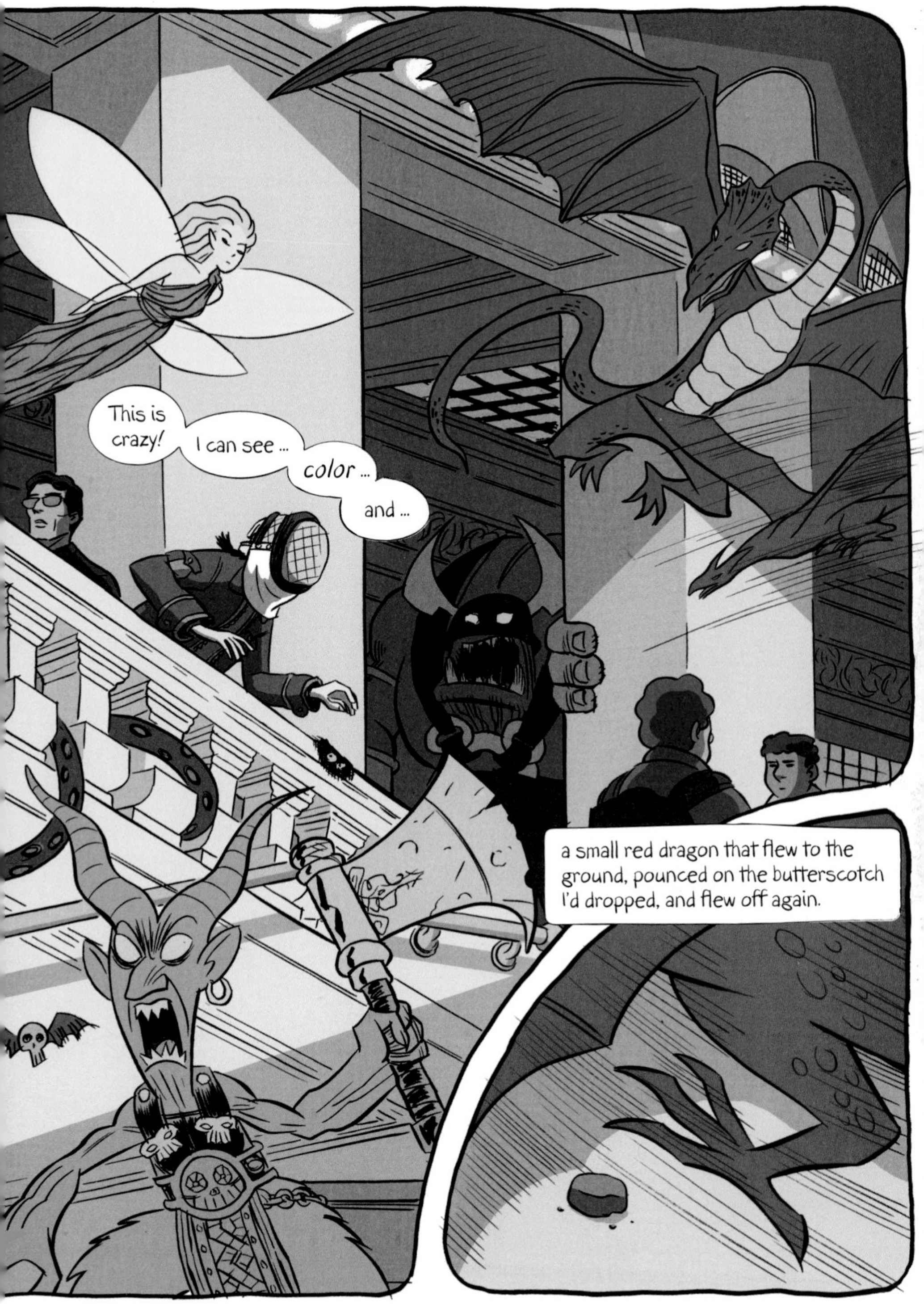

This is crazy!
I can see ...
color ...
and ...
a small red dragon that flew to the ground, pounced on the butterscotch I'd dropped, and flew off again.

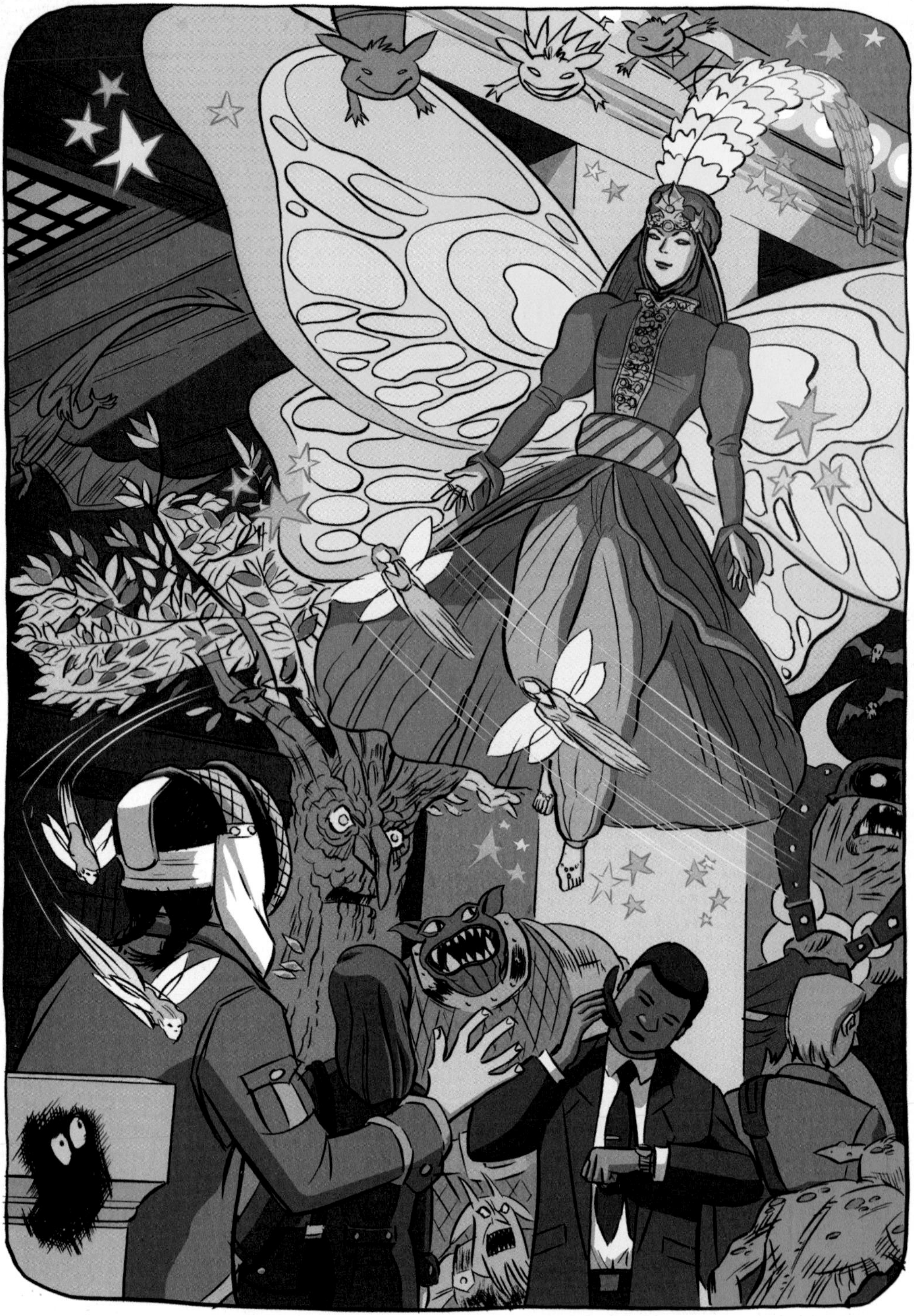

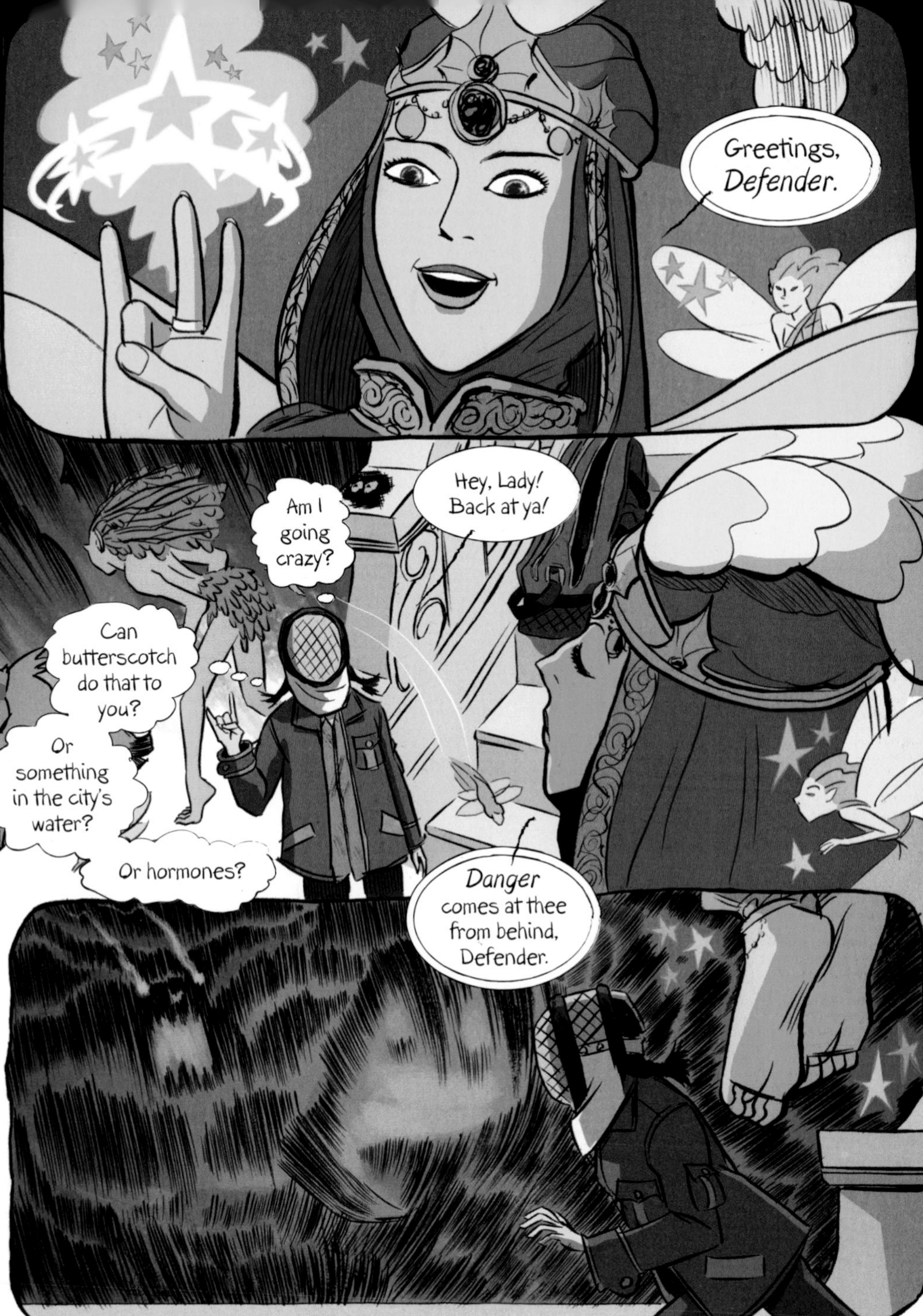
Greetings, Defender.
Am I going crazy?
Hey, Lady! Back at ya!
Can butterscotch do that to you?
Or something in the city's water?
Or hormones?
Danger comes at thee from behind, Defender.

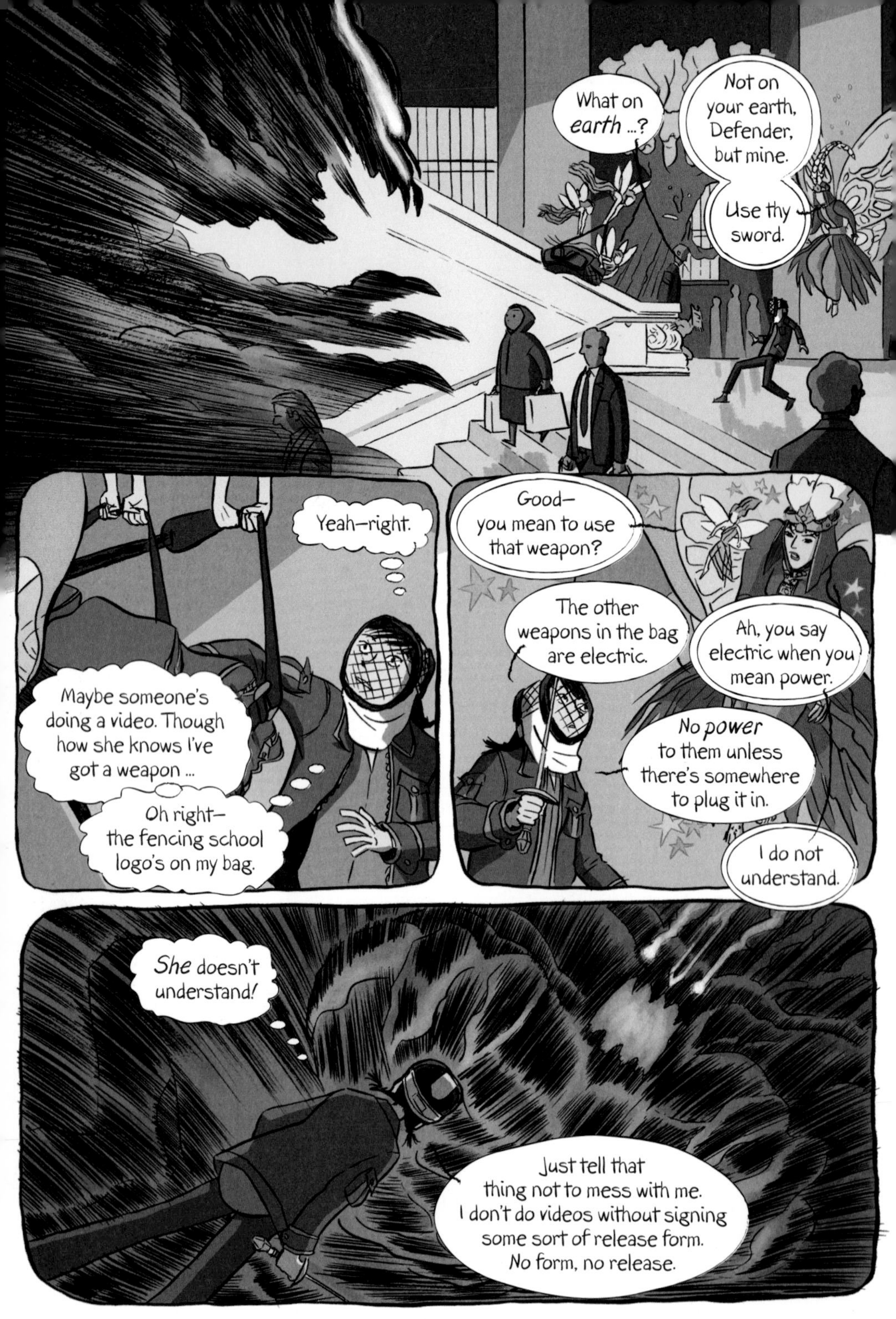
What on earth ...?
Not on your earth, Defender, but mine.
Use thy sword.
Yeah—right.
Maybe someone's doing a video. Though how she knows I've got a weapon ...
Oh right— the fencing school logo's on my bag.
Good— you mean to use that weapon?
The other weapons in the bag are electric.
Ah, you say electric when you mean power.
No *power* to them unless there's somewhere to plug it in.
I do not understand.
She doesn't understand!
Just tell that thing not to mess with me. I don't do videos without signing some sort of release form. No form, no release.

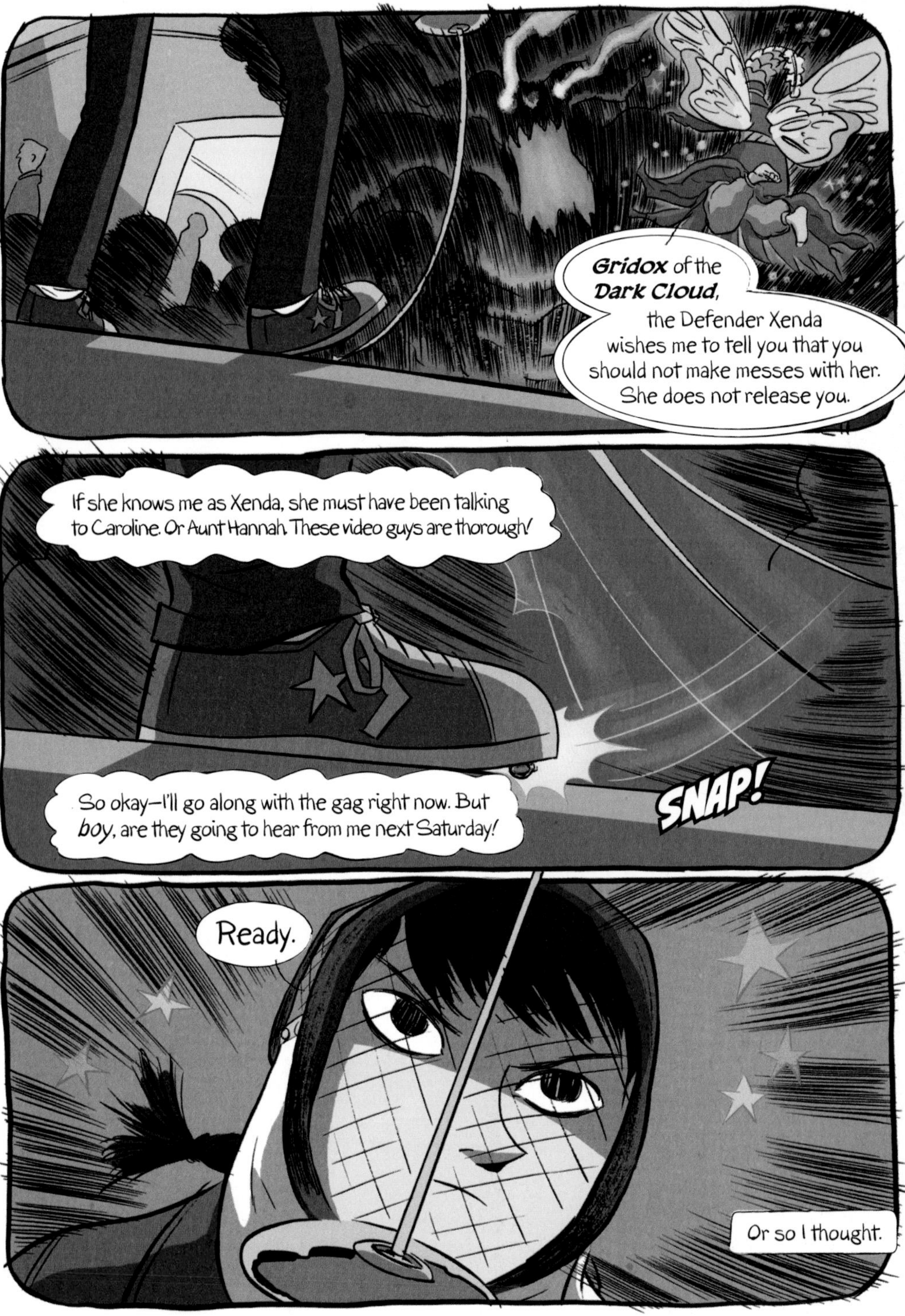
Gridox of the **Dark Cloud**, the Defender Xenda wishes me to tell you that you should not make messes with her. She does not release you.
If she knows me as Xenda, she must have been talking to Caroline. Or Aunt Hannah. These video guys are thorough!
So okay—I'll go along with the gag right now. But *boy*, are they going to hear from me next Saturday!
SNAP!
Ready.
Or so I thought.

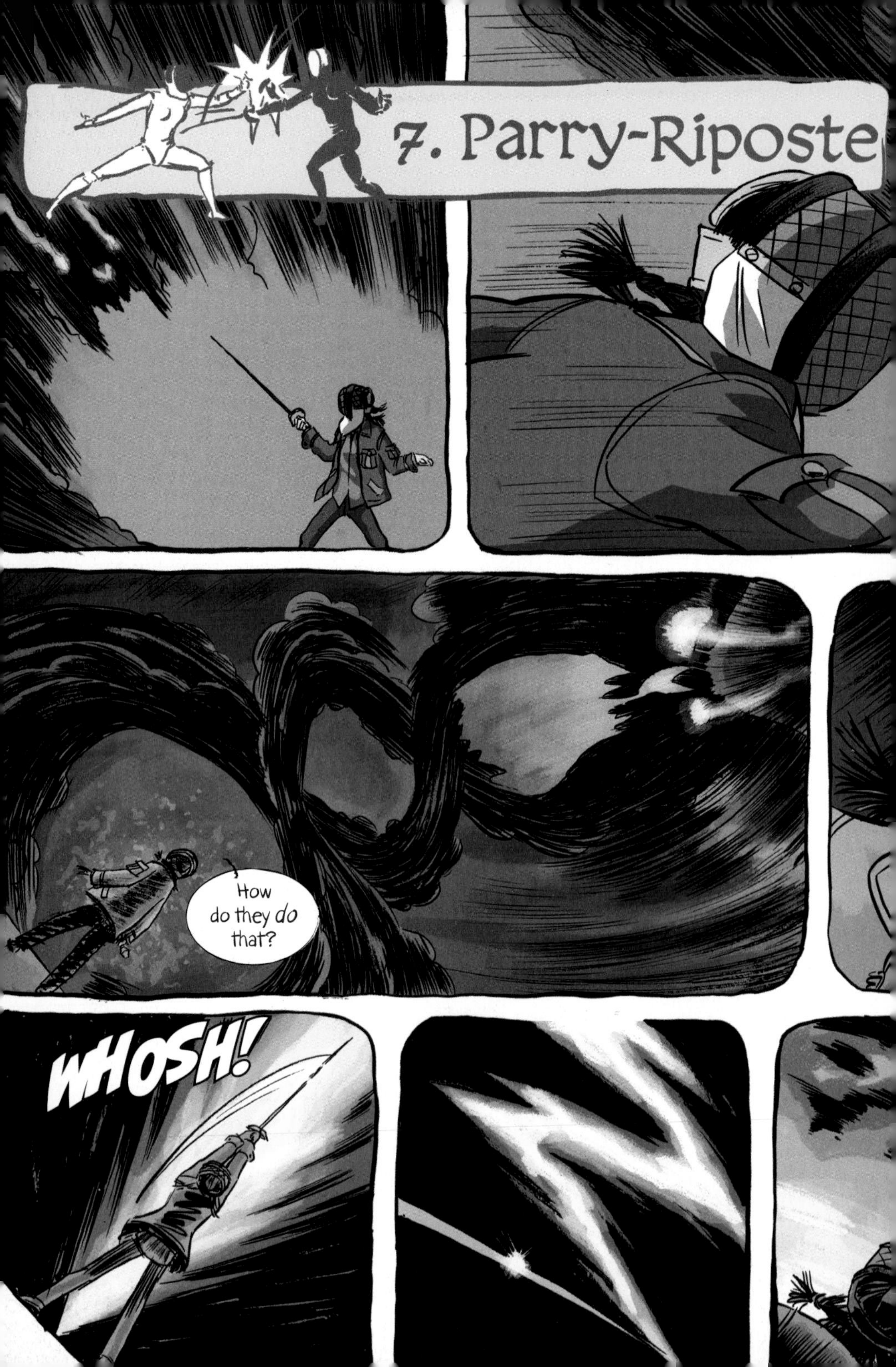
7. Parry-Riposte
How do they do that?
WHOSH!

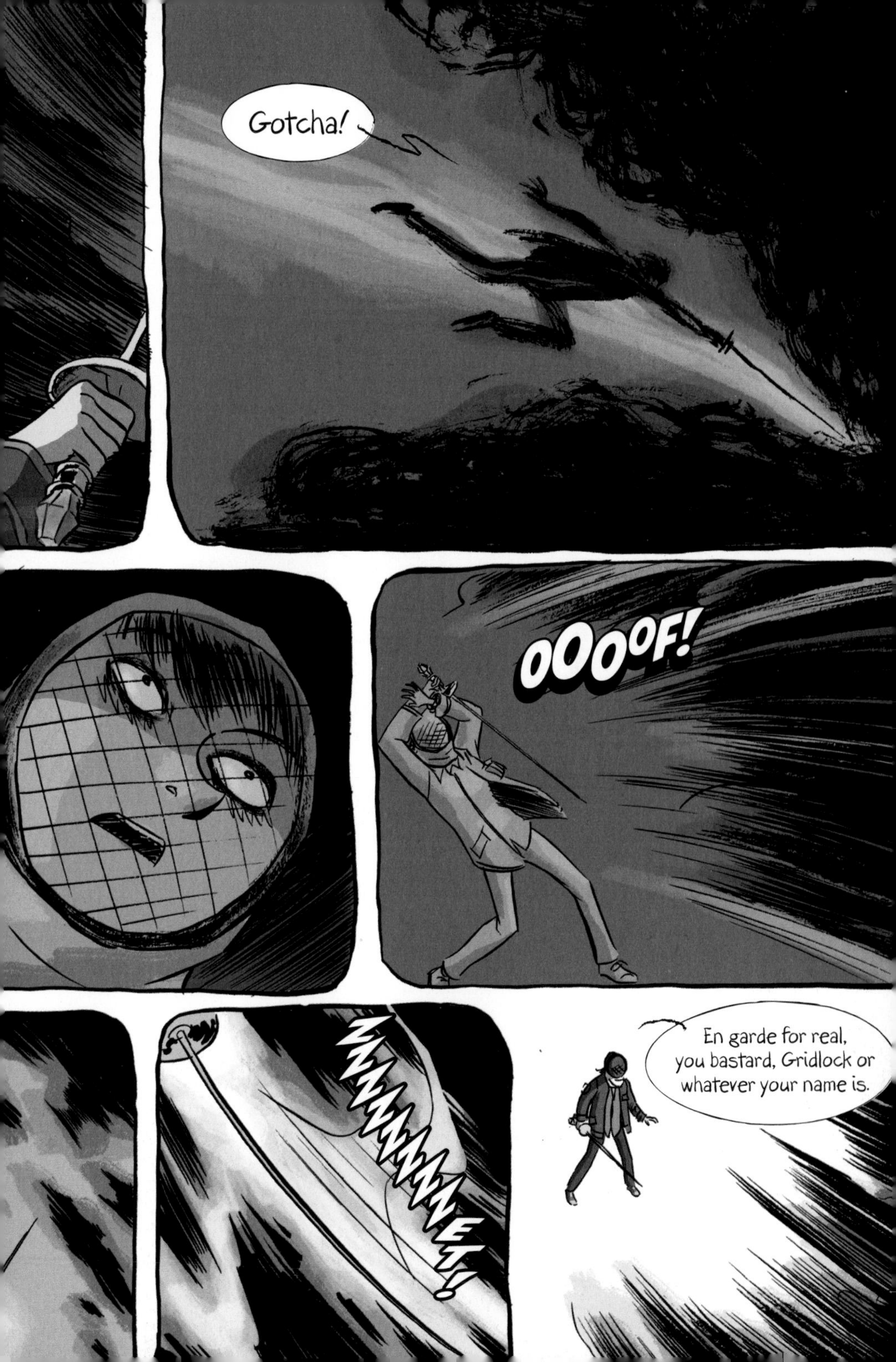
Gotcha!
OOOOF!
NNNNNNET!
En garde for real, you bastard, Gridlock or whatever your name is.

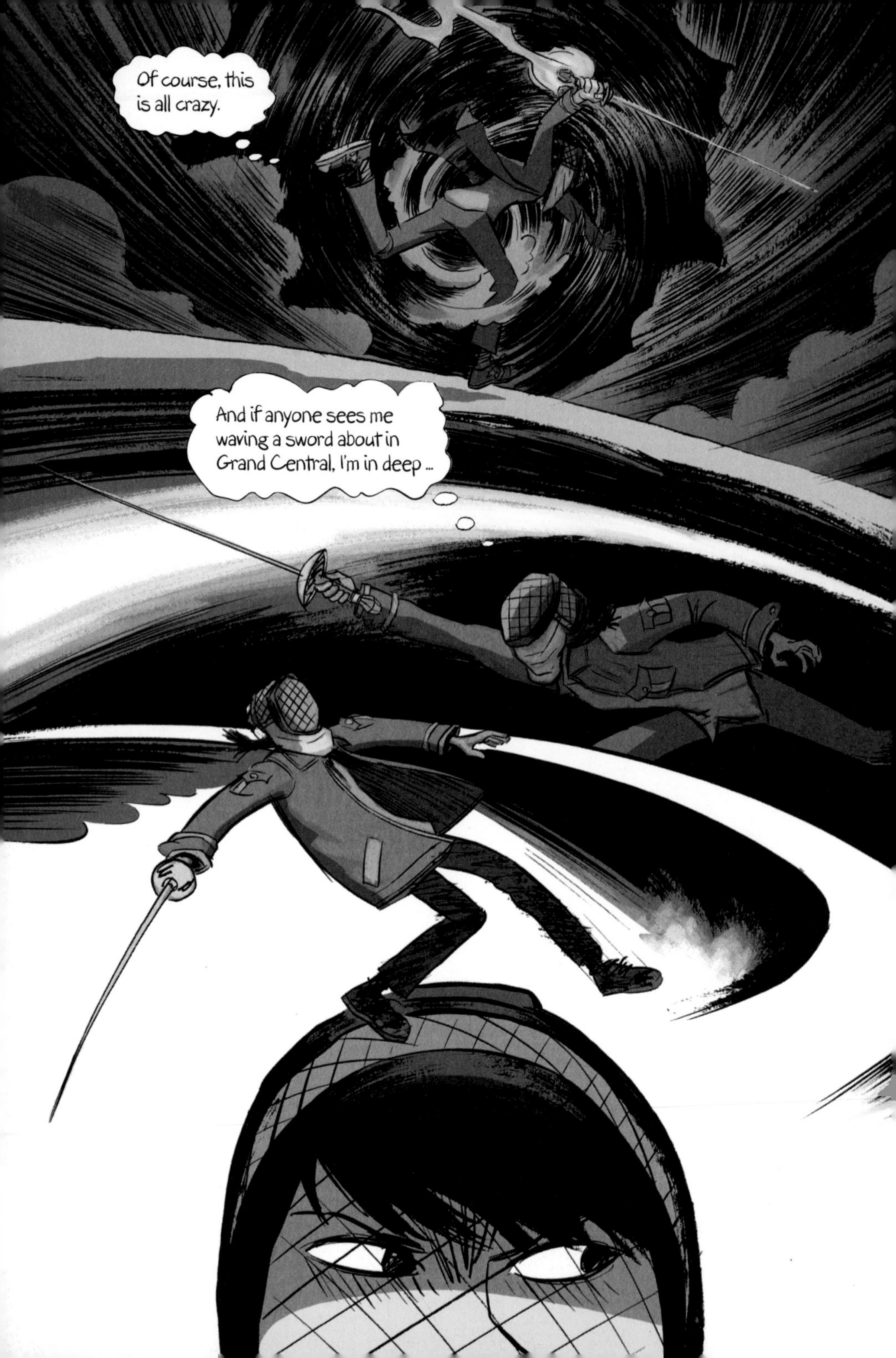
Of course, this is all crazy.
And if anyone sees me waving a sword about in Grand Central, I'm in deep ...

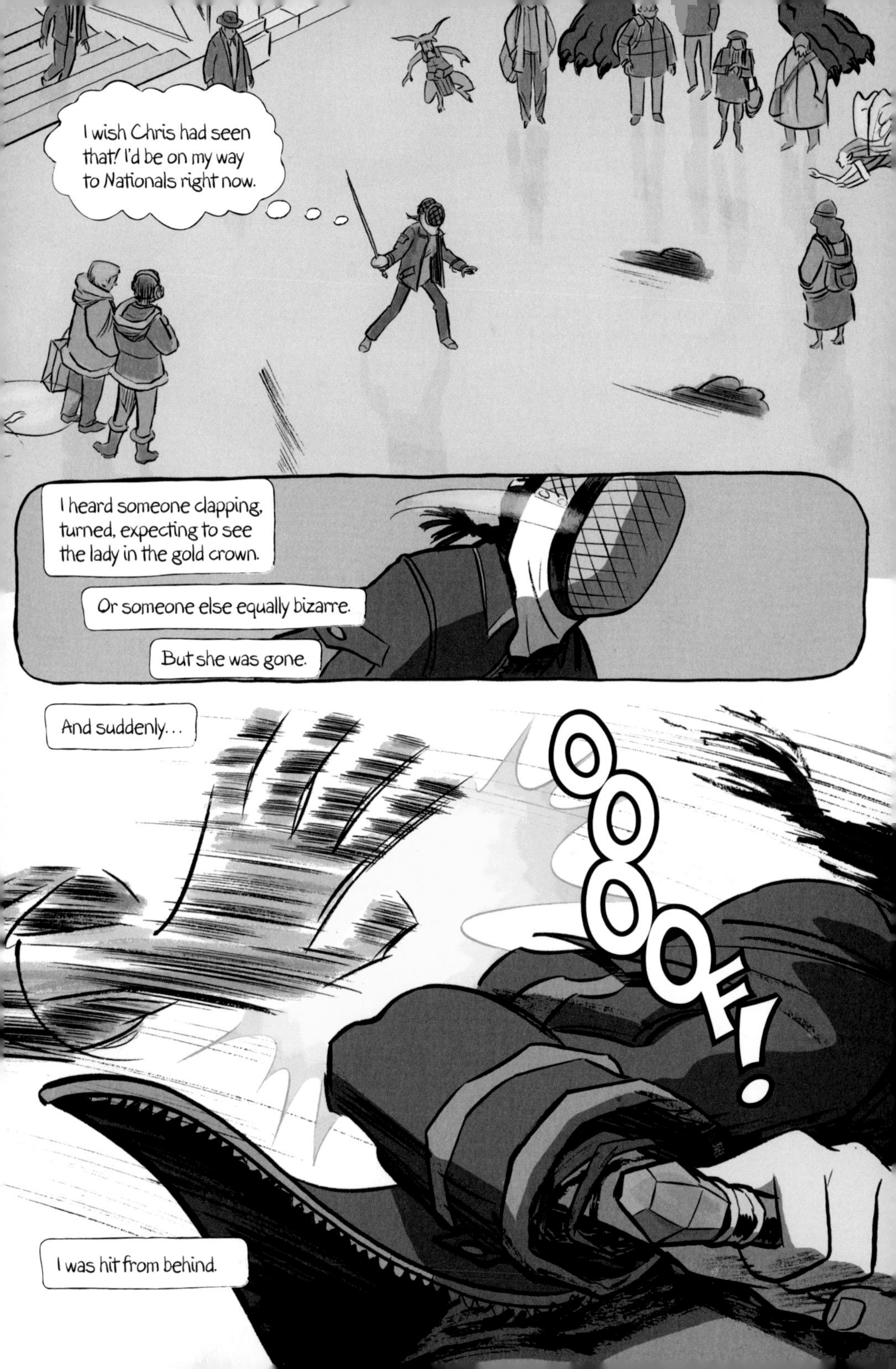
I wish Chris had seen that! I'd be on my way to Nationals right now.
I heard someone clapping, turned, expecting to see the lady in the gold crown.
Or someone else equally bizarre.
But she was gone.
And suddenly...
OOOOOF!
I was hit from behind.

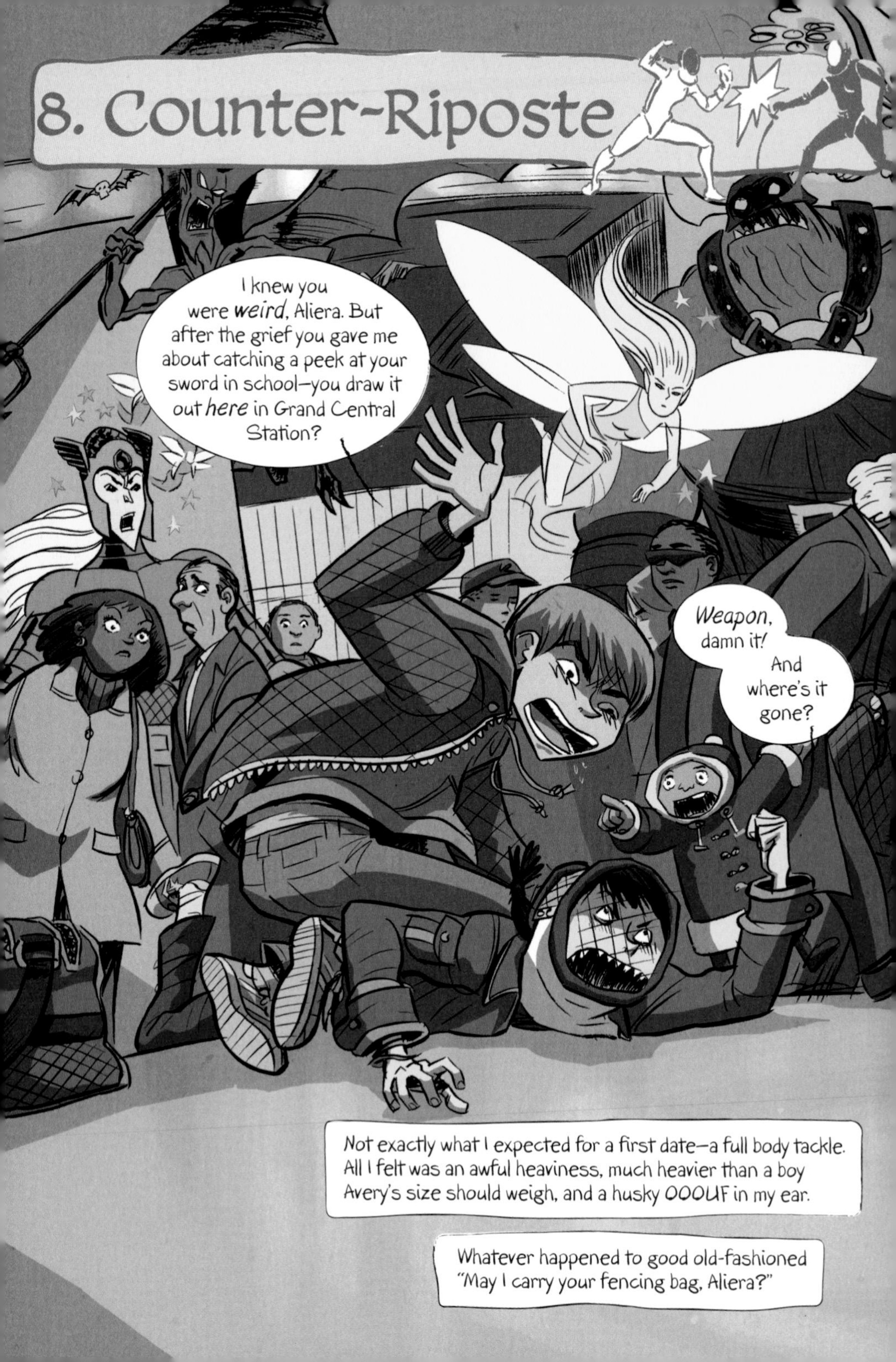
8. Counter-Riposte
I knew you were *weird*, Aliera. But after the grief you gave me about catching a peek at your sword in school—you draw it out *here* in Grand Central Station?
Weapon, damn it!
And where's it gone?
Not exactly what I expected for a first date—a full body tackle. All I felt was an awful heaviness, much heavier than a boy Avery's size should weigh, and a husky OOOUF in my ear.
Whatever happened to good old-fashioned "May I carry your fencing bag, Aliera?"

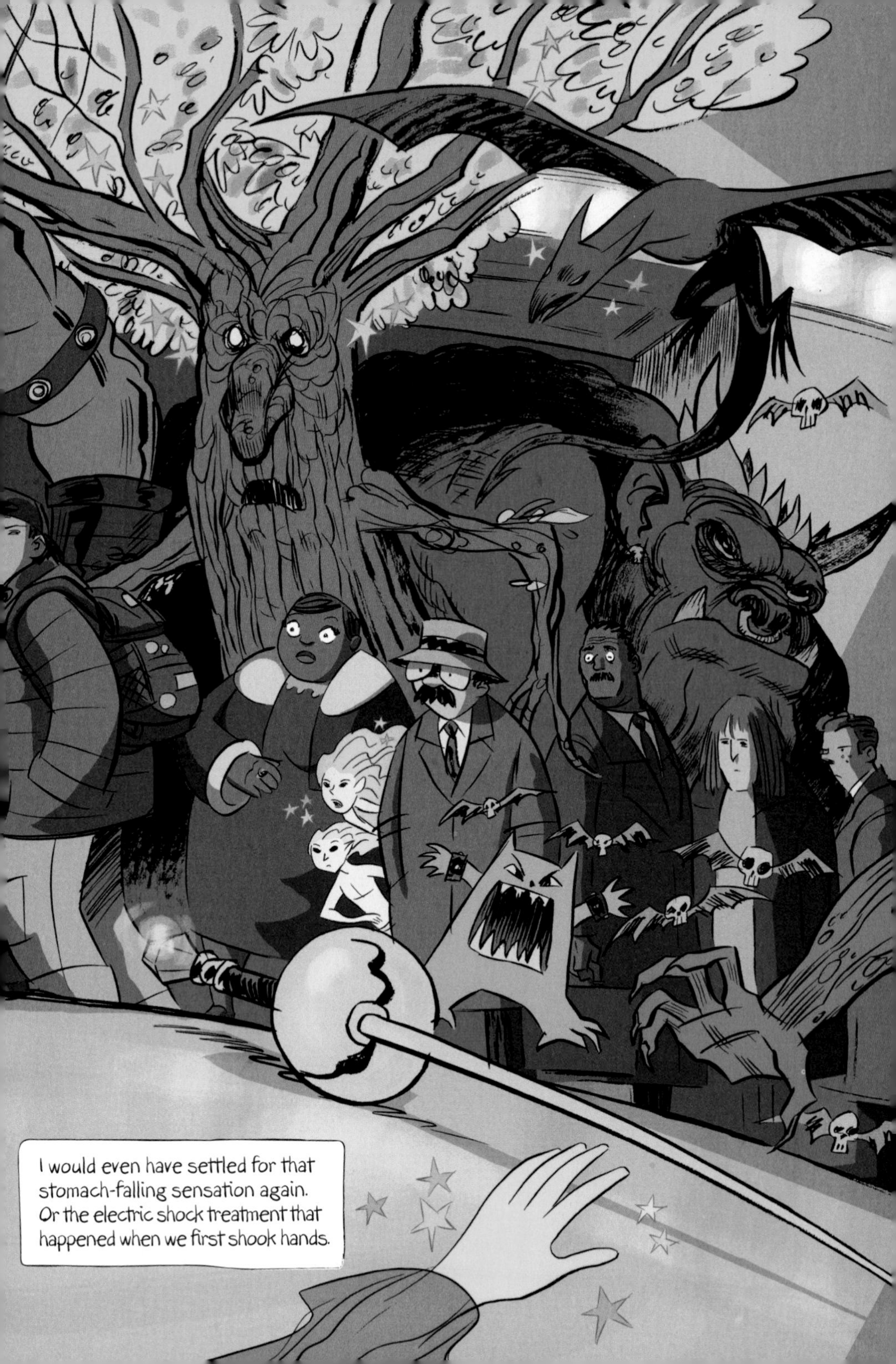
I would even have settled for that stomach-falling sensation again. Or the electric shock treatment that happened when we first shook hands.

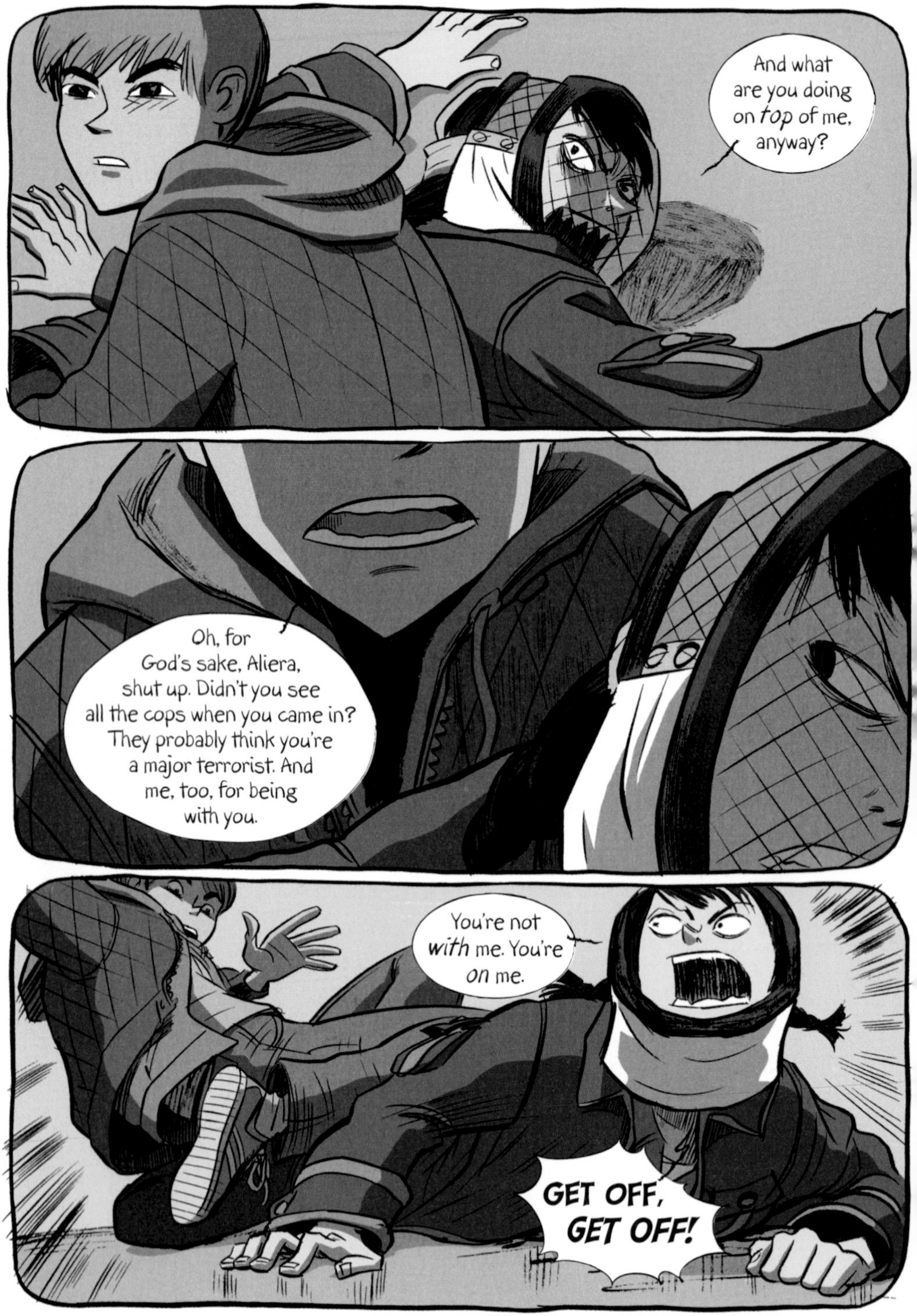
And what are you doing on *top* of me, anyway?
Oh, for God's sake, Aliera, shut up. Didn't you see all the cops when you came in? They probably think you're a major terrorist. And me, too, for being with you.
You're not *with* me. You're *on* me.
GET OFF, GET OFF!

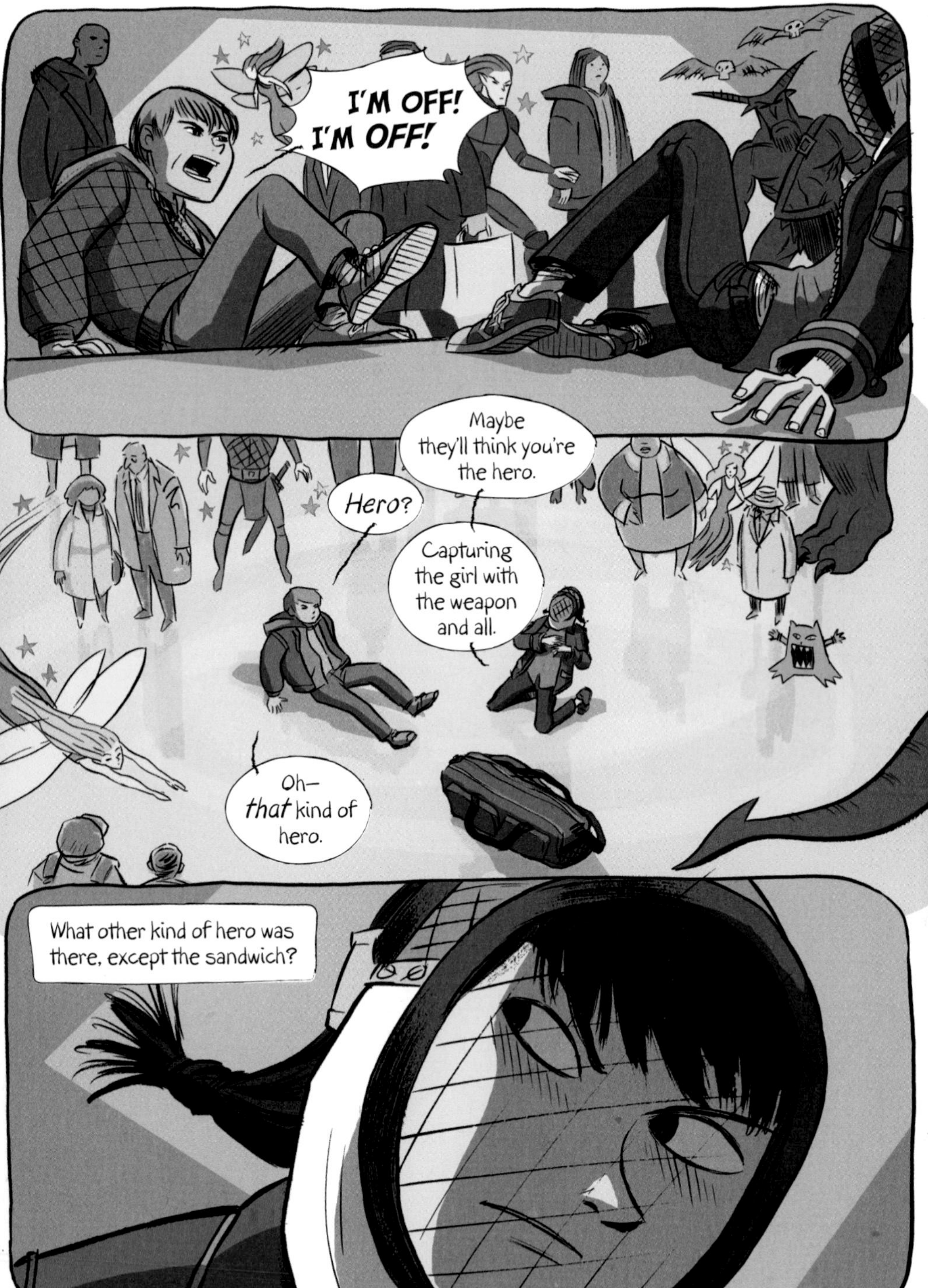
I'M OFF!
I'M OFF!
Maybe they'll think you're the hero.
Hero?
Capturing the girl with the weapon and all.
Oh— *that* kind of hero.
What other kind of hero was there, except the sandwich?

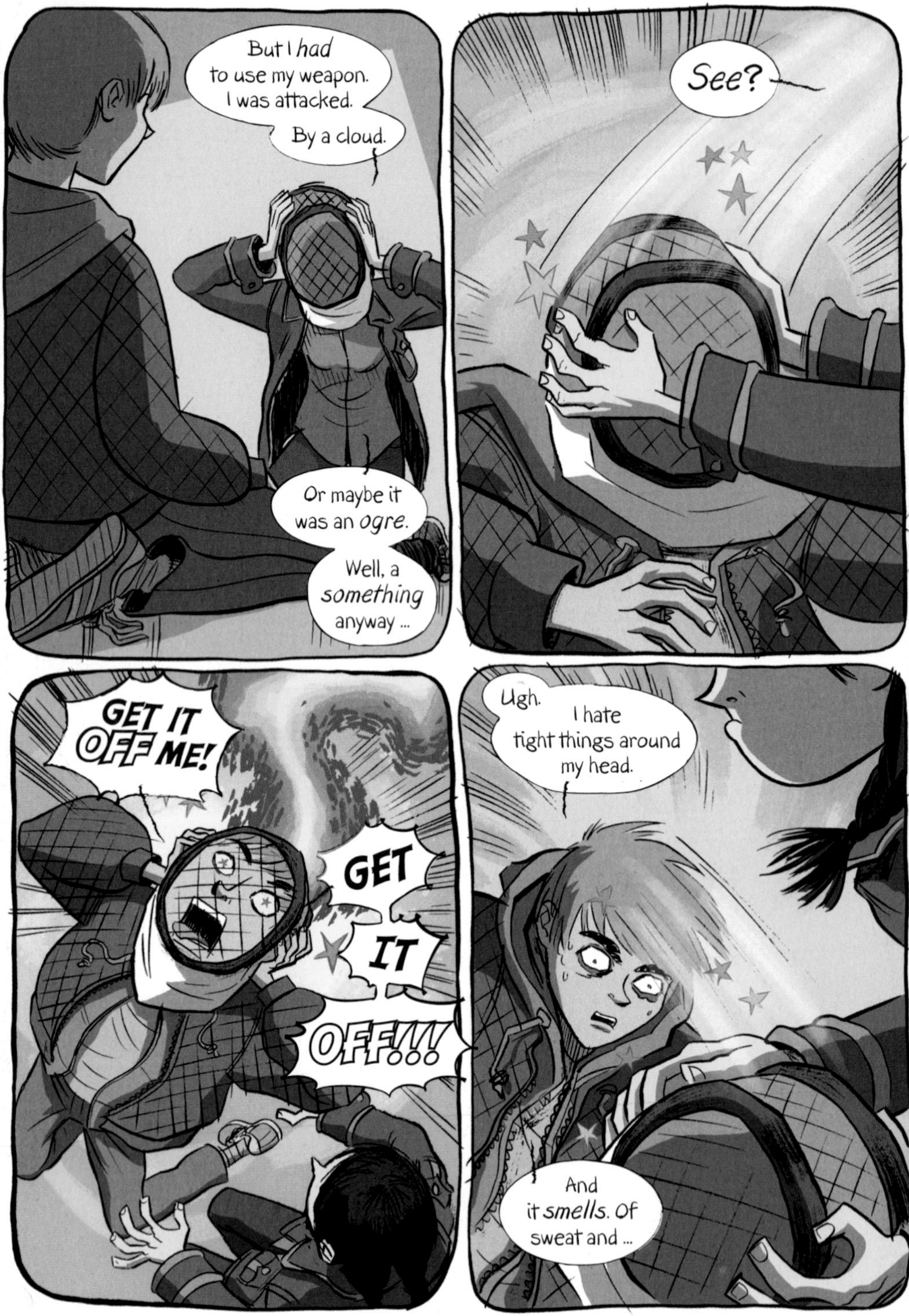
But I *had* to use my weapon. I was attacked.
By a cloud.
Or maybe it was an *ogre*.
Well, a *something* anyway ...
See?
GET IT OFF ME!
GET
IT
OFF!!!
Ugh.
I hate tight things around my head.
And it *smells*. Of sweat and ...

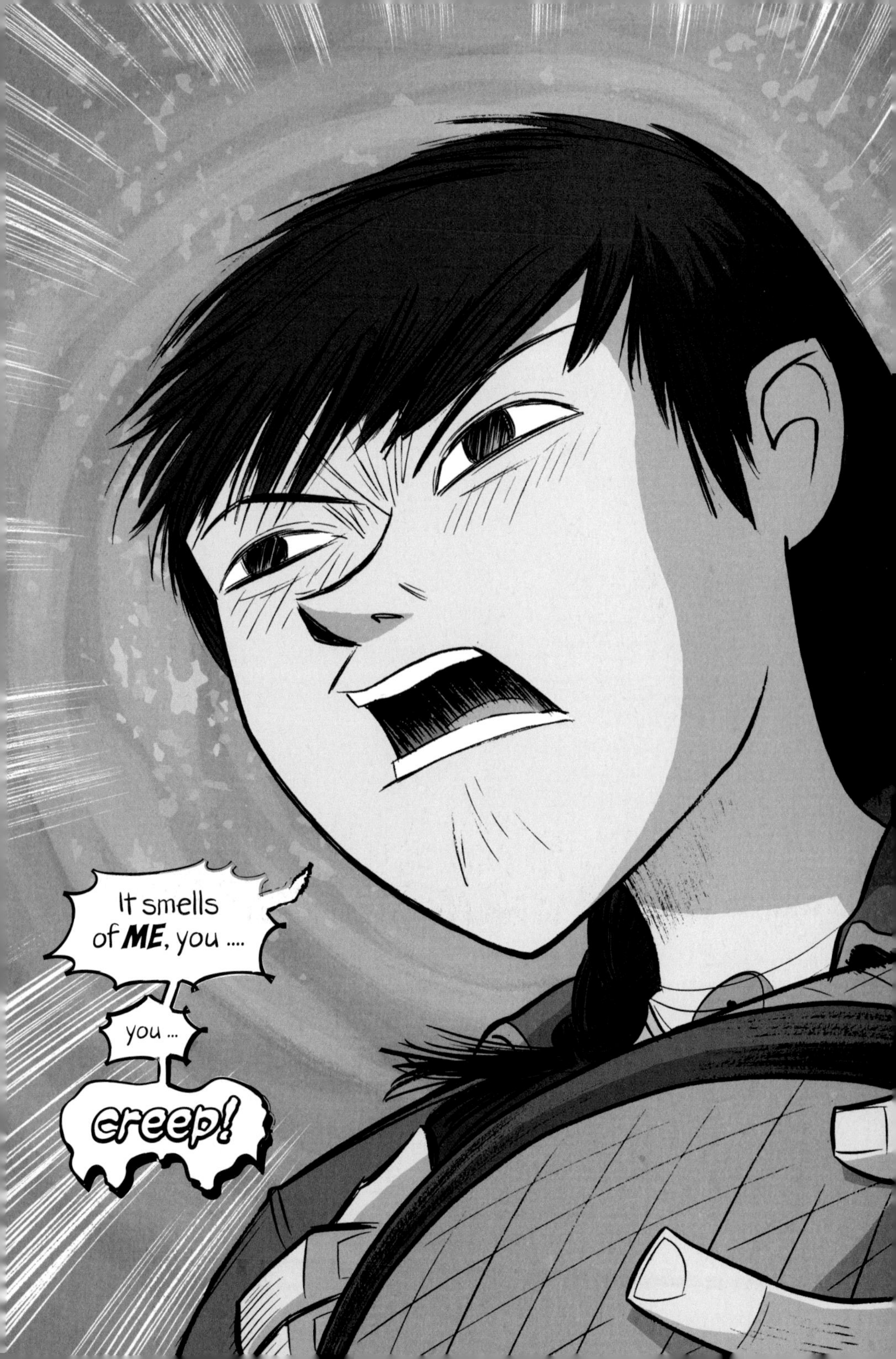
It smells of ME, you ....
you ...
creep!

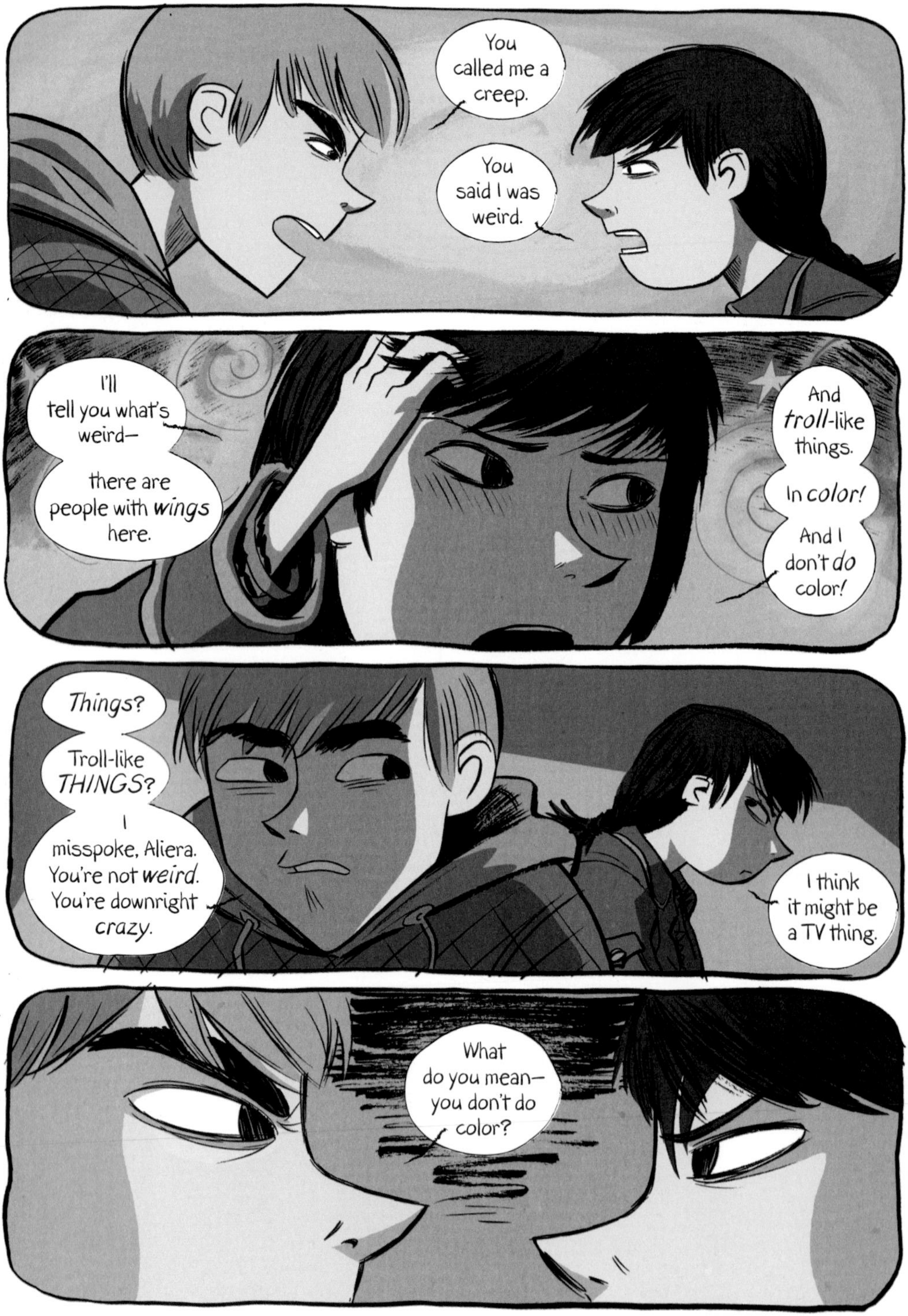
You called me a creep.
You said I was weird.
I'll tell you what's weird—
there are people with *wings* here.
And *troll*-like things.
In *color!*
And I don't *do* color!
Things?
Troll-like *THINGS?*
I misspoke, Aliera. You're not *weird*. You're downright *crazy*.
I think it might be a TV thing.
What do you mean— you don't do color?

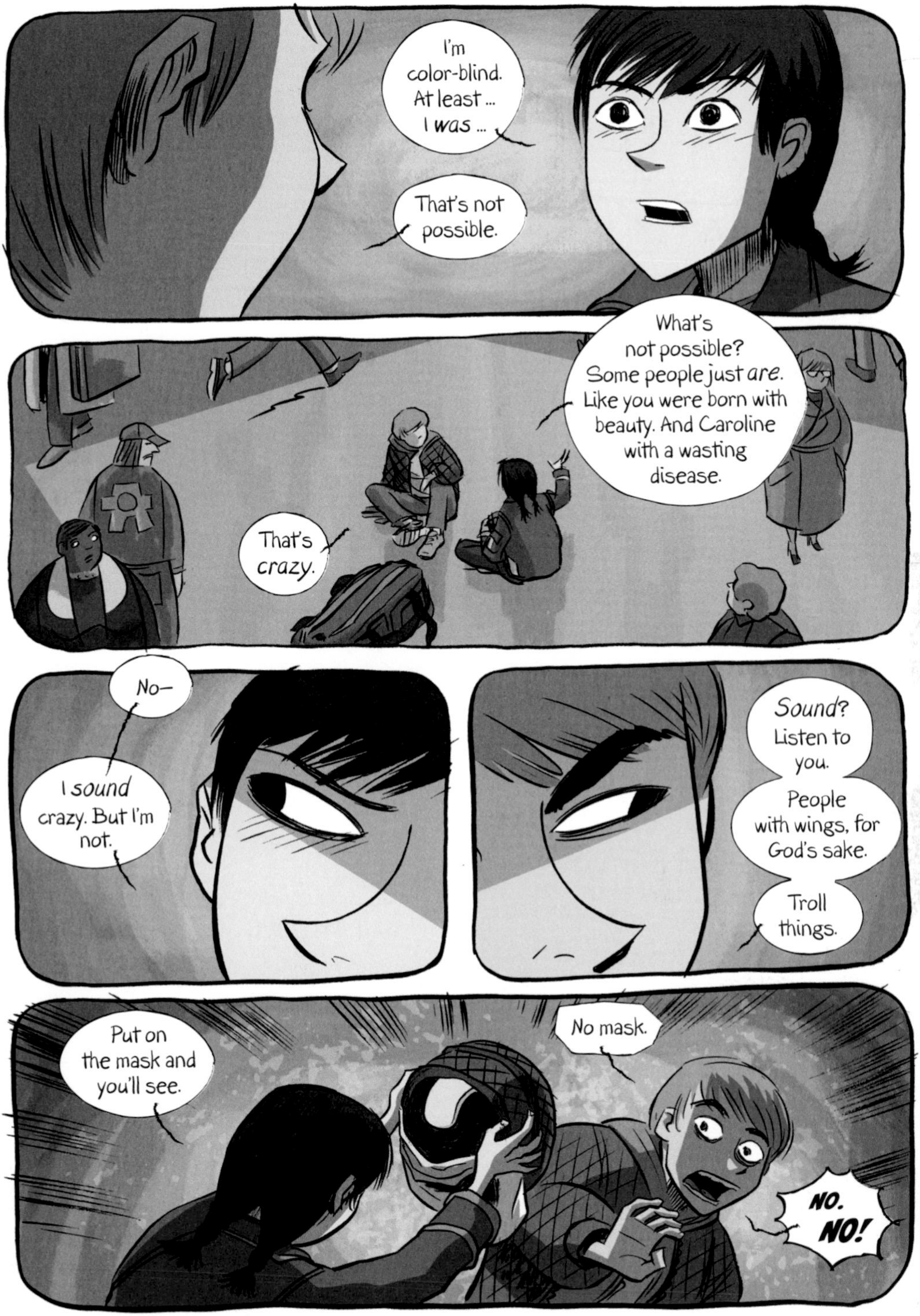
I'm color-blind. At least ... I *was* ...
That's not possible.
What's not possible? Some people just *are*. Like you were born with beauty. And Caroline with a wasting disease.
That's *crazy*.
No—
I *sound* crazy. But I'm not.
Sound? Listen to you.
People with wings, for God's sake.
Troll things.
Put on the mask and you'll see.
No mask.
NO. NO!

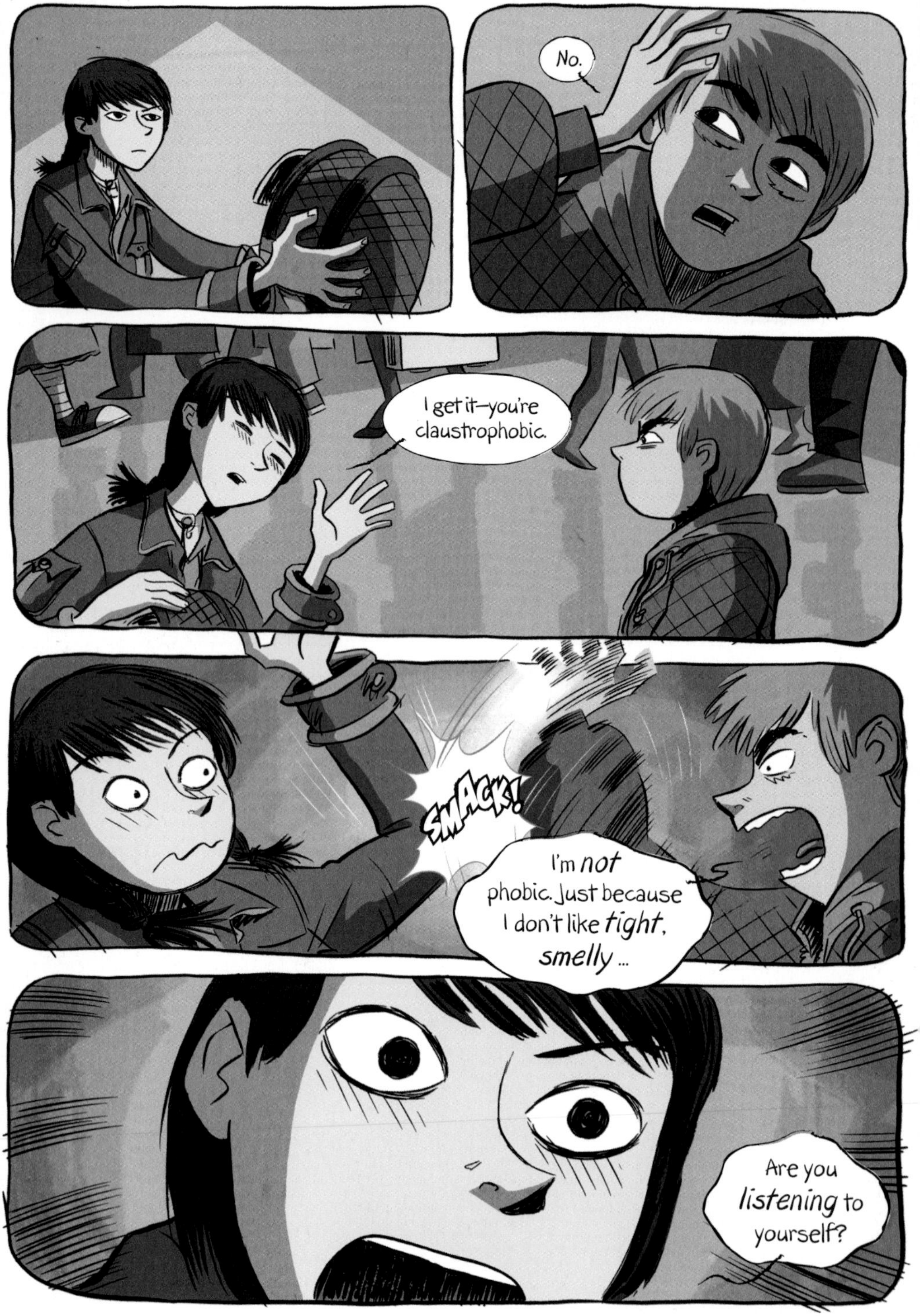
No.
I get it—you're claustrophobic.
SMACK!
I'm *not* phobic. Just because I don't like *tight*, *smelly* ...
Are you *listening* to yourself?

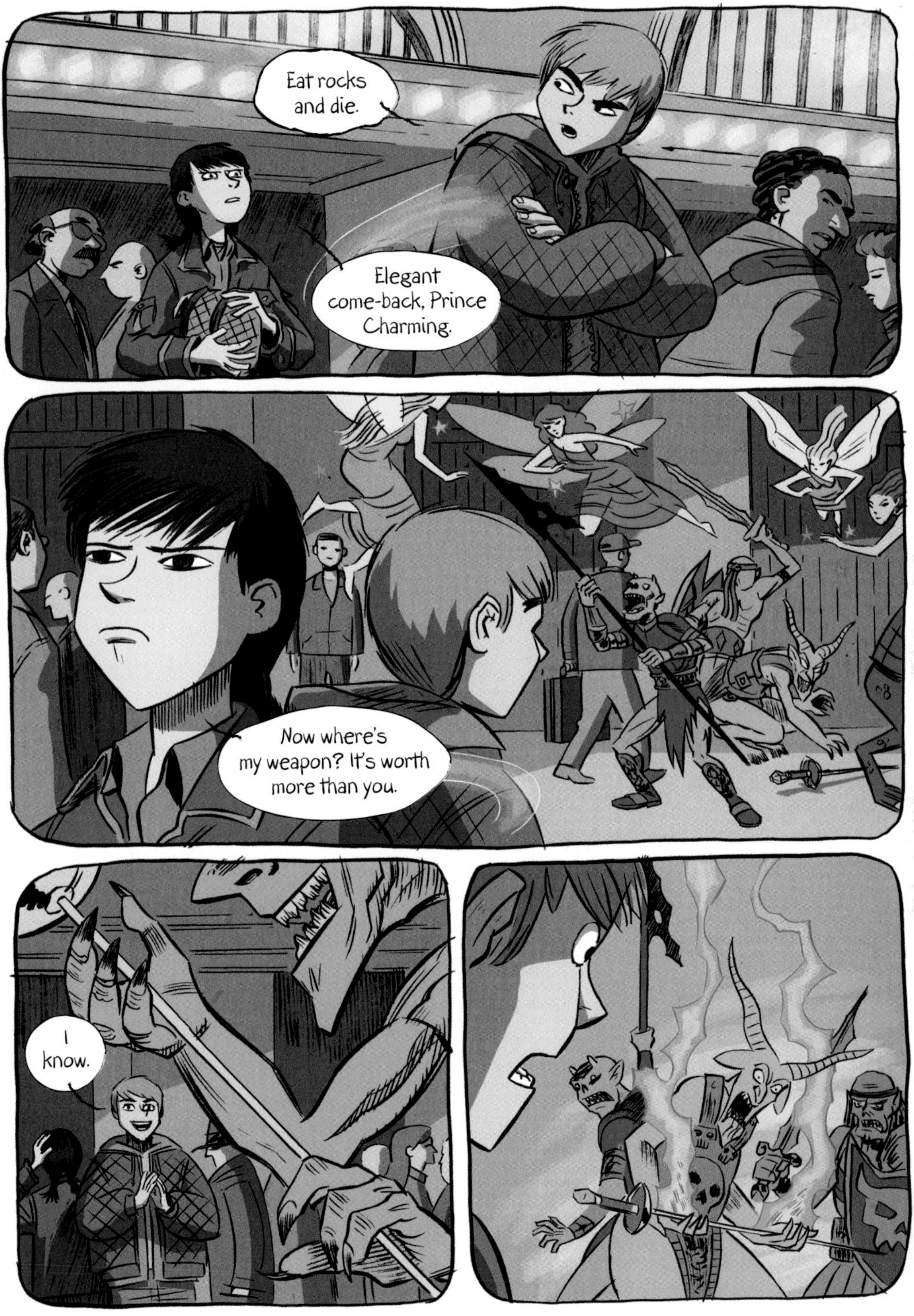

Eat rocks and die.
Elegant come-back, Prince Charming.
Now where's my weapon? It's worth more than you.
I know.

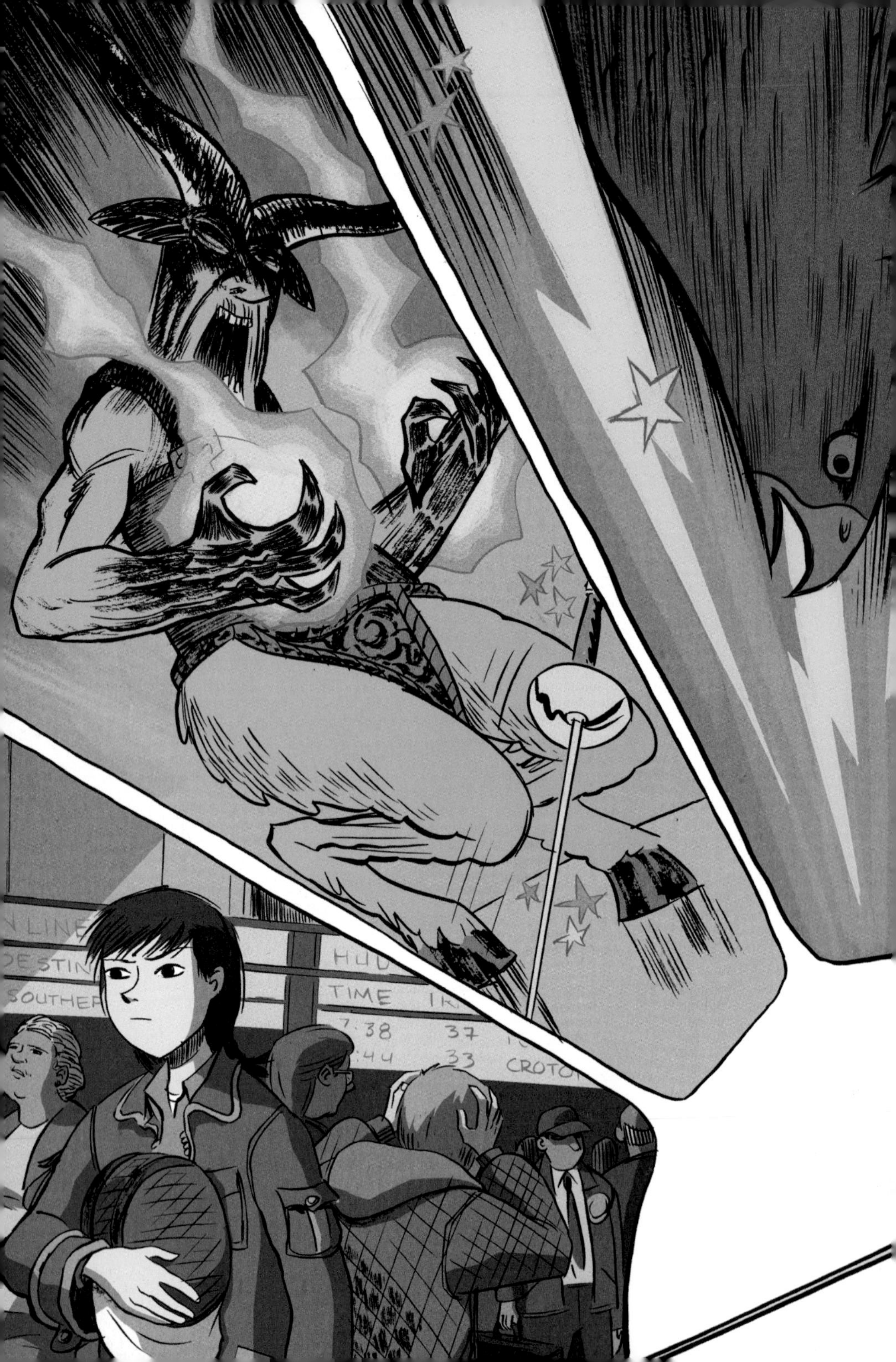

N LINE
DESTIN
SOUTHER
HUD
TIME
7:38 37
:44 33 CROTO

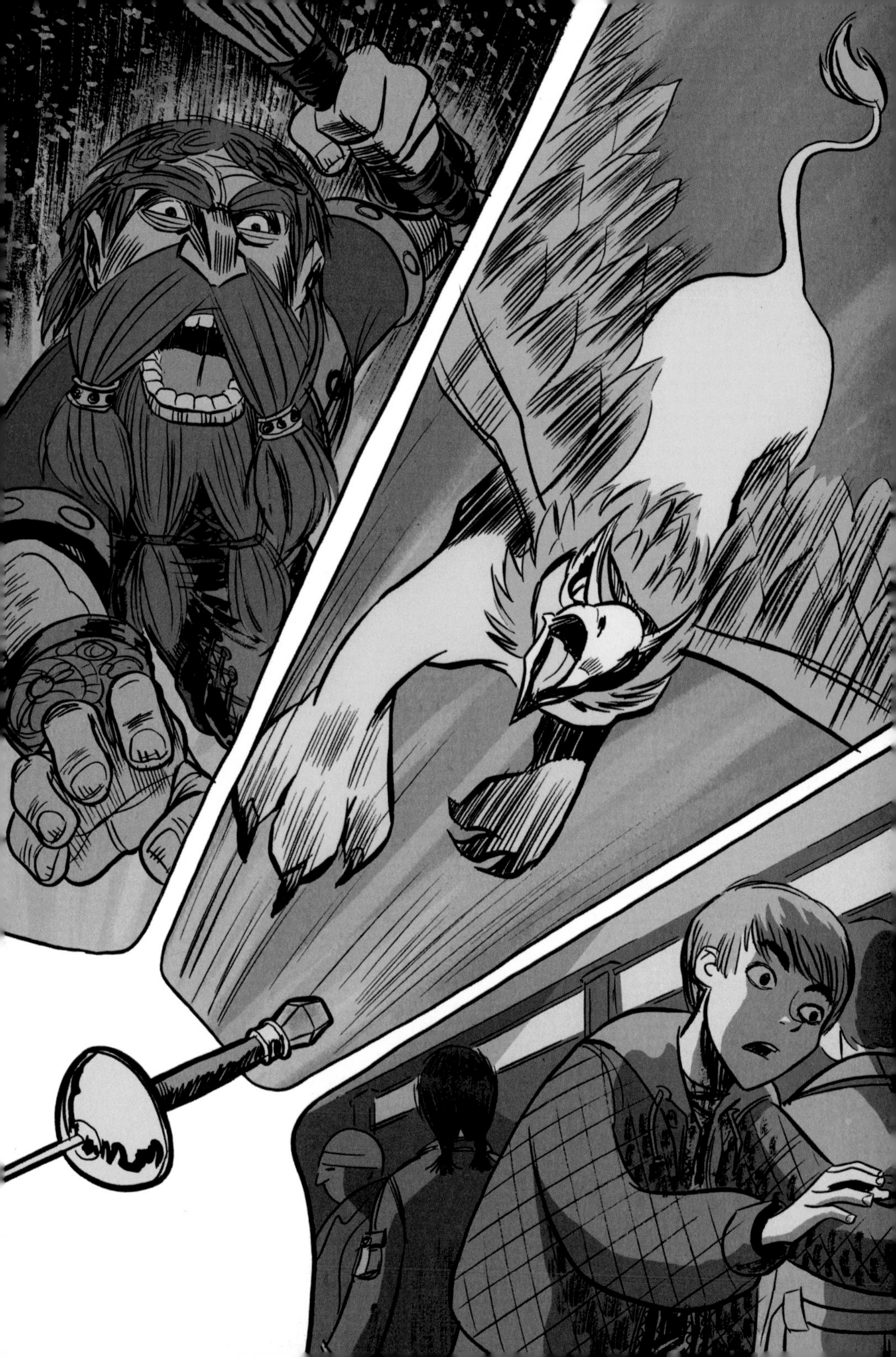

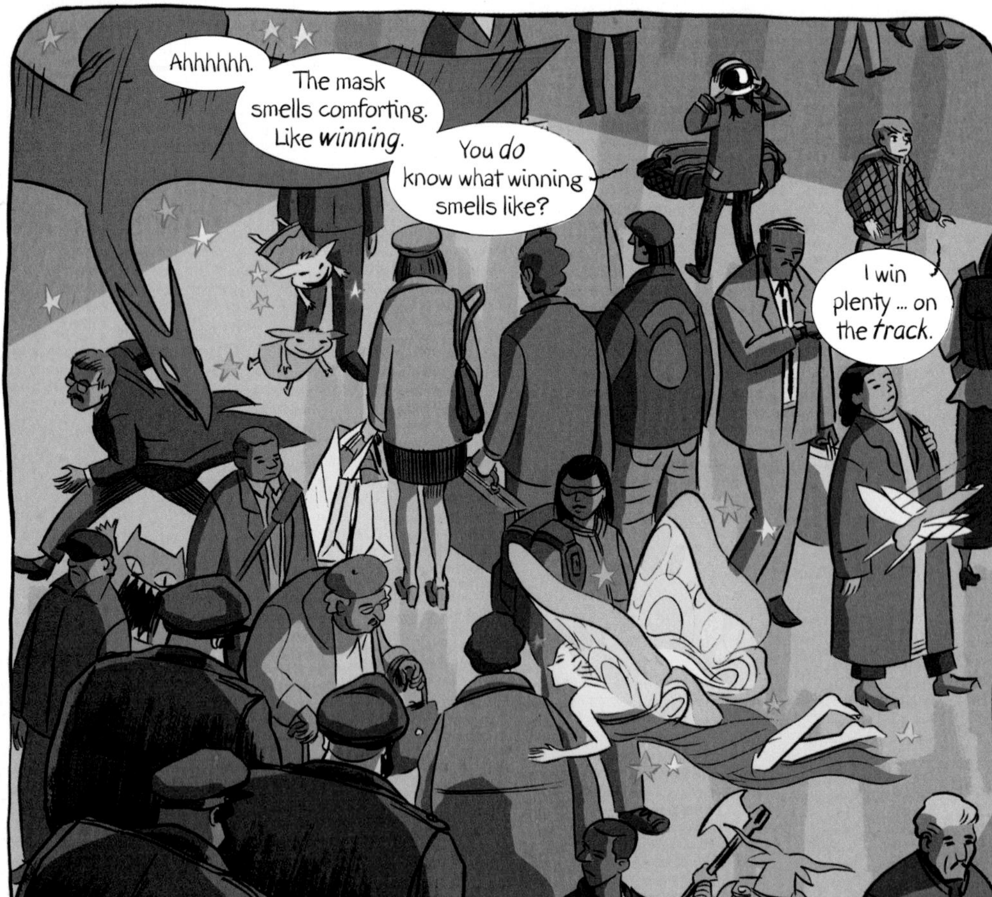
Ahhhhhh.
The mask smells comforting. Like *winning*.
You *do* know what winning smells like?
I win plenty ... on the *track*.

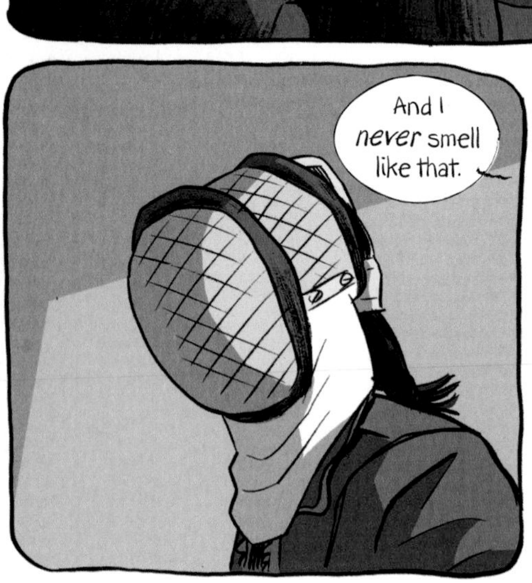
And I *never* smell like that.

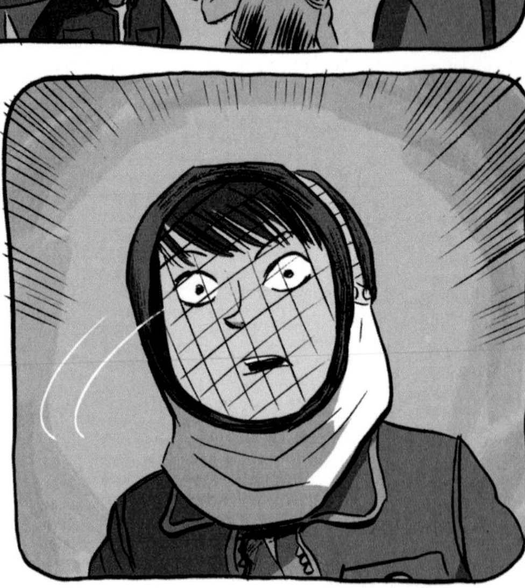

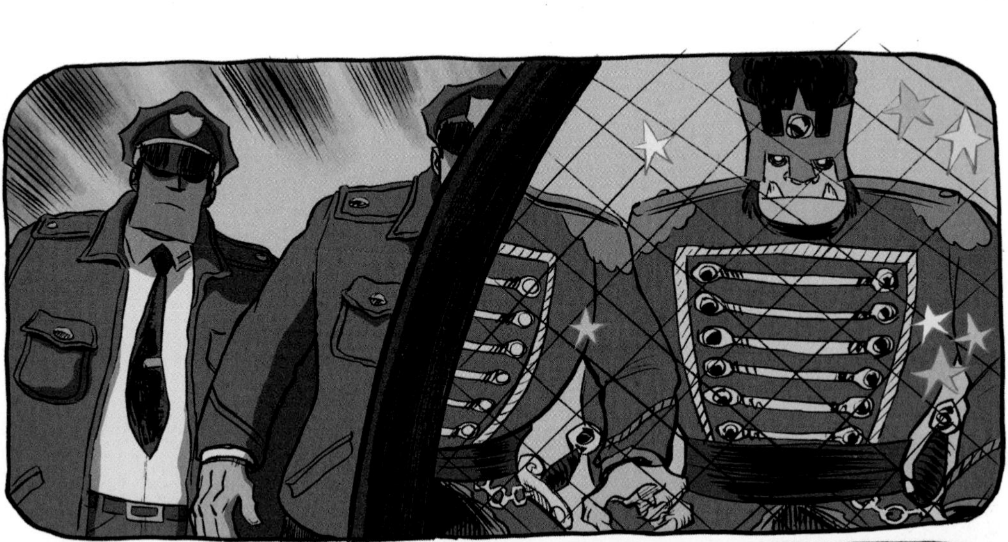

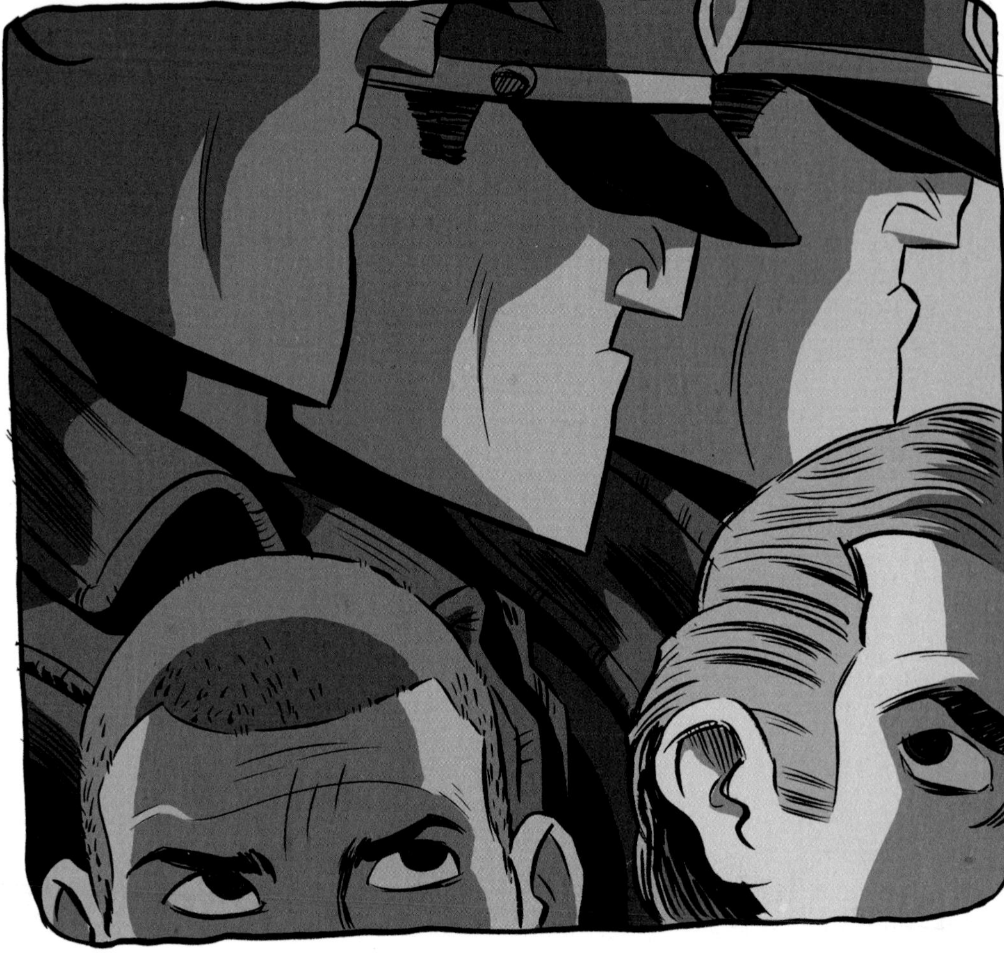

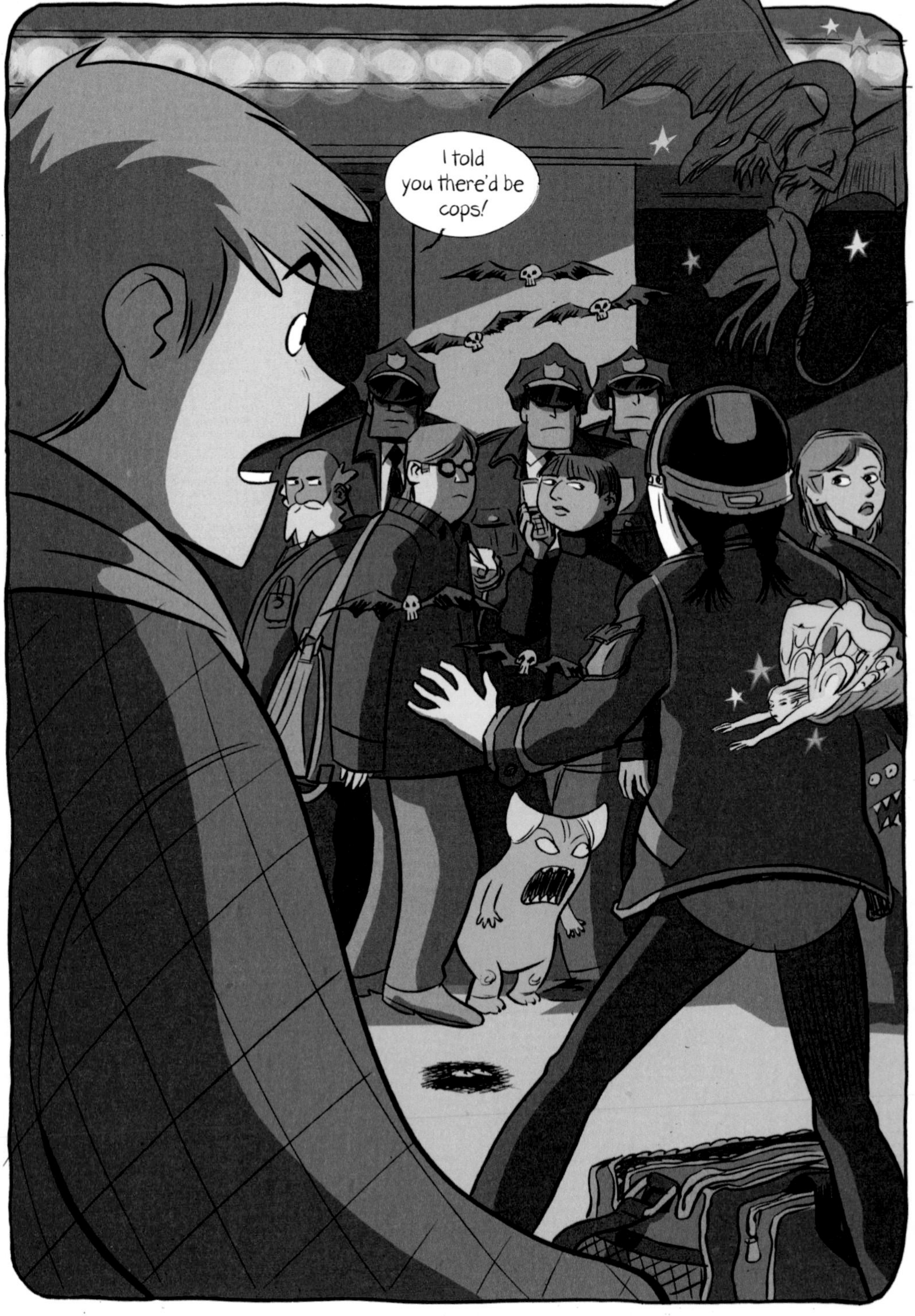
I told you there'd be cops!

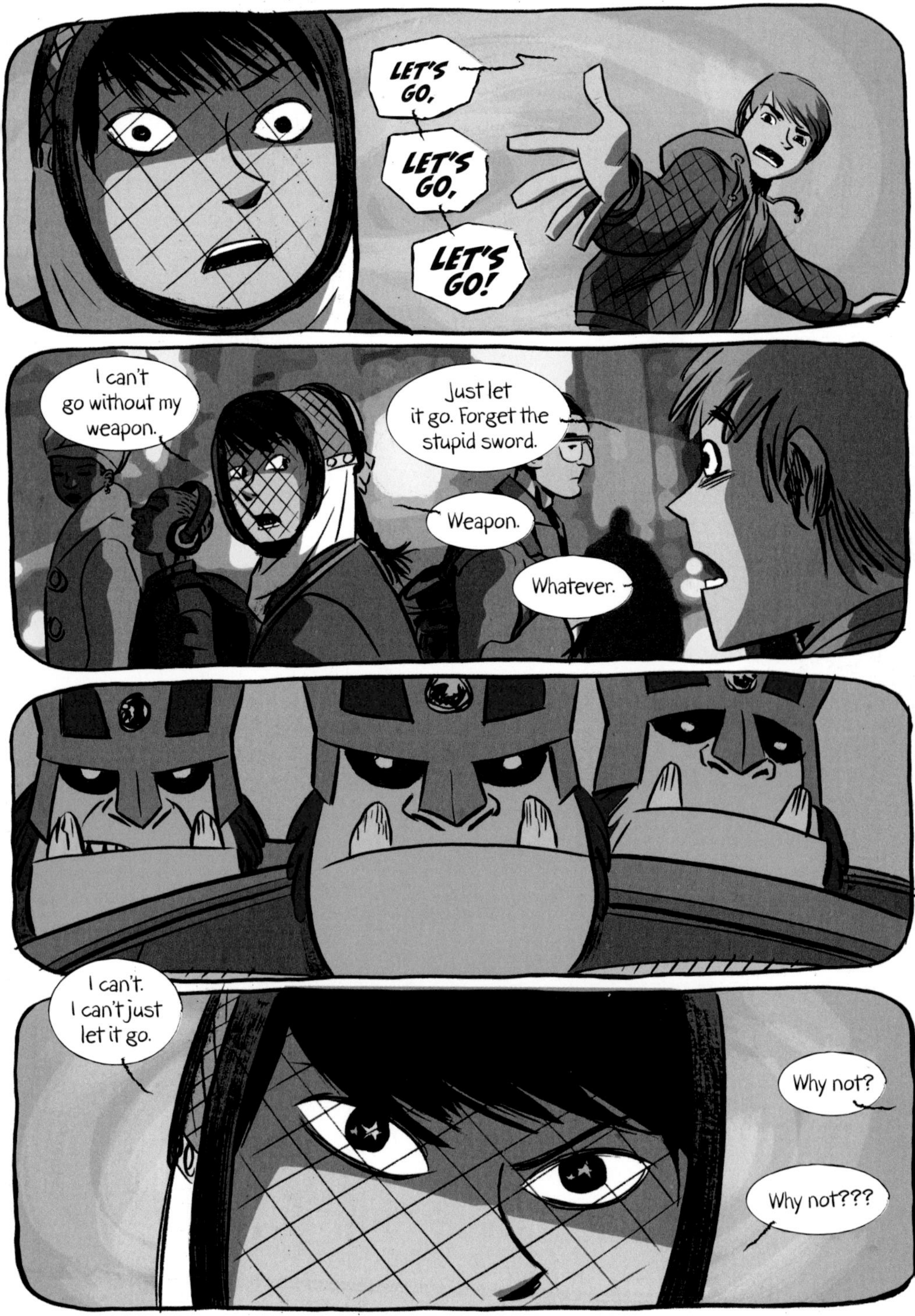
LET'S GO,
LET'S GO,
LET'S GO!
I can't go without my weapon.
Just let it go. Forget the stupid sword.
Weapon.
Whatever.
I can't. I can't just let it go.
Why not?
Why not???

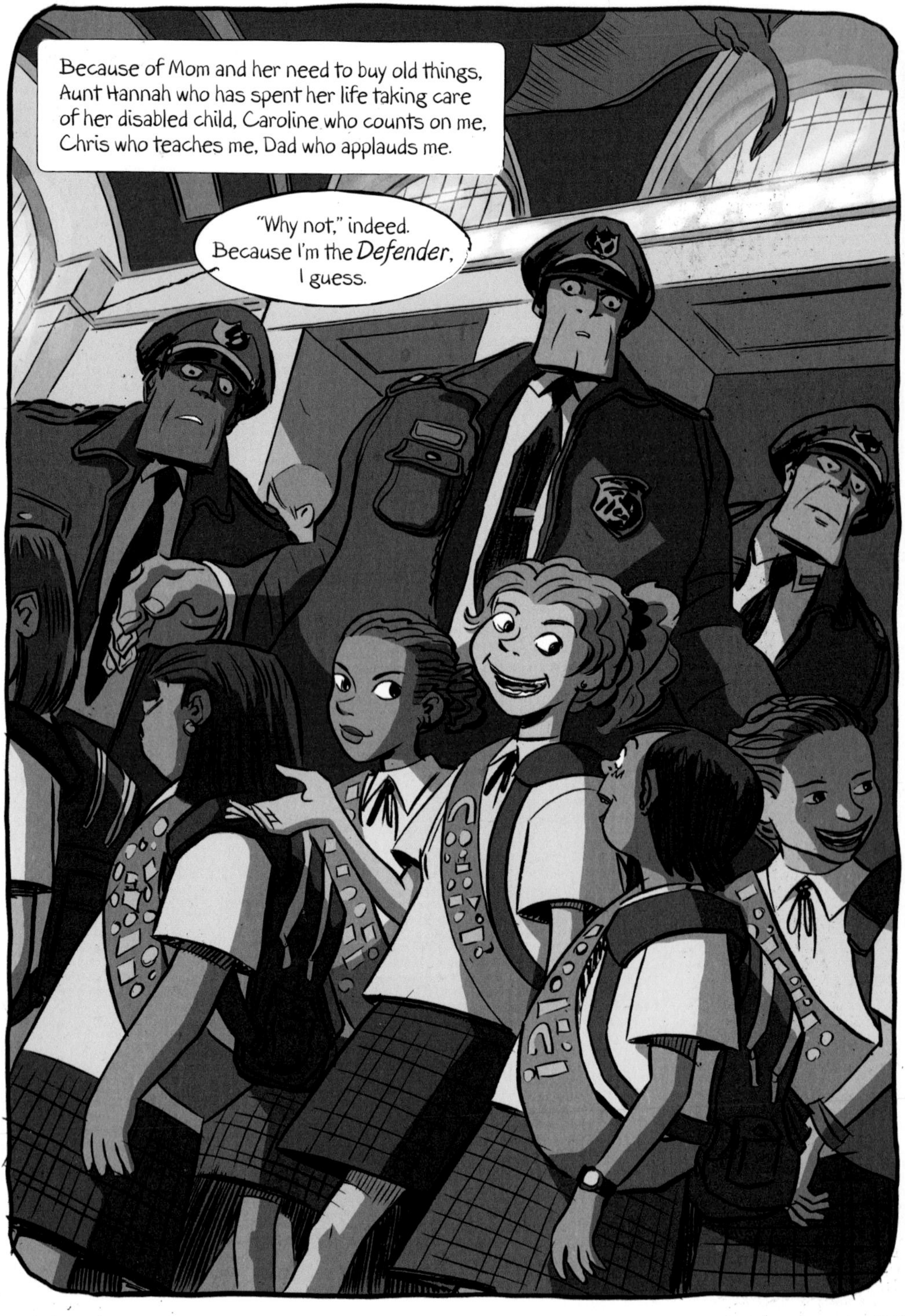
Because of Mom and her need to buy old things, Aunt Hannah who has spent her life taking care of her disabled child, Caroline who counts on me, Chris who teaches me, Dad who applauds me.
"Why not," indeed. Because I'm the *Defender*, I guess.

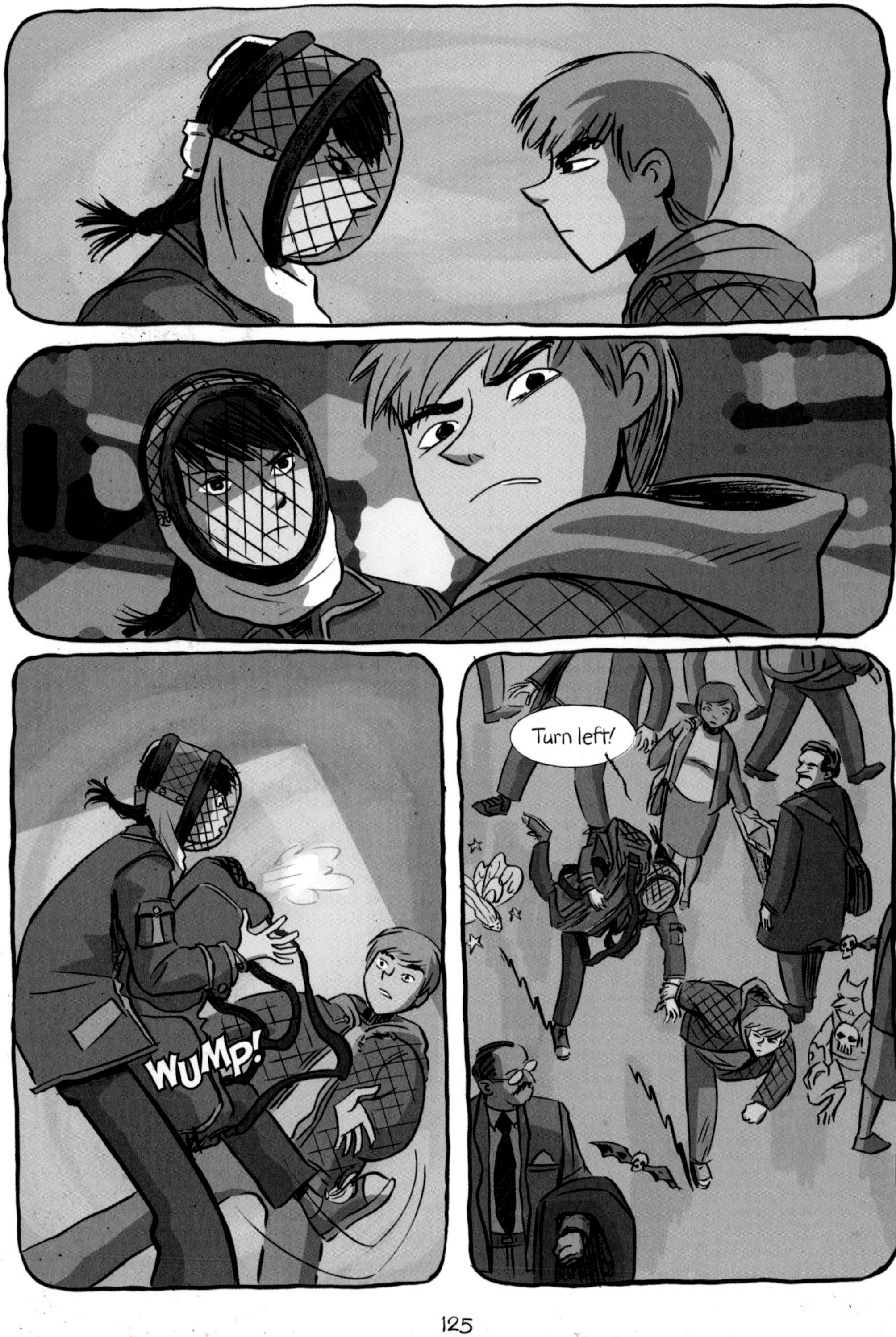
WUMP!
Turn left!

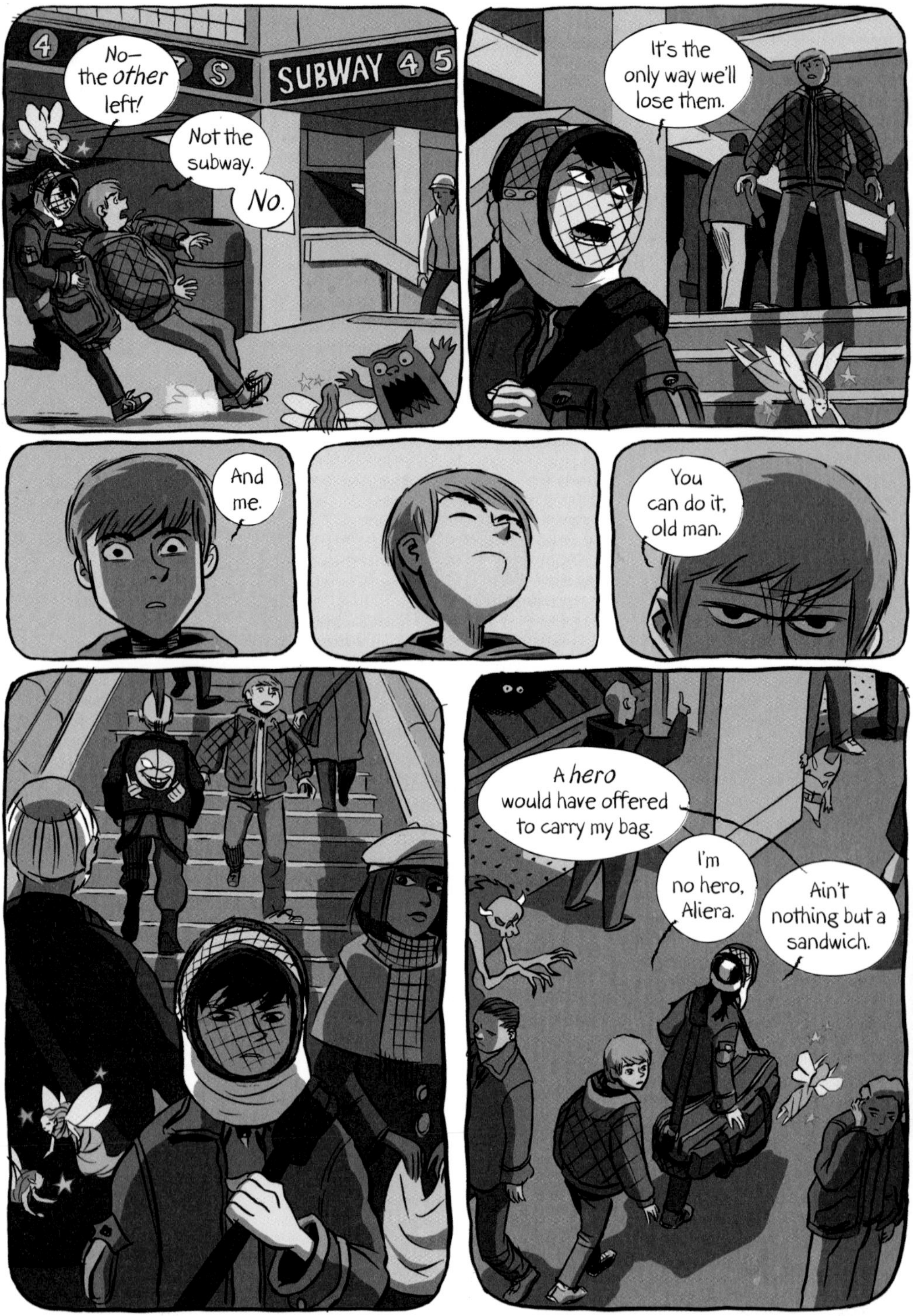
No—
the *other*
left!
SUBWAY 4 5
Not the
subway.
No.
It's the
only way we'll
lose them.
And
me.
You
can do it,
old man.
A *hero*
would have offered
to carry my bag.
I'm
no hero,
Aliera.
Ain't
nothing but a
sandwich.

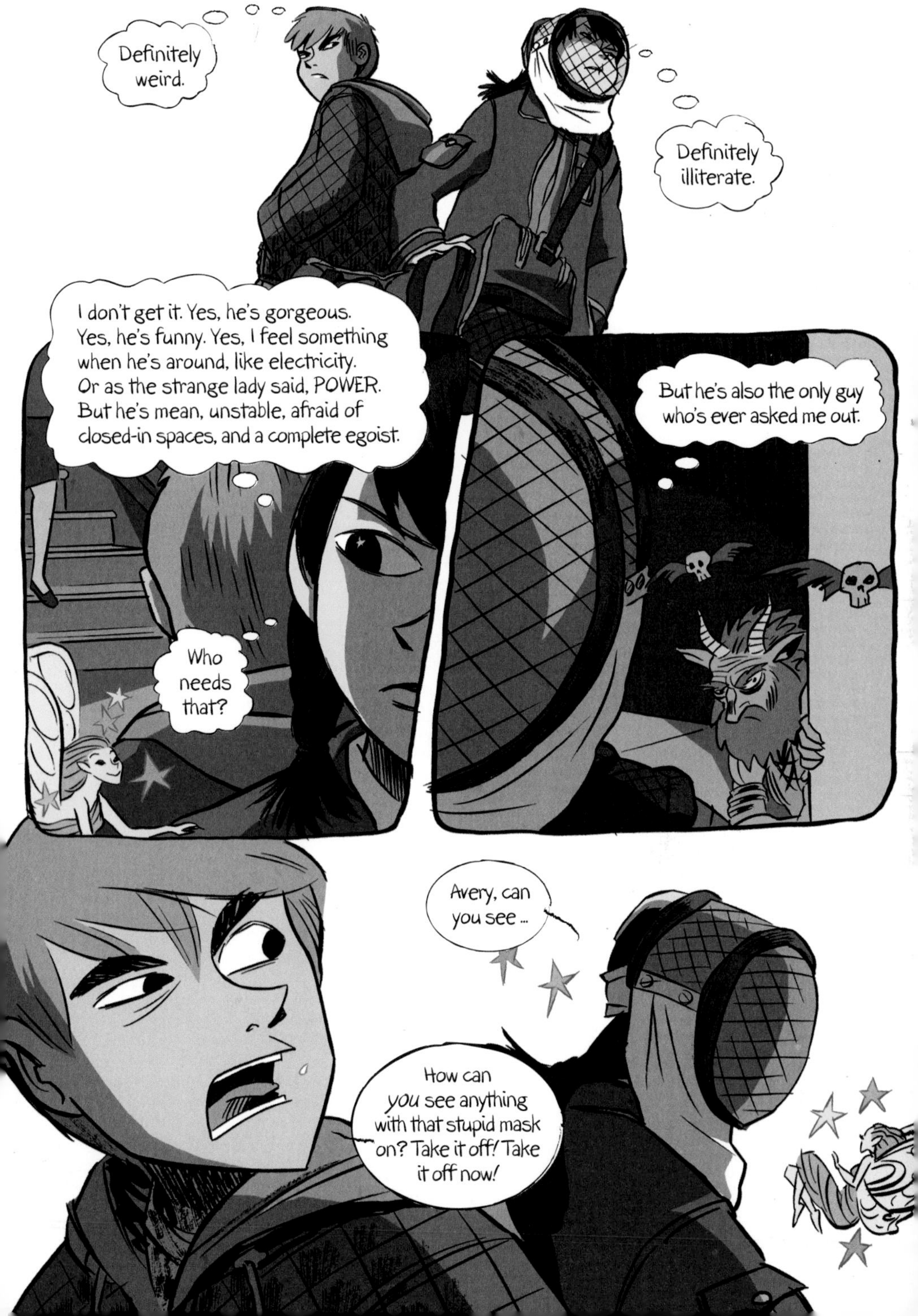
Definitely weird.
Definitely illiterate.
I don't get it. Yes, he's gorgeous. Yes, he's funny. Yes, I feel something when he's around, like electricity. Or as the strange lady said, POWER. But he's mean, unstable, afraid of closed-in spaces, and a complete egoist.
But he's also the only guy who's ever asked me out.
Who needs that?
Avery, can you see ...
How can *you* see anything with that stupid mask on? Take it off! Take it off now!

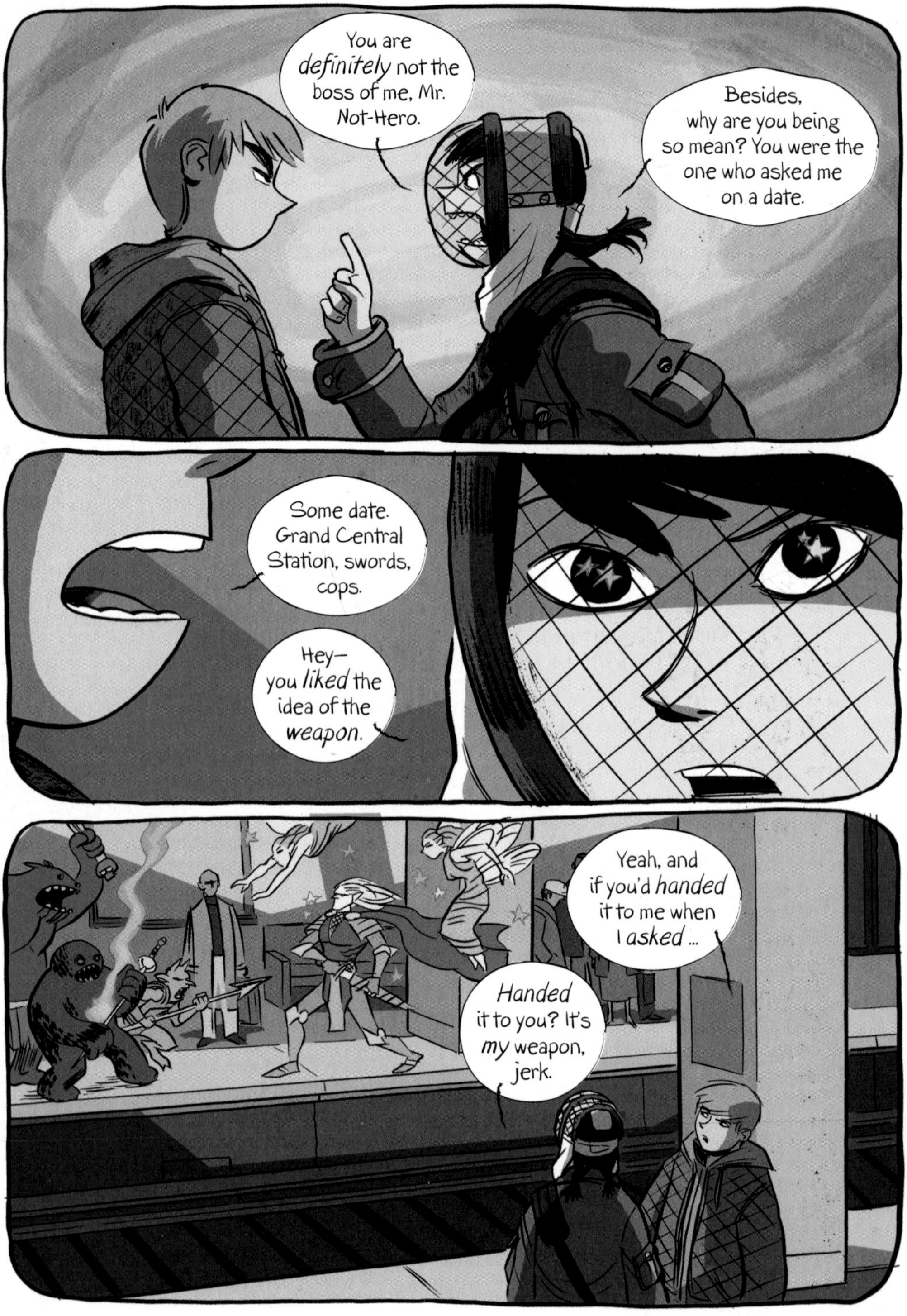
You are *definitely* not the boss of me, Mr. Not-Hero.
Besides, why are you being so mean? You were the one who asked me on a date.
Some date. Grand Central Station, swords, cops.
Hey— you *liked* the idea of the *weapon*.
Yeah, and if you'd *handed* it to me when I *asked* ...
Handed it to you? It's *my* weapon, jerk.

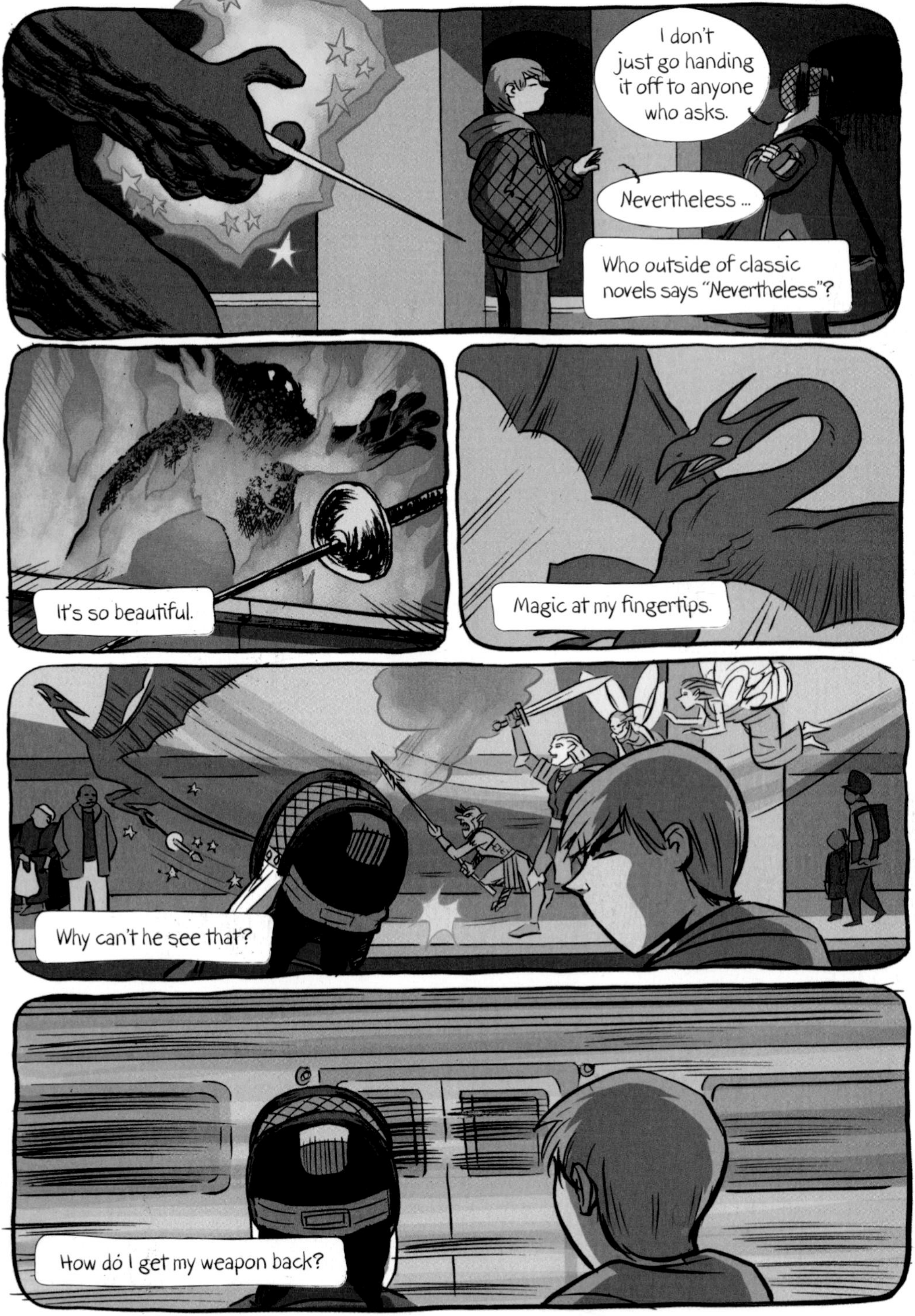
I don't just go handing it off to anyone who asks.
Nevertheless ...
Who outside of classic novels says "Nevertheless"?
It's so beautiful.
Magic at my fingertips.
Why can't he see that?
How do I get my weapon back?

9. Coupe de Temps

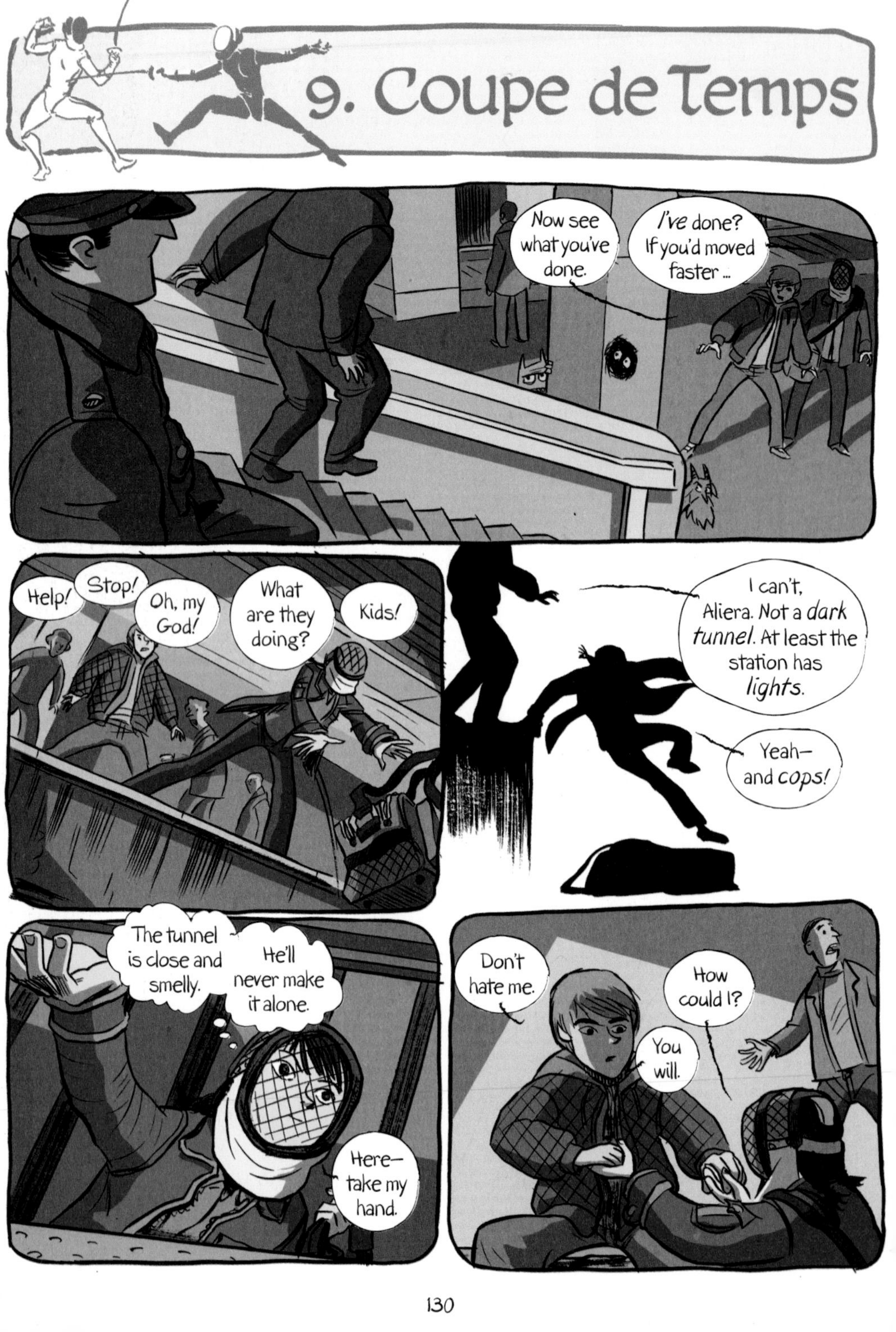

Now see what you've done.
I've done? If you'd moved faster ...
Help!
Stop!
Oh, my God!
What are they doing?
Kids!
I can't, Aliera. Not a dark tunnel. At least the station has lights.
Yeah— and cops!
The tunnel is close and smelly.
He'll never make it alone.
Here— take my hand.
Don't hate me.
How could I?
You will.

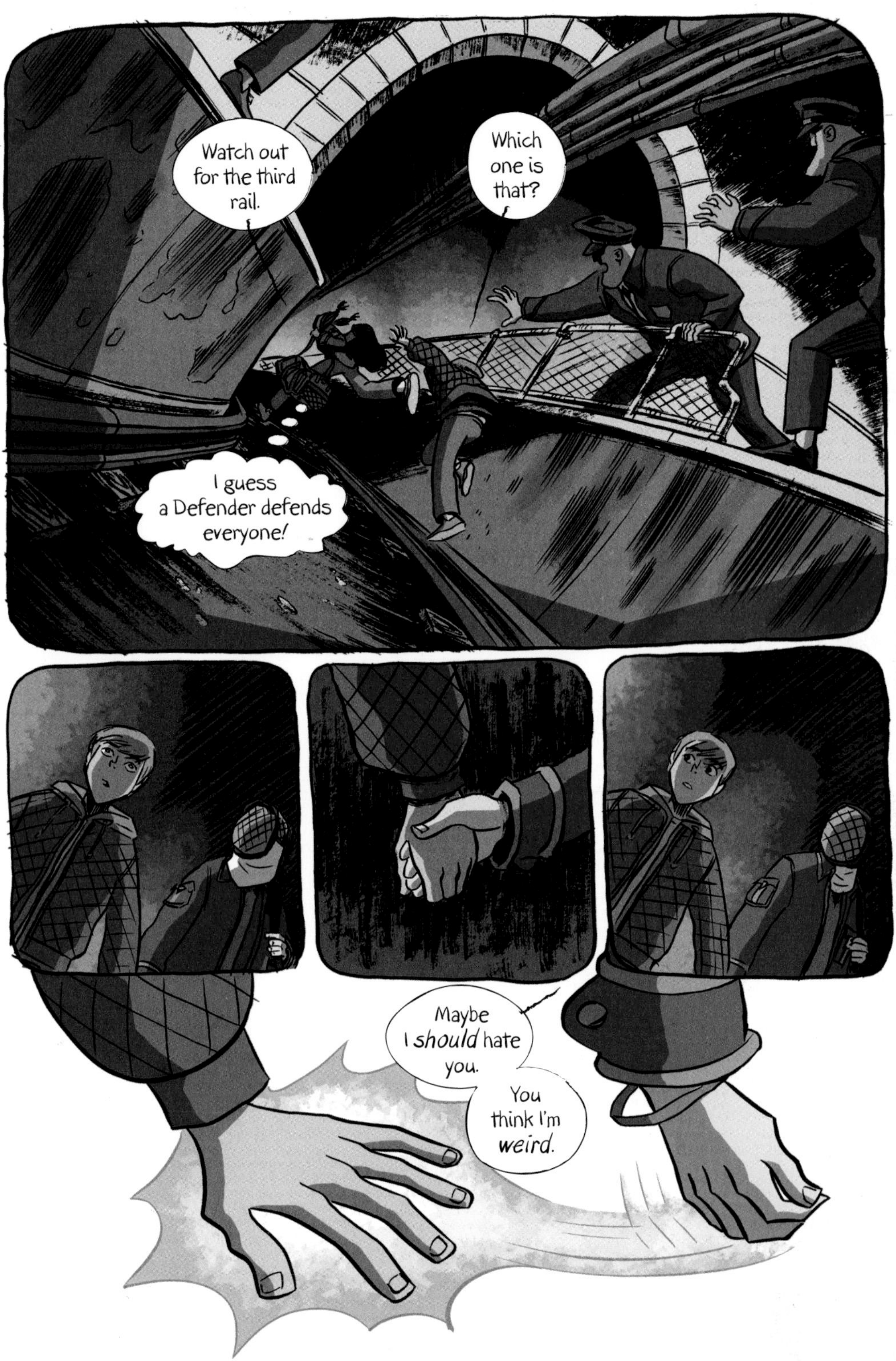
Watch out for the third rail.
Which one is that?
I guess a Defender defends everyone!
Maybe I *should* hate you.
You think I'm *weird*.

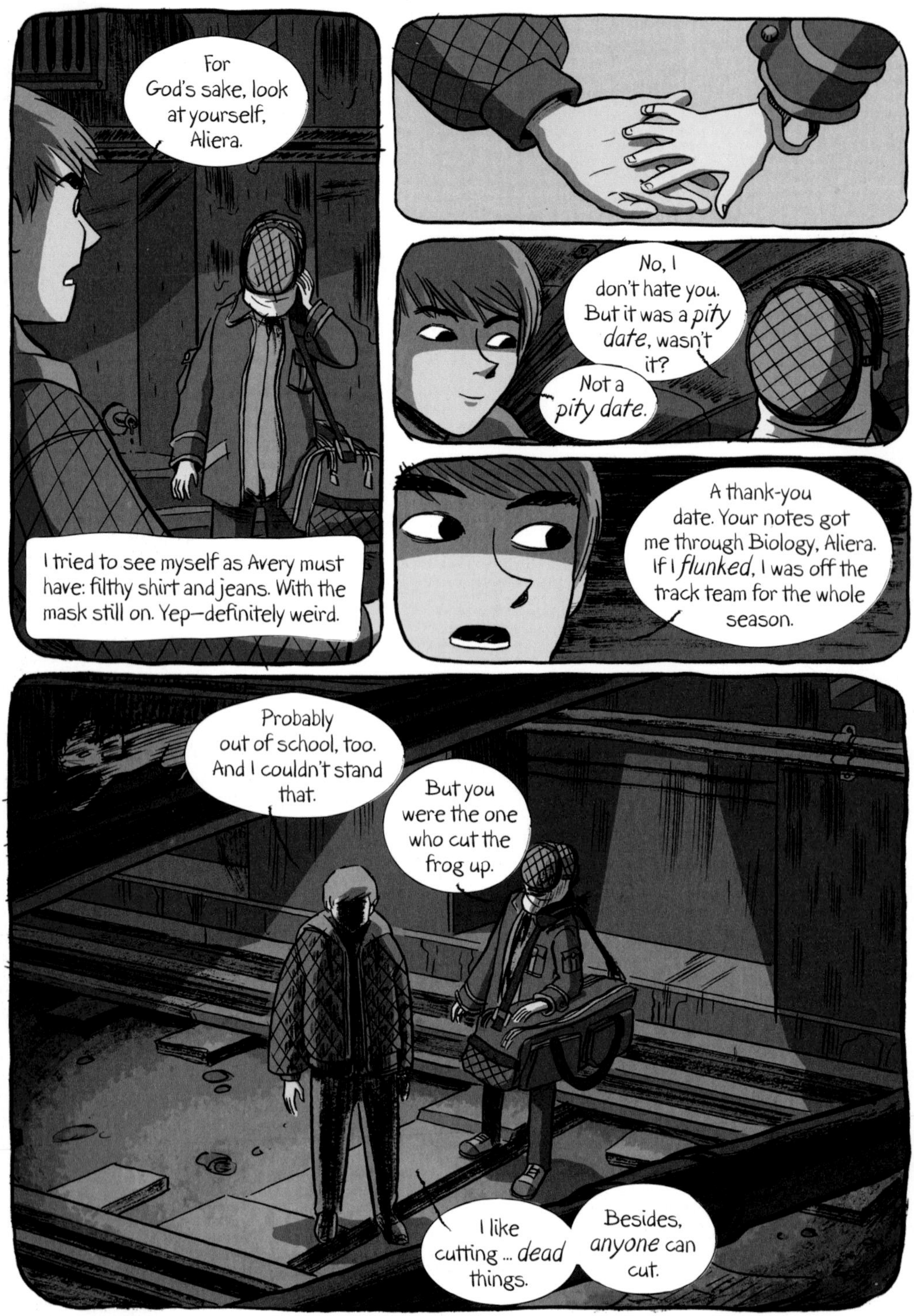
For God's sake, look at yourself, Aliera.
I tried to see myself as Avery must have: filthy shirt and jeans. With the mask still on. Yep—definitely weird.
No, I don't hate you. But it was a *pity date*, wasn't it?
Not a *pity date.*
A thank-you date. Your notes got me through Biology, Aliera. If I *flunked*, I was off the track team for the whole season.
Probably out of school, too. And I couldn't stand that.
But you were the one who cut the frog up.
I like cutting ... *dead* things.
Besides, *anyone* can cut.

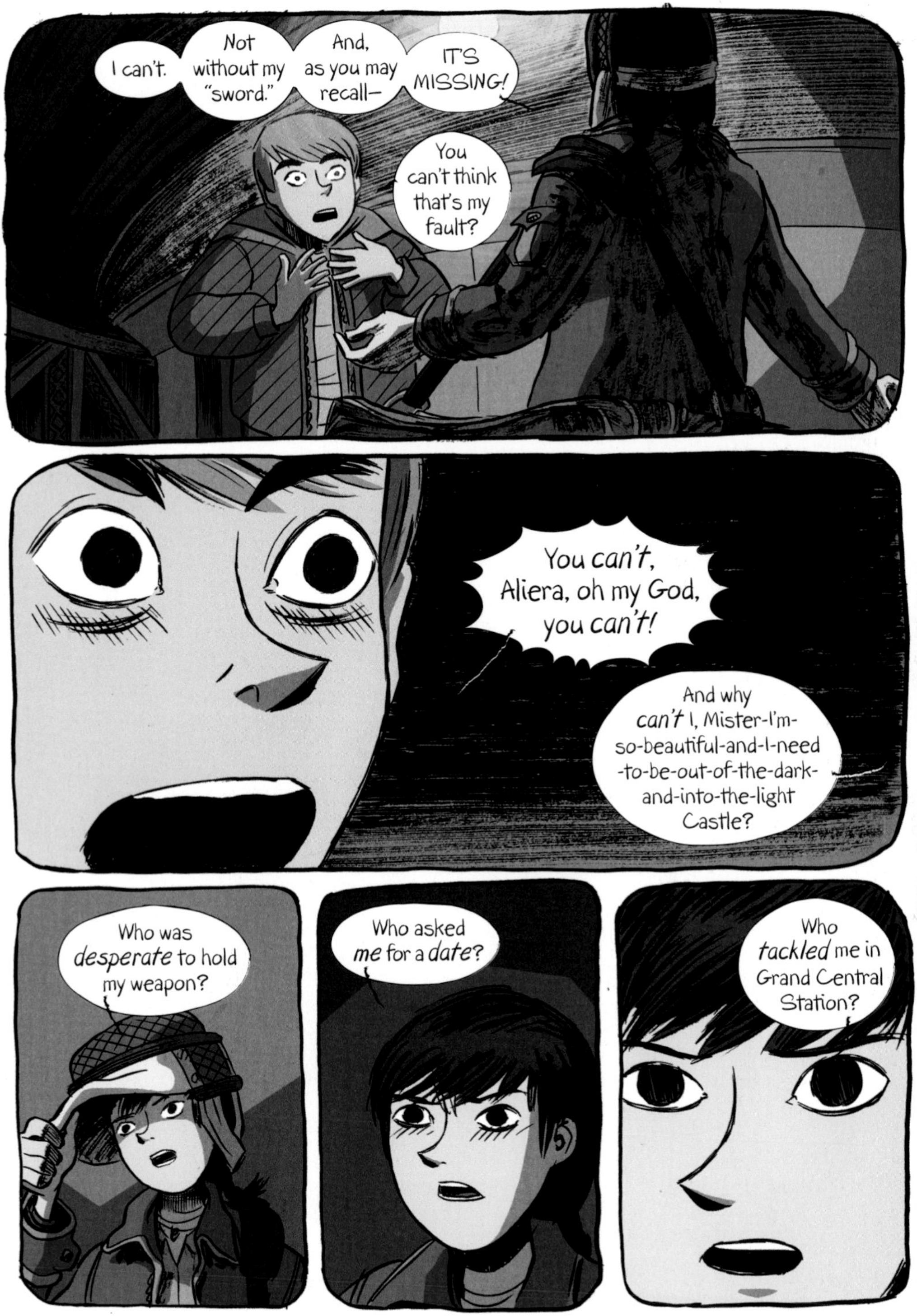
I can't.
Not without my "sword."
And, as you may recall—
IT'S MISSING!
You can't think that's my fault?
You *can't*, Aliera, oh my God, you *can't*!
And why *can't* I, Mister-I'm-so-beautiful-and-I-need-to-be-out-of-the-dark-and-into-the-light Castle?
Who was *desperate* to hold my weapon?
Who asked *me* for a *date*?
Who *tackled* me in Grand Central Station?

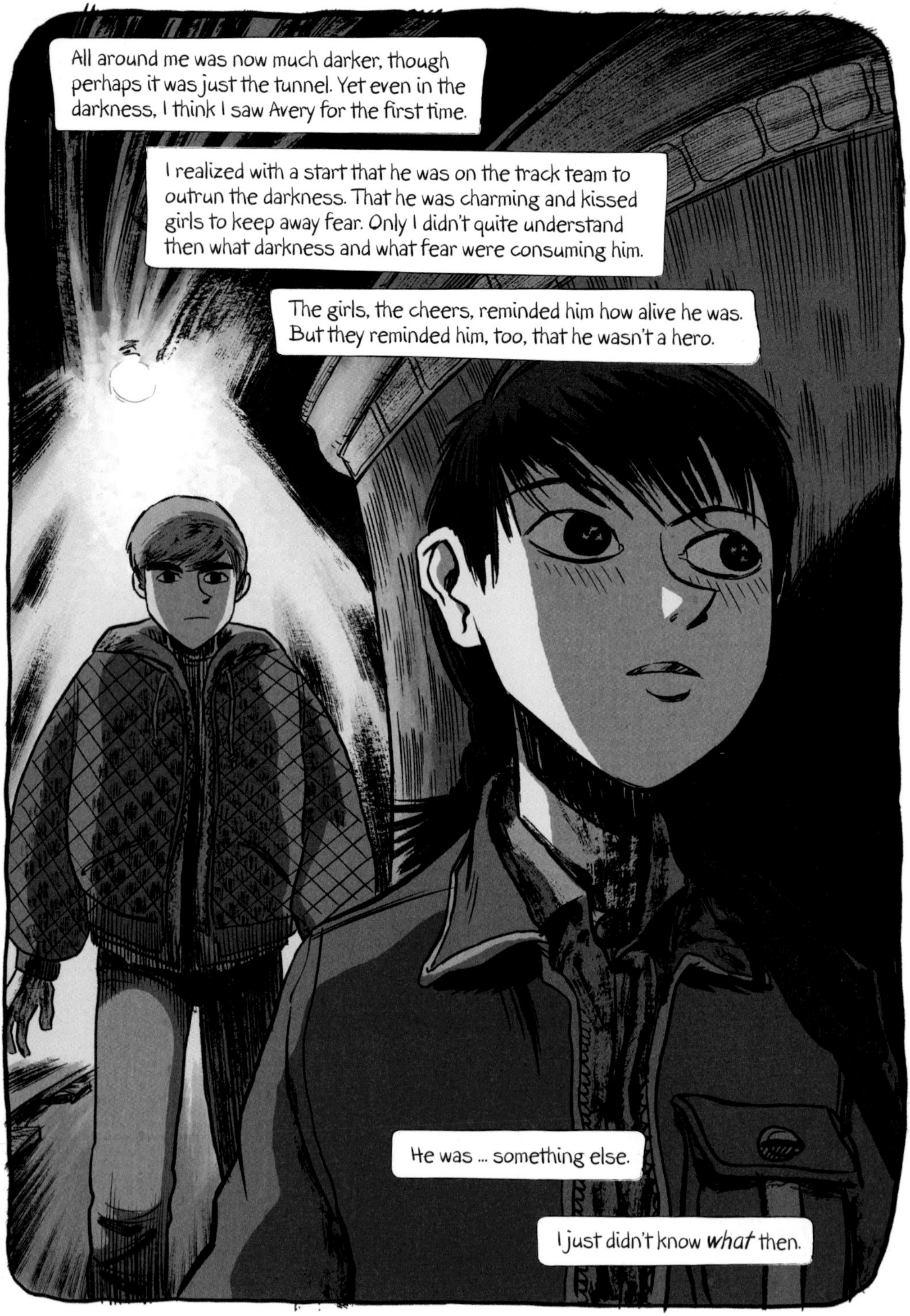
All around me was now much darker, though perhaps it was just the tunnel. Yet even in the darkness, I think I saw Avery for the first time.
I realized with a start that he was on the track team to outrun the darkness. That he was charming and kissed girls to keep away fear. Only I didn't quite understand then what darkness and what fear were consuming him.
The girls, the cheers, reminded him how alive he was. But they reminded him, too, that he wasn't a hero.
He was ... something else.
I just didn't know *what* then.

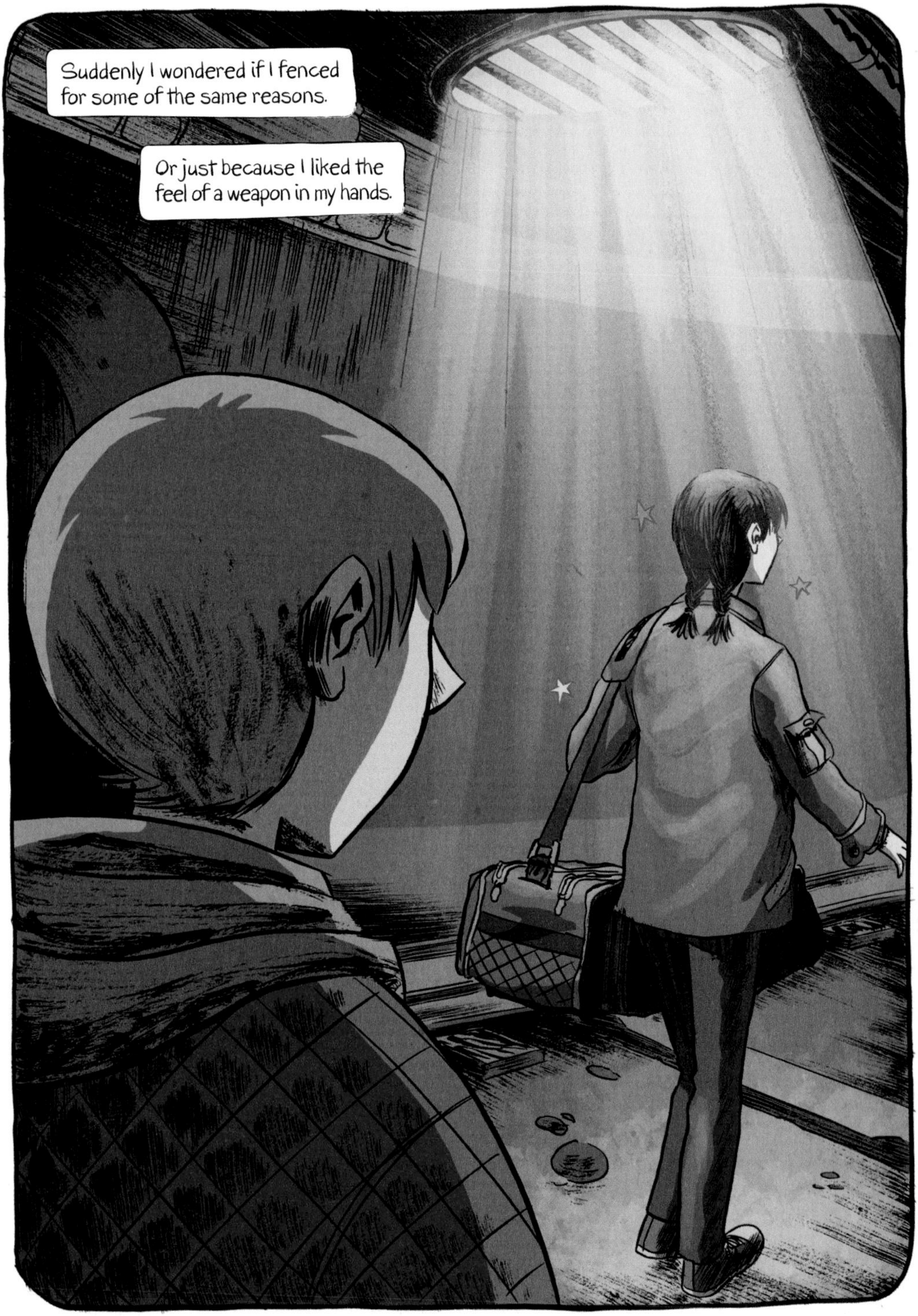
Suddenly I wondered if I fenced for some of the same reasons.
Or just because I liked the feel of a weapon in my hands.

10. Esquive

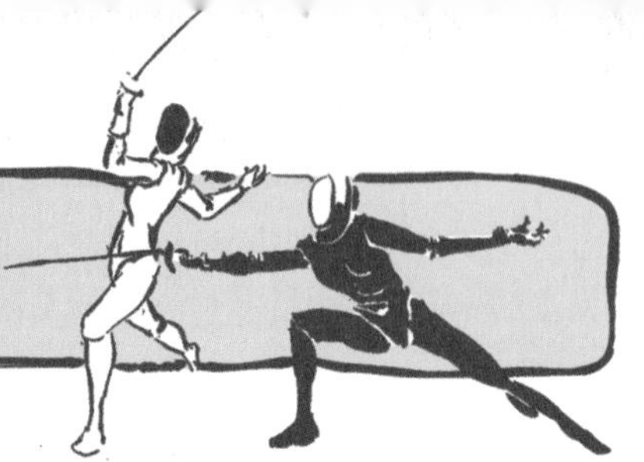

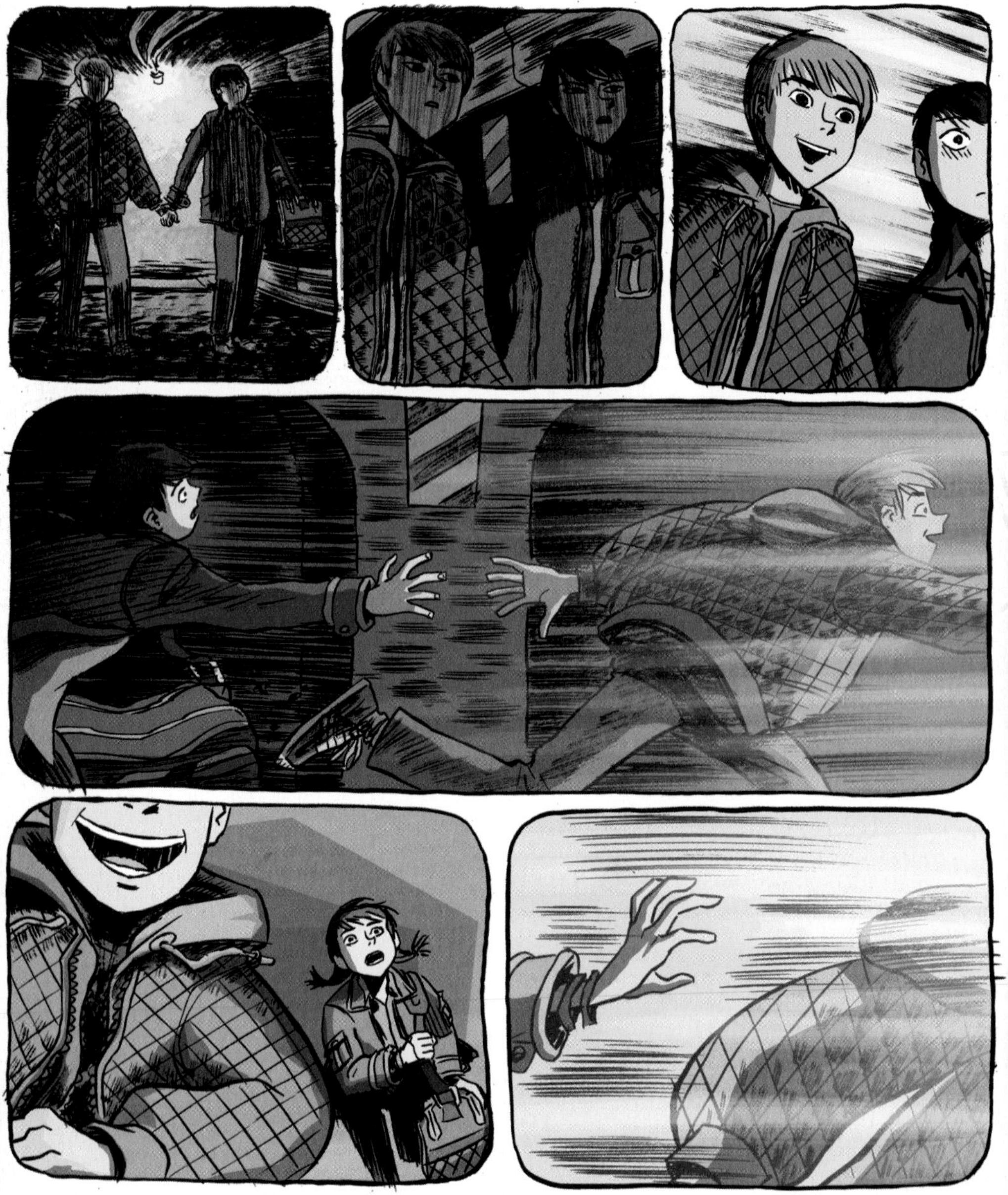

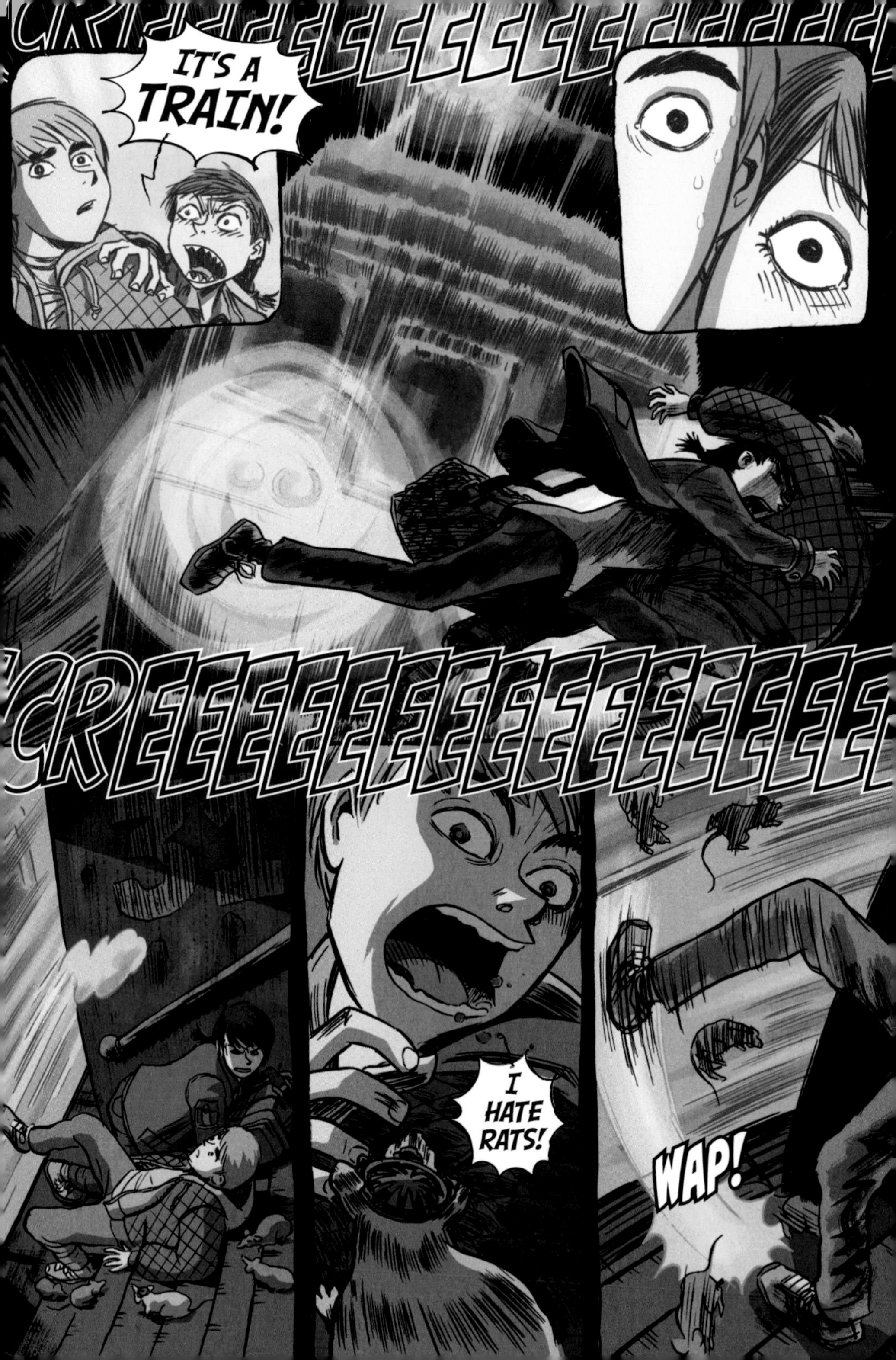

CRIIIEEEEEEEEEEEE
IT'S A TRAIN!
CREEEEEEEEEEEEEEEEE
I HATE RATS!
WAP!

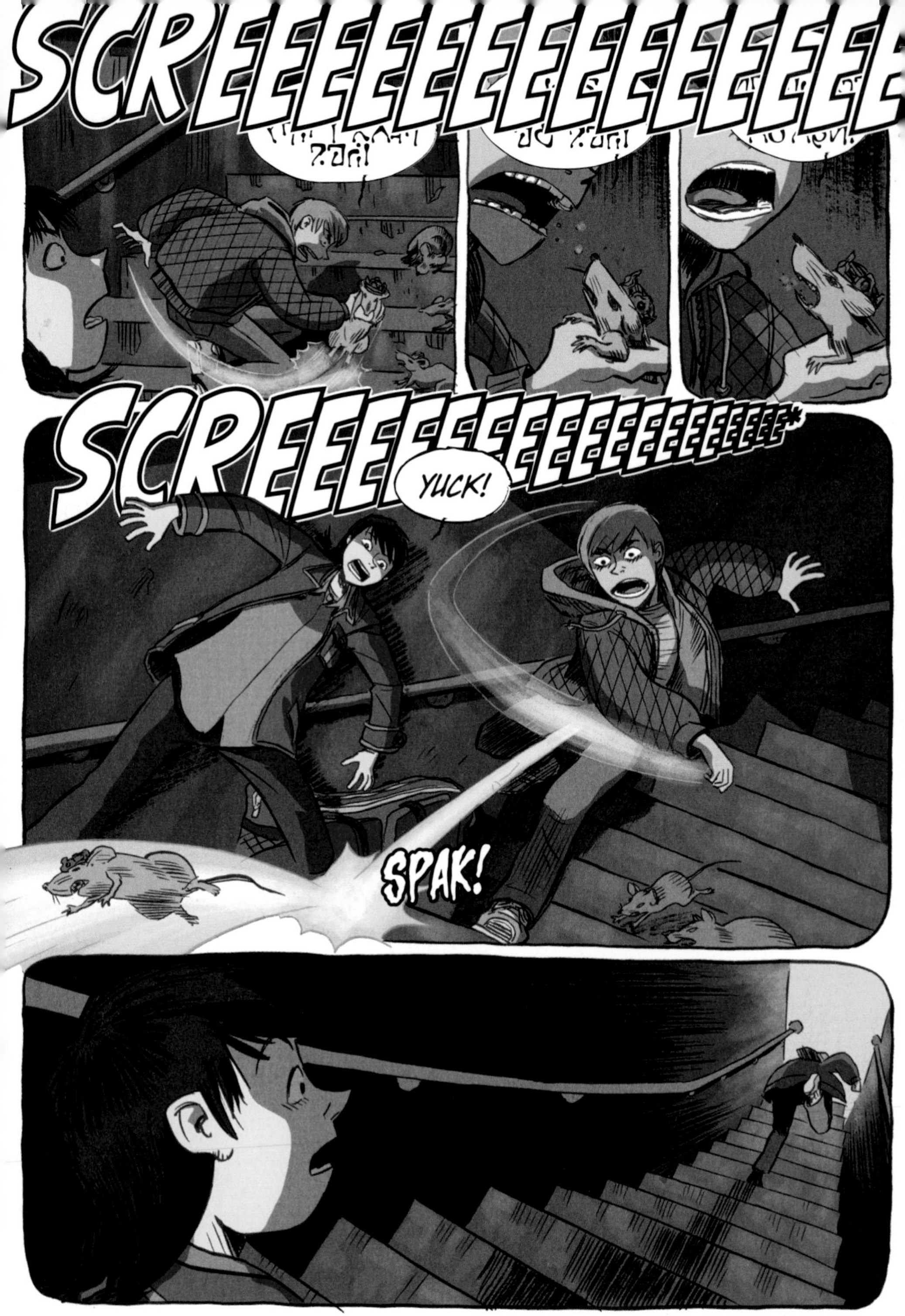

SCREEEEEEEEEEEEEE
SCREEEEEEEEEEEEEEEEE*
YUCK!
SPAK!

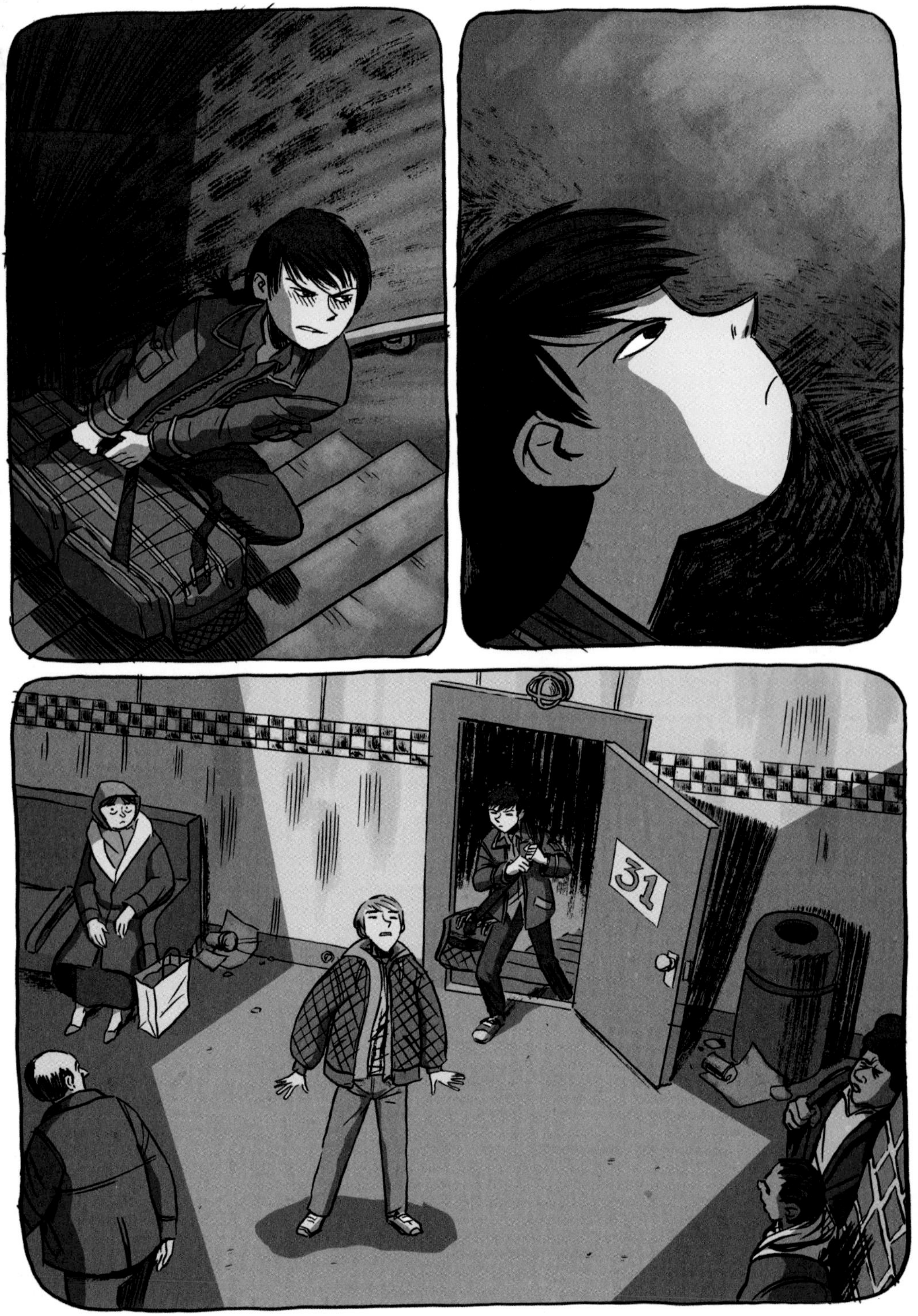
31

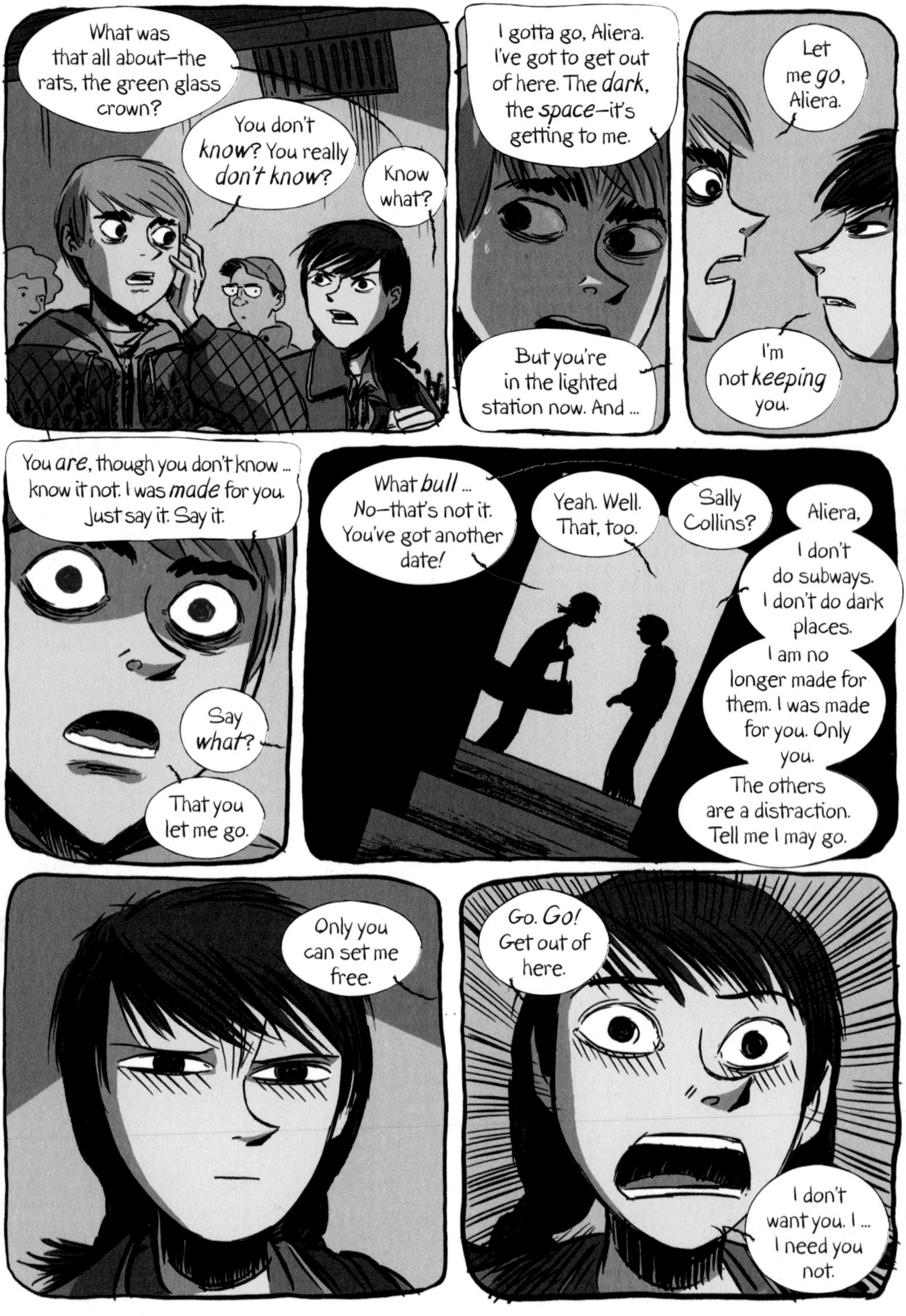
What was that all about—the rats, the green glass crown?
You don't know? You really don't know?
Know what?
I gotta go, Aliera. I've got to get out of here. The dark, the space—it's getting to me.
But you're in the lighted station now. And ...
Let me go, Aliera.
I'm not keeping you.
You are, though you don't know ... know it not. I was made for you. Just say it. Say it.
Say what?
That you let me go.
What bull ... No—that's not it. You've got another date!
Yeah. Well. That, too.
Sally Collins?
Aliera,
I don't do subways. I don't do dark places.
I am no longer made for them. I was made for you. Only you.
The others are a distraction. Tell me I may go.
Only you can set me free.
Go. Go! Get out of here.
I don't want you. I ... I need you not.

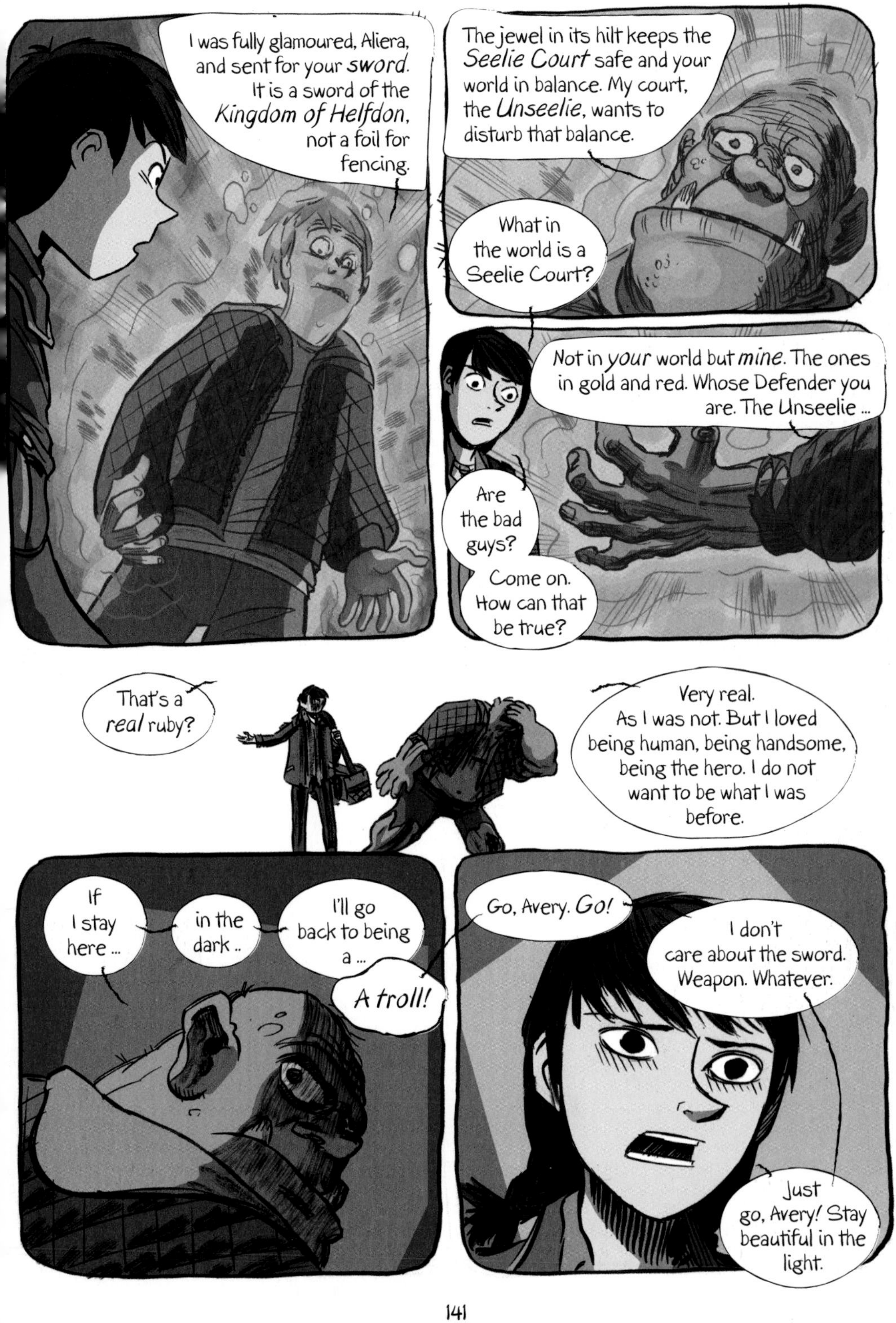
I was fully glamoured, Aliera, and sent for your *sword*. It is a sword of the *Kingdom of Helfdon*, not a foil for fencing.
The jewel in its hilt keeps the *Seelie Court* safe and your world in balance. My court, the *Unseelie*, wants to disturb that balance.
What in the world is a Seelie Court?
Not in *your* world but *mine*. The ones in gold and red. Whose Defender you are. The Unseelie ...
Are the bad guys?
Come on. How can that be true?
That's a *real* ruby?
Very real. As I was not. But I loved being human, being handsome, being the hero. I do not want to be what I was before.
If I stay here ...
in the dark ..
I'll go back to being a ...
A troll!
Go, Avery. *Go!*
I don't care about the sword. Weapon. Whatever.
Just go, Avery! Stay beautiful in the light.

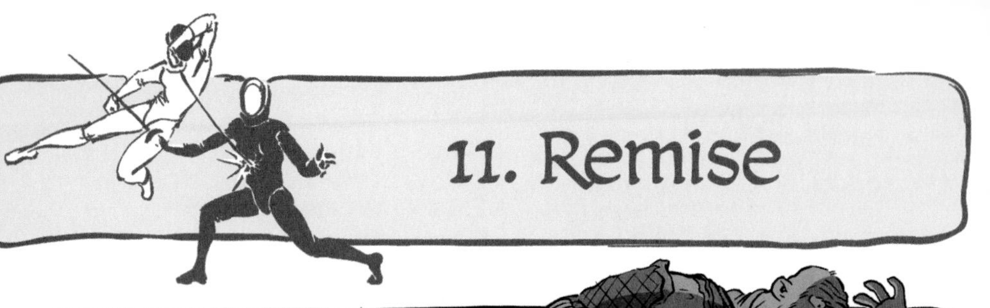

11. Remise

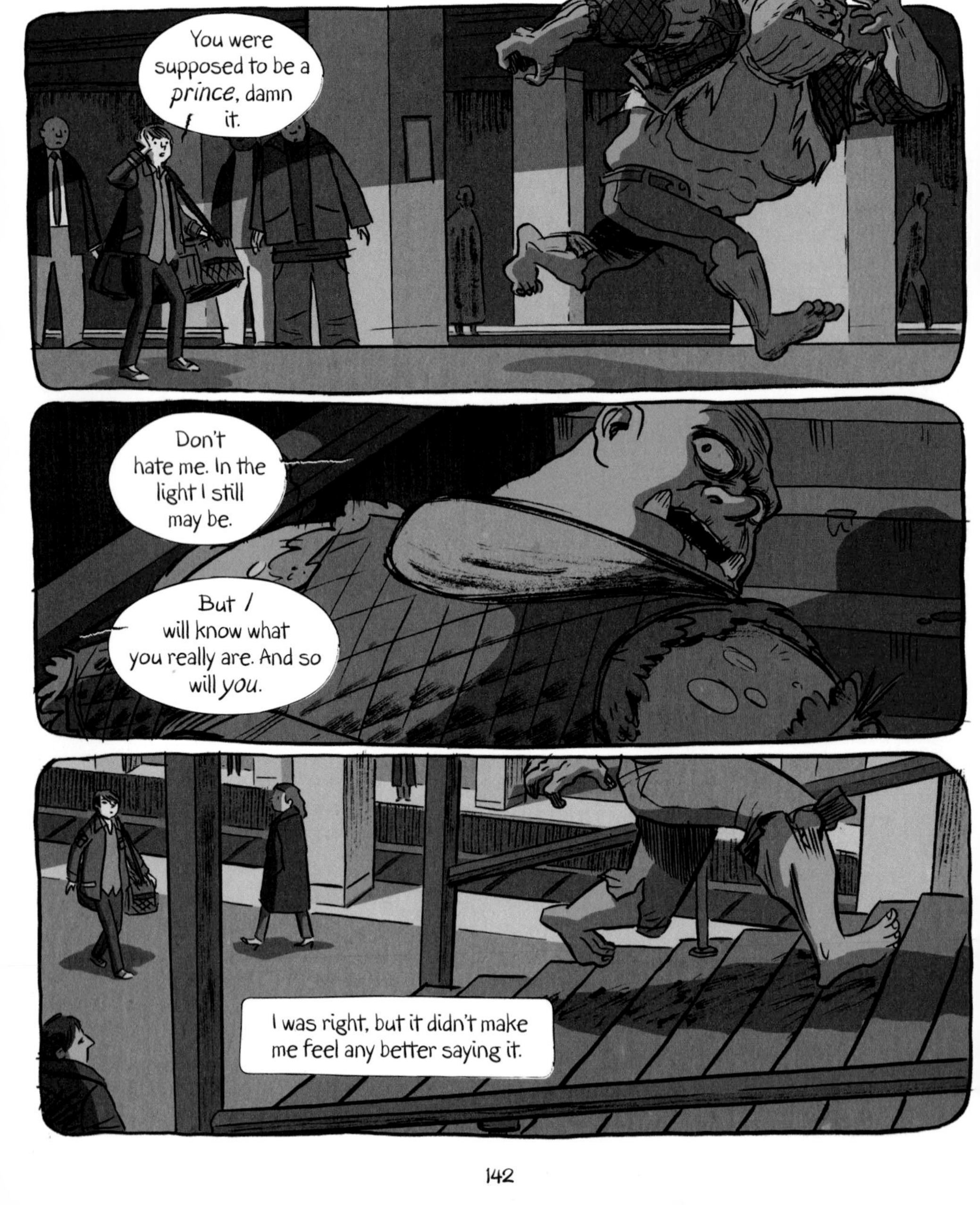
You were supposed to be a *prince*, damn it.
Don't hate me. In the light I still may be.
But *I* will know what you really are. And so will *you*.
I was right, but it didn't make me feel any better saying it.

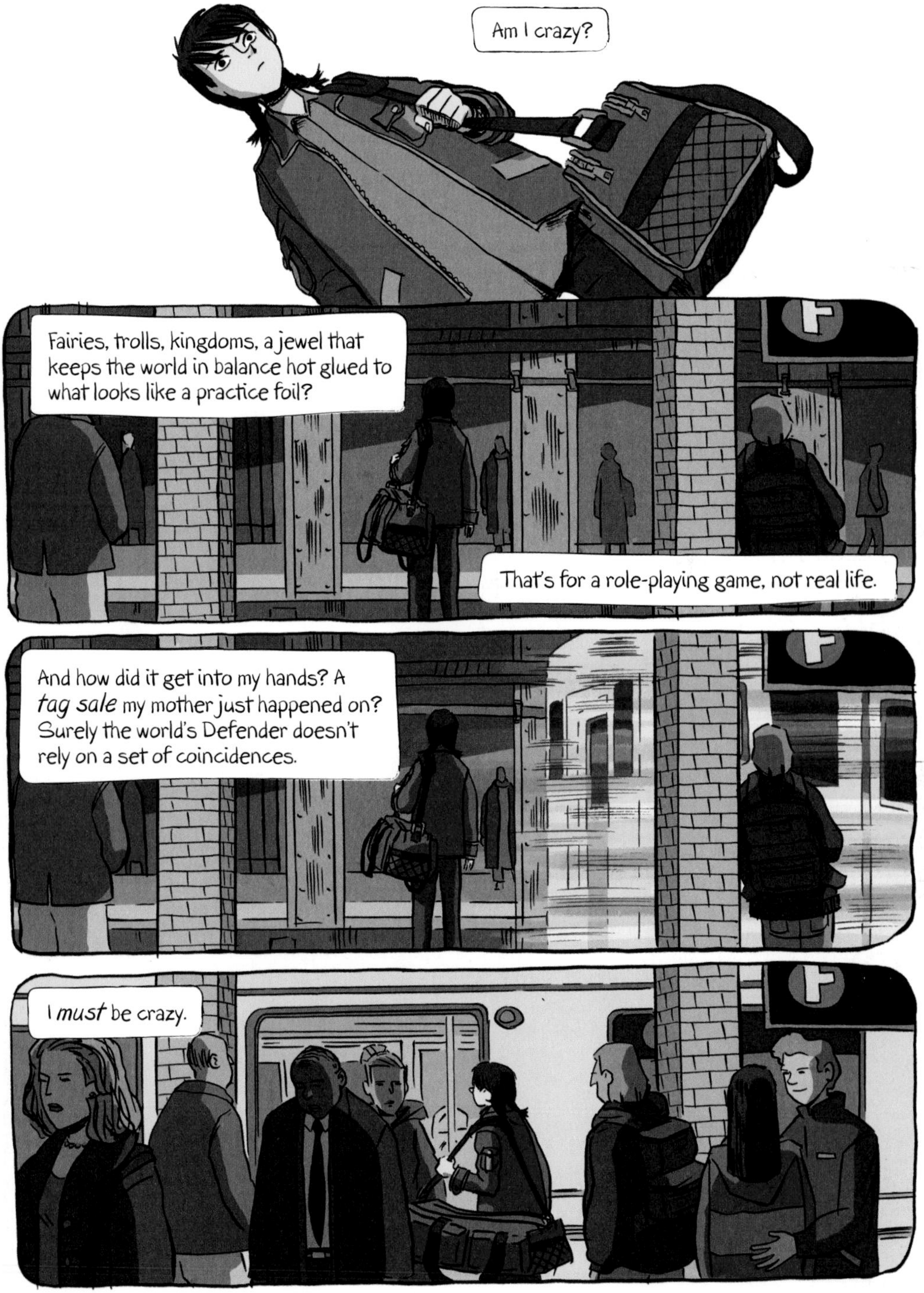
Am I crazy?
Fairies, trolls, kingdoms, a jewel that keeps the world in balance hot glued to what looks like a practice foil?
That's for a role-playing game, not real life.
And how did it get into my hands? A *tag sale* my mother just happened on? Surely the world's Defender doesn't rely on a set of coincidences.
I *must* be crazy.

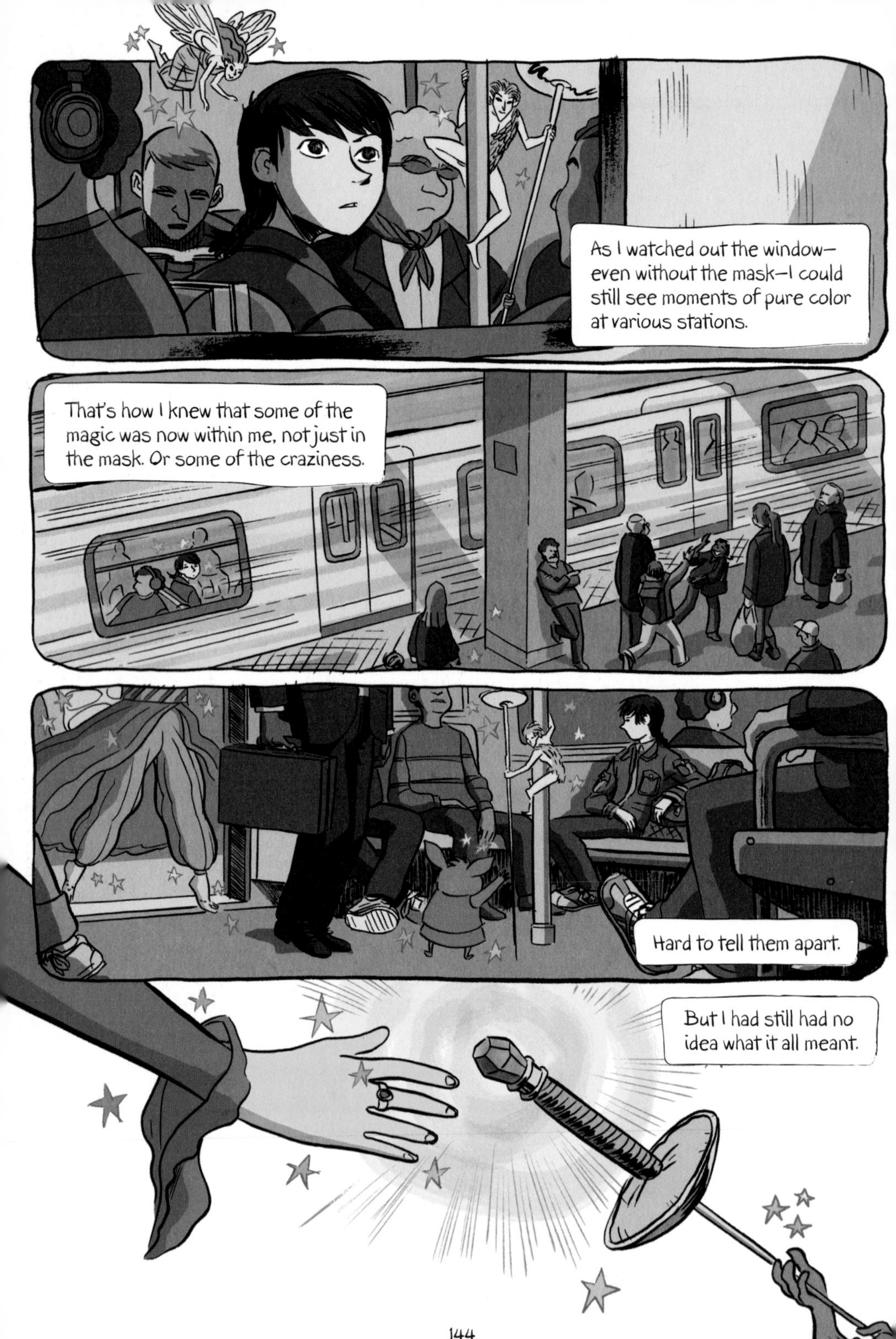
As I watched out the window—even without the mask—I could still see moments of pure color at various stations.
That's how I knew that some of the magic was now within me, not just in the mask. Or some of the craziness.
Hard to tell them apart.
But I had still had no idea what it all meant.

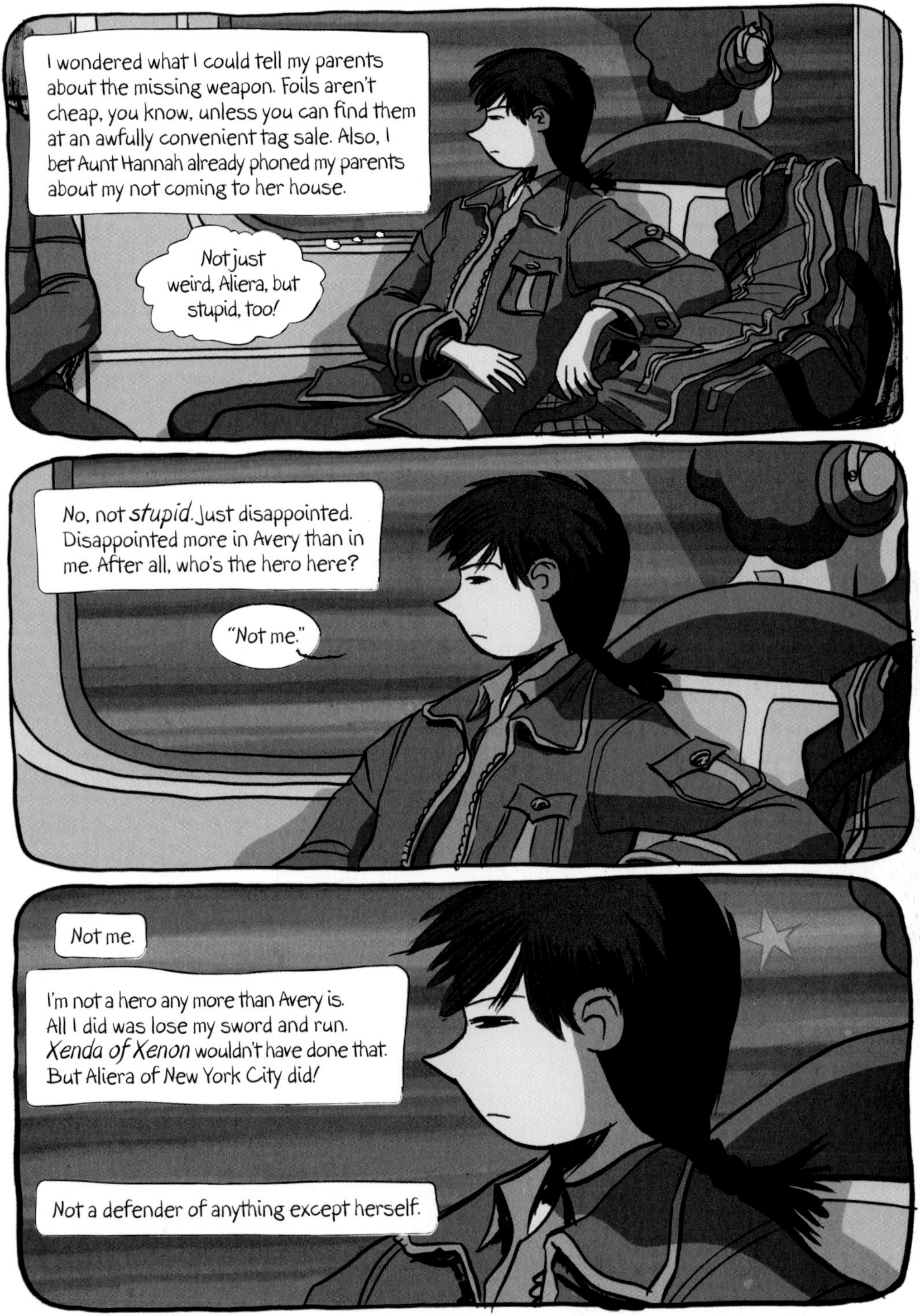
I wondered what I could tell my parents about the missing weapon. Foils aren't cheap, you know, unless you can find them at an awfully convenient tag sale. Also, I bet Aunt Hannah already phoned my parents about my not coming to her house.
Not just weird, Aliera, but stupid, too!
No, not *stupid*. Just disappointed. Disappointed more in Avery than in me. After all, who's the hero here?
"Not me."
Not me.
I'm not a hero any more than Avery is. All I did was lose my sword and run. *Xenda of Xenon* wouldn't have done that. But Aliera of New York City did!
Not a defender of anything except herself.

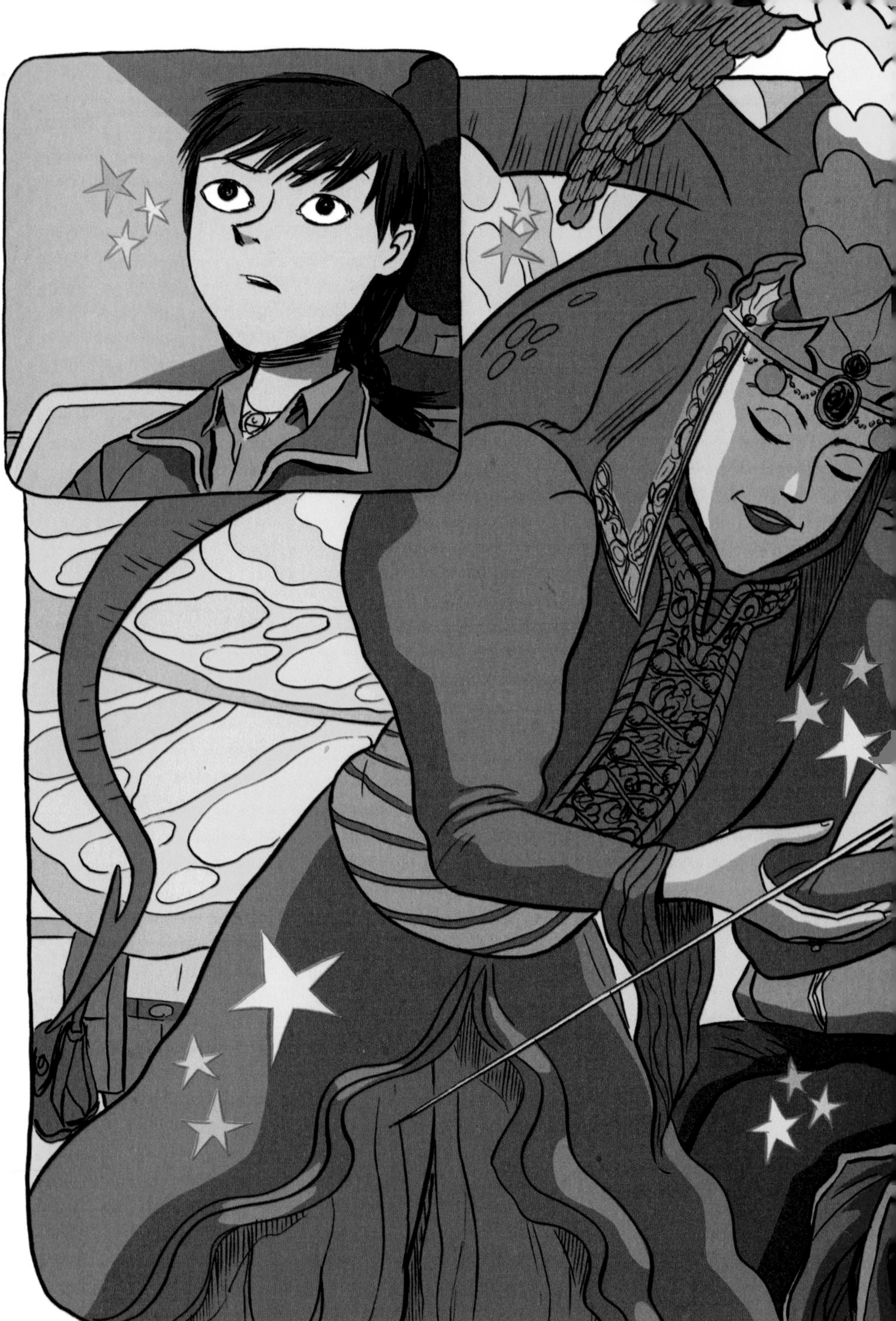

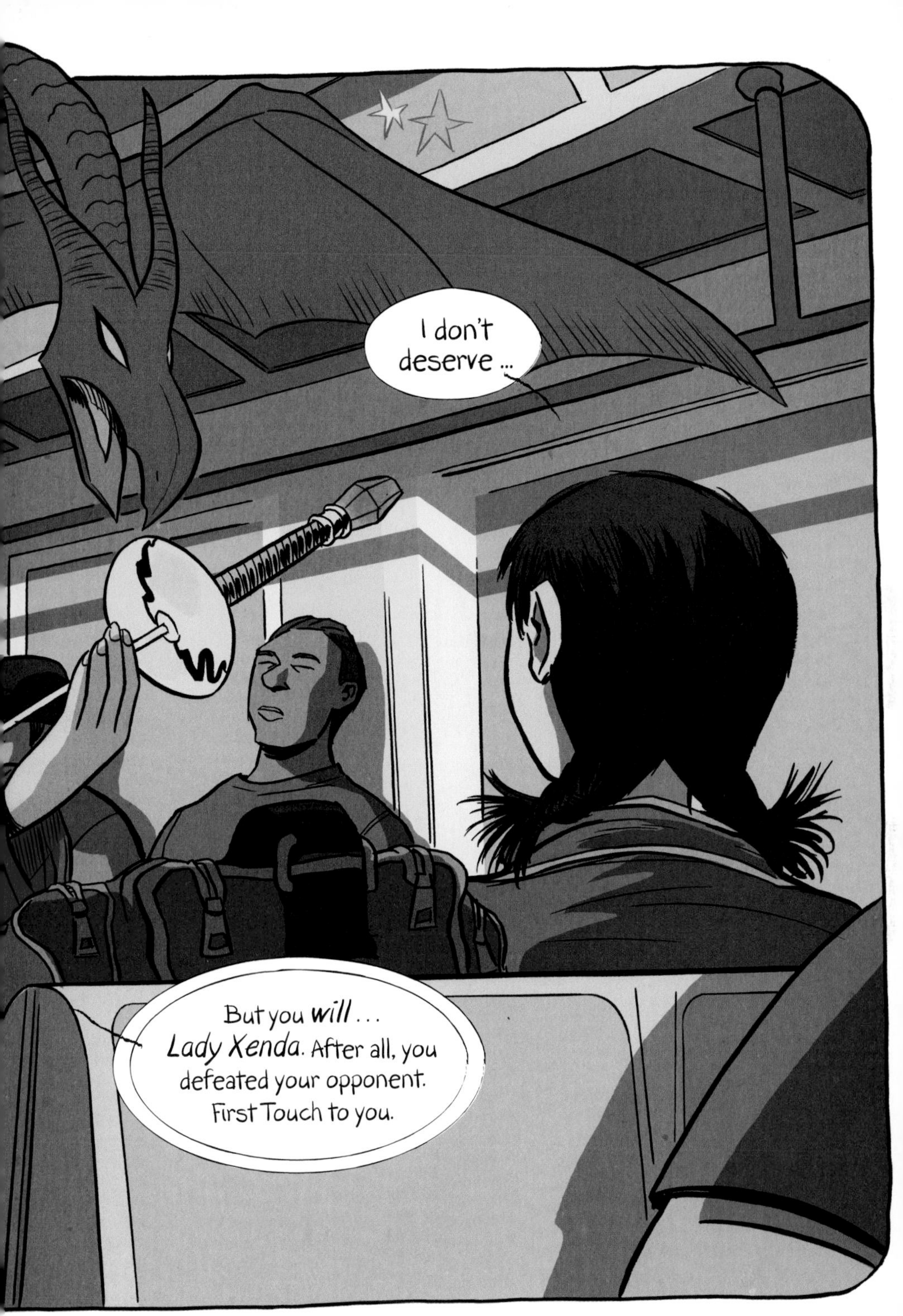
I don't deserve ...
But you *will* . . . *Lady Xenda*. After all, you defeated your opponent. First Touch to you.

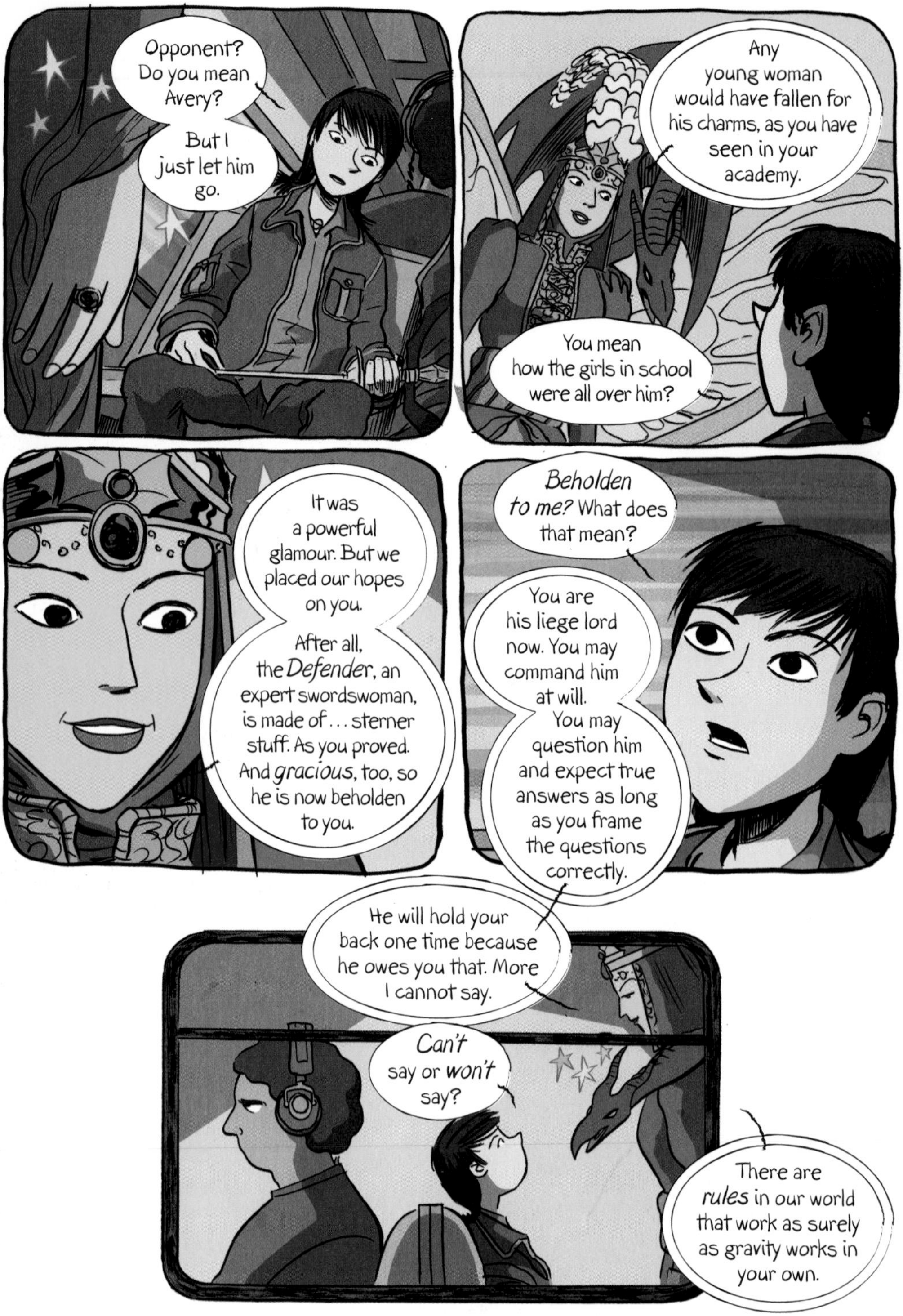
Opponent? Do you mean Avery?
But I just let him go.
Any young woman would have fallen for his charms, as you have seen in your academy.
You mean how the girls in school were all over him?
It was a powerful glamour. But we placed our hopes on you.
After all, the *Defender*, an expert swordswoman, is made of . . . sterner stuff. As you proved. And *gracious*, too, so he is now beholden to you.
Beholden to me? What does that mean?
You are his liege lord now. You may command him at will.
You may question him and expect true answers as long as you frame the questions correctly.
He will hold your back one time because he owes you that. More I cannot say.
Can't say or *won't* say?
There are *rules* in our world that work as surely as gravity works in your own.

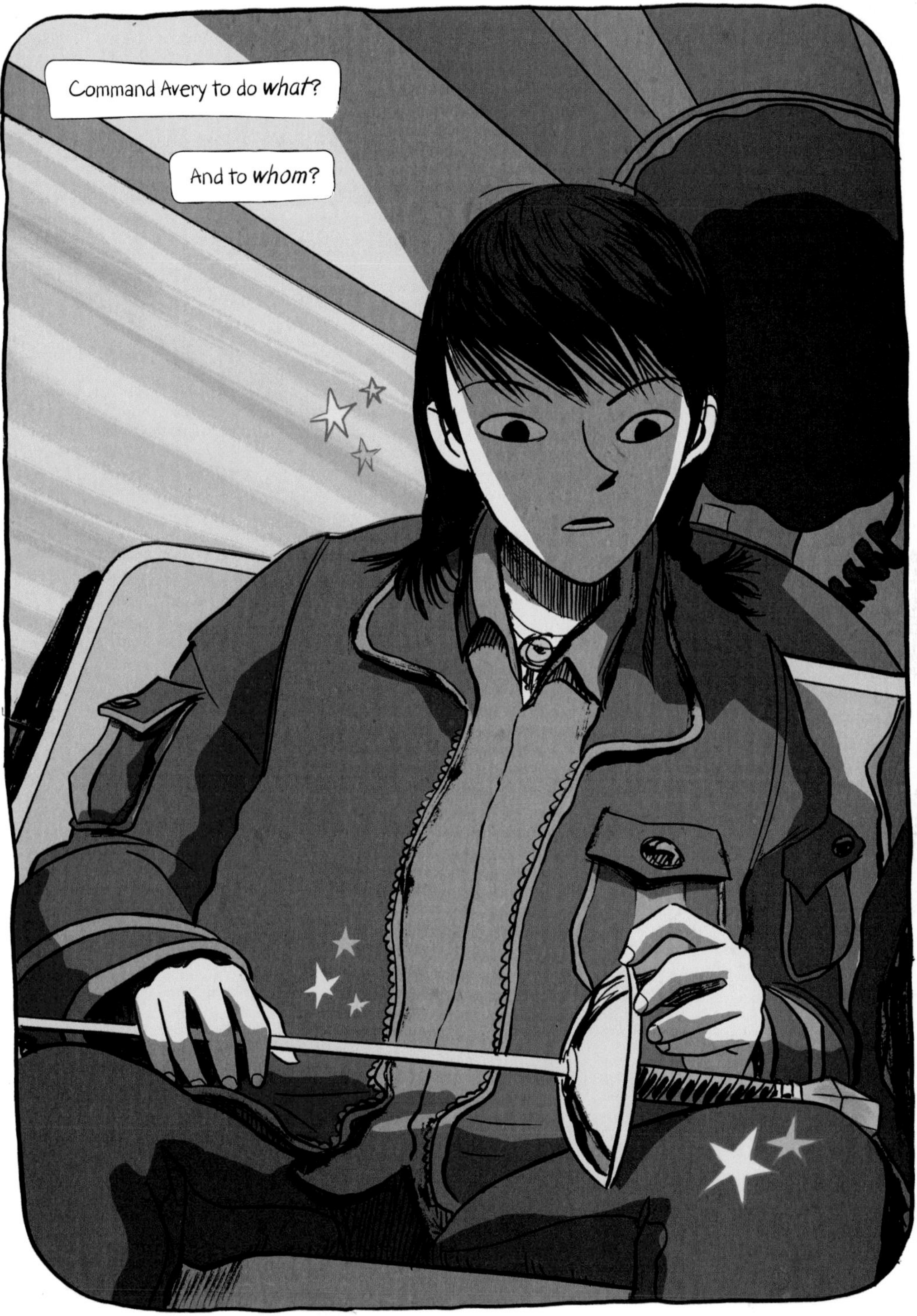
Command Avery to do *what?*
And to *whom?*

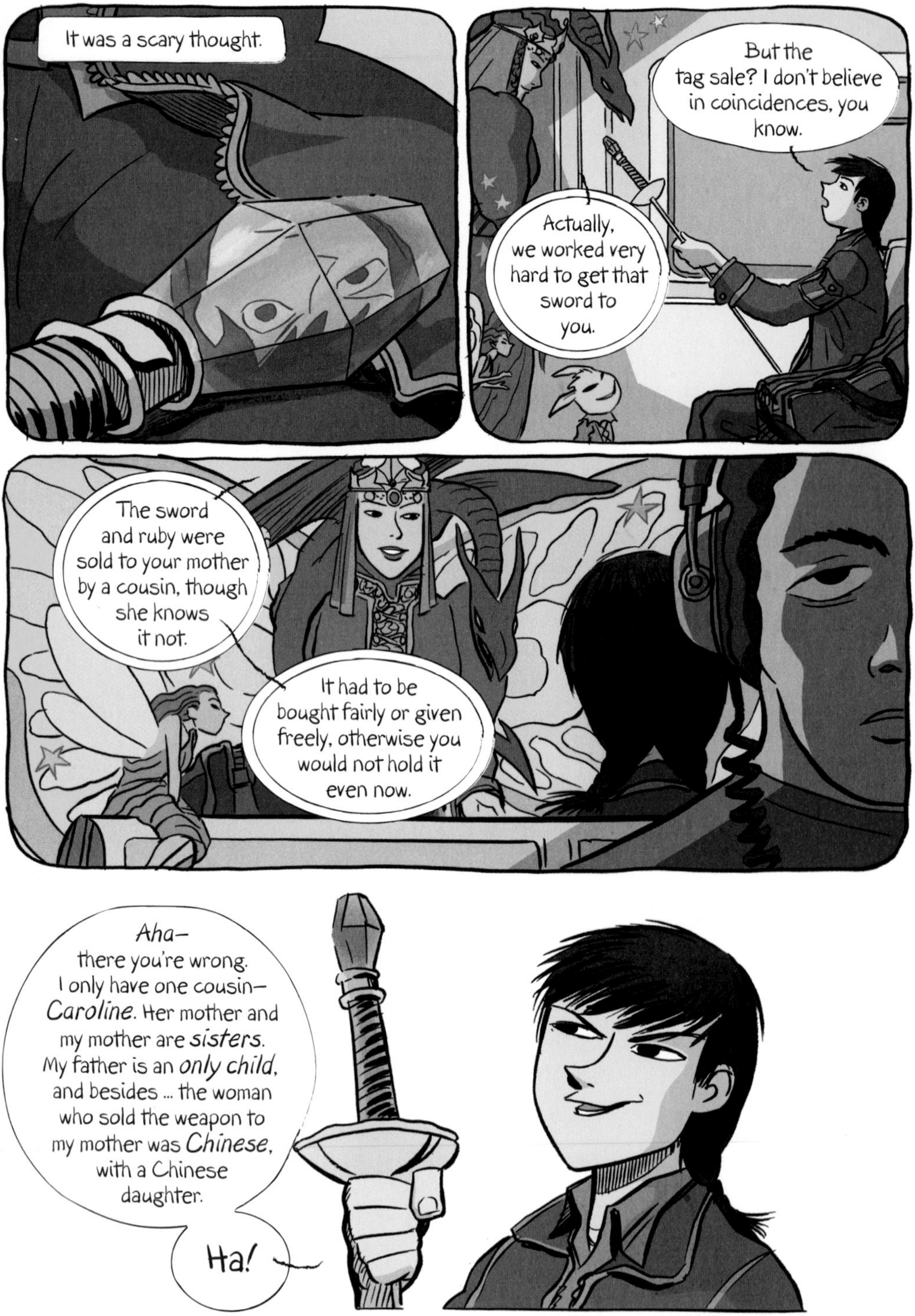
It was a scary thought.
But the tag sale? I don't believe in coincidences, you know.
Actually, we worked very hard to get that sword to you.
The sword and ruby were sold to your mother by a cousin, though she knows it not.
It had to be bought fairly or given freely, otherwise you would not hold it even now.
Aha— there you're wrong. I only have one cousin— *Caroline*. Her mother and my mother are *sisters*. My father is an *only child*, and besides ... the woman who sold the weapon to my mother was *Chinese*, with a Chinese daughter.
Ha!

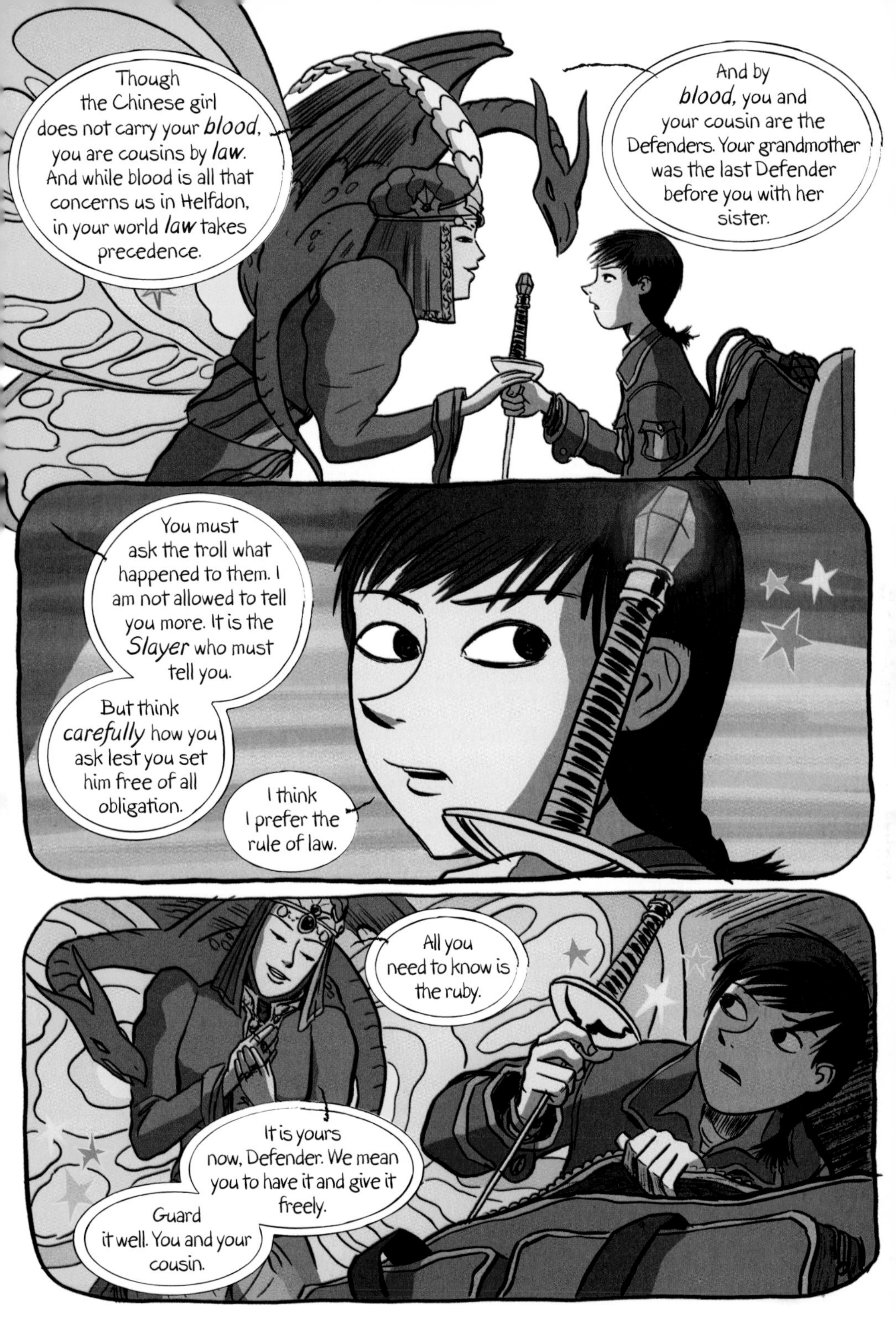

Though the Chinese girl does not carry your *blood*, you are cousins by *law*. And while blood is all that concerns us in Helfdon, in your world *law* takes precedence.
And by *blood*, you and your cousin are the Defenders. Your grandmother was the last Defender before you with her sister.
You must ask the troll what happened to them. I am not allowed to tell you more. It is the *Slayer* who must tell you.
But think *carefully* how you ask lest you set him free of all obligation.
I think I prefer the rule of law.
All you need to know is the ruby.
It is yours now, Defender. We mean you to have it and give it freely.
Guard it well. You and your cousin.

12. Disengagement

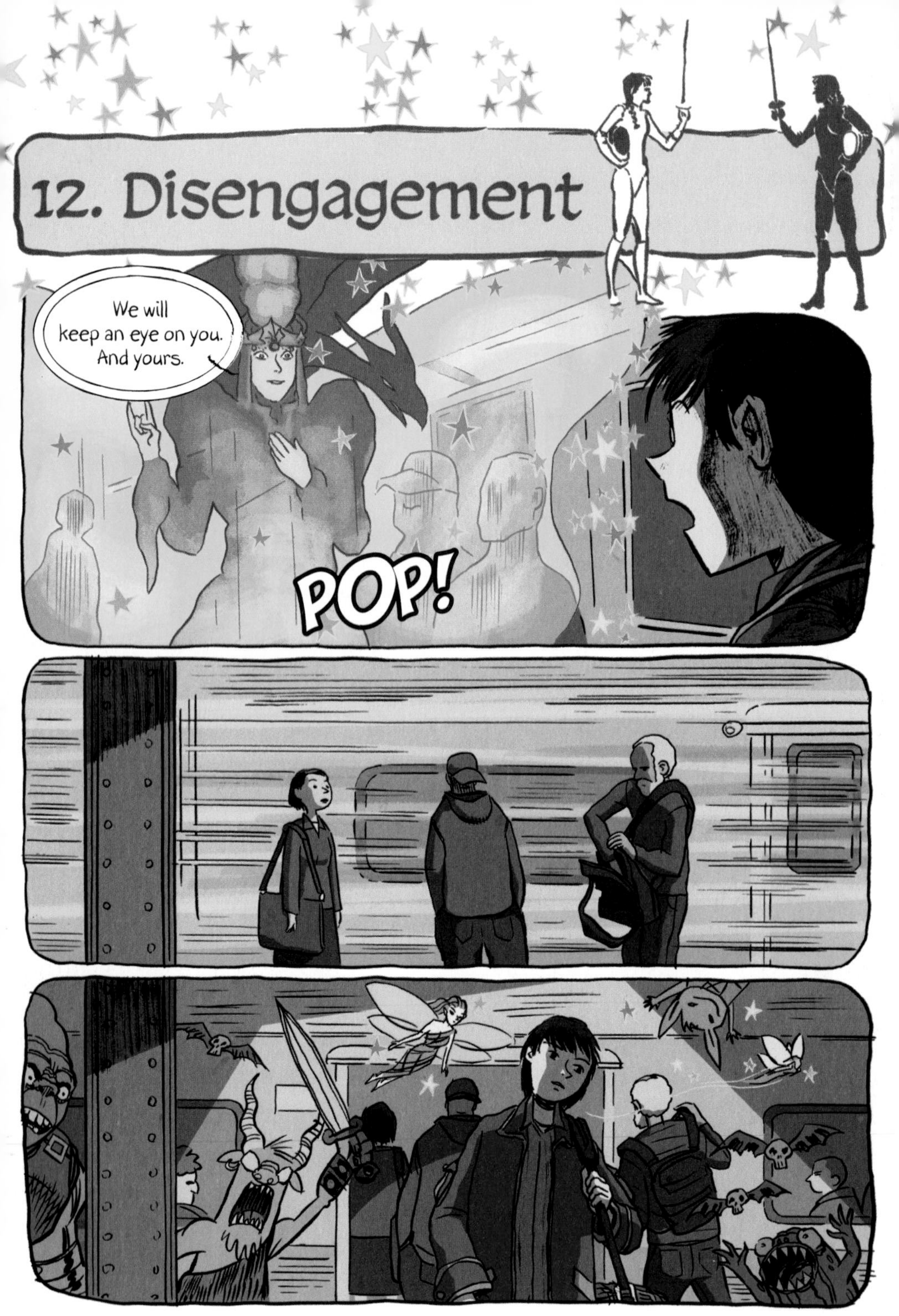
We will keep an eye on you. And yours.
POP!

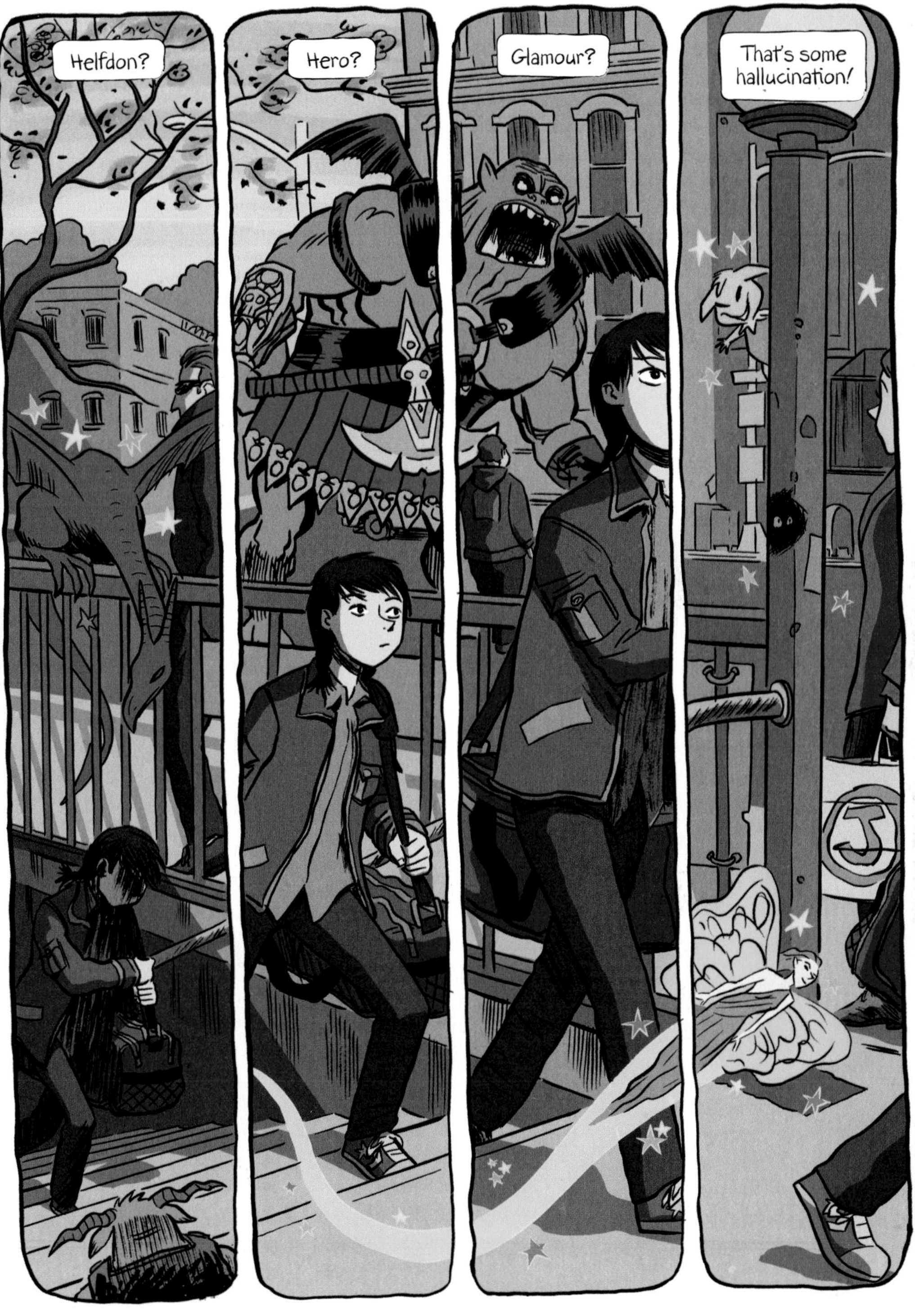
Helfdon?
Hero?
Glamour?
That's some hallucination!

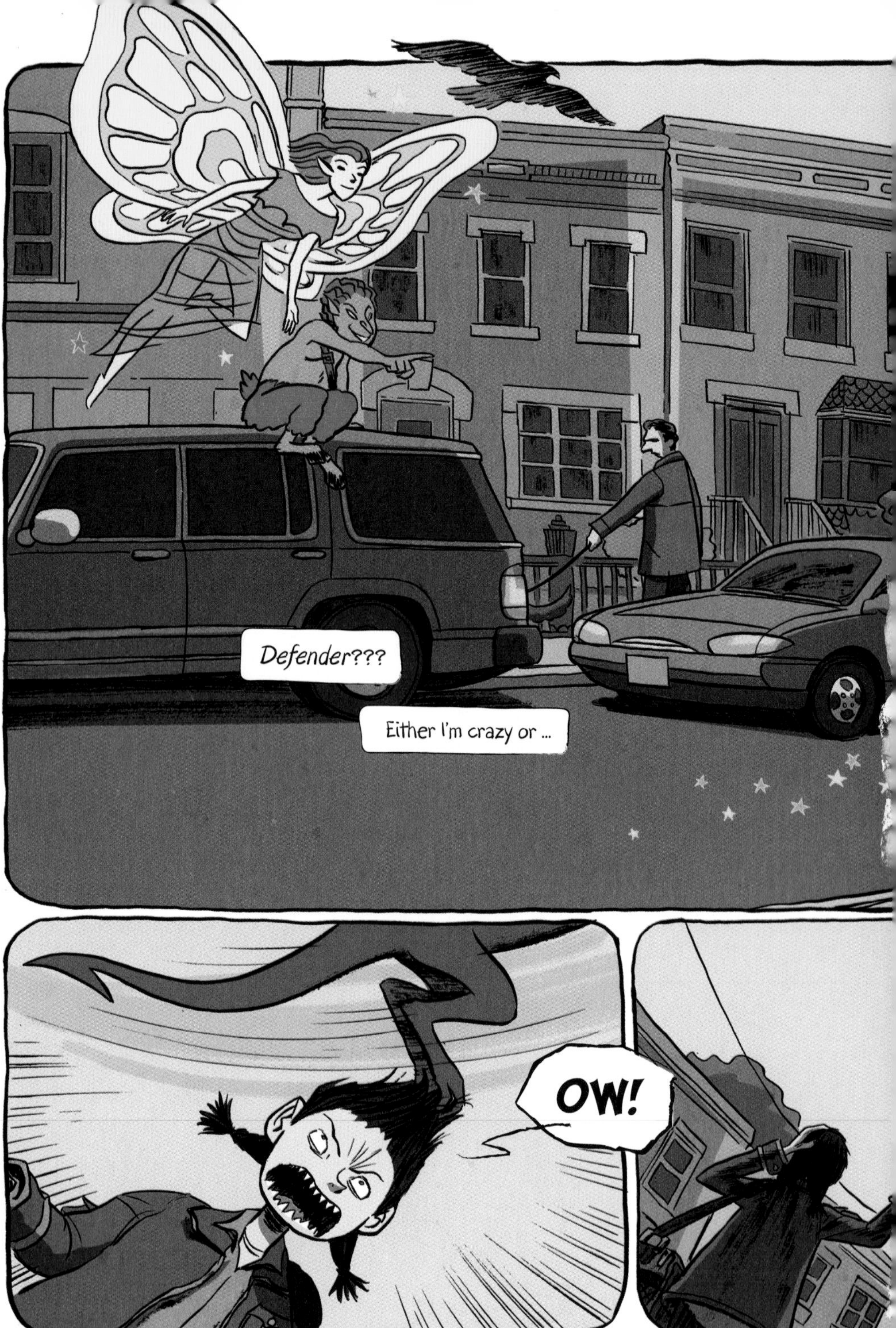
Defender???
Either I'm crazy or ...
OW!

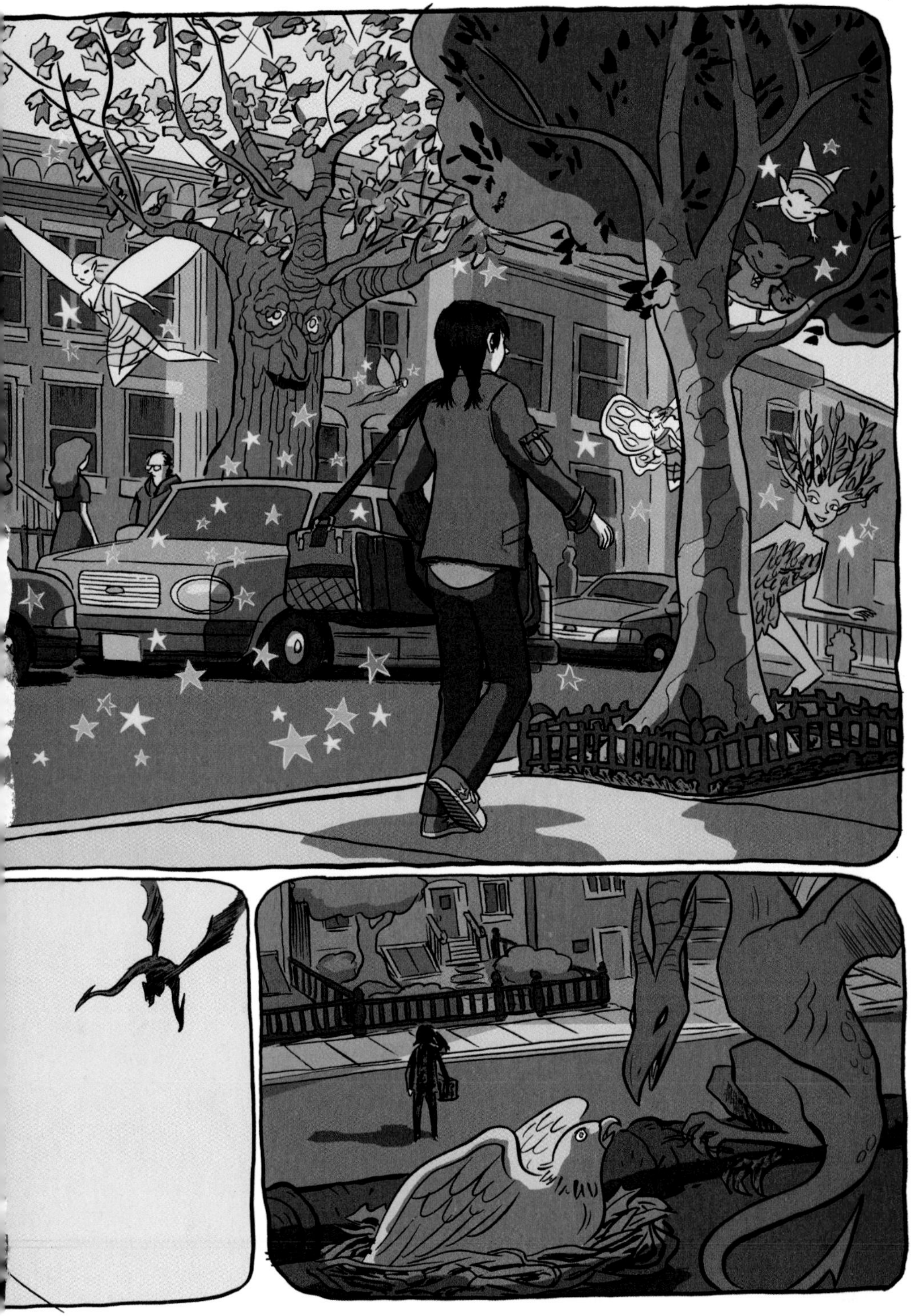

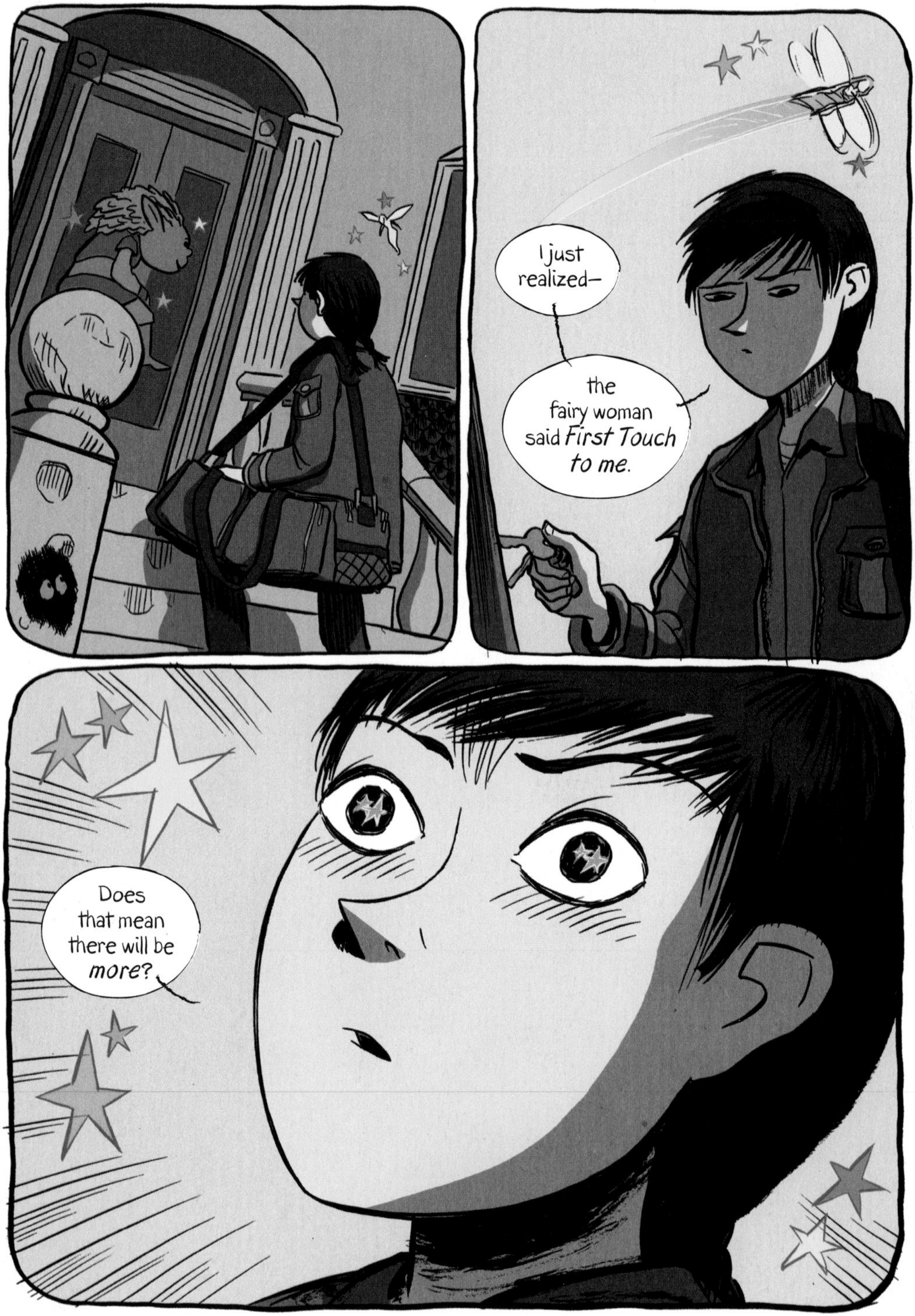
I just realized—
the fairy woman said *First Touch to me.*
Does that mean there will be *more?*

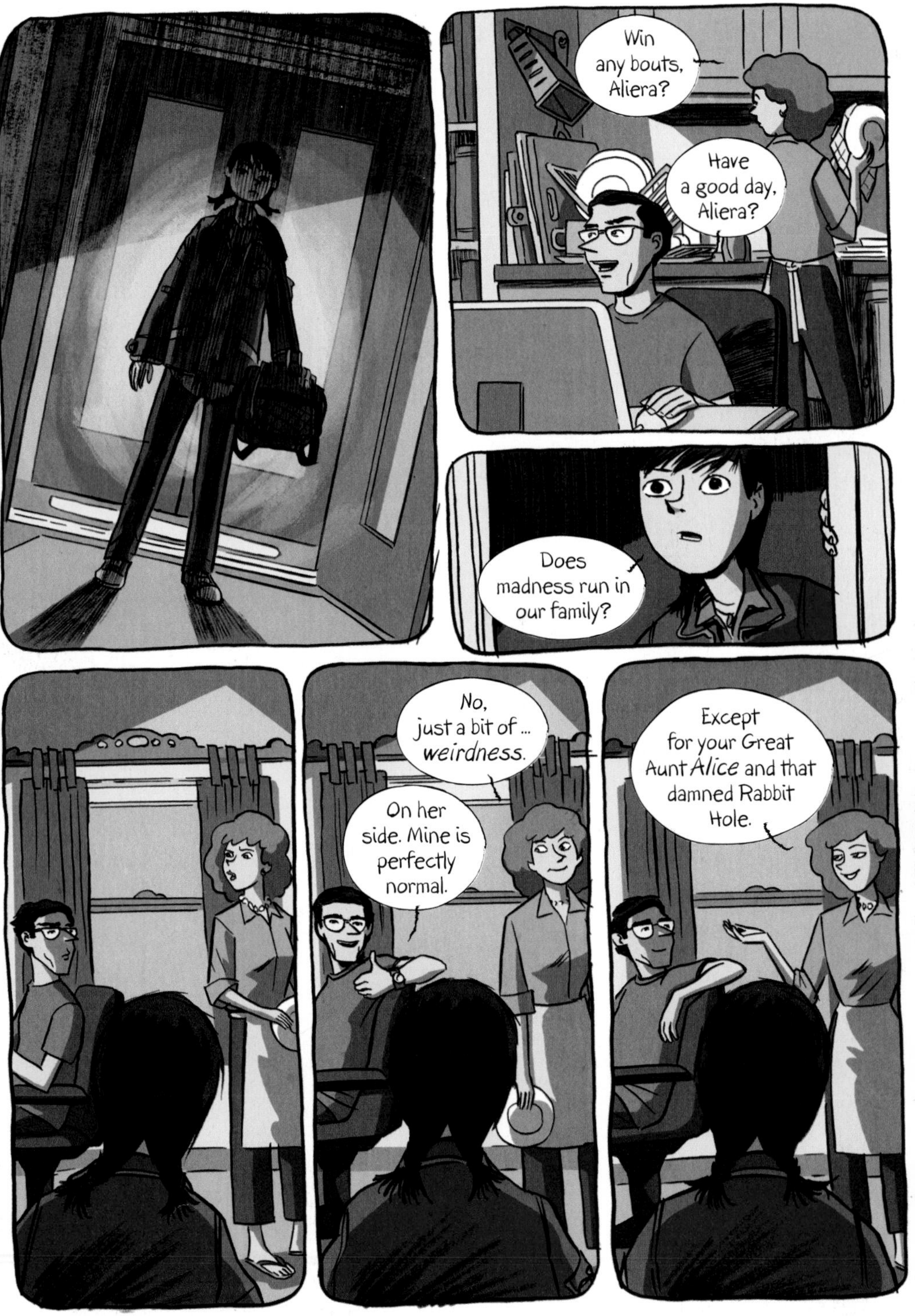
Win any bouts, Aliera?
Have a good day, Aliera?
Does madness run in our family?
No, just a bit of ... *weirdness*.
On her side. Mine is perfectly normal.
Except for your Great Aunt *Alice* and that damned Rabbit Hole.

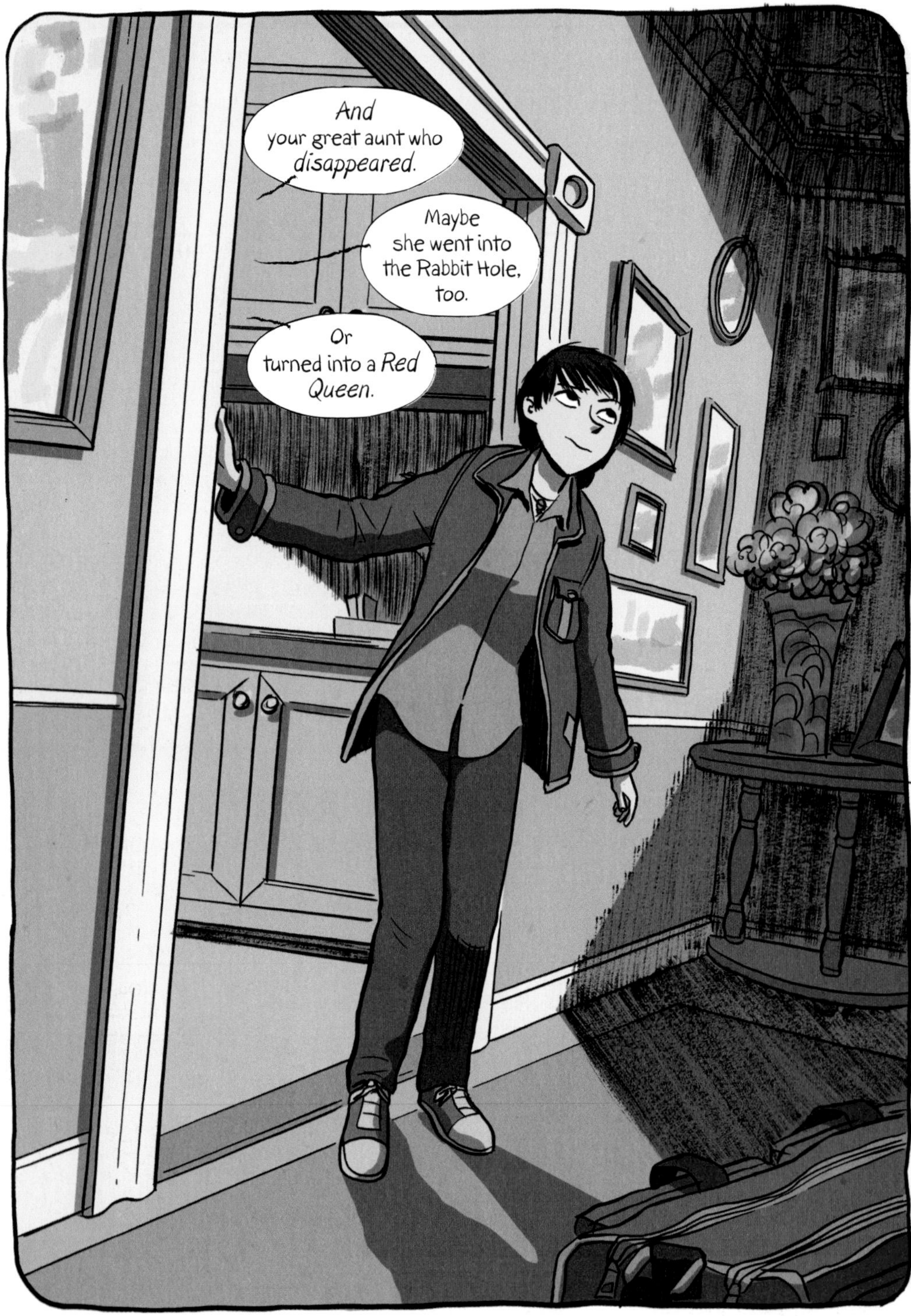
And your great aunt who *disappeared*.
Maybe she went into the Rabbit Hole, too.
Or turned into a *Red Queen*.

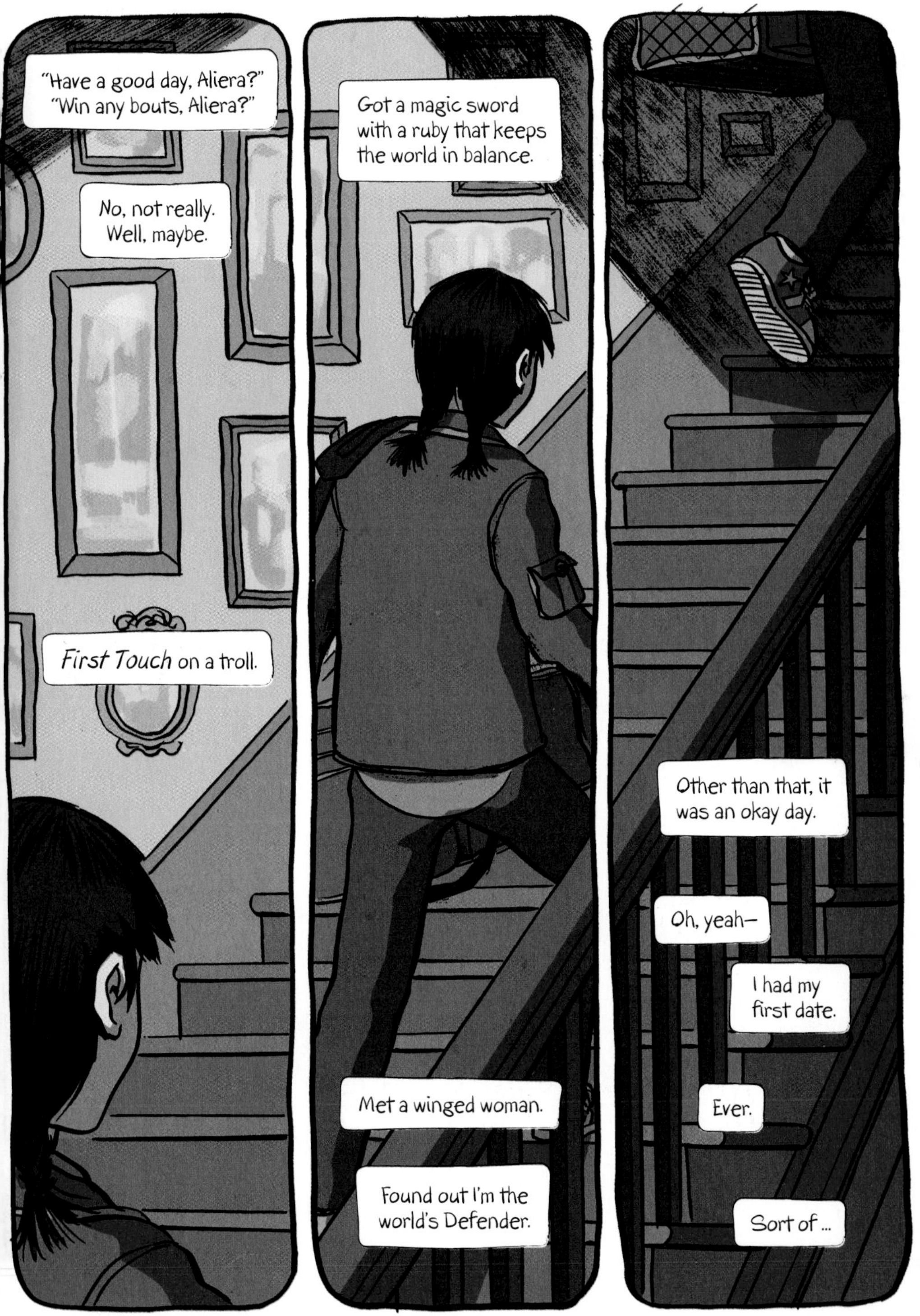
"Have a good day, Aliera?"
"Win any bouts, Aliera?"
No, not really. Well, maybe.
First Touch on a troll.
Got a magic sword with a ruby that keeps the world in balance.
Met a winged woman.
Found out I'm the world's Defender.
Other than that, it was an okay day.
Oh, yeah—
I had my first date.
Ever.
Sort of ...

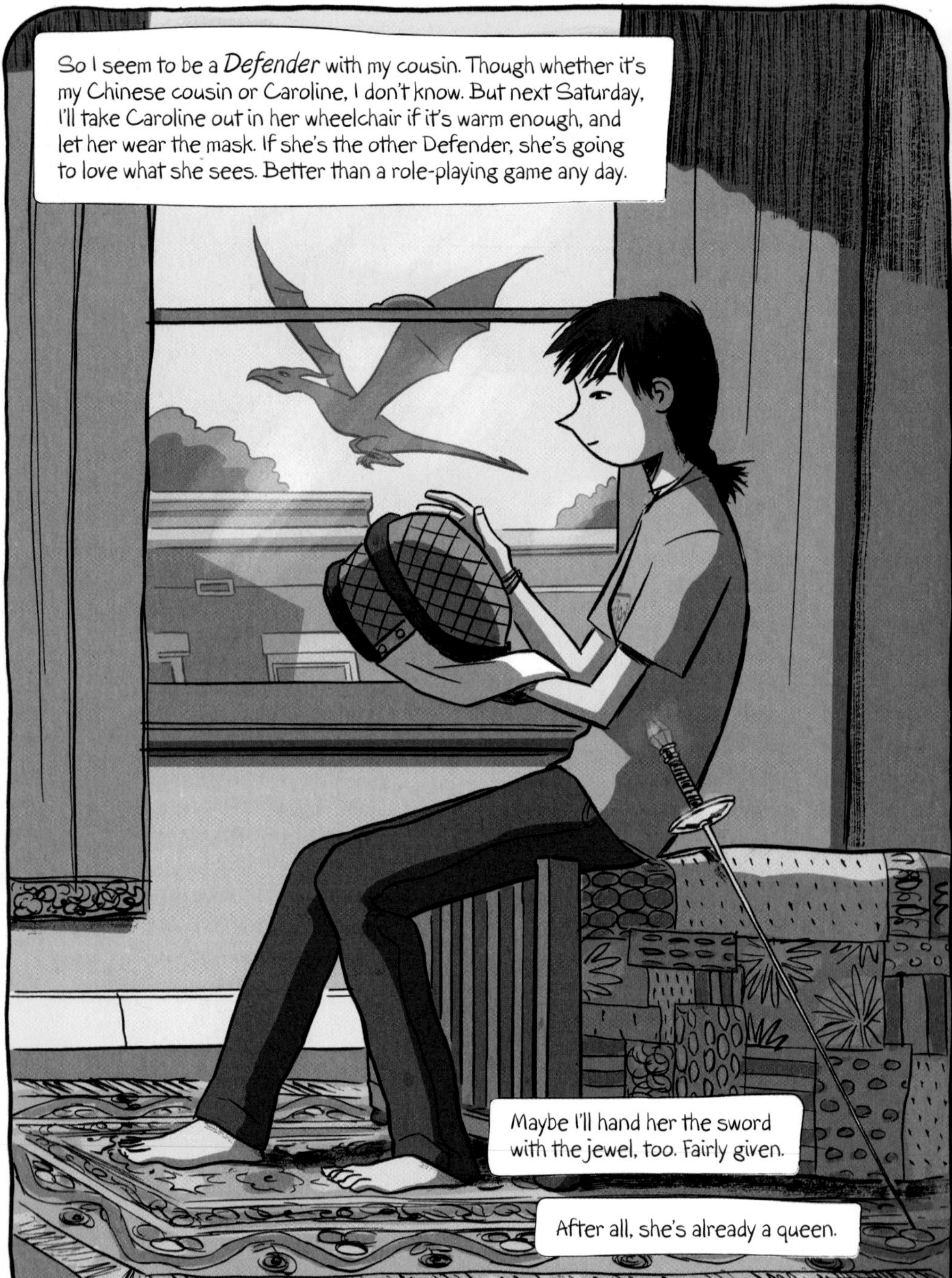
So I seem to be a *Defender* with my cousin. Though whether it's my Chinese cousin or Caroline, I don't know. But next Saturday, I'll take Caroline out in her wheelchair if it's warm enough, and let her wear the mask. If she's the other Defender, she's going to love what she sees. Better than a role-playing game any day.
Maybe I'll hand her the sword with the jewel, too. Fairly given.
After all, she's already a queen.
END
CAVALLARO '09